To Francine

A pleasure meeting you.
Thank you for your support

Gerry

GM-38

"What a wonderful story, heartbreaking and beautiful all at once."

April Grace O'Sullivan - Editor

By

Gerry Morris

Shield  Crest

ISBN: 978-1-913839-55-0

MMXXII

A CIP catalogue record for this book
is available from the British Library.

Published by
ShieldCrest Publishing,
Boston, Lincolnshire,
PE20 3BT England
Tel: +44 (0) 333 8000 890
www.shieldcrest.co.uk

It was akin to childish innocence
But as my years slip by
Due to unsuspecting ignorance
In my tormented shell I lie.

Acknowledgements

Without the support and encouragement of friends and close family this book would never have been written. It has been three years in the making and at times proved to be almost too demanding, partly due to my advancing years and various health issues. There was however a compelling reason for putting pen to paper, which spurred me on to finish the book when it all seemed too daunting. This is my first book and my last... well maybe?

A number of people have helped me in this endeavour and to them I wish to extend my heartfelt gratitude:

Anne Tuxford a very close friend who has been there from day one. Endlessly patient, with a good eye for detail and authenticity she offered help and support every step of the way.

Mary Coffey, my partner, for her gentle nagging in persuading me to stay on task when I would have much preferred to spend the time watching rugby in the pub! Also, for the all the hours she spent proofreading, compiling and typing up my somewhat illegible scrawl.

Ann Taylor for her help in picking up Mary's typing errors!

My first readers, two dear friends:

Ken Moody - a perceptive critic.

Rodney Henderson who could always be relied upon for research and accurate historical information.

Garry Kemp at Tower Design & Print for his valuable advice and assistance in bringing the book to print.

Last but not least, **Lizzie Huxtable** for editing, preparing the material for publication and of course for her delightful illustrations.

To all others not mentioned I am deeply indebted.

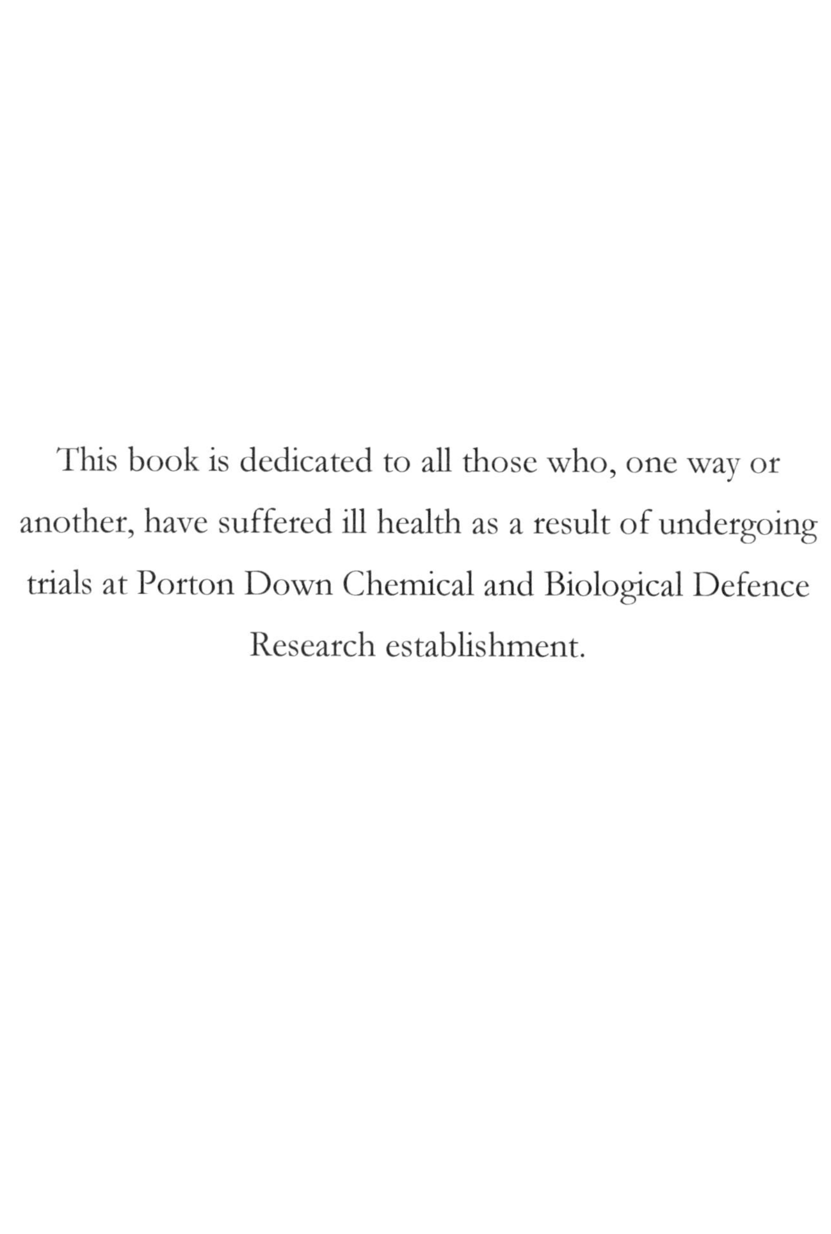

This book is dedicated to all those who, one way or another, have suffered ill health as a result of undergoing trials at Porton Down Chemical and Biological Defence Research establishment.

Prologue

At 10.00am on the fourteenth of February 1958 I had reason to feel excited. I was to receive fifty bob (£2.50) and a few days extra leave. All I was asked to do in return was to sit alongside four other National service men for just one hour and fifteen minutes.

The glass panelled door slid open, we all entered the room, totally unexpecting and unprotected as we took our seats around a table. In front of us, behind a thick, sealed partition, were a group of white-coated men. Bloody hell! What have I let myself in to!

Seventy -five minutes later we left the room. Staggering, needing assistance from other white coated men wearing gas masks. It was only then that realisation hit.

We had been sitting in a gas chamber.

This was a day I would remember and regret for the rest of my life.

Chapter 1

Spandau, Germany

Gerhardt got up from his chair, walked over to the small window overlooking the field behind the laboratory. It was just a few days before Christmas, which he was looking forward to, as it would be a welcome break from the long hours he had been working. This time of year always revived memories of family gatherings and shared happy times. He had lost several uncles and other relatives in the Great War, and so images of the past made him reflective as he saw the snow beginning to fall. Although the snow was settling, the sun continued to shine through small gaps in the clouds. The diffused sunlight caused the crystalline flakes to give off an incandescence, creating an almost surreal atmosphere, the first flakes to settle on the grass seemed to surrender themselves to their inevitable fate, as they slowly turned to water.

It seemed as though it were a sacrificial act. Although they had been transformed to liquid, nonetheless they had cooled the blades of grass allowing fresh, following flakes to retain their crystalline state. The landscape changed before his eyes, as flake after flake surrendered itself before others secured a sound footing. The process of one crystal leading the way so others might survive was, he thought, an exact analogy of what had happened on the battlefields. He wondered how it must have felt for the first men getting up, over the top of the trenches to face the onslaught of gunfire. They knew their chances of survival were slim. The strong possibility that they would never see their loved ones again must be forced to the back of their minds, surmounted by their determination to survive.

Knowing they were part of a dedicated team, they could rely on the support of their colleagues close behind them, as they took the brunt of it, clearing the way for them to follow. Follow they did, clambering, stumbling over their broken mates. Peering through the cold window, now misted with his breath, he imagined that the reflecting shards of light might represent the souls of those soldiers as they faced their end.

This had been a fiercely cold December, and he hoped to God it would not continue to be so. He had been working without rest in the laboratories situated near the Spandau Citadel, the centre of operations. His spirits low, his mind exhausted, the freezing conditions at his workplace did little to help his progress as his numbed fingers prepared the chemicals for his experiments. The laboratories were some distance from the town, isolated from prying eyes. It was imperative that it was so shielded, the work they undertook was sensitive and highly secret. A tall perimeter fence surrounded the laboratory, enclosing a copse of trees and a large meadow. The entrance was manned twenty hours a day, the security fence constantly patrolled by soldiers with dogs.

A sentry box situated between two barriers housed armed guards who admitted no-one without security clearance - trespassers were to be shot on sight. The present guard in his grey uniform could be seen brushing snow from his greatcoat; he was sporting the new emblem which all the government officials seemed to be wearing. Hitler himself claimed to have designed it. To preserve nationalistic fervour, he had used the colours of the German flag, but the emblem consisted of a red ground, with a black swastika contained within a white circle. To Gerhardt's mind it sent a powerful message to the supporters of the Third Reich, whilst at the same time appearing menacing and threatening to those alien to their policies. He sensed that something terrible was looming over his country, could almost smell the bloody miasma of war. The long hours at his work bench, the pressure being imposed on him to get results, were taking their toll. He desperately needed a break; he was looking forward to time with his family over Christmas. Face drawn with tiredness, he gazed through the window; seeing the sun shining again on the white fields, he relaxed for a moment and felt more at ease.

Gerhardt Schrader was born on the 23rd of February,1903, in the town of Vandenberg. He had studied Chemistry at Braunschweig University, was technically employed by the I G Fabian chemical subsidiary company but had been enlisted by the government for their research programme. He was assigned the task of developing chemicals for the preservation of foodstuffs and textiles. Despite misgivings concerning what was happening in society at large, he was still extremely patriotic, supporting the policies which Hitler and the Third Reich had adopted in their running of the country. He was proud to be working on their behalf. His appointed task was to produce an insecticide to eliminate lice, rodents and any forms of infestation. Large amounts of food stocks and textiles were being destroyed by these pests. Food and clothing were in desperately short supply, with people reduced to wearing thin, threadbare clothing in freezing conditions. Most of Germany's finances it appeared worryingly to him, were being diverted to rearmament programmes in preparation for conflict.

Imported supplies were few, and in transportation large quantities of food were being destroyed by vermin; the chemicals and repellents they had were ineffective, and in some cases were compounding the problem by damaging the goods. The use of gases such as chlorine were causing concern as they affected personnel. Inhalation of the gas had led in the past to lung damage and sadly in many instances proven fatal.

The trench situation of the Great War was familiar to him; soldiers had battled in filthy trenches filled with ankle deep stagnant water, polluted by dead rats, and even the remains of lost comrades. Lice crawled all over their bodies, no part sacrosanct from their bloodthirsty ravages. Soldiers exhausted from battle, starving, shell shocked, suffering unimaginable conditions, and had no respite. The scourge of constant itching caused them to scratch themselves until their skin and flesh were torn and bleeding. Then came infection, and septicaemia, with soldiers losing limbs through amputation. Many died in consequence.

If there was to be another war, Gerhardt was determined this would not happen again; finding an effective deterrent was of paramount importance. He turned away as the deepening snow mantled the buildings, trees and grass.

Finally settling at his desk, his mind reverted to his growing concern about the mounting tensions in Europe. He understood the grave misfortunes the last conflict had inflicted on the people around him. There were countless widows in the towns and cities, fatherless children, food in short supply - there were rumours people were dying of starvation. The politicians' propaganda laid the blame at the door of Britain, France and their allies. The Jewish sector were singled out for the same accusations. Germany needed rebuilding, and fast. Hitler had instilled a new sense of national identity, unifying the disparate states into a cohesive single nation. New roads, factories and housing were being constructed; the blame for the struggle was increasingly laid on the strength, power and influence of the Jewish community.

Yes, there had been problems, inevitably! The lack of direction, the deep-rooted archaic mindset of the Weimar Government had prevented change and progress; there were many who denigrated Hitler, even resorting, he thought, to lies and fantasy. Gerhardt was disturbed by rumours that officers of the Third Reich were suppressing the will of the people with force. It was said that citizens were now afraid to express their concerns, accusing their leaders of tyranny. The word on the street was that many dissenters were being persecuted, and Gerhardt had even been told of a newly designed guillotine to be used as a deterrent.

He thought false stories like these were undermining the good work the authorities were doing to change the antiquated infrastructure. People reported that loved ones who complained had been arrested and never seen again. To suggest that everyone was afraid of talking about issues for fear of retribution was surely not true. The supposition, that neighbour might betray neighbour, friends betray friends, and even family - Gerhardt found difficult to believe. He had no time for such rumours, often raised by his close friend and colleague Max. He needed to concentrate on more important matters. He had received a formal letter which impressed on him the urgency and importance of his mission. In the envelope was an article on the effects of poor sanitation in the Great War. The truth was that great numbers of their men had died not by shot or shell, but of the infections caused by vermin and insects.

This often led to typhoid, that killer disease. This note weighed heavily on his mind - if hostilities broke out... he must solve the problem!

Gerhardt checked the clock, wondering if Max would be delayed by the snow; as normally he could rely on him to be on time, and he began to shuffle anxiously as he waited. He couldn't begin the new project without Max's help. The preparation of mixing chemicals needed great care; they were highly toxic; one slip could lead to serious injury. Gerhardt had tried to manage an experiment on his own before, but with a small spillage of a single liquid he had experienced the painful effects of toxic chemical exposure. His chest tightened making breathing difficult. All turned dark as his eyesight faded. It was forbidden to conduct experiments on oneself, so he kept the incident from Max. Fortunately the symptoms subsided over time and a few days later he was as normal.

To keep fumes and vapour from entering the lab, the volatile liquids were mixed very carefully. Experiments were conducted in a large, triple sealed glass cabinet, so that any gas emitted from the evaporating liquid could not escape. It was constructed in three sections, allowing each part in turn to be exposed to the gas. The first section was where solutions were prepared, connected to the second chamber by a sealed panel. When opened, it allowed the gas to pass through, exposing small lifeforms such as insects, flies and other pests, in the second chamber. The third and last chamber, also accessed by a sealed panel, was the largest, for larger animals like mice, rats and rabbits.

To access the first preparation unit where the chemicals were mixed, a set of thick rubber gloves were hermetically sealed within the chamber. This insulated and carefully sealed construction prevented the escape of any vapour. Whilst it was a very efficient means of containing the gas, the thickness of the gloves made it cumbersome for picking up small objects. Then, on completion of experiments, there was the problem of removing any gas in the chambers. Each glass cabinet was fitted with an extractor fan enabling spent gases to be evacuated to the outside air. The cabinets allowed them to measure the lethal effects of the gas under trial. So far the results had been disappointing. In the past they had used a variety of substances including a new powder called Zyklon B. This produced a gas called cyanide when water was added; it had proved to be very effective, but it was clearly too dangerous to use in the holds of ships or storage depots. Curiously, for some unknown reason, large quantities of it were being prepared - presumably, he mused, for the extermination of rats and other vermin.

Gerhardt had no sooner left the window to head to his workbench than Max arrived, wearing his usual smile. Always happy and jovial, he was a pleasure to work with. Recently, however, discussions about what was happening in the new Germany were escalating into disagreements. A rift was forming between them, their diverging opinions about the Third Reich becoming more aggressive. They tried to avoid the issue, but Max often seemed to bring up the topic at the least opportune moment.

On his way to the lab, seeing what was happening to Jewish owned shops on the High Street, he would find it difficult to contain himself, but - "not now," he thought. For their important work, they agreed to defer on most things, and especially now when they thought they were close to a solution. They had a new formula and were keen to see if it worked.

Max was a tall, well-built man; having served in the Great War he knew first- hand the horrors of the trenches. He had been personally trained by the fearsome Oskar Dirlewanger as an elite storm trooper, he gained respect not only from his troop but amongst senior officers. Although the man appeared to be a gentle giant, he had volunteered for some extremely dangerous situations, particularly information gathering, and getting close to the enemy. Max, unknown to Gerhardt and the authorities, was descended from American stock; he spoke perfect English and had distinguished himself by crawling close enough to the enemy lines to gather vital intelligence.

On one occasion he had heard of a planned bombardment - the Germans had been able to retreat, and after the shelling, returned to their lines - ready to repel a frontal attack. Their idle chatter had caused mayhem for the British, but the sight of so many brave soldiers slain by machine gun fire had sickened Max; it would haunt him for the rest of his life.

Chapter 2

Spandau, Germany

Max walked to his desk, saying, "Let's get started!" with excitement brewing in his voice; they were both feeling a heady mixture of satisfaction that they had created an effective agent. The two men shared a tinge of apprehension - failure meant starting all over again. Max unlocked the drawer containing their folder of formulae, took them out and headed to the fume chamber for the chemicals. He checked liquid fluorine, sulphur, cyanide and phosphorus. Some other elements were contained in a separate sealed jar. The proportions had been very carefully planned. Max walked to the gas chamber, and checking everything was in the right place, signalled to Gerhardt to place the insects and mites into the second chamber, and two chickens and a rabbit in the third.

Max had been carefully mixing the chemicals in a glass jar with a tight ground glass stopper, he smiled tautly at Gerhardt as he swirled them gently together. He was attempting to remove the stopper, which had become too tight, when the telephone shrilled out, making him jump and drop the flask onto the work bench. He snatched at it, but the thick rubber gloves were clumsy, and some of the fluid spilled before he could get the stopper back – fortunately only a small amount and Max was safely behind a screen with his hand protected by gloves. Gerhardt grabbed the phone and listened impatiently to one of the security guards before grabbing both the black and green phone and laying them down with their handsets off.

"Come, Max, let's have a break and settle our nerves before the real work begins." Max hesitated, as he would like to get on, but Gerhardt was in charge, so he shrugged and went to sit with him. Gerhardt took a deep breath before explaining, "It's of great national importance, this work, Max - I feel so honoured to be carrying it through! How about you? Nervous? Concerned?" It was a spark that couldn't fail to ignite Max's annoyance at the current regime; he was soon in overdrive, complaining that the New Germany was ruining people's lives. After nodding in approval a few times, Gerhardt turned, apparently equally keen now to get back to their work. As they rose from the table, Max heard a click from the green telephone receiver; he was puzzled - had someone been listening? He grimaced; was everything being recorded? Were his views on the third Reich known? Should he fear for his life?

Max carefully opened the stopper on the flask of solution, and waited a few moments before sliding open the panel, allowing the gas to reach the second chamber. The men stared in amazement as they watched the small creatures die. Now they wanted to see its effects on the larger animals - "Good God!" Max and Gerhardt both uttered as they witnessed the immediate effects - the animals became instantly agitated, shaking and shivering, and racked with spasms before falling into a pool of their own urine and excrement.

"This is remarkable, Max! We've done it! This means we can protect food stocks, remove infestation... all of our targets!"

"Excellent!" crowed Max, shaking Gerhardt's hand and grinning, although a moment later, he was more thoughtful.

"We have to get rid of this mixture safely now, and it's quite volatile. We should evaporate it - warm it up so it goes faster, and put the extractor on to take the fumes outside."

Gerhardt agreed immediately and they set about the task. After an hour of pumping, they checked the chamber by putting in another rabbit. It was still alive half an hour later and they felt able to lock up the remaining chemicals and information and leave. They secured the lab carefully and went out into the cold, fresh air; the snow had stopped and they were in high spirits about their success, and the timing of it, with Christmas only two days away.

Then Max cried out, "Gerhard, stop!" And they stood, frozen in horror at the sight revealed by the floodlights across the darkened field. Sheep and horses lay dead in the snow.

"My God, what have we done?" groaned Max hoarsely. "Where is the guard? Is the gas still lethal? What must we do?" Gerhardt pointed at a group of pigeons sitting in the tree. "Birds have a rapid metabolism, if the gas was still present, they too would be dying."

The two scientists crouched to check the poor beasts - all had died with froth at their mouths, obviously in pain, and it was clear that their nervous systems had been attacked. Gerhardt said in an exhausted and colourless voice, "We have created something menacing, evil, Max - a new and powerful nerve gas." They returned in sombre mood to the laboratory. They needed to document what they had seen and were concerned about the guard.

Fortunately, the patrols had been stood down for Christmas, and they found the guard sitting in reception, apparently unaffected by the disaster outside. He told them his name was Frank, and he had seen them often, he said, although they had never really met... He was very well built, just the right physique for a guard, but with a scarred face, broken nose and partially closed left eye; his lip was damaged, revealing some of his lower teeth. "Don't worry," he assured them. "I know I'm not a pretty sight! It was a hand grenade in that bloody war!"

Max patted him on the shoulder and said, "Oh, comrade, I know, I was there too! I'm sorry you got hit."

Frank shrugged. "Yes, it was tough... I was lucky though, I kept my eyesight, and I'm alive, lots of my mates aren't. I sometimes envy them though - my body's stuffed full of shrapnel and it hurts like hell. Still, things are on the up now with the new lot. They've given me work and honours - letters commending my patriotism! I'm all for Hitler and his plans! Germany will be supreme again."

Max decided to cut the conversation before it became too provocative and get onto sorting out their nightmare situation. They now had a problem - how much were they going to reveal about what had happened? Gerhardt took the initiative; perching on the desk, he told Frank that they had been experimenting with chemicals to prevent food from being contaminated. To test this, they had put some in the food for the outdoor animals; regrettably the animals had died, and he should not go near them.

Frank was perplexed - he was fond of the animals, was used to them. How many had died? Max explained that they were sorry but it was all of them; Frank should understand that preserving food was of vital importance to the New Germany.

"Don't be concerned, Frank, we will return tomorrow and organise the removal of the carcasses, and we'll need to record the incident. You get off home, the relief guard are already overdue. Remember it's almost Christmas! Good times for us all!"

As they left, they saw Frank gathering his things and heading away; but they were in the laboratory in moments and didn't see Frank turn. He walked silently back down the corridor and slipped into the room with the Restricted Entry sign. He didn't turn on the light - he knew where he was going - he reached the green phone in the darkness - and listened.

Moments after they regained the lab Max noticed Gerhardt was hunched over and holding his chest. "Gerhardt - are you OK?" Max moved toward his colleague anxiously.

"It's my chest - I feel like I've got iron bands on my lungs," Gerhardt groaned.

Max was concerned - he had seen how close Gerhardt had gone to the poisoned animals to check their eyes and mouths.

"I'm getting a splitting headache, Max, and it seems to be getting darker in here."

Max, shocked to see Gerhardt was dribbling and looking unsteady on his feet, guided him into a chair, studying his eyes; the pupils had shrunk to pinpoints. "Look Gerhardt, you must rest - you obviously got a dose of that gas; let's see if you recover soon. I'll call a taxi, get you home, and stay with you. If you get worse, I will get you to hospital, but we can't let this leak out. We have to decide if we should stop this research... We've got something hideously dangerous... getting close to it is... tabun."

Max felt "taboo" was appropriate - they had broken some ancient moral code, had strayed into a ghastly breach of their scientific standards. He shuddered as he called the taxi, and noticed as he replaced the handset, that once again the green telephone clicked. He then went swiftly to secure the laboratories, checking each door as he swept through; he paused outside the Restricted Entry door in the main corridor and wondered again what was in there. Passing the entranceway, he saw the taxi flashing its lights at the gates; letting the driver in, Max asked him to come as close as possible to the entrance, then returned to help Gerhardt. As they reached the front door, Max was glad to see two guards approaching to take over security; he helped Gerhardt into the cab and they drove thankfully away from the buildings and into the moonless night.

Inside, the guards were surprised to see Frank coming toward them in the darkened foyer. He said goodnight to them and hurried away. He had gleaned some important information; it was time to tell the Colonel what he had heard on his important green phone.

Five days after Christmas, Gerhardt was feeling almost himself again. His pupils had almost returned to their normal size, his headache had cleared as well as his hyper salivation. His chest still burned slightly, but the tinnitus in his ear was gradually subsiding. He and Max decided to return to the laboratory two days earlier than planned. Gerhardt decided it would be more prudent to drive there and asked Max to get the car from the garage. There was a lot to be done; they hadn't yet decided how much information they should reveal about the effect of the gas on the livestock. They had decided it would be wise to include the deaths in their report.

Frank would be a problem - they concluded he had been spying on them, had by now probably passed on the result of their experiment to the new director, Colonel Schmidt. They would have to present their findings in a way which did not contradict Frank's version of events, and in future they would deliberately reveal only matters they wanted the authorities to know. Max was anxious - had Frank been listening to all the contentious conversations he had had with Gerhardt? His mouth felt dry, and his heart and mind seemed to pound in unison. As they approached the gates, they spotted a staff car parked at the main entrance, an armed soldier standing by it, and an SS officer at the wheel. They looked at each other nervously - this was someone important, there were dangerous shoals ahead.

Max cleared his throat before asking, "OK, so we're agreed right? If it's the Colonel, we proceed as if we don't know he's already been informed... go ahead with the report... we have got to handle this carefully, Gerhardt. This guy's known to be a total bastard - maybe we can dampen whatever rage he's already in."

They parked close to the labs, and were approached by the soldier, the officer and Frank, who had come out and was speaking quietly to him as they walked. The soldier unshouldered his rifle, holding it in readiness across his chest; the expression on their faces and the purposeful stamp of boots on tarmac showed they meant business. This was no friendly visit. The SS officer summoned a nearby group of soldiers to form up close by, Frank was sharply ordered back to his post and Max and Gerhardt were suddenly encircled by troops and hustled towards the building. Max was working hard to conceal his sudden rage - he wasn't afraid of these untested troops! But Gerhardt had turned pale and was shaking.

Escorted into the building, they were turned to the left and halted outside a door marked Out of Bounds. The SS officer knocked briskly and opened the door, marching inside and motioning Max and Gerhardt to enter, closely followed by the soldier. The officer barked at them and all gave the Sieg Heil salute. It was a ragged attempt, and they were made to repeat the gesture in front of the frowning officer. In a padded club chair sat a smiling Colonel Schmidt, slowly taking in every detail of their appearance, and addressing them by their Christian names as he welcomed them. He was in immaculate army uniform, and wore the Iron Cross on his left breast. Tall and slender, thin lipped and with a thin moustache, everything about him seemed lean and sinuous, reminding Max of a venomous snake. Max felt no fear of him personally - he felt he could snap the man in two given the chance, but Gerhardt continued to shake.

One of the Colonel's fists, clad in a black leather glove, clenched a roll of paper on the desk, while the other, casually holding a baton, rested in his lap. It felt like a long time until the Colonel, apparently casual and relaxed, began to speak. Max and Gerhardt intuitively knew this man had already been fully briefed about their work and actions - the sight of the green phone on his desk made them fully alert to what Frank had heard and passed on. When questioned, they would have to reveal the truth - but what about the way they had expressed their concerns about the new regime?

"I apologise, gentlemen, if my visit has taken you by surprise. My information was that you would not be back here for two more days - we are still technically on holiday. It happened that I was in the area, and I felt it would be a good opportunity to call in and see what is going on. I have been appointed to co-ordinate all the chemical research being carried out over this and other establishments. I am very curious to see how things are developing here. I believe you have been tasked with finding a solution to the problem of pests and vermin damaging our food and textile imports?"

Max and Gerhardt both nodded, their eyes fixed on his face, their shoulders taut.

"So! This is a most important project - vital work! I personally have no knowledge at present of the nature and progress of your research, but with both of you here, perhaps you will explain what has been achieved, and what problems may be encountered?"

Max had passed close to the Colonel's car as they came in, had felt the residual heat from the powerful engine on this cold winter day. This meant he had only just arrived, had been granted no time to investigate the laboratories. However, Frank had clearly communicated much of what had happened. He tried to organise his thoughts as the Colonel told them he wished them to show him their laboratory, and as they began to introduce their equipment, Schmidt studied the fume chambers carefully, as well as some notes they had left in the room, even examining the waste container.

Colonel Schmidt moved closer to Gerhardt, studying his every move and gesture; Gerhardt shifted his ground a little nervously and continued his explanations. There was no point holding back - Schmidt had clearly had a full report of the incident with the gas; Gerhardt tried to keep calm and present everything as naturally as possible.

"I see everything is in order here - now I want you to explain to me what recent experiments you have carried out, and what results you have achieved in tackling this infestation problem. What tests have you carried out, and when will you be ready to start testing on transit goods?"

Gerhardt began to outline the nature of the problem. "Of course, the biggest inhibiting factor, Colonel, is the need to preserve the food stocks from contamination while killing the vermin, and of course to protect those handling the goods, and the consumers, from chemical harm. Until recently we have worked without much success, but just before Christmas we had some heartening results. A solution which when evaporated had a powerful effect on insects and smaller animals. You may be aware Sir, that several animals were found dead in the field outside - this can only have been caused by an accidental spillage during the experiment on the small animals, and we must for safety's sake cremate the beasts. But they clearly died from a neurological poison which we had expelled. We were planning to write up our full report after Christmas, once we had had the chance to fully examine the results, and then bring it to the authorities. We are aware this gas may be far too strong and dangerous for the job intended, Sir, and we didn't want it to come to common knowledge - we were considering the best way of keeping the research secret until we could inform you - in the wrong hands this could be devastating."

Listening to Gerhardt, Max had his head bowed; he now became aware that Schmidt was watching him closely. Max shrugged his shoulders and stretched, trying to look as if this was all in a day's work.

Schmidt glanced across to the soldier and back to Gerhardt. He was clearly taken aback but had made up his mind on his next course of action. "It is very important that this be kept absolutely secret. I will go to see these animals; you will gather all chemicals and formulae, everything used in this experiment; it will be placed in a secure location and you will tell no one. You will give me a report down to the minutest detail. It is clear this substance could cause devastation, and if news of this leaks there will be a heavy price to pay, beginning with yourselves. Is this clear?" They assented numbly and were told to remain in the laboratory until they were sent for.

Max and Gerhardt slumped in their seats, wondering what would happen next.

They had been forced to reveal everything, but the Colonel had been clearly affected, and angry. Twenty minutes later, they were again taken to Schmidt's office. He informed them that he had spoken with one of the Chiefs of Staff, who had halted experiments on the product until further notice.

"I have decided that I do not need to see the animals - I must go at once to Berlin. However, I will return tomorrow to collect your report. Heil Hitler!"

The scientists came to attention and echoed his salute, then followed him from the room. The soldier locked it behind them. They wished the Colonel a good journey as he slammed his door shut and an armed soldier took up his place on the car running board.

Max and Gerhardt were feeling some relief as the gates were opened and the staff car moved through. Suddenly however, it reversed back into the courtyard, making way for a lorry full of armed soldiers. Schmidt once again left his car and hurried over to issue orders for the man in command. Soldiers descended smartly from the trucks and began unloading sandbags, which were quickly formed into walls on either side of the gate. Next, a group were sent to a large tarpaulin covering the carcasses of the dead animals which had been moved from the barn. They were thrown into the back of a lorry.

The soldiers deployed around the perimeter and the building while the Colonel shouted instructions, heightening emphasis with the pointing baton. When all was satisfactory, he jumped back into the staff car and sped away. The officer in charge approached Max and Gerhardt; they were to hand over their keys and leave, to return at 10am. tomorrow. The scientists felt bemused, taken aback by the speed with which the operation had been completed - no one had spoken a word to them, and they felt like pawns in the Colonel's new game. He was stamping his military authority on the laboratories, which would clearly be managed now under tight security, and he realised they would both now be monitored relentlessly.

Max turned to Gerhardt urgently and asked, "Did you notice that Frank and the first soldier disappeared? Did you hear two pistol shots? I did, and God help me, there were two large sacks in the back of that car when it left!"

Chapter 3

Spandau Germany

A deep dark cloud hung over Gerhardt and Max the following morning. They had talked over and over the significance of their meeting with Schmidt the day before; the possibility that Frank and the soldier had been executed because of what they had learned about the experiment, meant, they were sure, that Schmidt had been granted authority from a higher level.

The toxic gas they had created was of such importance and secrecy that this barbaric regime would murder at will to protect it - so what did this mean for them? They knew their conversations had been monitored, but Gerhardt had never expressed himself as passionately as Max had about the way the Third Reich was changing German society. Max had often been vocal about the sinister direction the new regime was heading. Here was a prime example - Frank had been a loyal and patriotic servant of the regime, yet was still callously eliminated to protect this research, a gas with potential for devastating effects in chemical warfare.

They had slept little, talking into the early hours, and woke in the morning light little refreshed and full of anxiety. With only strong coffee inside them, they set out to the laboratory to report as ordered, hoping the walk would clear their minds.

Approaching the gates, they saw evidence of much activity; trucks were parked along the front of the laboratory and were being loaded. "That's some of our stuff - they're clearing everything!" Max muttered. "So where does this leave us?"

For a moment they stood still and looked at each other. Then a Gestapo officer directed them to follow him. Inside, they were taken again to Schmidt's office, but found a more senior Gestapo officer in command of it; his expression was grim.

However, to their surprise, he stood and extended his hand to Gerhardt, shook it and clicked his heels. He saluted him and, ignoring Max completely, thanked Gerhardt warmly for his service to the Fatherland. He then signalled to two soldiers and ordered Max to stand to attention; he was suddenly seized by the shoulders and his arms pulled behind him - handcuffs snapped onto his wrists. Gerhardt stood motionless in shock, and as Max was marched away heard him shout, "Tell Ruth I love her! Tell her I will be back."

The door slammed. They would never meet again. The Gestapo officer turned back to Gerhardt. "Now! I should remind you that you are still employed by I G Fabian, but while your work is being monitored by Spandau Citadel, you will be transferred to Rambkammer near Munster. There, you will be working with a team to refine this substance you have created so it can be used as a pesticide."

Gerhardt knew that pesticide was not the true objective. He suspected that there could be a much more sinister motive underlying the experiments.

"I would like to know where my colleague is being taken, and what will happen to him?" It was a brave question and there was a silence in the room for a long moment.

"Your colleague will be taken to the Citadel for questioning; he was trained as a storm trooper and he will probably be better employed in that capacity. You will now have an opportunity to meet up with a group of other scientists in your field, at Falkenhagen; they are looking forward to sharing ideas with you - including on the product Zyklon B, which I am sure you are familiar with from its use as a de-lousing agent in the last war."

Staring intently at Gerhardt he suddenly snapped, "You have a name for your new discovery?"

"Tabun."

"Tabun! Why?"

"Because I wish I had never invented it, and because it should never be used in its present form... just as Walter Heerd never meant his work on Zyklon B to produce cyanide gas to be used on his countrymen." Gerhardt knew he was sticking his neck out, but his anger over Max's treatment had overwhelmed caution.

The officer stared at him long and hard; he could so easily have Gerhardt disposed of, but the man at present was valuable. He thought that one day, he would make him pay. "You will now return to your home and pack, sort out your affairs, and return as soon as possible for your transportation to your new quarters. You will not communicate to anyone about recent events, it would be foolish to do so, let me advise you."

As Gerhardt reached the door he turned. "Can I see Max before I leave?"

"No, where he is going, he will not be receiving visitors, Herr Schrader. Be glad you are in charge of this new opportunity to serve the Fatherland and be grateful for your situation."

Max strained at his cuffs and tried to wrestle them into a more comfortable position, only to receive a sharp blow to the back of his skull. "Where are you taking me? I'm a scientist here!"

Silently, the soldiers hustled him into a limousine, pushed his head down between his knees. "Shut up! Any problems with you, any attempt to escape, and you will be shot."

The car sped on for several miles and arrived at a narrow bridge which was the entrance to Spandau Citadel. The beautiful and elegant building stood at the junction of two rivers, the Sree and the Havel, which created its moat. An impressive symbol of power, it had been built in the late 16th Century on the foundations of more ancient structures. Its builder, Francesco Charamella de Gandino, had designed the castle to protect the town of Spandau, which stood on an important trade route East to West via Magdeburg. It enabled

Spandau to grow as an important trade and military centre. Boasting four bastions without blind spots, it was a daunting target to attack.

Now it was a popular tourist spot, with many drawn to its beautiful setting; but the passers-by knew very little of what was happening inside. The elegant and majestic exterior spoke of safety and peace, but the interior was a place of darker activity. Access was strictly limited, the entrances well-guarded. The cellars had been converted to laboratories dedicated to research for military purposes, mainly chemical weapons, while the upper floors contained offices. In one of these a sinister group awaited Max.

During the half hour journey, Max's mind was a compound of rage, anxiety and bewilderment. He wondered where they were taking him but knew there was no point asking questions. Anger flared at the way they were treating him, a scientist.

Then the thought came to him - it was time to stop thinking like a scientist and think like the highly trained soldier he had once been. He needed to consider, firstly, was he going to be in danger? Were they simply taking him to a different centre? Given the roughness of his treatment that seemed unlikely; he needed to keep as calm as possible, and as aware of details which might help him escape. Seeing the Citadel, he felt relief for a moment, that he was going to be put to work in a different laboratory here. But that thought quickly darkened; he sensed that interrogation was the purpose of bringing him to this stronghold. He wasn't going to give in easily.

He was dragged from the car and frog marched up two flights of stairs and into a tobacco smoke filled office. Through the haze of smoke, he saw different ranking officers sitting round a large square table. A senior Gestapo officer was flanked by two further officers each side. Then he caught sight of someone he knew from Army days - he wondered how his old friend Fritz, now a Captain, came to be sitting with these Gestapo and SS bastards. He exchanged a fleeting glance with Fritz - this was no time for acknowledgement or pleasantries. Max could see a glimmer of recognition on Fritz's eyes before he lowered his head to hide his surprise.

Max was seated in a chair as the senior officer studied him grimly; with a pale, thin lipped face with half closed eyes, he was clean shaven, in his forties and had a sharp pointed chin which seemcd to suit his office. Max, staring back, thought there was something faintly ridiculous about the way his hat perched above his pointed ears. Nevertheless, he sensed something tyrannical and nasty about the man.

The thin shoulders and bony wrists belied the power this man had.

"You have been brought here accused by several agencies of being a traitor to the state," the officer announced, with no introduction of himself or the others.

"You were entrusted with work vital to the security of this country, but you are a subversive and dangerous enemy of the Third Reich, and undeserving of their protection. You will be transferred to an area of correction and rehabilitation. It is hoped that you will then return to your work with honest endeavour after your re-education. It has been noted that as a storm trooper you distinguished yourself in battle, therefore it is felt that when you can be trusted, you may be returned to your old regiment. This is the opinion of all on this panel and will be enacted immediately."

The officer stood and stretched out his arm, looking sternly down at Max who rose to the salute and an echoing, "Heil Hitler! Zieg Heil!"

As the officers filed out of the room, Max tried to rally his thoughts, feeling that it could have been worse. He had often missed the comradeship of his army unit, had only been assigned to laboratory work because of his scientific background, especially chemistry. Now, only Fritz and another stormtrooper remained.

As Fritz approached him, he flicked his eyes as a signal not to reveal their friendship. The other officer turned to leave the room. Max felt he had also seen this man before, then remembered they had served together in World War 1.

The corridor was empty - it was a Saturday, and most people had gone home for the afternoon.

Fritz checked the corridor and focused on Max. "I have orders to kill you."

Chapter 4

Spandau Germany

They moved together along the corridor, Fritz removing Max's handcuffs as they went. Max eased his shoulders and arms, stiff and bruised. Too soft a life as a scientist he thought wryly. They came to the door leading down to the laboratories - a massive one of solid oak, strapped and reinforced with iron bands. It was locked, but it seemed Fritz had been overseeing security for several months, and possessed all the keys to the Citadel.

They heaved a sigh of relief as they locked the door behind them. Security was tight when the scientists were at work, with guards at all the doors, but at the weekend guards were at the front of the building only, though, with regular armed patrols of the building.

Max and Gerhardt had worked here initially, but as their experiments began to require more space and secrecy, as well as grazing for larger animals, they had been moved. As Fritz was securing the door, Max was able to take a look at his old friend - looking just as lean and healthy as always. He was very tall, slender yet powerful; his fair hair was close cropped and the tanned face accentuated his light blue eyes. Close shaven, and impeccable, his appearance gave the impression of self-discipline - he would be firm in his commitment to any task.

Fritz had exceptionally large hands, scarred by hand-to-hand combat in the battlefield. He had studied in Berlin, but like so many had not completed his course in mechanics, but had been removed from university to fight. He had earned several commendations in the field, and had experienced first-hand the hell of survival in the trenches. The smell of death, the constant fear, had hardened his resolve; he would never be free of the anguish of loss and waste of so many lives. All the responsibility of stupid warmongers and inept politicians. A cauldron of disenchantment and foreboding had been left from the loss of so many friends and the bitterness of the final outcome of war. He seemed well suited to the position he now held.

He feared no-one, trusted few; he secretly loathed the new regime, finding himself constantly at odds with those around him. Fritz was confused as to where he stood in society, unable to reconcile his beliefs with the evil ideology he was now forced to follow. He had no idea where his future lay, or which direction to follow. But one thing he was certain of - that one of his close friends, a man he had trusted with his life during the war, enduring with him the ravages of battle, should not suffer at the hands of these depraved extremists.

Fritz introduced Alex, the other soldier, to Max and as they shook hands Max remembered where they had met before. During a battle Alex had helped him to carry a wounded comrade back from the front; he had noted the stocky strength in the young man as he took the injured man's legs, and Max the shoulders. Their common bond was experiencing the sickness and horror of that war, and they felt alike the sadness and disgust at the direction the new Germany was taking.

Alex was short, but with thick, strong arms and legs. In his round face, his smile revealed missing front teeth - knocked out by a British rifle butt which had rendered him unconscious and presumed dead. Coming round when the battle had ended, he had crawled back to his trench, to find it full of British infantry. He was treated well and released just weeks after the war ended. His mother had been raised in London, so his good English helped him communicate well in his makeshift prison camp. He had never forgotten their kind treatment - perhaps he thought, it was because they all knew the war was ending, and just looked forward to peace in Europe.

Down the steps they went to another massive door, made entirely of iron and centuries old - it was sealed with three padlocks, and as he easily undid the highest one, Fritz joked that Alex was designed to open the lowest. They all chuckled with relief as the well-oiled and finely balance door opened easily for them. On the other side, they bolted it and felt safe for now. They had to devise a plan of escape, but could relax a little.

Unknown to them, a security guard had observed them in the corridor, and was on his way to alert the guardroom at the front of the castle.

Max suggested they go to his old laboratory where they could try to work out what they could do. He was perplexed about why his old comrades had put themselves in such danger on his behalf. They faced a possible death penalty for their actions, and now were trapped in the basement laboratories... How were they going to get out?

"Our biggest problem is going to be finding a way to get past the guards," said Max, "the place is crawling with them, especially the front of the building. Let's get to somewhere we can get a minute to think - my old laboratory's still in use, there's always some food and drink about for the scientists working late... we can get a coffee and start planning."

Fritz suddenly remembered something - he'd neglected to secure the door at the top of the stairs. Dashing back to it, he half turned his key in the lock - that would prevent them inserting another key. He found a pencil in his pocket and rammed that in so they wouldn't be able to turn his key either. He returned to the others and they set off, following Max. Fritz and Alex were taking in their surroundings as they walked, there were a mixture of service rooms and labs, with half glazed doors. At the last laboratory, Max stopped.

"I think all the lab doors are opened with one key, Fritz - have you got it?"

Fritz handed his bunch of keys to Max, who quickly recognised the one he needed; entering, he switched on the lights and went straight to the cupboard holding the kettle. Coffee was ready in a few minutes, and they relaxed a little.

"Max, is there a master switch for the lights in the laboratories?" Asked Fritz, looking keenly about him for ideas.

"Yes, there's a storeroom at the end of the corridor with a set of switches, lots of equipment in there too."

Max looked at Fritz and Alex. "I can't tell you how grateful I am for your help - but why are you putting yourselves at such risk? And why come down here? Aren't we more trapped underground? Couldn't you have just let me go without becoming implicated?"

"We had no idea who it was being interviewed, we just knew whoever it was would be executed - no proper trial - a done deal. It's happening all the time! When Alex and I saw it was you, we were totally shocked. Max, we couldn't let them do this to you - we are all stormtroopers - that's a bond stronger than loyalty to this bunch of murderers. But Meyer said we were to take you to the cells, shoot you, then put you into a body bag. He said he will personally inspect the body tomorrow, he's under orders from on high. It's about the experiments in these laboratories - they'll kill anyone who's a risk of breaking the secrecy. He was off to some urgent meeting, that's why we waited until they'd all gone before bringing you out. We had to opt for the labs because we had to wait until most of the security have knocked off - we heard you had worked here before - we hoped you might know of other ways out." Fritz appeared tense and eager wondering if they would ever find a way out. He went on, "We thought maybe we could smuggle you out in a body bag - common enough! But Meyer wanting to see you dead tomorrow means we'd have to explain. The guards here don't just distrust outsiders, they're all trained to distrust each other... security is really tight."

Max dropped his head, staring down at his old workbench, he felt humbled by the loyalty and bravery of his two former comrades, it fuelled a surge of inner strength; he raised his head to look steadily at the others with tears almost brimming. "If we get out of here, I will repay you with my loyalty, If we are destined to die, then I will be proud to do so in your company, with old friends I trust and love."

They all tried to shake off the emotion and muster their thoughts - were there other exits, other service tunnels they could use? Max knew of some manholes in each laboratory, which carried away wastewater, and also serviced the toilets. They immediately started to work on raising one of these - they were heavy and rusted in place. When they finally managed to heave one away, they were desolate to find only a narrow pipe, stinking of waste and only large enough for cleaning by brushes or rods.

"It seems we can't escape this place - we need to think of some other way of tricking the guards?" Alex said, as they gathered around the workbench to reconsider their options.

"We don't know how long we have before they start looking for us - or how long before they can get through the doors." Alex took out pen and paper from a desk. "If they take us, I would prefer we shoot ourselves than be taken."

They were a brotherhood now, not ordinary men. Their military training began to assert itself.

"We should go through the equipment here, make a list of whatever may be useful."

"Three brains are better than one," said Fritz, grinning, "even if one of them is Alex's."

"We need to collect anything we can use as a weapon, and Max, think - are there any places we could remain undetected for a while?"

Max mentally walked the corridors - telling Alex as he thought of possible hiding places, including an old bricked up tunnel near the iron door, a cloakroom, and the storerooms. They split up to investigate. In the cloakroom, Alex found uniforms similar to theirs and he grabbed a set for Max; he also spotted gas masks and took three. In the storeroom Fritz selected candles, cord, buckets and mops and brushes. He made a mental note of any other equipment, but there wasn't much of use. Max, meanwhile, was going through the chemicals in the laboratory, wondering how they could be effective in their escape.

They reconvened - with some amusement at Fritz's mops and buckets. "Is it a clean-up operation?' laughed Alex.

Max said he had enough chemicals to make explosives, and quite a few nasty surprises.

"When they break in, we have to ensure complete darkness. We need somewhere to hide where we can then work our way out in the blackout. Max, you should get into the uniform," Fritz was wondering aloud. "Can we think of a distraction, something pretty scary?"

The plan was beginning to crystallise in their thoughts, but at that moment they heard sounds of pounding and hammering at the upper wooden door, followed by gunshots. Grabbing his pistol, Fritz ran to the iron door to listen; he examined a light switch close to the door and switched it off. The effect was dramatic - the only light was coming from the lab windows. He saw another, larger switch beneath the other, and flicked it off. The whole underground zone became pitch black; it was the kind of darkness to chill the soul, he thought - it could be useful.

He checked the recess, the blocked off tunnel Max had mentioned - when opened the door would partially block it; Max said he had a plan now, but they needed to move fast. "We can hide in the recess, then put out the lights as they break through - that will confuse them."

"I'll get working on the lights," offered Alex, "just need a screwdriver and some string." Fritz also had an idea: "I can put piles of chairs, buckets and glass on benches along the wall - tie them together with string so they bring it all down."

Max was to get together something chemical to create alarm and fear. The banging on the iron door had begun. They got to work.

Chapter 5

Spandau Germany

The banging at the door had stopped, thankfully, but also worryingly. The noise had been deafening even with the laboratory doors closed. Perhaps this change of attack would buy them some precious time. Max had been busy making a concoction from some violet crystals and what smelt like ammonia. Collecting several jars of crystals, he had poured them into several beakers forming a layer around two cm. deep in the bottom. He then poured the liquid over them to a depth of around four cm. He now had five standing ready in a row, the mixture not stirred but allowing the crystals to settle.

Fritz was busy piling chairs and stools onto the benches nearest the doorway; he then gathered as much glassware as he could and balanced that on top of the furniture. He looked around for anything else that would make a lot of noise if it hit the floor. He had found a ball of strong twine and was attaching it to the legs of stools and chairs; when he was satisfied with his mounds of objects, he trailed the twine in amongst them and then along the corridor to the recess behind the iron door. Carefully he took up the tension, then hooked the twine to a nail projecting from the wall. At the right moment he could tug on the twine, setting the whole thing crashing to the ground, and creating a noisy distraction as the guards entered the corridor.

Alex, meanwhile, had been busy with the electrics; removing the panel which accessed the wires to the master switch controlling all the lighting for this section of the cellars - he felt confident it would work. Returning to the lab he found Max intent on a further project, mixing powdered chemicals together in a mortar.

"Glad to see you Alex, I could do with some help here! Can you weigh out these three powders and keep them in separate piles?"

He indicated the three - one white, one yellow and one black.

"It's really important they are the same weight, then you can mix them together in a mortar."

It was clear to Alex that the mixture was gunpowder - he was intrigued to know what Max intended to do with it. Looking at the crystals which Max had transferred onto blotting paper from the beakers, he asked what they were for.

"I found some violet iodine crystals - and put ammonia over them. After a while the crystals react with the ammonia to form nitrous iodide crystals, which is what is drying on the paper." As he talked, Max was carefully transferring the piles of crystals in small heaps along the corridor. Then he took the gunpowder and made a trail along the side of the passage, with smaller trails to the crystals.

"If anything touches the crystals, they'll set off the gunpowder, making a nice big flash! It should temporarily blind them and give them a nice suntan! I really don't want to kill these guards - I've worked with quite a few of them, they're like me, veterans who didn't choose to work with this bastard regime and monsters like Mayer. If I die making sure he gets his just desserts, so be it."

Fritz had taken three sets of uniform, padded them with towels and propped them up with mop handles, completing the illusion of three men with gas masks. He thought, just perhaps it would be an extra diversion if the guards mistook them for the three of them in the confusion and darkness. He set them up further along the corridor, beyond the diversion heap of chairs and glass. As he hurried about, he narrowly avoided treading on the purple crystals, and gave himself a shake - he needed to focus! He went to the iron door and listened intently; the sound of the guards discussing what to do next was muffled but he heard the name Mayer more than once. The guards were obviously feeling they needed Mayer to decide what action to take, once he got back from his important meeting. Fritz frowned - having dealt with Mayer for some time, he knew he would stop at nothing - would probably blow the door up to get to them, and then their preparations would be for nothing.

He had his own reasons for hating Mayer, and business to settle - even if it meant killing colleagues he had worked with for years, it was worth it, to get Mayer.

He called Max and Alex to a table to talk through what they were going to do, and the sequence of events. He told them what he had heard about Mayer; with him in charge their hope of being captured and surviving was nil; he would probably enjoy doing something extremely nasty to them himself. He confided his worry that Mayer would blow the door, ruining their escape, and worse, preventing Fritz getting close to Mayer.

"Right! The plan - as they come through the door, they will look down the corridor, see the three dummies and hopefully charge forward. At that moment, we kill the lights; and bring the chairs and glass down. The guards will be setting off the dynamite flashes, and the bangs will sound like gunfire. Now we get the chance to join at the back of the group, then as everyone moves back out, we get away in the dark. The best way will be out the back, away from the guard room; it's not as closely watched because it has high security locks... But I still have my keys!"

After Fritz's briefing, the other two smilingly shook their heads - there was only the slimmest of chances they would get to the door, but it was their only chance and they would give it their best shot. At this point, Alex asked Max why he had made so much gunpowder; Max turned to them both, rested his palms on the table and, speaking slowly but passionately, began to share what was in his mind.

"Realistically, we all know our chances of pulling this off are minimal... We don't need luck so much as divine intervention. We've all agreed we'd prefer to die by our own hands than give Mayer the satisfaction. I've worked here before, and around these labs are many toxic materials in preparation - sulphur dioxide, chlorine and other gases. Plus, every bench has a gas supply for the Bunsen burners and other equipment."

The other two men looked at him gravely, seeing where this was going, what the end game might be. "If we turn on all the taps, the gas will create a potential explosive force capable of destroying these cellars. If all else fails I could seal the end laboratory and use the ring main to ignite the dynamite and the whole damn thing."

"How will you ignite the gunpowder?"

"I would turn off the electricity supply in the storeroom, remove an appliance and connect the ends of the wires - make a bundle of wire wool laced with magnesium powder. At the right moment, I turn the power back on. The explosion would destroy these laboratories and all the research files, putting back their work months. The building would need complete restoration. If Mayer survives, he's not going to be popular with the authorities. I would deem it an honour, my friends, to be the one to ignite this explosion."

They all smiled, Fritz and Alex placed their hands on top of his for a moment. "So be it." Fritz had one concern - the fate of some of the guards - some were veterans like themselves, and the younger men relied on them. It weighed heavily with him that they would all be killed - but he understood it might be unavoidable. They agreed that the detonation would be the point of last resort.

"Do you think we'll survive the blast while we're in the recess? Mind you, we're dead men walking, what's the difference!" But Fritz suddenly had a thought about how gas masks could help them. "Max, could we release some gas under the door? They'll think the place is full of gas and wear gas masks..."

"And we can wear them and mingle in better! Yes!" exclaimed Max and went for a gas canister, while Alex made for the storeroom. Max brought a cylinder of chlorine and rubber tubing and Alex brought the masks... suddenly their spirits lifted. Maybe they could do this!

Then the banging began on the iron door.

Time for a quick celebration - Max knew there was often some alcohol to be found in the lab refrigerator, and came back with a bottle of Alsace, which happened to be his favourite. They grabbed three beakers and toasted their new plan. As they banged their fists on the table, one of Fritz's dummy contraptions clattered to the floor. They all laughed for the first time in a long while; the dummy looked even more real in a heap on the floor, as though they were all dead. Fritz told them he had another idea and would explain it later.

A large staff car screamed to a halt before the Citadel; someone was in a hurry.

The powerful headlights poured light over the bridge and castle walls, but the Citadel seemed indifferent, serene in its splendour. The driver leapt out to open the rear door, and Lt Mayer thrust it open so fiercely the driver was thrown back.

As Mayer pushed past him furiously, the driver fell to the ground. Unseeing, Mayer was stamping and waving his arms as if fighting a swarm of bees. He stormed into the Citadel and kicked his way into the guardroom. His rage was out of control; he hurled his swizzle stick at the unfortunate clerk sitting at his desk; it missed the man and clattered off the wall. His words were being spat out of a face twisted and contorted with venom. He was incoherent and rambling, with froth at his mouth as he snarled, his body writhing as if it wanted to tear free of his uniform. Like an angry viper preparing to strike, he turned on the guards.

They had never seen him as angry as this; they all stood rigidly to attention, frozen with fear. They didn't want to have to speak to him in this state, remembering the young guard he had thrashed for failing to open a door for him.

Mayer demanded to know where Fritz and the others were holed up. He had received a phone call from a Spandau guard while he had been with senior SS officials, to be told that Max had not been executed as Mayer had promised his senior officers, but was at large within the Citadel. It made him look a failure, and they were angry at possible leaks about the research work. What should have been a routine matter was turning into a catastrophe. The Spandau Citadel was valuable to the war effort, one of the principal laboratories; it must not be compromised or damaged.

Mayer was quickly taken to the site of the oak and iron door, he heard that apparently Max and the two guards were within the laboratory complex - this meant getting them out was going to be difficult, the research laboratories must be protected. The SS had made Kurt Mayer personally responsible for ensuring that no damage or delay would hamper the vital research going on in Spandau. As Mayer had left that meeting, for the first time in his evil and destructive life, he had felt the steely claws of fear digging into his body.

He was going to make people suffer, and Alex, Max and Fritz were in his crosswires.

Chapter 6

Spandau Germany

Mayer ordered one of the senior guards to ensure all entrances and exits were sealed - when the man replied that this had already been done, he instantly regretted having spoken. Mayer seized him by the throat and snarled at him to do it himself and be quick about it. As the guards turned, they almost crashed into two men in civilian clothes; the men had spotted Lt Mayer and felt a chill sensation of anxiety. They had dealt with him before, and on one occasion Mayer and his henchmen had burst into a laboratory and seized a Jewish scientist; he was hauled off, never to be seen again.

The men introduced themselves to Mayer, explaining they had been instructed by central office to come to the Citadel and help with the situation in any way they could. Mayer recognised them as senior scientists, important people who must be treated with respect. Middle class and cultured, he thought, with concealed rage. People who had had all the advantages he had never had, and whom he envied and despised. He would adopt an appearance of warmth and co-operation, but it irked him that he would have no control over these favoured specialists. It irked him even more that he was desperately in need of their help.

Hans, the taller of the two, approached him without saluting; something which made Mayer long to be able to strike him and demand his respect. Holding his resentment at the superior intellectual accomplishments of a man taller, younger, in check was going to be hard. The man was well built and athletic, blond and good looking with a confident relaxed manner - all the attributes Hitler admired.

"We will do all we can to help, Lieutenant," he was saying. "We have worked with Max Ackermann here in the past, before he and his colleague were moved to a different facility. Max is highly intelligent, quick minded, with a broad knowledge of chemistry. Although he was appointed as a research assistant, he is very capable of coming up with his own ideas independently, but has often shared these with the lead scientists for improvement. I know a little of his past, he was trained for special services as a stormtrooper; he didn't speak much of the War, but clearly suffered. It made him sometimes a little reserved with others, perhaps, but he was always ready to volunteer his services, sometimes without pay. He has spoken of his opposition to Germany going to war - but he is a patriot, and I am sure he would volunteer again!"

This was not what Mayer wanted to hear - in his mind Max Ackermann was an agent provocateur who needed to be taken out. "What kind of items are stored in these laboratories? Things that would enable them to create weapons against our security guards? I must get through that door! Are there places to hide, or get out by other means?"

"No, the piping etc. was all made secure some time ago, and there is simply a corridor of storerooms interspersed with laboratories."

The lieutenant turned to the second man, relieved to find him shorter than himself, rather plump and wearing glasses. He was however, well dressed. Mayer knew he was called Klaus - he had heard him spoken of by Colonel Schmidt as a brilliant scientist. Mayer was pleased to see Klaus was looking much more nervous and intimidated by an SS officer than Hans, and immediately felt more in control. Klaus also offered more detailed descriptions of the rooms in the basement, including the power and lighting control systems. Mayer thanked them for their help and crisply requested them to wait in the guardroom until they might be needed.

Hans and Klaus held a whispered conversation as they made their way to the guardroom; they were concerned to hear that Max had been joined by Fritz and Alex, two members of the staff they knew and respected.

"Knowing Max and his inventive mind, he'll have some tricks up his sleeve, and they are battle trained so they won't go without a bloody strong fight, but I can't see them leaving this place alive." Hans shook his head thoughtfully.

Mayer inspected the iron door again, and the amount of room they had to work with. They needed something heavy to get through this thing. He left three men to guard the door, then called together all the remaining security guards. Some were young, having trained with the Hitler Youth, while some were veterans of the last conflict.

Mayer posted the three young men, with weapons, at the top of the stairs, then turned on the seven veterans and ordered, "Go at the double to the courtyard, remove one of the cannons from its mountings and get some rope." They were to practice swinging the cannon, in preparation for using it to batter the door, "Even you old men can be useful sometimes. Get a move on!" he screamed.

Outside the veterans grouped around a cannon; talking bitterly about Mayer; they hated him and the arrogant way in which he treated them. Bruce, who had been in the same company as Fritz, gathered them together. He was a huge man, well over six feet tall, who could probably pick up the cannon on his own. He was a person they always listened to when he had something to say, and he had something important to say now.

"We all know Fritz and Alex well, we share that bond of pride in our regiment, compared to that jumped up little shit Mayer, right?" He spoke softly but with conviction. "Mayer has never served, he got to be Lieutenant because he was helpful to the Nazis; he pretends to be strong and in command, but he's a weak, bullying sadist. Remember what he did to conscripts if they didn't meet his targets?" They all nodded, grimly. "I am going to pay him back for all of it, I don't expect you to get involved, but if I get the chance during this attack on the cellars, I'm going to take him down. I will report him as killed in action. If possible, I want to get Max, Alex and Fritz away. If that works, I'd be grateful for your silence"

Without a word, the men set to work on the cannon and rope. It was clear they were in agreement - if the opportunity came, they would get rid of Mayer. Returning to the cellars, they were castigated by him again, for being slow. Mayer banged on the door, asking to talk with Fritz, who eventually called from the other side.

"Listen, Fritz, I have been talking to command; we realise we've made a mistake here; Max's sentence was too harsh. If you give yourselves up, Max will be given a choice: he can go to a rehabilitation unit, then return to scientific work, or he can return to his regiment; his war service is respected, and he will gain easy promotion, we are sure. Because you have all served, you and Alex will not be punished, we understand your position and you are of great value to the Reich."

Max, Fritz and Alex came in turns to the door and told him to rot in Hell. "You think we are that stupid?" shouted Fritz. "Germany has lost its direction under vile, evil people like you. Now, for once in your life, show some understanding. We know we can't escape alive - give us ten minutes to make our peace with God, and we won't blow up the labs. We are going to shoot ourselves, then you can do as you like. Knock three times if you agree."

After a few moments, came three raps on the door.

Running along the corridor, Alex tapped Fritz on the back. "The dummies were a great idea! When the lights go out, Mayer will have torches if he's got any sense - in the torchlight they might just be convincing enough to give us time to mingle!" Max hefted the chlorine cylinder, and after putting his gas mask on, opened the valve, jamming the rubber tube under the door.

Shouts of, "Gas!" and coughing came from the other side, and a panicky retreat up the stairs.

"Good," thought Max, "when they come back down, they'll all be wearing masks." Fritz and Alex got their masks on and added final touches to the "bodies" on the floor. Max and Alex took their places in the recess, and at a signal, Fritz fired one shot, followed by another two, and sauntered toward them, giving a silent thumbs up, just as an enormous crash on the iron door made the top bolt fly off. As he squeezed into the recess, Max suddenly raced away to the end laboratory - he had forgotten to turn on the wall switch connected to the magnesium powder! Leaving the laboratory, he changed his mind about turning on the gas taps - it would kill too many men he had known as comrades. Another thunderclap as the cannon hit the door, the sound reverberating through the cell almost deafened him. The door was now giving way, hanging on the loosened bolts.

He ran, dancing around the heaps of crystals. Another crash, and the door was hanging on the final bolt. Fritz shot out an arm as Max dived, and pulled him in. He tugged on the switch and the cellar was enveloped in complete darkness.

The lieutenant shone his torch along the corridor, he thought he could see three bodies, but had to be sure. He ordered the three young guards forward, telling the veterans to stay at the top of the steps. This was not what Bruce wanted - he had planned for his guys to be with Mayer in there. He would have to bide his time.

Mayer was gabbling promises to the young men of how well rewarded they would be for their action in protecting this vital work; the capture of the three traitors would get them a medal for sure. Then ushered them past him, being careful to stay out of the firing line himself.

The door crashed back against the wall, almost touching Max, Fritz and Alex. They froze and held their breath. It was up to their booby trap now. The young soldiers moved along the sides of the corridor, cautiously approaching the bodies.

Max wondered why none of the crystals had gone off yet? Had they become damp? Then one of the soldiers stepped into the centre to get a better look, and set off the first explosion. The other two flung themselves to the ground before setting off two more. Following what sounded like gunfire, a blast and a brilliant, billowing flame shot up the side wall and across the corridor roof. It was over as soon as it began, but then the screaming started. The soldiers leapt up, their clothes on fire, and fought to get out of the doorway. Their gas masks were protecting their faces, but their hands would bear the scars for life. They crashed into Mayer, almost setting him alight. As they struggled upwards, the veterans grabbed them and quenched the flames, stripping their clothes from them. One of the older guards ran to get more water. Bruce saw his chance, and shouting to one of his men, dived into the cellar, grabbing Mayer and pushing him further in. Mayer shouted, and Bruce apologised, saying he had mistaken him in the darkness.

"I'll go ahead of you sir, and we'll have another behind to protect you." Mayer was hustled forwards. Suddenly Bruce shouted "Vouchercodes!" Fritz and the others recognised his voice and the stormtrooper code for a manoeuvre involving heavy firing followed by troop movement.

Bruce moved forward, and Max, Fritz and Alex came out from their hiding place to join at the back. Max tapped the last trooper on the back, who turned and nodded approval. The second part of their plan was now in full swing. As they passed along the corridor and came to the storeroom, Max stepped in and tapped Alex, signalling to follow. After a moment, he asked Alex to get Mayer as close as possible to the bundle of wire and powder in the end laboratory. Alex was puzzled, but nodded, and rejoined the group in the corridor. Progress was slow, as they checked each room.

Looking around him with his torch, Mayer caught sight of the clothing that had been one of the bodies. He suddenly felt trapped, and panicking, thrust his pistol into the back of Bruce in front of him. He screamed "Halt!" and tore off his gas mask.

"I am returning to the entrance! If anyone tries to stop me, I will shoot this man! The traitors have not died, they are here," Bruce spoke up.

"You're right Lieutenant, and now you've given away our position! If they are still behind us, you will run straight into them.

Better move forward with us, so we can protect you - we have to do our duty and protect these laboratories, those are our orders!"

Mayer put his mask back on, choking from chlorine gas and dust, and decided he had better stay with them.

Fritz was searching along the side of the corridor to find the twine he had attached to his next booby trap - the flames had burned through the upper line, but the lower one might be intact. He found it, nudged the others in front of him, and pulled hard. His heap collapsed with an enormous clatter; Mayer fell to the floor in fright; Bruce rushed into the lab and surveyed the rubble in the torchlight, grinning. "Clever stuff!" he thought.

The commotion gave Alex a chance to get close to Bruce, pulling off his gas mask; the closed door had stopped most of the gas, and it was bearable. As he too pulled off his mask, Bruce gave Alex a huge smile. There was no time for niceties; Alex quickly explained to Bruce what was set up in the end laboratory, still not sure what Max was planning. They returned to the group, with Max now at its head. As they reached the last doorway, Max, pretending not to know it was empty, told two guards to protect Mayer while he and two others went in. As they entered, Max and Bruce fired randomly into the room, Bruce emptying his revolver and making it sound like a battleground.

Bruce shouted, "It's over!"

Mayer got off the floor, brushing himself down, stamped into the laboratory, shining his torch around. He saw only shattered glass. Turning, he found he was now surrounded by the other men, most shining their torches in his face, but Alex and Fritz illuminating their own. A deadly fear was gripping him now. Surely, they would not dare kill him? He waited for them to speak first. Showing his face, Max came in; the two men looked at each other, then Max went to speak to Bruce in whispers. Nodding a farewell, Max left. Bruce spoke then, solemnly, almost like a priest giving final absolution to one who had committed many crimes.

"We know if we leave and leave you here alive, we will soon be captured and killed; if we kill you, there will be an enquiry, which will come to the same end. However, if you are prepared to give your solemn oath as an officer of the Third Reich that you will give us time to get away, we will not take you as a hostage. You won't have a good time anyway, with that lot."

Mayer was thinking, rat like, how much he wanted to destroy them all - whatever they offered he would accept.

Perhaps he could achieve both, get free of blame, and get his revenge on these traitors.

In the dark and sheltered by the circle of men, Fritz moved a telephone closer to the bundle of wires, and half concealed it so it looked as if it had been overlooked.

He found a large stop clock which he had set nearby.

He moved to Bruce. "Trust me, we can all get away with this if you leave matters to Max. I will deal with the Lieutenant."

They moved out of the room, and Fritz explained, "We need to leave Mayer tied to a chair facing the explosives. His legs and feet will be properly bound, and one arm, so he can't move - but his other arm will be loosely bound so he can wriggle it free." Bruce knew Fritz as a good strategic planner, so he nodded agreement.

Fritz now took a man back in to tie Mayer up, having a quick whispered conversation on the way. He was told to whisper to Mayer that not all the guards were traitors, he should remember that, because he was leaving his right arm loosely bound. Once the Lieutenant was bound to the chair, opposite the explosives and close enough to the phone, Fritz sent the others out and closed the door. Moving to Mayer, he gripped him by the collar and thrust his face close.

"I loathe and abhor you, but I'm not going to kill you. For which you can thank Max and the others who have persuaded me not to. These men I am with have been bound together through battles, they believe in honour, and you are not fit to give them orders; you and your filthy Third Reich are destroying everything Germany stands for. We will get away, and we will rejoin our regiments and prepare to lay down our lives, while you and your like sit about barking orders, prostituting yourselves to power hungry madmen. You have the rank of officer - can we rely on your word of honour to give us two hours before trying to escape?"

Mayer raised his head and nodded agreement.

Fritz pointed to the stop clock and tapped significantly on the two hours; he laid a torch on the bench. "If you do get free, you'll be able to get out without setting off more booby traps."

Leaving the room, Fritz told the guards to take spare gas masks and form a cordon at the entrance; they were to wear the masks at all times, and if anyone came, tell them the cellars were filled with chlorine gas.

Keeping the Citadel empty was crucial - the laboratories and corridor must be free of prying eyes.

Chapter 7

Spandau Germany

Fritz had assured the men that Bruce would be looking after them all, but absolutely no one was to contact the outside authorities yet; he asked them to send Bruce down to him - there was a lot to do to protect the guards from the SS.

He flashed his torch over Mayer, who still had his head down, as he locked the door, hoping he would never have to see the man again. Max arrived, and they moved away from the door to discuss their next move. Fritz said he would stay close to Mayer, and if he picked up the phone to betray them, would flash his torch several times to tell Max to turn the switch on. In the unlikely event of Mayer doing nothing after half an hour, Max was to leave, taking Alex with him. "When you go back to the end Max, shout goodbye - hopefully Mayer will think it's me leaving; and then you need to get back to the storeroom without making a sound!"

Next Fritz had quiet words with Bruce; he outlined his plan but made it clear that after half an hour he and his colleagues should disperse. "God willing, it will all work, and the blame will be put completely on Max, Alex and me; if it works, I'll join you - but don't wait around for me."

Bruce shook his hand warmly. "Good luck Fritz - let's hope for the best. It's been like the old days, working as a unit! Maybe we'll all meet up again in the Army - they need some experienced guys, and I'll take it over being cooped up here much longer!"

Fritz settled down against the door, to listen to what Mayer was up to; Max made a good noisy farewell, then slipped into the storeroom. He had gone into all the labs and turned on the chlorine gas cylinders. The gas would permeate the cellars, making the whole area impenetrable. His own mask was beginning to give way to the gas, the carbon filters becoming saturated. He found a fresh mask, and taking a deep breath, replaced his with the fresh one. He took another for Fritz, who would be in the same situation. He waited, screwdriver in hand. It was close now to the thirty minutes they had agreed - Max wondered what Fritz had in mind if their plan didn't work.

Inside the laboratory, Mayer was wondering if the guard's action had been genuine, or another trap. He had untied his bonds without too much difficulty and was quietly groping around in the darkness for the phone he had spotted. He found the torch and began checking the room over; he had been here nearly half an hour, and the silence was unbroken. He started to search for anything he might be able to open the door with; he studied the pile of wire wool and cable, but it didn't seem to make much sense. It was connected to an electrical plug secured to the wall, and the switch was on, but touching it with the torch there seemed to be no current. It was probably part of some experiment, he decided. He switched off his torch and groped his way to the door, being careful not to bump into anything and make a noise.

Reaching the glazed door panel, he peered out into complete darkness, then turned on his torch towards the end of the corridor, seeing nothing, but alerting Max to the fact that he was on the move. The Lieutenant could see, flicking his torch along the part of the corridor it could reach, the dummies still on the floor, and the scorched walls and ceilings, black with carbon, which suggested gunpowder had been used. Not intended to kill however, as it had not been packed in cylinders, but spread along the floor to flash and flame up. It had certainly caused disruption and fear, and burned some of the guards. He was wondering, had they really overlooked the phone? They must have known that every laboratory had one - but it was dark, they were in a hurry, and it was almost obscured with papers. If it was an oversight, it was a stupid one, putting him in a strong position - and he would make them pay for their stupidity!

He had never thought that Fritz, though popular and well organised, was particularly clever; he had risen up the ranks because of his war record... he wondered if the phone was connected. He sat back in his chair and turning on his torch, turned to inspect it. It was the modern type, with a button to press to get an outside line; he picked up the receiver, heard the connecting click and replaced it, feeling triumphant. He turned the torch on again and had another look round, checking the door. It was still locked, and he gave it a ferocious kick.

Pain shot through Fritz's head. He almost fell backwards but stood the shock and didn't move. He hadn't expected that, as it wasn't in the script.

"Two hours!" Mayer thought. "How bloody naive of them - just one call was all it would take." Even if they were still in the castle, at least one of the guards was on his side, and they were all in fear of him and what his superiors would do. The traitors were probably well away by now - he picked up the receiver and dialled. He was feeling confident now, as he was no longer alone.

Fritz heard the dialling of the phone. "Now for some fireworks!" he thought, jumping up and aimed his torch through a small window directly at Mayer.

For a moment Mayer was shocked... they had been there all the time! The shock quickly turned to anger; with the phone he was restored to power, if they harmed him now, they would be hunted down, as his was a position of strength not weakness. He shrugged and grinned as he stared back down the light beam, which was suddenly removed. The light now flashed down the corridor, Fritz's signal to Max, who was almost on the brink of leaving. He swiftly moved to the panel on the wall, and pausing for the briefest moment, turned the switch.

There was no thunderous explosion, just a solid sound, like the first piston thrust of a locomotive. Pressure on Max's ears and the rattling of everything in the storeroom confirmed that the wire wool and magnesium powder had fulfilled its deadly purpose.

What the effect might be on Fritz caused Max to rush down the corridor in concern to get to him. His torch shone through a myriad of tiny dust particles, a cloud that clung to everything, glowing in an eerie silence. He saw Fritz prostrate on the floor, there was glass everywhere, and the laboratory door hung partly open, illuminated by a red glow of burning embers from inside the room. He knelt close to his friend, and found that thankfully, he was breathing, then saw his eyes flickering as they gradually opened.

Fritz took a deep, gasping breath as his consciousness returned, his confused mind returning to normality. His forehead was covered with a multitude of small cuts and he was peppered with debris. Slowly mustering his energy and sitting up, he wryly commented, "The second time that bloody door has got the better of me - maybe next time a bit less magnesium?" Then he told Max to get to work with the screwdriver, "We need to get out of here quick, everyone in the building must have heard that go off." Inside the room, the torch light barely penetrated the mist of smoke, water vapour and dust. An acrid stench of burnt hair, clothes and chemicals assaulted their senses. Lieutenant Mayer had been blown several feet away from where he had been sitting and had come to rest, still upright and attached to his chair, propped against another sturdy bench. Clearly, he must have died instantly, his gas mask fused to his face, his clothes smouldering, and his hands blackened with the heat. Max had no time or inclination to inspect him further, that was for others. He now had to fudge the evidence of how Mayer had died.

Everything around the bench was seared, the clock partly burnt, the wires, stripped of their insulation were brittle grey threads. This would be advantageous to their story. The electric plug in the Bakelite socket below the switch had been pimpled by the heat but was otherwise intact. The switch nearby had partly melted but kept its shape. He examined the screws holding the assembly to the wall, and thankfully they were intact too. With a little effort he was able to unscrew the panel and pull it from the wall. The switch was still in the on position; he very carefully turned it round and repositioned it on the wall; it now appeared to be in the off position. He intended this to suggest, under examination, that it was another booby trap. He scattered some dust over the plug so it wouldn't appear to have been disturbed, and crossed himself, sending a silent prayer that this would exonerate everyone else from Mayer's death. He had every confidence in Bruce's ability to spin the line they had agreed when investigations began. Max and Fritz had concocted the story, it was Bruce's job to make it convincing.

Max returned to Fritz. "How are you feeling?"

Fritz managed a grin. "Stirred but not shaken, I would say."

Max grunted in amusement and helped Fritz along the corridor and up the stairs where Bruce and other senior guards took them along to the guardroom. Bruce had done his job, the young guards had been patched up, they had blistered hands and necks but apart from that seemed generally fit.

Outside the entrance to the Citadel a crowd had gathered; amongst them were two medics with an ambulance. Bruce had called them, but denied them access because of the gas. Alex was covered in bandages, his face completely hidden; Bruce said he must be taken immediately to the hospital by Max and Fritz, while the medics tended to the injured left behind, who had been prepared for transportation and would be brought out to them. Fritz, still in his captain's uniform, and Max, shouldered Alex between them and made for the car park. Just as they got close to Fritz's staff car, they heard running footsteps and turned in alarm - thankfully it was Bruce, almost out of breath, with his gas mask perched on his head. They all embraced, Max and Fritz thanking Bruce over and over for his help. He had had no choice, he said. Wasn't their comradeship a bond for life? Forged in the furnace of the Great War, facing danger and under the shadow of impending death at every moment, their brotherhood had been one of support and reliance on each other.

Once again, they had banded together in a common cause, and if the need arose, they would do so again. It seemed everything was working out well, but if things went wrong, they urged Bruce to get away, and they would all make their way to their old regiment to serve their country.

Fritz suddenly thought of another possible escape route for them all, and he asked Bruce to contact his old friend Eric and ask if he would meet with them at the old barn they knew. Bruce asked why, when it was so important right now for Fritz and the others to distance themselves as fast as possible from the area.

"Eric and I were brought up together, enlisted together, and fought together in the trenches. He and Mayer crossed swords several times, and Eric was demoted at Mayer's instigation for some made up reason... he'll help, I'm sure! And who would think of looking for us in their own barracks? It will give us time to prepare our escape properly too."

"I think it's too risky to use the phone, I'll contact him directly... But will he be prepared to put himself in that kind of danger?"

Fritz smiled. "Better to die with friends than live unhappily without them."

Bruce made his way back to the guardhouse and found that the young guards had been taken away, and the older guards were busy opening windows and doors to disperse the chlorine gas. It would be days before the laboratories would be finally free of gas, and they would be able to remove the remains of Lieutenant Mayer - he shrugged, the guy wasn't going anywhere. He was worried though; he felt his three friends were putting themselves in a terrible position.

The treads tore into the gravel, smoke plumed and rubber scorched. Fritz was in a hurry. Heads turned as the car sped along the road to a T-junction; Fritz revved the engine and made a noisy right turn, attracting the attention of the onlookers; Max and Alex knew Fritz was laying a deceptive trail for anyone following them soon. He made a left turn a mile along the road and backtracking along a parallel road, he rejoined the original route heading out into the countryside.

For the first time in a long and arduous day, they began to relax - but they knew the Nazis would soon be after them. A few miles down the road, the traffic began to slow, and they could see flashing lights some way ahead. They gloomily grasped that roadblocks had already been set up. There was no point turning around, they all realised; it would just attract attention, and there was probably also a roadblock behind by now. It was just a matter of time before soldiers would come down the queue, checking every car. Fritz got out to see if there was any other direction they could take. There was no possible exit.

"You'd better grab anything important - we'll have to abandon the car and try to get away on foot."

"Hang on." Alex was gazing down the road - his senses, trained in conflict to distinguish anything out of the ordinary - had drawn his attention to the sound of a bell... an ambulance now trying to make its way through the queueing traffic. "It's the one we left at the Citadel - some of the guards were suffering from the gas... get back in the car!"

Fritz nudged the car in front, reversed into the car behind, and pulled into the empty lane created by the roadblock. He ran up to the ambulance and spoke to the driver urgently, "We'll help you get through! Follow me!"

The driver recognised Fritz as an officer from the Citadel without appreciating that he was one of the men being hunted. With horn blaring and lights on full beam, Fritz's staff car forced a route through to the barrier; Max flung open his door and screamed at the soldiers, "Lift the barrier! The ambulance is full of soldiers who've been gassed - we have to get to the hospital." Seeing his officer's uniform, the soldiers obeyed, and car and ambulance raced down the road toward the hospital.

They all sighed with relief as they reached the hospital driveway, the ambulance driver turned in, waving his thanks, and they headed out into the countryside. Half an hour later Fritz slowed, dimmed his headlights and turned onto a gravel track; one he obviously knew well, since he followed it perfectly in the dim light. A further fifteen minutes and they were on an unmade road and could just discern a small cottage and a large barn. Its doors had seen better days and hung awkwardly on rusty hinges.

Max and Alex pulled them open and the car moved gently in as Fritz killed the lights. "This was my grandfather's house." Fritz nodded to the cottage. "It's only a small farm, he scraped a living here. My grandmother died but he stayed on alone. I used to like being here, Eric and I had all the woods and fields and streams for a playground. The barn was our Castle to defend; I think my grandparents liked hearing our noise and games.

They left the farm to me, and I come when I can to keep an eye on it. Nothing has been touched for thirty years, but it isn't derelict.

We'll be warmer and more comfortable inside while we wait for Eric." Fritz pulled out a set of keys and they pushed through long grass to a faded green door. It opened smoothly; inside it smelled faintly musty, of damp and cobwebs, yet was at the same time peaceful and inviting. They could imagine why Fritz's grandfather might have felt at ease here.

Fritz went to turn the water supply on in one of the cupboards, then walked to the sink to turn on the tap and let it run for a while. From another cupboard he brought a dusty cup, rinsed it and filled it to the brim. Taking the first sip, he closed his eyes as the spring water filled his mouth and memory. Nothing had changed, the water was soft and clear, bringing a flood of childhood memories. Alex and Max eagerly drank, also glad of the refreshment after their ordeal.

They dusted off three stick-back chairs, and sat by the old pine table, glad for now just to have respite from the cold and a chance to rest. Fritz broke up some worm-eaten chairs to use as kindling, and they gathered close to the fire, gazing pensively into the flames. They had escaped the snarling teeth of death against almost impossible odds, and with, it seemed, a gracious dose of Dame Fortune's help.

The future before them was unclear and fraught with danger; they needed to take stock and make decisions which would influence the rest of their lives. Hounds were on their scent, and they needed to go to ground.

Fritz took them upstairs and invited them to see if they could find useful outfits; the wardrobes and cupboards were still full of undisturbed garments from the past. Fritz found a suit of his grandfather's which fitted him perfectly - obviously he had followed in his footsteps with his height and size. Alex and Max looked comical in their ill-fitting outfits, and even more so when they added an assortment of hats.

For a moment the tensions slid away as they danced around the room; Max called to Fritz, "Now if only you could work a miracle and turn water into wine, couldn't we enjoy it!"

Fritz looked inspired for a moment, then dashed downstairs and dragged the table and rug to one side, revealing loose boards forming a trapdoor. He lifted this and climbed the steps leading down to a small cellar. His torch revealed huge cobwebs hanging almost like stalactites down to the floor, and dust settling anew on dust. He groped his way to a wine rack, old bottles with their feathering of dust, containing the home-made brews from elderberry, blackberries, gooseberries and plums. Their corks were sound, and the wines remained, patiently waiting for glass and lip. Soon they were gathered around the fire again, the wines delighting their eager palates. Time was moving on, and with no sign of Eric, which was worrying, but all they could do was sit it out until morning. In the darkness before dawn, they would start trekking across country.

They took it in turns to watch from the window which commanded a view of the barn and the approach road; they would see any movement. Each took a one-hour turn, but there was no thought of going to sleep, they had to be on their guard.

"If we are discovered," Fritz suggested, "we should split up, head for the woods about a mile from here. At least one of us might get away. If we succeed, let's meet up in the old city in Spandau, at ten p.m. tomorrow, at St Nikolai's church."

They nodded agreement.

Around midnight Alex saw dimmed lights approaching and summoned the others. Fritz ordered the others to hold the carpet before the fire to dim the light, opened the door and crept outside to get a clearer view. Suddenly returning, he told them, "There's something big coming down the track, I can't make out exactly what, but if it's a truck full of soldiers, so we need to split up. Grab your stuff and come outside!" He showed them a thicket which would be a good vantage point and pointed out a track which would take them away, toward the woods.

"If everything's O.K I'll signal with my torch; if you hear shots, run for it, I'll hold them for as long as possible." Seeing them about to protest he whispered fiercely, "That's a direct order!" Max and Alex melted into the darkness and took up their positions; they could now see a jeep and a large lorry getting closer. Had they been betrayed? The lorry pulled over between the cottage and the barn and turned out its lights. Dense darkness cloaked the entire scene.

Fritz was crouched behind a pile of stones he and his grandfather had pulled from the fields. He kissed his fingertips and touched them in hope. They felt cold; he gripped his pistol and waited.

Chapter 8

Spandau Germany

The jeep door opened slowly, and a figure cautiously lowered itself out of sight, then darted into the barn close by. No movement from the lorry; the driver was either still at the wheel or had moved into the back. The moon had hidden behind the clouds, it was almost impossible to see anything. A beam of light waved in a circular movement from the barn. The lorry door was flung open, and Fritz made out a shadowy figure running into the barn. A few moments later, two figures left the barn, the torch lighting their way toward the cottage. One was limping badly, the torch light swinging unevenly. A sigh broke from Fritz, and a wave of elation swept through him. Shouldering his pistol, he jumped up and called out, "Eric!"

Hearing Eric's loud, "Hello," in reply, Fritz rushed to him, and they embraced.

Fritz told him how relieved and glad he was to see his friend. Max and Alex, disobeying orders, came to join them and all five men entered the house together, into the warmth from the fire.

Once they had all embraced and shaken hands warmly, Eric introduced his companion, Ben. They had met at the end of the War, when Ben had just been drafted. He was several years younger than Eric and stood head and shoulders above him. His appearance was extraordinary, and he wasn't the type you would like to meet in a dark alley, thought Max privately. His ears stood out almost at right angles from a lean, clean-shaven face with an elongated nose and slightly protruding teeth, which had a slightly comical effect. His long thin neck made his Adam's apple stand out starkly, and his wrists showed several inches of very pale skin below his sleeves. His uniform hung on him as if on a coat hanger. Yet when he spoke his voice was soft, and for all his odd appearance outwardly, he gave the impression of being both confident and intelligent.

It transpired that Bruce had contacted Eric as soon as Fritz's car had sped away. Eric was the quartermaster at the military base a few miles away, in charge of moving supplies and sending documentation to other depots, as well as issuing arms and uniforms to new recruits. Due to his long military service he had been promoted to Captain, and was well respected as having made his way up through the ranks. Answerable to the Colonel in charge of the depot, he had the complete run of the place, the Colonel happy to leave the daily organisation to him. He and Ben had worked together for years, and had an almost father and son relationship.

When a request had come to move Ben to an active regiment, Eric had successfully quashed the transfer, arguing that Ben's encyclopaedic knowledge of all the thousands of items in the depot would take years of retraining for a new man. Eric now told them he and Bruce had come up with a plan to enable Max, Fritz and Alex to lie low and then escape. There was always risk, but if the plan worked, they would be able to get away with new identities, safe from pursuit. They could even re-enlist and offer their services again to their country. "We've got some things in the lorry, but we have to go to the chemicals factory at Falkenbeig near Berlin."

"Falkenbeig!" Max muttered. "I've been there, it's not a place I'm keen to see again! They manufacture bloody dangerous stuff, highly secret as well."

"Yes," Eric agreed. "It's such dangerous stuff they use, captured Poles for labour... quite a few die from inhaling the products. Access is tightly restricted; security is really tight." Eric looked at Ben, then the others.

"We've got three bodies in the truck." It was time to mobilise - Eric pointed out that the authorities would soon trace them to the smallholding. He looked at the three men, almost shaking his head in disbelief at the situation they had got themselves into. But, once a stormtrooper...

"Let's get out of here - you get your stuff together, especially the uniforms, and get in your car."

As they bundled in Eric gave them instructions - he would lower two ramps from the back of the lorry and they should drive into it, he would then close the tarpaulin at the back. Ben was driving Eric's jeep, and pulled aside at the junction for the lorry to go first. They were heading toward Berlin, but the first obstacle was the roadblock on the road to the Citadel; when they arrived at the barrier Eric stuck his head out to ask the soldiers to raise it. The men immediately recognised Eric and Ben, and had a few jokes with him about how he was going off to a comfortable night, while they were freezing cold. All because of some sodding runaway soldiers - if they caught them, they'd shove the barrier pole up their arses!

"All right for some!" they jeered as he drove off with a friendly wave, following the lorry.

A couple of miles beyond the Citadel, they turned for the army barracks. A couple of armed men came out at the barrier but raised it immediately as they saw Ben; he returned their salute and wished them a good evening. "I can't wait to put my feet up with a bottle of Schnapps!" He was popular with the men and highly esteemed by all. The lorry carried on ahead as Ben peeled off to park the jeep in the compound, then walked some distance to the rear of the barracks and on to the storage area. The stores contained a wide variety of clothing, bedding and kit to support army personnel; close by were the armoury and administrative offices.

Further along there was a fuel store and a large engineering compound, then the barracks for the soldiers adjacent to the parade ground, the canteen, and the officer's mess. Eric's office was at the rear, between the stores and the engineering complex. It was self-contained, with all the amenities needed to make it independent of the barracks. He and Ben were on call twenty four hours a day, with extra personnel working in the stores during the day. Guards were on patrol, but to a strict timetable, which would make it easy to evade them. The patrol inside the perimeter fence in contrast to the outside, which was thoroughly patrolled and covered by searchlights, was considered low-key, so the guards would often stop for a chat with their mates or to have a cigarette. Ben arrived at the office and knocked with three rapid taps followed by another two, he could hear Eric's irregular footsteps approach. As the door opened and he stepped inside, blinded for a moment by the bright lighting, he found Fritz, Alex and Max seated round a table in one of the back offices. Three mattresses had been placed on the floor, with blankets and pillows stacked to one side. There was a smell of carbolic soap, quite refreshing after the experiences of the last few hours. Ben made hot fresh coffee as Eric came in with a large map; as he approached, he could see Max sitting with his elbows on the table, his head in his hands, apparently miles away.

"What's the plan going to be from here? Here we are, surrounded by hundreds of soldiers - I feel like a butterfly in a wasp's nest!"

"Yes," said Eric, "but if you want to hide a marble, put it in a bucket of marbles! You need to lie low until the time is right to get you away. Disappear from the face of the earth. You're as good as dead men now, so we need to make you appear to be just that." He unrolled the map on the table and they could see the local area with Eric tracing with his finger the route they had followed, then pointed to where the road made an almost ninety-degree turn. "It's a famous accident black spot, high ground and poor visibility. This is how we start your new lives with new identities!"

The caffeine from endless cups of coffee began to reinvigorate the three escapees who were exhausted mentally and physically from the events at the Citadel. Max began to put together what Eric's plan meant. "Presumably, we stage an accident?"

"That's right, we can substitute the three Polish prisoners' bodies for yours; the problem is how we make their faces unrecognisable; we're depending on you for this Max, you're the scientist."

Max and the others thought sadly about the fate of those three Poles - taken prisoner and treated so badly by their captors, worked and beaten to death. At home wives and children would be missing them, wondering about them. Their deaths would cause grief and loss - but then to have their bodies disfigured and abused further, to enable three Germans to escape? Max felt anger surge inside him. He had assisted in producing a chemical weapon which in the wrong hands could wipe out cities. He wanted to do his best for his country, but there needed to be a balance, he needed to survive and try his best to prevent this happening. If it entailed an act of blasphemy, of desecration, so be it.

"I know how to use chemicals to destroy human tissue; it will rest on what chemicals you can get your hands on Eric."

Eric got up. "We had better get going, we should get the bodies from the lorry."

"I need highly concentrated sulphuric acid - it's used to top up batteries, so you probably have it in the engineering supplies - but will it be concentrated enough?"

Eric shrugged. "I don't know - topping up the lead accumulators is something I leave to the engineering crew, but we'll find out. Ben, can you get a bottle of acid, but make sure no-one sees you over there?"

Making sure there were no guards outside, he ushered them into the lorry, where the bodies lay beneath a blanket. Gesturing silently to their clothes, he pointed to the staff car at the front, and they scrambled over to it to get their uniforms, brought from the cottage, and lay them beside the bodies. They would never forget the strangeness of this process, the poor thin white bodies, the paper-thin skin covered in bruises and weal's from blows they had received. Rigor mortis had not set in, so they awkwardly dressed them, the uniforms folding like blankets around the emaciated forms of these who were once proud soldiers. They had just finished when Eric returned carrying two bottles marked in red "DANGER! CONCENTRATED SULPHURIC ACID"

Max asked Eric to bring a glass of water, and an empty glass, making sure the second was absolutely dry. In the dim light within the lorry, Max, asking the others to move back, carefully poured some acid into the water. It gave off steam and was almost boiling. "This will certainly do the job, even though it's a disgusting job to do."

"I remember now," Eric said. "We had a new recruit who poured the water into the acid instead. It all boiled over and burnt his hands so badly he had to be discharged from the service."

"Yes, the concentrated acid absorbs water incredibly fast, creating heat in the process. Poured onto skin, it will absorb the water, the heat will burn and create a chemical reaction reducing the skin to black carbon. We had best do this with the bodies already in the staff car. We'll put the acid on faces and hands, and if we also set fire to the car, the chances of definitive identification will be nil."

Silence followed this description, broken by Eric asking them to hand over any personal effects to place on the bodies. Selecting the closest size to themselves, they did so. Fritz had his keys, a bold ring, his wallet and reading glasses. Max and Alex followed suit. Ben took the dry glass and poured acid into it; after a moment he applied it to the bodies. Max was right, the acid acted quickly, the skin turned black and bubbled, steaming. Eric noticed tears were running down Ben's cheeks, it was a dreadful task.

Checking all was clear again, the three went back inside; all had the same sombre expression. Eric dashed in, "We need your boots... three barefoot men in a staff car is going to cause questions." Taking the boots, he said, "Ben and I are just building a wall of storage chests at the back, if we get stopped it will just look like a transport run. He's thought of a way to make it difficult for them to look inside as well. The acid has worked really well, Max." Max only shook his head with a mixture of sorrow and anger.

"We're ready to go, so all the lights need to be out - probably a good opportunity for you to get some shut-eye. We've got fuelled up, and we should be back before daybreak." The friends went to him, shook his hand and wished him God Speed.

There had been a light dusting of snow, which might be useful in some ways, but the thought of steep icy hills was not so welcome.

Ben took the wheel and they passed through the first two barriers without any difficulty; there was little traffic on the road - with luck they could make the Hartz mountains in three and a half hours; he knew of a particularly nasty bend on a tree lined road. After another hour they saw lights ahead, yet another barrier. Here the guards were not looking friendly. Eric told Ben to leave the talking to him, as the torchlight flashed into the cab and he was asked, "Where are you going?"

"Where are you going, Sir" snapped Eric. The soldier stood to attention and saluted. They could hear the sound of the tarpaulin being pulled back, and the rays of torch lights were questing through gaps.

"Ben, go and see what they are doing... we have important machinery to deliver." Eric included the guard in his comment.

Ben found two guards trying to drag a crate from the back. "Be careful, we have some very heavy but delicate machinery, removing it could damage some very expensive and vital instruments!" Ben went on, "This is for a most important project, it's imperative that it arrives safely and in time."

Eric had now got down from the cab, demanding to know what the delay was. They were told that three soldiers were on the run, and checks were needed to prevent their escape by road, but the guard, noticing Eric's Quartermaster insignia and that he was becoming agitated, decided that he really did just have a delivery to ensure, and invited them to proceed. Back in the van and underway, Eric asked what had gone on at the back - the crates were empty and should have been easy to move.

Ben grinned and explained he had taken the precaution of nailing them down.

Eric smiled, thinking, "This Ben, I like him more and more!"

Chapter 9

Spandau Germany

The snow was not settling, which was lucky, but the roads were still slippery, making their progress frustratingly slow; an hour had passed when Eric instructed Ben to pull into a slipway. They quickly got to work unfastening the nailed down crates with a crowbar Ben had brought. "He thinks of everything!" thought Eric.

They bundled the crates out of the lorry and assembled the ramps, then reversed the Jeep out into the road. Ben drove it to a bend in the road, pulled on the handbrake and put the Jeep in gear. Eric drove slowly up to the car and began to push it; the sliding car made black tyre marks as it went, and Ben was pulling on the steering wheel to create a zig-zag track. As they approached a stout tree, Ben started the engine and released the hand brake, hopping out of the car. Eric continued to push the car and it crashed into the tree, making a satisfactory mess of the car. Now Ben attached a rope and Eric dragged the car into the centre of the road, blocking it. They doused the interior with diesel, then Eric brushed away their footmarks with a tree branch, while Ben turned the lorry around. Sending a small prayer heavenwards Eric took his lighter and set the fuel alight. The fire grew slowly at first, but soon took hold, turning the Jeep into a blaze emitting fierce heat. They had done it!

They drove back the way they had come, heading back to Spandau - it had taken them four hours, longer than planned, and they had to get back as soon as possible. At the road check, they told the guards they had had to turn back because of a burning car on the road. "You guys had better get up there and clear the road - we'll have to find an alternative route, we're late already."

Safely through, they began to relax; Eric thanked Ben for his ingenuity - without him they might not have got through that checkpoint! Hopefully the guards would find the car totally burned out, and clambering about and moving the Jeep would further disguise any evidence of their handiwork.

At last, they turned into the barracks, were waved through with no problem, and parked the lorry. Letting themselves into their offices they found the three fugitives tucked in and fast asleep. They had made it back before daybreak, mission accomplished - but would the "accident" stand up to an SS investigation? If the three corpses were not accepted as being those of the escapees, they themselves would be in the spotlight. They shrugged - it was almost day, and they just had to wait and see. Ben offered to make more coffee, when there was a thunderous pounding on the door; the two men froze, while the noise alerted the three in the back room, who scrambled their bedding together and dived into a large storage cupboard, hearts thudding. Lieutenant Hans Muller had been an investigative police officer before the war, stationed locally, and had been drafted into the SS when hostilities began. Well respected locally, he was often called "the monk" because of the shiny bald patch on his head, made even more distinctive by the shock of black hair surrounding it like a black halo. Bareheaded, he did look as if he had just stepped out of his monastery.

He was a short man, only just topping 5'2" and was self-conscious of taller people looking down at his bald crown. He constantly wore his peaked SS cap, which added a little to his height and dignity. However, this peculiar idiosyncrasy concealed a cunning and methodical brain, with an almost uncanny ability to unravel criminal cases of great complexity; his success rate at apprehending the most devious of criminals was well known. Thanks to his skills, crime in the Spandau area had been kept well under control, so it was no surprise that the SS had recruited him.

His curious appearance often led culprits into underestimating him, to their cost. During interrogation he was able to play both good and bad guy, one minute appearing gentle and understanding, the next angry and aggressive. Soft talking and angry volleys were effective in getting to the truth. Criminals who knew him knew to keep their distance.

His recruitment into the SS however, made him ill at ease, the insignia he had to sport did not match his inner character - he was a man feared by the bad but respected by the good. As he was based locally, he had come to know the guards at Spandau Citadel, and he knew Fritz and respected him. During their chats he had come to notice a ring on Fritz's right hand, as he noticed so many things. Fritz would twist the ring on his finger as he was mulling over a situation. One day Hans noticed the ring had been transferred to the left hand - it was the sort of small detail that lodged in his memory, maybe to be useful one day.

This morning his telephone rang and he was ordered to investigate a burned- out car found in the Hartz mountains; he hated being distracted from his normal work, and the thought of a drive up those mountain roads was even worse. The weather was making the roads dangerous and there had been a lot of accidents. However, this call was different - they wanted him to try to identify the driver and two passengers, who had been badly burned. He hoped nothing would be moved or touched, it was imperative in such cases that nothing should be interfered with.

He arrived four hours later, to find the car had been dragged to the side of the road to allow traffic to pass; this was annoying, but he was able to study the deep skid marks on the road, and also the tyre marks of the truck, which puzzled him. He inspected the car and was taken aback by the amount of burning to the bodies; it would clearly be hard to identify them so he began a search for personal items which might help. When he saw the ring on the almost fleshless finger, he had a sudden thought of who this might be. The finding of a watch and other items would be important. He was aware that Fritz and two friends had escaped from the Citadel; this was evidently Fritz's car - it seemed inescapable that these were the three men. He had been informed that if apprehended they were to be shot on sight, not taken prisoner. Hans took the ring and other objects back to the Citadel; he knew Bruce was a friend as well as colleague of Alex and Fritz, and was fortunate to find him on duty.

After a few brief pleasantries, Muller went straight to the point, "I need to ask you about something - do you recall the ring Fritz always wore, and do you think you would recognise it?"

Muller noticed the uneasy look on Bruce's face, but he answered immediately, "Yes, I would. I was there when Fritz's wife Eleanor put it on his finger at their wedding. He was proud to wear it as a token of his undying love for Eleanor, even after she died. Lately, though, he has met a local lady, and to avoid any confusion in his relationship, he moved the ring to his left hand - although he always said that while he hoped for a new beginning, it would be impossible to replace the love of his life. That ring was very important to him!"

Hans nodded - over the years a special bond grew within those who worked in the Citadel as they shared things with one another and kept separate in their dealings with the ordinary town's folk. There were confidential aspects to their work, which made them wary of too much reliance on outsiders.

"I am sorry to have this unpleasant duty." Hans showed them the ring as he spoke, "I am investigating a fatal accident to Fritz's car - we found three of them, and I believe the other two to be Alex and another man called Max Ackermann."

Bruce was deeply shaken - Fritz, his closest friend, was dead? Fritz had guided him and many others through the hell of the trenches, through the stench of bodies as men were torn apart by a hailstorm of metal. Men like him could not be replaced, and now he was dead. Typically, to the last, he had been protecting one of his own as if still on the battlefield. Only a few moments earlier Bruce had believed Fritz had gotten away, would start a new life.

Now, that life had been lost in the cause of helping others. Bruce felt a hand on his shoulder, words were spoken but he didn't hear them; Hans went to leave, stopping at the door to say how sorry he was that things had turned out this way. He walked back to Bruce, extending his hand in friendship, and as he shook hands, Bruce felt the ring being pressed into his palm.

"Perhaps you should care for the ring; it would be a pity for something so special to be worn by anyone who did not know of its significance."

Stunned and silent, Bruce sat on the chair and looked at the ring - he tried it on his left hand. Of course, it was far too big for him, he thought, since Fritz was big in life and character. He needed to gather his thoughts; he wondered if the others knew of Fritz's fate. He went to make some coffee.

Outside, Hans had walked away, but before turning down an alleyway he took a sideways glance to see if anyone was watching him; he took up a position in a doorway where he had a clear view of Bruce's office. His plan was to stay there for some time and see if any response was precipitated as a result of his conversation and his actions. He was clear that Bruce's response to the death of his friend indicated he had been unaware of the accident, but it could well be the case that there were others who did, and he was hell-bent on finding out who they were!

Bruce wondered whether Eric and the others were aware of the accident, if not, they urgently needed to know, and it was best coming from him. Hans had told him that a lorry had been making an urgent delivery; in the Hartz mountains they had come upon a blazing car; the guards from the checkpoint had been sent to put out the fire and clear the wreckage. Three bodies had been in the burnt-out car, and having been sent to investigate, Hans had searched for personal items to identify the dead. Amongst the items was Fritz's ring, and he had named the other two bodies as being Max and Alex.

The winter sun had long since dipped below the horizon; the chill in the air had brought with it a flurry of snow, and without a wind, it wouldn't be long before it settled again. Clutching the ring in his hand, Bruce made his way toward the military section of the complex where Eric's Stores Depot was situated. The snow was settling fast, leaving footprints as he walked. As he approached, he was surprised to see no light coming from the windows, since Eric was normally there at this time of day. Taking a deep breath, he banged on the door with a clenched fist; minutes went by with no response, and he was just about to bang on the door again when Eric appeared, appearing more than pleased to see him. One look and Eric knew Bruce had heard about the accident and the three bodies. Dusting off the snow, he entered to a warm welcome from Ben, "That'll change when I tell them the news," he thought. He slumped down in a chair, and putting his hand on the table opened his fist to reveal Fritz's ring. His eyes glistened. "They didn't make it out; they crashed the car... Burnt out, it's horrific... They were burnt to cinders..." his distress silenced him. He stared at the wall opposite, seeing and hearing nothing. He was trying to make sense of what had happened, his brain was in a kind of vacuum. He thought how only a few hours ago he had seen the three escape - he was partly responsible.

Eric placed his hand on Bruce's shoulder, and bent to whisper in his ear, "My friend, they are not dead, but very much alive and just a few metres away!"

"What? How? How have they got his ring, and the other's things? They were actually in the burnt car." Ben sat by his side and intervened, explaining what they had done without too much detail. Ben had noticed the ring on Fritz's hand and put it on the body of the dead Polish man, on the left hand. "It's important because most people didn't know he had recently moved it from his right to his left hand."

Bruce looked closely again at the ring and mused, "The little green stones have survived the heat so well."

"That's because emeralds don't burn like diamonds, they can survive hot temperatures," the familiar voice made Bruce shoot up from his chair, and he found he was looking at Max, Fritz and Alex.

He shook their hands feverishly and said, "I know a famous resurrection story, but I didn't expect one on my doorstep two thousand years on!"

Eric reminded them to keep their voices low, since there were always prying eyes and ears around the Citadel. They gathered round the table, drinking copious amounts of coffee augmented with the occasional Schnapps, as they explained in detail the events of the night before.

"I'm amazed you got away with it," Bruce said, "but The Monk is on the case now, and very little gets by him. What are your plans now? I can't believe you're here hiding in the Citadel complex - can't decide if it's a stroke of genius or total stupidity, but if it works it will certainly be an achievement! So far I've seen a transformation followed by a resurrection - let's hope for an evacuation!"

They all agreed that being too hasty would be foolish - if everyone thought they were dead the hunt would be called off. "With a bit of time we can build new identities and begin new lives." They raised a glass to this, then Bruce said he had better be getting back to his office.

Fritz, Max and Alex disappeared into the back room. Ben opened the door for Bruce and looked out; the snow had stopped, but Ben pointed silently to Bruce's footprints leading to the door - another set of footprints led to the door and away again.

Suddenly he held Bruce back and quietly asked him who had the ring? "You should keep it; the Monk may have set a trap to see if you would return it." He fetched the ring and Bruce stowed it safely in his pocket. "Goodnight Bruce, and trust no-one!" Ben said as Bruce waved and strode off into the darkness.

Chapter 10

Spandau Germany

Several days had passed since Bruce had met up with his friends, and he was overjoyed knowing they were still alive and well. He went about his business as usual but with an extra enthusiasm as he thought of them safely secreted, and hopeful for the time they would be able to get them away. He was conscious however, of the vital need to keep them safe from prying eyes, and the sudden inspections which occurred without warning.

To this end, Eric and Ben had turned one of the store cupboards into a safe hiding place in case of an emergency; they had sawn a large cupboard in half, so that when opened it revealed shelves full of blankets. Behind the blankets was another compartment, entered from the back; once inside they could slide another panel across and lean against it to form a perfect seal when examined. The fugitives walked about in their socks, and to avoid attention kept well away from all openings and windows, always staying in the rear of the building.

He had heard nothing further about Hans Muller's investigation, so they could only assume it was still underway. The lack of feedback was beginning to give them concern - his reputation for an analytical mind and his attention to the minutest detail was well known to lead very often to him discovering the truth. They all knew that discovery of the three men would have terrifying consequences, and it did little to ease the tension of not knowing. During their travels, Bruce and Eric were able to see the roadblocks still in operation on the highways and minor roads; vehicles and passengers were rigorously scrutinised.

At last, the snow had melted, and the passageways and walkways inside the citadel garrison were clear. It was a bright day when Bruce arrived at the guard room, and to his surprise found one side of the corridor lined with his guards. Facing them and standing at ease were an equal number of heavily armed SS troops.

Trying his best to conceal his uneasiness, and appear calm, he entered his office. A mixture of both relief and anxiety assailed him when he saw Lieutenant Hans Muller sitting at his desk. He was shuffling through a pile of paperwork which must have been removed from one of his locked drawers. Bruce hurriedly tapped his jacket pocket to make sure his keys were still there; he instinctively knew they would be, he felt angry at himself for the stupidity of the action. Without looking at him, Muller motioned him to a chair opposite, and as he sat, Bruce noticed Hans had new insignia on his lapel. He had been promoted to Captain. It seemed to Bruce that a lot must have happened in the interim since their last meeting. His feelings began to change from annoyance to anger. Someone was sitting at his desk, rifling through his notes, and occupying his chair without seeking his permission. As far as he was concerned, Hans was trespassing and demeaning his position of authority.

"For God's sake!" he thought. "This is my desk and my office! What the hell is he doing here?" He bit his tongue, however, and tried to conceal his anger; there must be a good reason for this, he thought, and the last thing he wanted was to create tension between himself and the man who appeared to be holding all the trump cards.

Brushing the papers aside, Hans smiled, folding his arms, and congratulated Bruce on the efficient manner in which security arrangements at the Citadel laboratories had been conducted. He added, with a rueful smile, that his chair was a very comfortable one, and he knew he could rely on him to carry on the good work.

Bruce relaxed.

The Monk went on, explaining that over the last few weeks he had made exhaustive enquiries and conducted a thorough investigation of the security and procedures at Spandau, and was pleased to see everything was in good order. He had been authorised by the authorities to congratulate him on his good work, and to tell him, unofficially, that he was to be promoted to captain!

"This promotion, however, comes not without a certain price... the work in these laboratories is to be upgraded, very sensitive but important work. This will entail an increased level of security here - a new influx of senior scientists will be arriving to carry out work which will require security of the highest level. High command has detached some of the finest SS security agents to assist you - we trust you will welcome this new venture of sharing the security task between the SS troops and your existing guards."

It was abundantly clear to Bruce that despite the pleasant manner in which these changes were presented, he had no choice in the matter, and it was a direct order. A chill went down Bruce's spine. Despite the pleasantries, he now had an SS captain sitting at his desk, a parade of SS security officers encroaching on his domain, and the problem of working with troops whose brutal training came with a history of intimidation and Nazi indoctrination. He was now being put in the hot seat with a vengeance - he felt a sort of viral infection of panic rising in his spine as he thought of the enhanced importance of these laboratories, and the increased focus of the SS, while just a short distance away were three most wanted men. The panic subsided a little as Hans went on to tell him he himself had been assigned to the Gestapo HQ in Berlin; there had been a possible security leak involving high ranking officers; he was to investigate, and would not be returning to Spandau. He had no details to give, but someone would be appointed in his place, and he felt sure the new SS investigator and Bruce would work well together.

"I would like to take this opportunity to formally say goodbye, and to wish you well," Bruce was about to stand but the Monk gestured him to remain seated. For a moment he gazed ahead in deep thought, then began to speak in a different tone to his usual manner. He was no longer the abrupt automaton, the SS trappings of severity and coldness seemed to fall away, and he looked directly at Bruce, speaking in a sincere and humane tone. "Germany has changed; traditional values are being replaced with aggressive doctrines. Joy and friendship are being replaced with fear and intimidation; people no longer feel free to voice their opinions, even within families. People are disenfranchised, Jews are being persecuted, even our schools are under attack, with books burned and the curriculum dictated by the Reich. Our churches are also coming under their control - they are being used to indoctrinate..." He tapped Bruce on the shoulder. "I know your feelings, Bruce, I can empathise with them; I have often felt that in a different time we would have been friends. But now... survival will depend on how we can adapt to the changing times. In my line of work, I see many injustices and it sickens me to be a part of this; but I am forced to follow the script, as it were." Hans had been walking to and fro, but he turned to Bruce to ask, "Do you still have Fritz's ring?"

Bruce fished it from his pocket to show him.

"Good - it is best you do not pass it to anyone else. You understand, psychological propaganda is a powerful weapon; it is seeping through the streets, under doors and into windows. It devours homes and towns and cities, and soon the whole country will be under its spell. The Trades Unions will be taken over, the Bible will be replaced with Hitler's "Mein Kampf", individualism will be snuffed out so they can attain the Aryan ideal, a new breed, the masters of the planet. They believe in this."

Bruce silently shook his head, then rubbed his forehead, slowly realising the reality presented in this strange interview.

Hans went on, "It has been a consequence of the Great War - the German people wounded in their soul, were hungry for change; but justice was the price for a new direction, and now people are too afraid to challenge the new regime; to still pursue the truth has consequences, so people are wrestling with their conscience versus the danger. You know, it's a bit like walking in virgin snow - a set of footsteps reveals a clear direction of intent, retracing one's steps would signal a change in the way forward." Bruce tried to subdue his emotions at this hint, then Hans finally pointed to a folder on the desk. "Here is a copy of my report on the car accident, and the demise of the three occupants. As far as I am concerned Fritz, Alex and Max were killed in the fire and the case is closed. I have recommended that the roadblocks be lifted." With a final glance at Bruce, he walked briskly out into the corridor. The guards and SS troops snapped to attention as he regarded them sternly, especially the SS men, issuing orders.

"You will secure these laboratories with the utmost diligence, and any failure to do so will meet with the harshest penalties! Heil Hitler!" the troops responded with precision, the guards a little raggedly, as he marched out.

"The albino leopard has regained its spots!" thought Bruce.

Chapter 11

Spandau Germany

Lieutenant Bruce Vogel lined up the citadel guards along the corridor just outside the guard room. It would be a proud moment for him, young and old, the guards had pulled together and restored the laboratories to their former state. In the aftermath he had met with the Colonel and senior members of the establishment. He had impressed them by his efficiency, dedication and the manner in which he had organised the guards in the rebuilding work. Today was the day where he and the Colonel would be presented to the citadel guards to receive commendation for their efforts. He had taken over the role of Lieutenant Mayer, and hopefully would soon be promoted to the same rank. He had been at pains to make sure that the men presented themselves to the highest possible standards and had given them strict instructions on observing the correct protocols when addressing a senior member of the third Reich.

The guards were lined up so that the tallest men stood at the ends with the shortest in the centre. There was to be no separation of old and young guards. As the new officer in charge, Bruce had gained the respect of all of the men irrespective of age and seniority. The authoritarian, often brutal leadership of his predecessor had been replaced by cooperation and teamwork. Bruce's management approach was to encourage everyone to work, to assist those who were the weakest and learn from those were most knowledgeable. He would not stand for bullying, he found value in everyone, encouraging all to work to the best of their ability and capacity.

He delegated as much responsibility down the line as circumstances permitted, whilst at the same time keeping overall authority to himself. As a platoon sergeant under the command of

Lt. Fritz, he had seen how men responded to strong leadership which was fair and seen to be fair. During action Fritz would be the first out and over the trenches in attack and the last to return in retreat, often risking his own life helping the wounded or stragglers back to safety.

Bruce was now leading his men just as he had learnt to lead a platoon of storm troopers when fighting in the trenches of the First World War. The storm troopers had followed him then without hesitation or question, and now the citadel guards were responding in the same manner.

Inspecting the guards for the last time, he felt very proud of the way they had turned out. Young and old were now working in close partnership and what had been a divided group was transformed into a cohesive unit. The older guards were bound together by events and secrets they shared, and by the responsibility they shared in training and protecting a group of youngsters. This would serve as the glue and catalyst that would now bind them all together. They were now a team.

Bruce congratulated them all on their turn out, but deliberately singled out the youngest member as being the smartest on parade. With a rueful smile he glanced at the veterans and told them they could learn a lot from him. Turning his back on them, he walked toward the guard room, while the veterans jokingly gesticulated crudely behind his back. Without turning, Bruce told them he had seen their gestures reflecting in the glass door in front of him, warning them that the next time they were on parade, he would line them up, one behind the other and order them to stick their fore fingers up the arseholes of those in front. As for the last man in the queue, who was missing out on a digit, he would personally thrust his swizzle stick right up his rectum so far that it would lift his helmet, by way of an apologetic salute.

They all laughed. He turned and looked at them and reiterated the importance of the occasion. Senior officers had to be treated with the utmost respect, and if addressed, they would keep their replies to the basic minimum, preferably limited to just a few words. The Colonel had come to inspect them, and hopefully offer congratulations for what they had achieved. He hadn't come to dry their eyes, wipe their noses or change their nappies. Bruce meant to keep a tight rein on subject matter, he had already given the Colonel as much information as he wanted him to know. The laboratories had been restored to their original condition, some of the scientists had returned to their workbenches; a sign that things were returning to normal.

The Colonel was making this a final inspection, giving him the opportunity of meeting all the guards who had been involved in preserving the building. He had been very impressed at the speed in which the laboratories had been repaired and delighted that the fact they were up and running again. He had personally come to commend them for their industry, bravery and dedication.

Bruce had been put in charge of managing all operations at the Citadel. Having on the one hand the support of superiors and on the other the respect of those under his charge, he felt he was making a positive contribution to the war effort. For the first time for a long, long while, he felt at ease with himself, comfortably adjusting his persona from one level to another whilst at the same time contributing as much as he was able to his country. He was now a man for all seasons, changing his apparel as the weather suited.

In the aftermath of the events in the laboratories, and the escape of the three men, there had been an enquiry into the death of Lieutenant Mayer, and questions were raised about the manner in which the three men had escaped. Colonel Schmitz had personally conducted the enquiry and interrogated all involved. He had assigned Bruce to assist him gather information, Bruce ordered all the guards to draft their personal account of what part they had played, detailing what they had seen and experienced. It was vitally important that there was a high degree of correlation in their reports. To ensure complicity each guard was then interviewed with their reports, if there were discrepancies, he would encourage them to make subtle changes to their reports of events, persuading them to differentiate between what they thought they had seen as opposed to what actually happened. This wasn't too difficult to achieve; the young guards were totally inexperienced and untrained in volatile situations; they had been exposed to violent shocks. In their confusion, persuading them that events had been distorted in their minds confusing their memories was an easy matter. For most of the time the young guards had not been present at the scene when crucial events had taken place.

Carefully, Bruce orchestrated their accounts through subtle suggestions. This tactic ensured these reports aligned and supported those written by the veteran guards. Everything on record would now confirm that the security guards had done their utmost, by supporting Lieutenant Mayer in his brave attempts and leadership in trying to capture the three escapees. The preservation of the laboratories had always been uppermost in the lieutenant's mind. As luck would have it, for the last moments leading up to Mayer's' death there had only been two people present, Max and Fritz. Whilst the veteran guards would be prepared to be compliant, they were only aware of what might have happened, as they did not actually witness anything. All the younger guards had been taken away from the scene and were being treated for the injuries and the trauma they had suffered from the heat of the burning gunpowder, smoke inhalation and exposure to the chlorine gas. They were unaware of what had happened and not in a position to see or recall anything.

The veteran accounts were written in such a manner that they substantiated everything that was written by the young guards. By the time the different accounts were bound together they provided a coherent and conflict free document. Everyone had followed the same script albeit some without knowing it. Everything now depended on how convinced Colonel Schmitz would be from both the written reports, and Bruce's first-hand account of what he had supposedly witnessed.

When interviewed by Colonel Schmitz, Bruce was at pains to elevate lieutenant Mayer to the status of a hero. He told the Colonel that Mayer had pleaded with the three men to open the iron door and to give themselves up, adding that no harm would come to them. He had sounded convincing and had communicated with clarity and reason. The lieutenant had explained, that although they would be arrested in the short term, his main concern was the preservation of the laboratories. If they surrendered, he had been authorised to inform them that the punishment for their indiscretion would be very lenient. The options available to them were outlined by the lieutenant and were supported by the young veterans. In their reports they had intimated that the lieutenant had been sincere and exceptionally fair under the circumstances.

The three fugitives had turned him down. Lieutenant Mayer then ordered the veteran guards to break down the iron door. This had entailed using a heavy cannon. The laboratories were now in complete darkness and filled with chlorine gas. Some of the older guards were exhausted and affected by gas; they were ordered to leave the scene and secure all exits and passageways. Lt. Mayer then mustered all the young guards, ordered them to get fitted up with gas masks and equipped them with torches. Lt. Mayer with revolver in one hand and torch in the other leading from the front, entered into the corridor. Bruce detailed the mayhem which confronted them, stressing the stress and panic caused during the commotion. This catastrophic event, resounding with the noise and screams of the injured had given a window of opportunity for the three men to escape. They were probably wearing gas masks similar to those worn by the guards, these camouflaged them allowing them, in the confusion, to escape without notice. The young and inexperienced guards had all rushed up steps pushing aside the two remaining older guards as they fled away from the gas and the fire. The lieutenant ordered some of the older guards to take them post-haste to a place of safety and to treat them as best they could.

It was at this point explained Bruce that he equipped himself, directed the older guards to secure the top entrance leading to the laboratories, then joined Lieutenant Mayer. Bruce then recounted how they had travelled down the whole length of the corridor checking each room and laboratory as they went. In all this time Lieutenant Mayer had led from the front and had shown great courage.

After what appeared to be an age with only torchlight to help them, they had surveyed all the laboratories, except for the one at the end of the corridor. Lieutenant Mayer had demonstrated great resolve and bravery by putting himself into very dangerous situations.

Thus far they had not seen any trace of the three men, and they were now entering the last place of hiding. Mayer, with a pistol in one hand and a torch in the other continued Bruce, told me to stay back as he shone his torch through glass panel of the door. As he scanned the room his torchlight fell upon what looked like to be a timebomb. Turning the handle of the door he kicked it open and rushed in firing shots in all directions before realising the three men were not there. He concentrated a light beam on to a ticking stop clock.

As he approached the clock, he told me to stay where I was whilst he examined the contraption. The bezel of the clock had a mark on the point of zero, with the minute hand close to it. The minute hand had about thirty seconds before it reached the zero point.

He ordered me to stand clear whilst he tried to disarm whatever it was. Mayer had made it clear throughout that saving the laboratories was his prime objective.

He called out that he was concerned that there was very little time before the minute hand reached the hour hand. Frantically, he traced the wires leading from the clock and found they were connected to a plug on the wall behind it. He saw it was switched on. Satisfied and with triumphant aplomb, he sat down on the chair in front of it, reached over and said, "All I have to do is switch it off." They were the last words he spoke. The blast was so strong that I was knocked backwards from the doorway," declared Bruce. "I was left semiconscious on the ground. On recovery I went into the room and was shocked to see that Lieutenant Mayer had been killed from the heat of the explosion.

Later on, examining the switch I found it had been tampered with. One of the three men must have removed the back plate and turned it upside down so the switch appeared to be in the on position. Thus, an unsuspecting person would think they were switching it off, when in reality they would be switching it on!

Colonel Schmitz, shook his head and looked totally bemused. He stared straight into Bruce's eyes and spoke in almost apologetic quietness and exclaimed he had totally misunderstood and underestimated Lieutenant Mayer. It seemed now that he was a man of great courage and resolve. With that, the Colonel placed his hand on Bruce's shoulder and with watery eyes, told him he would never make that mistake again. He then ordered him to assemble all who were involved.

Once the men had gathered Colonel Schmitz had arrived with his entourage. His tailored uniform, pressed to perfection, patterns and buckles highly polished. He made an impressive entrance. Every inch of buffed leather shone as if made from lacquered ebony. He represented the very epitome of confidence in power. The walls, ceiling and the very building itself seemed to be affected by his presence.

As the Colonel approached, Bruce responded with a smart click of his heels and the mandatory exaltation of, "Heil Hitler." The Colonel inspected the young men as they shook their hands, and congratulated them on saving the laboratories. Noticing that some of them still bore the scars from their experience, he told them he would not forget what they had done. He made a very special commendation to the veterans, saying he was encouraged by the loyalty and the courage they still had for the Fatherland.

Turning to Bruce, he called him forward, shook his hand, and in front of all the others expressed his gratitude for the way he had tackled the problems of restoring the laboratories to their present condition, and the manner in which he had encouraged cohesion amongst his men. He then to the delight of all those present awarded Bruce with an Iron Cross medal. The Colonel then turned to the youngest member of the group, who could not have been more than eighteen years old, short and thin dressed in a uniform that seemed to dwarf him. Young and fragile as he seemed, he smartly saluted the commandant and stood upright and confident. The colonel beckoned to one of his assistants who handed him a framed medal, inscribed with the name of Lt Mayer. He had been awarded a posthumous gallantry medal for his gallant efforts in preventing the laboratories from being destroyed, and the manner in which had led from the front. He told the young guard to make sure that it is was hung in a prominent place in the ward room. He then proceeded to make an examination of the laboratories, after which he left taking his entourage with him. Bruce and his band of young and old guards were more than pleased with the outcome.

As time went by and the war progressed, they were to see more action. Colonel Schmidt was put in command of a depleted army and set the task of defending the battered city of Berlin. The Russian Army had surrounded the capital and were advancing toward Hitler's bunker. With little food, experience and a depleted store of ammunition they held out as long as they could against overwhelming odds. Toward the end they had been holed up in a derelict building, as the Russians advanced the older guards had attempted to save the younger guards by waving a white flag of surrender to the oncoming enemy.

They had ceased firing, Bruce ordered the young guards, now stiff with terror and shaking with fear to leave, with arms upright. The lead youngster, who had once been so pleased to accept Mayer's award from the Colonel, carried the flag of surrender. It seemed for an instant that all the noise of war and the crash of gunfire had ceased. Most of the young guards looked like bedraggled ragamuffins and had tears in their eyes, but all walked with their heads held high.

Then the noise and screams of battle shattered the silence once more as each fell where they stood from an onslaught of bullets.

Bruce and the others who had been watching, felt the burning heat of blood pounding firstly with sorrow and then with tortured anger grabbed their bullet-less rifles and rushed out toward the Russians. They each in turn surrendered their souls, tumbling helplessly on the lifeless bodies that lay before them.

Bruce's last act was to brush away the white flag from the young man's face and run his fingers through his blood-soaked hair. Such was the futility of that war, when an ounce of cheap lead could stop so many men all young at heart and with lovely minds.

Each in turn had faced fearful odds, given their lives on the earth of their fathers, all as a result of a single man's ruthless ambitions.

Chapter 12

Spandau Germany

The three of them sat around a table, it was apparent from the expressions of their faces and the atmosphere in the room that they were utterly fed up with being locked away. "Let's put our hands on the table, it's obvious that we can't possibly stay here indefinitely, we need to come up with a plan to make our escape. It won't be easy, where the hell can we blend in and integrate without attracting attention to ourselves? Don't look at me like that, I know it's been on your mind as much as mine, any ideas?"

A long silence followed but was eventually broken when Bruce entered the room.

"What's the problem with you three? You look pretty glum, isn't the food up to scratch or something?" They laughed at him. "You can stick those German sausages, or whatever you'd like to call them up your arse, they'll probably taste much better up there!" someone muttered.

"We're trying to resolve a problem," explained Fritz, "we can't possibly stay here any longer; we're struggling to come up with a plan of escape."

"Have some fucking patience, won't you!" exploded Bruce. "I've already worked out a plan for your escape, but it comes at a heavy price which you will have to be prepared to pay."

He could see from their expressions that they were more than keen to know more. Alex, his enthusiasm growing with the thought of getting away, punched his arm into the air. "Great! How long do we have to wait?"

"Calm down!" came the reply. "I need you to listen carefully, don't interrupt until I am finished! A large quantity of vital equipment - not including those bloody sausages - is to be delivered to Tunis, which as you well know is under a great deal of pressure at the moment from Britain and her allies. This is a serious matter which needs urgent attention. Rommel has returned to North Africa; things are looking pretty grim out there. There is a desperate shortage of equipment, ammunition, food and fuel, and vitally many technical instruments need replacing as a result of enemy bombing. I have orders to take charge of delivering these particular items. As I speak an aircraft is being loaded to take them from Berlin to Tunis. It will be departing tomorrow night and you three will be on board. Your role is to guard the vital supplies and ensure that they get to the depot in Tunis in one piece."

"Precisely," came the reply, "that's the rub, it's up to you. Do you want to stay here or risk sacrificing yourself in fighting for your country? There is and can be no future for you here, knowing your skills and the vast experience the three of you have it is evident that you would be a great asset in the defence of Tunis. I will give you time to think matters over, when I return, I will bring three sets of uniforms. We will prepare new passports and documentation. It's your choice, whether you use it to help you cut and run and take your own chances, or you can leave on the plane and help Rommel repel the British and Americans. Don't forget to smile at the camera. Oh, by the way your presence here has come to the attention of some of the delivery boys, and questions are being asked about who you are. I can't keep matters secret for much longer. So, whatever you decide you have to leave as soon as possible."

With this he turned and walked away, and he was about to close the door behind him Max spoke, "I don't know about the other two but count me in. I'd like to take a pot shot at Montgomery. "Count me in!"

"Me too, I will be on that plane tomorrow," chorused the others.

Fritz added, "I hope you give me a rank suitable for my age and experience, I don't want to be pushed around by some young squirt. I'd rather kick arse rather than have mine booted!"

"I've already thought about that, Lieutenant Fritz."

"What about us, do we get something?"

Bruce smiled. "I'll think of something" he shouted over his shoulder as he went, leaving the men to ponder on their future.

Max's thoughts were troubled. Would he ever see Ruth and his baby son again? He was already sick with worry about what was happening to both of them. Questions filled his mind: Were they safe? Where were they? Are they worried about me? Whatever the answers to his questions there was very little hope they would see each other until the war was over. He had long since realised that if Germany won their chances were slim. If the British won, would they have the freedom to move around and meet up? He'd have to try to push these matters to the back of his mind, he had to focus on what lay ahead in the next few days. Fritz's gaze was fixed on his fingers as he strummed them on the table. His thoughts lay in a similar direction. What would happen to his farm and family if he did not return?

He had nieces who depended on him. He realised that in his present situation, he had few options. As for Alex, the thought of returning to military life excited him, and he looked forward to the challenge. Despite their different views, one thing was certain: they would always be held together by the strongest bonds. All three were determined to make the most of a very challenging situation. After all this was a second chance for the three of them to have a future. They had already escaped once, and they would do so again.

That evening they spent their time preparing for their departure. They had written letters to their loved ones in the hope that somehow, when the world eventually settled down, Bruce would be able to pass them on. In the event of them not returning the letters may prove of some comfort for those that they had left behind. They retired early, there was a very busy day ahead. The next day they were woken early. Bruce was accompanied by two Spandau guards, well-known to them, arrived armed with a camera and the paraphernalia needed to develop mugshots for their new identities. The old ones were destroyed since they were no longer going to be civilians. They were heading for battle in one of the most hostile environments in the war. They were kitted out with used uniforms, Fritz bearing the insignia of Captain, Max as Lieutenant, whilst for Alex the stripes of Sergeant. He was a bit peeved off with this rank.

"Does this mean I have to salute and address the other two as sir?" He stamped his feet, stood to attention and saluted. "Heil Hitler, I am here to serve you. Which one of you wants your backside licked first?"

Fritz answered, "I think it should be the Lieutenant after all his is the largest arsehole."

Bruce frowned and shook his head; he reminded the men that this was serious business and they needed cut the jokes and focus their minds. He then stood to attention and cried out, "The only piece of anatomy I wanted to kick is Montgomery's brain. It's a much bigger target than his arse I am told." They all laughed. It was mid-afternoon by the time everything had been done.

As the two Spandau guards left, they told them they were so pleased to know they were still alive and swore they would keep this knowledge to themselves.

The situation in Tunisia was that fortunes were going backward and forward. Sometimes the Axis Army were making advances, only to concede to the British Allies who had increased their force with a large number of American, Indian and Greek soldiers along with their weapons. A contingent of Charles de Gaulle's Free French army had joined them. They showed little mercy toward the Germans they had a point to prove. The day dragged on, and at ten o'clock that evening, Bruce made a last-minute check. He then drove them toward Berlin airport.

Before their arrival, they were well briefed that they were to guard the technical equipment, making sure to avoid face to face contact with anyone. The plane was heavily guarded, and the guards consisted mainly of young soldiers who were unlikely to ever have met them. It would still be foolish to take any chances. The three of them were driven as close to the plane as possible, where Bruce bid them farewell, passing an envelope to Fritz. This contained brief notes about each of them. He thanked them for their service saying their services as true patriots of Germany would be of great benefit in the defence of Tunisia. He strongly suggested that the three of them should remain together as one single efficient unit. He then abruptly turned and walked away. He got into his car without looking back, feeling sick at the reality of leaving the three men. Sick with fear, that he was sending them to their death.

The noise of the plane's engine made it difficult for anyone to speak, so they each spent the journey with their own thoughts. As they closed in on Bore airport, they discovered an early taste of what was to come. They hadn't gone to war; the war was heading for them. As they neared the airstrip they were set upon by enemy fighters. Bullets showered in through fuselage as they tried their best to take cover.

Fortunately, the firing didn't last long, as German fighters came and repelled the attackers, and they later learned that the airport was heavily defended. After the unloading of the plane, they were ushered to the guard room where they settled down for the night.

Early the next morning, the three of them met up with a commander, who interviewed them. He was pleased to see that these three volunteers had served in the Great War. He was also very impressed with their credentials. For the time being he assigned them to the regiment that defended the airstrip. He explained that they had lost several men from air attacks, including some officers. Fritz was made second in command of the troops defending the perimeters, and it was decided that he would be assisted by Max. He then turned to Alex; who he believed could become useful as a general factotum, employed wherever necessary.

As they were escorted to the barracks, they heard the sounds of heavy gunfire seemingly not so far away. It was a sound they'd heard so many times before.

The airstrip was constantly under attack from British fighter aircraft. This was getting heavier and heavier as the months went by, culminating in a parachute raid in November. With great fortitude they managed to repel the attack. The three men led a small detachment of troops, their bravery, leadership and the manner in which they fought came to the attention of the commander. There had been heavy losses, including two senior officers. Fritz was promoted to lead a detachment which was seconded to a tank regiment. Max was promoted to second-in-command, whilst Alex was promoted to staff Sergeant. They left the airstrip and headed toward the battlefront.

The battle for Tunisia went on for several months with heavy casualties on both sides. Fritz was aware that the ebb and flow of successes and losses was taking a heavy toll on all the men. This was compounded by the fact that the number of German casualties was far greater than that of the Allied forces. To begin with his command consisted of some two hundred troops but it was joined almost every day by others who had lost their commanders thus swelling their numbers. Thanks to sound leadership they had won several skirmishes, gaining a great deal of respect from other command leaders. When on such deployment the platoon came across a large group of Italian and German soldiers who looked bedraggled, downhearted, and short of food and equipment.

Fritz took over the command. At first the newcomers were very reluctant to allow this. A junior officer from the group, approached Fritz, saying, "Please, Sir, may I have a word with you? There's an issue that is causing my men and others I have come across to be disaffected and dissatisfied. It is causing much dissent and low morale amongst the troops. Many of the junior NCOs are tired of obeying orders which direct them to perform impossible tasks, ending in high mortality rates. Often, when totally outnumbered they were still ordered to charge at impossible odds. The men are half starved. They receive scant protection due to the shortage of tanks, guns, and ammunition. There is much unrest. Large numbers are now threatening to surrender themselves rather than be killed as a result of overwhelming odds." Fritz looked anxious and was about to speak but the Lieutenant continued, "Our previous commander, who was well liked and respected, was sent a signal from the Nazi SS. It ordered him to report anyone who surrendered without due reason, stating that they would receive maximum punishment. Worse if any NCOs who were close to the soldiers encouraged the defectors or turned a blind eye, they would be treated as enemies of Germany, and as such their families at home would face consequences."

On hearing this, Fritz ordered all the new men to gather together with those of his own company and using a battered old tank as a platform made an address:

"Men, you know as well as I do, we will often have to fight against all probability of success. I, and the men of my platoon, have made a vow. We would rather die for our country, our loved ones and their freedom than surrender. Losing the war would mean that your families, friends and neighbours would be in jeopardy of losing not only their lives, but the whole culture of our great country. I ask you, to follow me. I give you my word I will lead from the front, I will face the same hazards as you. I also promise you this. Should a situation arise where we are heavily outnumbered and outgunned by their tanks and heavy guns and we are ordered into battle. Should we succumb to the overpowering strength of the enemy and they offer a truce I will seriously consider accepting it. The one thing I have learned from past experience when I fought from the trenches in the First World War is that I've always been mindful for peace rather than slaughter. So, if these conditions present themselves, and we are given the choice to surrender, I would probably take it.

Why? Because in the past I have seen the other side of the coin. I have offered and received the acceptance of a truce from the enemy. I am not here to turn you into compost. Whatever you face, I face. Have pride in yourselves and count those closest to you as friends who will look after you in times of trouble. So, I am beseeching you to follow my company. We are aiming to turn the tide and in so doing we will make our country safe and free again. May your God go with you!"

He jumped off the tank as he walked away a trickle of applause swelled by his own platoon members, gained in volume. It turned into a massive cheer as with rifles held high the men all joined in chanting, "Germany!", "Germany!", "Germany!"

With many skirmishes and battles behind them, his platoon gathered new members and increased in size on a daily basis. More and more foot soldiers joined them. They came from other regiments that had been disassembled as they made an escape from capture. An urgent message arrived from HQ. Much needed supplies of food and ammunition would not be arriving. Fritz's troops had successfully fought back when attacked by the French forces a few weeks earlier.

Fortunately, they managed to secure some of their supplies. The 34th infantry division moved into the area, heading to the Atlas Mountains. Fritz's platoon joined the 168's Regiment combat team. Many other regiments joined them and were scattered over a large area. As a result of this dispersion, they became isolated, giving rise to poor communication and difficulty in maintaining supplies. They were also in serious danger of being overrun. Fritz's regiment was in the same predicament. Although isolated, Fritz' managed through sheer guts and good leadership to push back the Allies on several occasions. The success of his regiment came to the attention of not only the British but also his German commanders.

The war vacillated from success to failure for six long months each side losing or gaining ground. A date Fritz would always remember is 13th May 1943.

A dispatch rider skidded to a halt, calling out, "Where is the officer in charge?"

He'd come in at such a pace that someone cried out, "That bloody bike could have killed me!"

"Never you mind about that. I have an urgent message, take me to him now."

Fritz hearing the commotion, moved through the crowd that had gathered around the dispatch rider.

On seeing him approach the man stood to attention and saluted. "An urgent message from HQ, Sir. Please sign here. I have a large area to cover and must move on."

Fritz looked at the rider. He looked exhausted, and there was mud splattered all over his leathers. The jerry cans secured to the sides of the bike suggested he'd come a long way and still had a long way to go. "You're not going anywhere just yet; you've been in that saddle for long enough." Fritz ordered that he should be taken to the field food kitchen and given some refreshment. He then signed a document acknowledging that he'd received the communication.

However, the messenger was not to be released until he had rested for a while. Although the dispatch rider protested, Fritz told him that if he didn't have a break, he would never finish his round. As Fritz walked back to his tent, a large group of soldiers silently gathered around him. Clearly there was something important afoot. Arriving at his tent he beckoned Max and Alex to join him. On the front of the missive were the words, "URGENT, For the attention of the Commanding Officer."

He quickly tore it open, the first thing he did was to look at the signature, it was from General Jurgen Von Arnim. The letter declared that his regiment was to stand down from all military activities forthwith. A truce had been agreed between Germany, Italy, Britain and their allies. The orders were: "*Lay down your arms and surrender yourselves to the nearest British command post or any of her allied regiments. You are guaranteed safe passage and reception. You will be held as prisoners of war where you will be treated in accordance with the Geneva*

Conventions." Max and Alex stood, feeling dismayed yet at the same time somewhat relieved, as they had seen it coming for some time.

The three exited the tent to be greeted by a large crowd of soldiers. They parted as Fritz walked between them, he headed toward the nearest vantage point which happened to be a half truck. They gathered around him.

"Men, the battle here is over. We have surrendered!" Almost to a man, they bowed their heads. "As from now the fighting is over for all of us. All of you will now be able to return to your homeland and your families. As you walk away, hold your heads up high, as every one of you has fought with patriotic fervour. Whatever the conditions, when you were outnumbered, you stood your ground and held them back. When you were half starved you fought on, calling on a deep energy reserve. You have not shied away but have all done the best you could for your country. Again, I say, do not regard today as a defeat. There will be honour again when together we will rebuild our country in times of difficulty. I salute each and every one of you, for the great effort and sacrifice you have made. We will be leaving behind many broken comrades, but we will honour their souls by rebuilding our nation. Do not regard today as a defeat but the beginning of a new era where Germany will rise again.

This time without conflict but in unity with all our European neighbours, and indeed the rest of the world. I must order you to collect all your weapons, munitions and any instrument that may cause harm. We will stockpile them for collection. There is a British contingent on its way to escort us to a holding place. When we arrive there, we will march with pride and dignity. You have all served your country with distinction. It has been my good fortune and absolute honour to have served as your commanding officer. Remember those words I spoke to you before. At the end of the day, it would be folly to give up your life when you're facing certain death because of overwhelming odds. You should do what any soldier would do, and accept a truce. This is the position we will find ourselves in. Britain and her allies are no longer the enemy, in time they will become peaceful neighbours and hopefully friendship will develop. God bless you all!"

Fritz turned to leave and everyone cheered, but he didn't hear the noise his heart and mind was too full of remorse. Hitler and the

Third Reich had a lot to answer for, and he hoped the bastard was dead.

A few hours later, a large group of British soldiers headed toward them. They had been drawn to the sound of cheering and applause. A small scouting party was sent forward to ascertain the cause of all the noise. The young Lt leading them, viewed them through his binoculars and could see their white flag of surrender flying high. He wondered if it was real or a trap, and then he saw the cache of weapons piled as in defeat. Still uncertain, he returned and reported back to his commanding officer, who decided to send a small force forward, they were to report back but on no account to make an attack. They were to hold their position, assess the situation, discover if the enemy were indeed standing down or setting a snare to attract unsuspecting soldiers.

He'd never come across such a situation before, he needed to be cautious. He decided to send his experienced second-in-command to lead the advance party. Since the ceasefire, Fritz had reduced the number of guards around the perimeter, consequently there were fewer guards than usual. The small advance contingent took up a defensive position, the Lieutenant selected half-dozen men to accompany him, they needed a closer look.

The others were ordered to stay in their positions and act as cover in case they had to retreat quickly. Because of a breakdown in communication, they had not received the message that a truce had been declared, so were unaware that the war was over. What was known was that this German Regiment was flying a white flag as a sign of surrender. Signalling to his men to stay and provide cover he tapped the soldier next to him and whispered to him to follow. The officer would crawl ahead and the soldier should follow a short distance away. The soldier looked blank, he gesticulated angrily. Understanding at last, the soldier obeyed and they crawled onward, keeping as low as possible. Initially they had some cover from the odd boulder and the occasional tree. Now there was nothing between them and the German soldiers ahead. He had to take his chances. It certainly looked as though they were unprepared for battle. He hadn't brought with him anything to signal with so searched his pockets. He had nothing. If he surrendered himself, surely they wouldn't shoot him. He stopped thinking about this for a moment then got to his feet, arms high in the air. As soon as he came to the edge of the clearing he was seen. He stopped. The soldier accompanying him rushed up, pointing his rifle in a threatening manner. All the unarmed German soldiers stood but didn't move. Alex, seeing the situation unfold, picked up the letter they had received, and frantically waving it in the air, moved quickly toward them.

The closer he moved, the more agitated the armed soldier became. Just at the point he was about to present the letter, a shot rang out, breaking through the silence. Alex was dead before he hit the ground.

The Lieutenant froze. Damn stupid fool! Bloody idiot! He began to wave his arms in the air, he turned around grabbed the soldier and threw him to the ground.

Fritz had seen all the action. He casually walked into his tent and pulled out his revolver. Truce or no truce, he wasn't giving his weapon up, as it might come in useful. There was a stillness outside, and no one was moving when Fritz moved forward, pushing the men aside as he went. He stood in front of the officer, levelled his revolver at him, then abruptly turned to the soldier on the floor and shot his brains out. The sound of gunfire had alerted the rest of his company who rapidly came to his aid. The English officer apologised profusely and extended his hand. After a brief pause, Fritz extended his in return.

"You are a very brave man; you have saved many lives. Lying before you is one of the finest of soldiers. His kind will never be replaced. We have now served two wars together, but ironically his demise the result of extending an arm of peace."

The English Lieutenant went through his dead comrade's pockets and found his identity card. He turned to Fritz, "It seems he was a traitor, a German defector and murderer of a brave German officer. Alex's body was taken and buried with dignity. They had managed to find large stone which they rolled over his grave. There was little time remaining before they moved on, however one of the German soldiers who had been a monumental mason before being drafted, managed with the few tools available, to engrave the words "ALEX" 13, signifying that as a German soldier he had given his life to his country, and he would serve as an example and solid rock for others to follow. This was not a tombstone but a monument to him and others who gave their lives to their Country. It remains there to this day."

Chapter 13

Spandau Germany

Pockets of war still continued, but it was all over for Fritz and Max. After a long trek they eventually arrived at the Prisoner of War camp on the outskirts of Tunis.

There they joined other POWs who were being held in a very large Bull Pen situated in a wheat field. They were all treated very well, fed and made as comfortable as possible. Before any of them could be released, each was interviewed to glean as much information as possible. Comprehensive records were made that would help Britain and her allies in the war effort. Eventually it was the turn for both Max and Fritz to be interrogated. Fritz had very little to say, anything of significance he did know he did his utmost to keep to himself. He was aware however that Max had different ideas, he was extremely worried that as Germany lost the war Hitler's regime might well use the nerve agent he had helped to formulate. Countless loss of lives of innocent families weighed heavily on his mind. What if bombs containing the deadly nerve agent were dropped on the cities of Europe? Would Senior Officers of the Third Reich use this weapon as a final resort, he wondered? He felt torn between the duty he had to help his country and the slaughtering of millions of people. There was only one possible conclusion. When interrogated, he would tell them everything. He was interviewed by a very young Intelligence Officer. He explained that he had been a scientist working in laboratories based in Spandau.

Initially the project was aimed at eradicating insects, vermin and anything that damaged food stocks and fabrics. Inadvertently, they came up with a product which was so powerful that it killed both small and large animals instantly. Evidence suggested that the substance either in aqueous or gaseous form attacked the nervous system thus incapacitating and killing all forms of life exposed to it. It was shown that it could be absorbed through the body, and gas masks therefore would prove ineffective. They had called it Tabun which means taboo in English, implying that it should never be used. Unfortunately, large quantities were made, and a more deadly variant called Sarin was also manufactured.

Max spoke in a serious and passionate way, "The reason I'm telling you all this must be clear to you. If Germany is heading for defeat she may well resort to using this chemical as a weapon. If it were delivered by aircraft or shelling it could easily wipe out a city in the matter of hours. London would probably be the first of many cities. There is nothing that would stop it. As a matter of urgent priority, you must inform your superiors to make preparation for the defence against such an attack. If I am given the opportunity, I would be prepared to travel to England to assist in analysing and treating the effects of this nerve agent. Throughout Max's statement, the Intelligence Officer found it difficult to take Max seriously. He drafted some notes in which he indicated his conclusion. He believed that Max was suffering from some form of trauma resulting from battle fatigue. After almost an hour's interrogation the interview concluded, Max was thanked for his contribution and dismissed. The Officer typed out his report as accurately as he could. He included reference to the possible aftermath of using this substance such as the annihilation of the population of Britain. He wrote across the top of the paper these words in heavy print. "I think this man is crazy," then placed it into a pile of non-important documents.

It wasn't until sometime later, that a Senior Intelligence Officer happened to be reading through some notes, he came across Max's statement. It made him feel very uneasy. Should any of this be based on fact it could have serious repercussions. He immediately ordered a group of soldiers to find him, but Max could not be found. The camp was in a state of disorder and confusion, it was impossible to pinpoint one man amongst the hundreds of thousands of inmates. The war continued until eventually Germany was close to capitulation as one campaign after another surrendered. The downfall of the Western front in April 1945 was the beginning of the end for Germany.

It was abundantly clear; Germany was losing the war. The days grew into months, there was no chance of them being repatriated until matters came to a final conclusion. Daily bulletins came over loudspeakers, giving information concerning defeats and surrender of German armies. Each report was painful for all the POWs. It was almost impossible to escape. Despite valiant efforts Fritz and Max could not get away. On April 25th. 1945 they heard of the death of Mussolini; he had been executed. This was followed on the 29th of April by the surrender millions of German soldiers in Italy and Austria. Then on the 2nd of May the POWs were stunned into silence. Hitler had committed suicide! Despair and humiliation spread amongst all the prisoners. Fritz and Max could almost anticipate what was in store. The Battle of Berlin was lost to the Russians.

They feared for the safety of all the civilians who were left to the mercy of the merciless Army. North-west Germany, and the Netherlands unconditionally surrendered on the 4thof May. The same happened in Bavaria on the 5th May then on the 8th May the Channel Islands surrendered this brought nothing but total dejection. Finally, on the 7th May 1945 the whole of the German Army surrendered; this was known throughout the world as Victory in Europe Day where every nation celebrated the heralding of peace throughout the world.

When German POW's were finally released, the responsibility of repatriation was down to the Germans, but individuals were offered scant help and had to make their own way by any means they could find. Max and Fritz decided they would start walking, making their way toward Germany. They had to take care; they were still wanted men it would be inevitable that someone would identify them when they reached their homeland. Fritz decided to take his chances, he would head back for his farm. Max told him he would accompany him as far as he could. He then intended to head for England. This was not going to be easy.

Eventually they got to the point where the road forked, one way leading to Berlin, the other toward Britain. They shook hands and embraced as they parted, hoping one day they would meet up again. Fritz took to the road; he couldn't help recall the long discussions they had had with each other. Max's argument for going to England was embroiled in a mixture of having produced such a potent weapon, which could then be used to annihilate a country so easily. He had argued that it would be likely that in the last-ditch defence, a nation under threat would use any means possible to save their people. Whatever conventions that were in existence would be ignored.

The bombing of nerve agent gases on cities and towns would be far more effective than trying to defend in a traditional manner. Should a country have a weapon destructive enough, and proven in its effectiveness, it would be unlikely that they would be willing to give it up. On the contrary, it would be a powerful deterrent. Max was also unaware of any convention that stated that in peacetime research into chemical warfare was illegal. Indeed, it was necessary for producing antidotes and treatments which might prove effective in the event of such attacks. What had struck Fritz, which somehow made good sense, was that in a desperate situation where a country was about to be annihilated, they would have nothing to lose.

The final solution would be to use the most powerful weapon they had available, spraying hundreds of tons of nerve agent onto towns and cities of her enemies. A country armed with such powerful weapons would hold a deterrent making potential aggressors fear reprisals. These thoughts perturbed Fritz. He was jaded by war and all the carnage he had witnessed. He was troubled by the decision Max had made to go to England but never the less he wished him well in his travels, he hoped he'd make it in one piece.

Perhaps he had a point! Either way there was no doubt he would miss him. They had come through a lot together. Max bade him farewell, telling Fritz that the small town he was heading for was called Porton Down.

Chapter 14

London

The river Thames was beginning to move more quickly, black, smooth yet forceful. It was seven thirty, and the light was rapidly fading. Rodders gazed over to the far side of the river as he stood under a large willow tree on the small pier, a short distance from the Prospect of Whitby Inn. He was there to make contact with an underground agent code named GM 38. He had met several other agents at this place, he used to drink frequently in London's oldest riverside inn which dated back to 1520.

Since the war the beer had tasted awful, he had a feeling it must have been distilled there. His gloved hands clenched the rusty railings, causing leather and metal to grind together. He contemplated the historic river. Mighty and forceful, nothing could or would stop it. It was hell bent on reaching the sea taking with it spoils of cities, towns and villages, notwithstanding the pollution of industry and any other form of silt or dross that either wilfully or accidentally ended up in its waters.

Maybe this accounted for its unpredictable nature as it vacillated on its course, yet, there seemed to be something graceful and dignified about its form. The river had travelled a long way to reach the nation's capital, London, speeding on its way to its inevitable end. Its destination had already been determined even before the first drops of rain had fallen on high mountains. It would soon merge with the brackish waters of the estuary, surrendering itself to the vast oceans where it would be caught up in an endless cycle. Much of what got caught up on its way was either deposited on banks serving the lower reaches or dissolved in the water. The insoluble materials hitched a ride on the tide and were set free in the waves.

Wouldn't it be wonderful if the enormous problems facing Britain at war could be taken up by a similar force and be dumped into some large abyss? The sickness of war, the heartache, destruction and death were tearing the tormented soul out of the nation. "Why, oh why couldn't its water wash away the carnage caused by an insatiable appetite for power of the Third Reich?" Rodders wondered to himself.

There was however no escaping it, the war would continue until the last drop of blood was spilt. Everywhere he looked was shrouded in darkness, all lights had been switched off, and this city was now engulfed in a black shroud. All was quiet apart from the sound of the moving water, which led his mind to more peaceful thoughts. A light breeze stirred. There was a chill in the air, causing his eyes and nose to run and making him shiver. He buttoned his coat as he thought back to a few days previously when he had celebrated his birthday with friends. They had gathered together, enjoying each other's company, dismissing thoughts of the present situation as they appreciated the rare opportunity to take a little time off and relax. They were however mindful that there was little to celebrate and in these times of shortage few luxuries to celebrate with. Nonetheless hope was glimmering. The allied forces were making substantial inroads, perhaps just perhaps, the end might well be in sight.

Rodney was born in India near Calcutta in December 1909; his father was a British diplomat, working in the Calcutta Embassy in the Bengal province. At the age of nine, Rodney was sent to live with his grandparents in the village of Aylesbury. His father's role at the embassy was not clear other than that it involved dealing with the Indian government at that time. When war broke out, he was assigned the war department overseeing the supplies of munitions and armoured vehicles. Supplying the British and Indian armies demanded an extensive range of supplies. This drained resources available to the local inhabitants, leading in part to a terrible famine in the Bengal region of Fort William. Millions of people died from malnutrition. Rodney's father Richard Preston assisted in importing large quantities of food and relief money to ease the problem. Many lives were saved but the losses were still countless. Much of the blame for the famine was directed toward the British for diverting power supplies to be used to keep the combined forces war effort going. Richard Preston never spoke about this dreadful time, he would however never for a moment forget it.

At his christening, Rodney's mother Anne was disappointed to find that her ancestral maiden name of Tuxford had not been included in his name. This had been agreed during her strenuous labour in order to preserve the family name as she was the last of her line. The name Rodney was given after his maternal grandfather but to her dismay, his father never used it, preferring to call his son Rodders. Anne did come to accept this but sadly succumbed to malaria and died whilst Rodney was still an infant.

Short haired, brown eyed, with squared shoulders, the older Rodney became the taller he stood and the wider he grew. While a student at Cambridge he excelled in both academia and sport. He represented the light blues at rugby in addition to becoming a champion in Judo. His studies came easily, he excelled in History and Greek, gaining a double first. Wherever he went his demeanour and stature ensured he stood out, his presence emanating an air of confidence and power. On leaving university he enlisted, volunteering to join the Special Operations where he quickly demonstrated leadership, self-sufficiency and great prowess in both physical and mental challenges. Keeping his eyes and mind alert he was constantly aware of all that was happening around him. Anyone would feel confident in having him at their side. These qualities led to Rodders, as he was affectionally called, being sent by high command to meet with a new contact who had sent cryptic messages through an overseas agent.

Rodders felt uneasy about the meeting, he had been waiting for thirty minutes and was becoming suspicious. He had concerns about how the meeting had been arranged, he had had no direct contact with GM-38 he was due to meet or any information about the source of the original contact. This seemed to indicate a high level of security involving a matter of great importance and urgency. Intelligence had classified the situation at the highest level but frustratingly all contact with the agent had been lost due to careless management. Whilst he waited, he pondered the possibility that it could be connected to a rumour he had recently heard but had no way of knowing if it was fact or fancy. It concerned a powerful gas in German hands.

A German prisoner had escaped some years ago and was on the run from German high command, who had gone to extreme lengths to pursue and capture him, suggesting he had information of great strategic importance. It was thought he may have been involved in scientific research on poisonous gasses. Under an assumed identity he had managed to travel to Italy along with other escapees. Here they enlisted with a small German force and were posted to Tunisia, facing troops from Britain, America, Greece and France. Despite being wanted by the German authorities his patriotism and loyalty was still strong, he was prepared to take up arms for his country. He was posted to an infantry battalion, involved in the fiercest of battles defending Germany's occupation of Tunisia against Britain and her allies. The fighting was long and hard, much of it hand to hand. The engagement lasted for six long months, casualties were high and both sides were exhausted but after determined and forceful resistance the Germans, drained and dejected finally capitulated and surrendered. Two hundred and thirty thousand soldiers were to be handed over to the enemy. Two of these had distinguished themselves in battle, often leading from the front, displaying courage and tenacity. They had gained the respect not only of their comrades but also of many of the British soldiers.

The two soldiers came to the attention of the British intelligence, the younger of the two having volunteered to speak to someone about a new gas which was under development in Berlin. He was interviewed by a young intelligence officer of little experience. During the interrogation he disclosed that he had been involved in experiments which had led to the production of an extremely potent and toxic gas. Trials exposing animals, and possibly humans, to this gas had shown it to be so efficient as a means of killing that it would change the whole outcome of the war if put into effect. The young officer after listening carefully formed the impression that the soldier was suffering delusions caused by battle stress, and he dismissed him as a crank. What he was saying seemed beyond comprehension alternatively it could be a deliberate attempt to spread fear undermining British morale. The soldier had, therefore, been dismissed and returned under escort to the prisoner's compound.

The following day, however, a senior officer doing a routine review of notes from previous interrogations came across the German soldier's submissions. His concerns were raised, and he was keen to hear more. He ordered the man to be brought to his office as a matter of urgency. Guards were sent to fetch him but he and others could not be found in their compound. An extensive search was put into operation to no avail. A full-scale hunt throughout the whole camp yielded nothing. The compound was very secure, surrounded by a cordon of wire guarded by armed soldiers. Despite these measures they had somehow managed to breach the boundary. Why they would choose to escape was puzzling, there was nowhere to go. The men were extremely weak and fatigued, they were being well looked after. The war was over for those in captivity so where was the rationale in trying to escape? It seemed to the officer that they were missing something significant. A troop of men were sent on a mission to search with the order not to return without them.

The young officer who had been responsible for the interview was summoned; it was made clear that his commanding officer was not impressed by the manner in which possibly important information may have slipped through their fingers. If the reported events had indeed happened, it would have been a long time ago. The question now was: did Germany still hold a store of this chemical? If so, why had it not been used?

A worried frown spread over his forehead as Rodders began to pace, turning details of the rumour over in his mind. Hopefully the soldier would be found soon and the matter could be cleared up. He was also feeling irritated because he had had to cancel a meeting with his old friend and fellow agent, known as Cloughie.

Rodders' mind wandered to their early days together. They had trained together as special operatives, both men distinguishing themselves. They were the only commissioned officers on the programme, the others being specially selected privates or NCOs. Everyone was treated equally, judged only by the way they completed the varied tasks that were thrown at them. Cloughie was slightly shorter than Rodders but broader and tougher, muscular but very agile. With his receding hairline, blue eyes and permanent friendly smile, he gave the impression of being a friendly sort. This could be misleading as he was capable of dealing harshly with anyone or anything in his way.

An unusual talent was his ability to mimic voices, whatever the dialect. During training he would provide light relief by impersonating those in charge. He did this well and would often call out commands as they marched along, countermanding the genuine thing. This would cause great confusion with troops who would suddenly halt or change direction. He particularly enjoyed the 'turn around' command which caused turmoil in the ranks. The drill sergeant was not amused by these antics but took delight in having reason to dress an officer down. Even so, the two men had great respect for each other. On one memorable occasion Cloughie ordered the men to remove their helmets and urinate in them, but it was only at the last second that the sergeant countermanded the order. Cloughie was reprimanded by the commanding officer who tried in vain to suppress his laughter. He was ordered to clean the latrines for a week in the hope he would learn the appropriate way of disposing of unwanted fluids. His sense of humour often got him into trouble but that didn't stop him.

After completing their training Rodders and Cloughie went their separate ways but still managed to stay in close contact. Rodders' thoughts drifted to one of Cloughie's missions. There had been a lot of activity in the North of France, and clearly the Germans were up to something. Cloughie spoke French fluently.

On one occasion he had asked a German soldier for a light, mimicking the voice of Charles De Gaulle. The soldier obliged. For this assignment he had been parachuted into France close to Arras where he met up with a member of the French resistance in the dead of night, and the man led him inland in an attempt to discover what was afoot. He had seen some heavy construction, a huge thick concrete building and large bunkers and underground tunnels were being built using forced Polish labour. Their treatment was inhumane in the extreme. He was told by the guide that those who did not die from beatings usually succumbed to exhaustion and the lack of nutritious food. The structures were being built at an enormous pace. Cloughie had taken photographs of the construction sites and slipped out of France as slickly as he had slipped in. His venture was invaluable in obtaining intelligence for night bombardments.

These kinds of memories tended to come to Rodders' mind in situations such as this, when he was unoccupied and alone. With a shake of his head, he cleared his mind and focused on present matters. He was angered at finding himself waiting for an agent who was now very late. He had been waiting nearly an hour. Had he not had strict instructions to do all he could to make contact with the new agent he would have left by now. It had been made clear that the information the carrier had could be of significant importance so he was duty bound to stay. The darkness was encroaching around him, he shifted his head quickly as he saw some movement near the trees. Someone or something had moved across the end of the passageway leading to where he was standing. Was this the agent? He had a feeling he was not alone and put his hand in his pocket to grip his revolver. He moved over to one end of the railing so he would be partly obscured from anyone approaching.

The Thames was picking up pace, the water around the edges of the bank rising. Rodders looked across the water to the bank which was vanishing in the distance. If the movement had been the agent, he would surely show himself soon. He tightened one hand on the rail, tightening his grip on his revolver with the other. Time was now drawing close to the danger zone. It was dark but despite the movements he had seen no one had revealed himself. Either the person due to meet him had cancelled, been delayed or the whole thing was a set up.

A plan to take out another operative. If this was the case, they would be waiting for darkness. Rodders had been in this situation before. It was possible he was under surveillance, so he lowered himself to make the target smaller. As he crouched, he could just see through the lower gap in the railings. There was something in the water amongst the usual flotsam carried on the current. He froze in horror as he made it out. There, almost totally submerged, he could see what appeared to be a body floating amongst the debris.

Chapter 15

London

The body was moving, and there was no time to waste. Rodders got up and clambered over the railing. Taking a firm grip on the lowest rail he stretched out as far as he could, but the body was just out of reach. Dammit, he said to himself. If this was the agent he was supposed to meet, he may well have some information on him. He thought about diving in, and racked his brain, wondering what he could do. "His umbrella!" he could use that; he had left it by the willow tree. The tide was slowly moving the body.

"Do I have enough time?" he muttered to himself. He decided to try, with a torch in hand he rushed along the railings to the narrow pass that led to the tree. As he got there, he distinctly heard someone or something brushing against the lower branches on the opposite side of the tree. He considered investigating, he had no time, and without further thought he picked up the umbrella and rushed back to the river's edge. He could not spot the body. Sweeping his torch angrily he spent some anxious moments peering onto the dark water, with all lights out because of the Blitz he could see only water. He shone the light further down the side until with relief he saw the body resurfacing. It was now opposite the end of the concrete steps leading down to the river edge. He rushed headlong down almost falling into the river.

However, the body had moved further out just beyond his reach, and so without hesitation, he stepped down onto the submerged steps. He stretched out, attempting to use the hook at the end of his umbrella as a grapple. He tried to hook the back of the overcoat which was still just above the surface. The weight of the body, with the force of the moving tide was simply too much. The small handle just slid across the clothing. He stepped deeper down into the river; he was now almost waist deep. He leaned out as far as he dared, he had almost given up hope of fishing the body out when the hooked handle anchored itself on the coat belt. It almost pulled him into the water. Leaning backward, his body now half submerged, he held on tightly to the umbrella and half crawled with one hand on the steps and the other pulling at the body. He gradually hauled it out. Finally, it reached the bottom of the steps, he clambered down, caught hold of the overcoat and heaved. To his surprise the body was much lighter than he had expected. He turned it over, and slipping his hands under the armpits, he slowly dragged it up to the top of the steps. "Umbrella!" he exclaimed, and splashing down the steps he retrieved it. This was no ordinary umbrella; it was designed to be used as a weapon. The sharp pointed end could inflict a nasty wound, it could also be unscrewed to reveal the end of the small-bore barrel whilst the handle end could be loaded with a single .22 bullet. He sat down, totally drenched, next to the body. He needed to regain his breath. He shone the torch on to the face. The eyes were covered in hair, which he gently brushed to the side. Staring up at the sky before him now was the face of a beautiful woman.

Rodders had been ailing for some time and the effort had affected him, his legs were beginning to ache. He stood up and rotated his head, trying to relieve himself of his stiffening neck. His mind went back to the willow tree, as he was sure he had seen some movement around there. He put his hand in his coat pocket just to make sure his pistol was still there, and gripped it in readiness. He moved over to the railings, flashing the light toward the trees. As if from nowhere he heard footsteps, but before he could react, he felt the pressure of something pushing into his back and stiffened. He had felt the barrel of a pistol before, and knew he was feeling it again. In a broad East London accent, a voice broke the stillness.

"I'll take over from here, mate!"

Rodders half raised his arms in the air and straightened himself to his full height. "His first mistake." he said to himself. The pistol pressed harder into his back. "His second mistake." Thinking this chap is not a pro, if he was, he would have stepped back and kept his distance. Standing this close to him would give him the opportunity to take him out. "Must be my lucky day," thought Rodders as he told the man he didn't want any trouble, explaining that he had been out for a walk when he had seen a body in the water. "Leaving it in the water would be foolish since it would have been carried away." He didn't get a chance to finish the sentence.

"Shut your fuckin' gob," was the response, accompanied by a sharp jab into his back.

"That hurt!" Rodders blurted as though frightened, promising himself his assailant would pay dearly for that. He attempted to speak again but stopped when the thug drove the pistol deep into his ribs, causing him to buckle in pain.

"I told yer once, now shut up and wind yer fuckin neck in."

Rodders straightened himself again, and he estimated that the thug stood about eighteen inches shorter than him because the voice came from behind his shoulder. "It is time to sort this thick arsed cockney out," he thought. He leaned back as though fainting in fear, and pressed himself against the barrel, causing his assailant to momentarily step back. Rodders was confident he would not press the trigger, that this man was no professional. With that in a split second Rodders turned sideways whilst simultaneously crashing his elbow into the thug's face. He was very pleased to hear the sound of cracking signalling the cockney's nose had been crushed. More importantly, very much to his relief, the gun did not go off.

As his assailant staggered backwards, Rodders delivered a karate chop to his windpipe. The man now semiconscious, was writhing in pain and fell to his knees as he gasped for air. Rodders picked up the gun, caught hold of the man by the scruff of the neck and raised him so his feet were off the ground. He could see his eyes rolling in his head, he knew he would cause no further problems. To make doubly sure, Rodders raised his foot and slammed his heel down on the thug's ankle. He screamed in pain. "That's for sticking the barrel on my back, you bastard!" With reluctance, Rodney untied his old school tie, threatening the now terrified thug to keep still or have his neck broken as he tied his ankles together. "That's to make sure that you ain't fuckin goin' anywhere mate," Rodders said, imitating the best Cockney accent he could produce.

He now turned his attention to the dead body, knelt beside her and shone his pencil torch once more at her face. He was still surprised that he was looking at such a beautiful woman. He felt so sorry for her and wished he had come to meet up with her earlier than planned. Touching her cheeks, he looked at her, thinking she was probably in her thirties. There was heavy bruising around the side of her forehead and deep scratches on her wrists. It was clear she had not given up lightly and fought hard against her assailant. One leg was obviously broken as it lay at an awkward angle. He wondered if she had broken it as she'd tried to escape from her attacker by jumping over the railings, falling onto the half-submerged stones below.

He examined her hands, there was a ring on the third finger of her right hand.

It was a thick golden wedding band, he thought for a moment that she could be a married German. He began searching her coat pockets, one contained a purse which had a bundle of notes, some in sterling but mostly in a mixture of French francs and German marks. He surmised that the brute on the ground had been disturbed, otherwise he would have pocketed the cash. The sight of her lying there angered him, and so he got up and shone his torch into the face of the wretched Cockney.

He looked terrified as Rodders approached him. "I didn't mean to kill her guv, as we struggled a bit, she freed herself and jumped over the rail, falling on the stones hidden under the water. She probably thought the water was deep but it ain't." It took little persuasion, as a result of Rodders' heel pressing on his throat to get to the truth. His voice rasped as a result of the pressure on his neck,

"Please guv, I meant her no harm, I begged her to give me the papers she had."

"What papers?" Rodders asked as he pressed his foot firmer on his neck.

"I'll tell you guv, please on my 'onour. I'll tell yer everythin' I knows, please on me muvver's life."

Rodders released the pressure, grabbed him by his ears as he sat him upright. He groaned in pain, his ankle broken, he tried in vain to rub his throat with mangled fingers.

"I'm listening, you better be singing the right notes," Rodders spat the words into his face, he was close to killing him but couldn't; he needed to know why the thug was there, and more about the papers he was talking about. "Down the pub, its down the pub, I meets this guy, he sez ees 'elpin the coppers get stuff from Mosley's mob, the brown bastards as 'e calls 'em. He points out people and I follows 'em, then I tells 'im wer they go. Fo' thar he gives me a few quid, honest guv it's all I does."

"What about tonight you little shit?" Rodders bellowed at him nose to nose.

"I'll tell it all, guv on my life, I'll tell yas."

Rodders backed off, keeping the torchlight in the cockney's face.

"He tells me t' follow 'er from the post office just off Farringdon Road. We meet at The Surprise there. He ses that she's got papers, if I gets them he'll give me a fiver, that's a lot of dosh for me guv. Cut a long story short, I follows 'er, he knows where she's at, the post office, he knows everythin' he duz! I follows 'er, I pulls out my shooter and asks her for 'er papers, polite like, I didn't mean to 'arm er. By the way gov this is not a real gun it's what you call a replica. 'armless it is. She suddenly gets angry, she whacks me one so I whack her one, she knows 'ow to 'andle herself, she then dived thro' the rails, banged 'er 'ed as she went. Then jumps into the water. There's rocks down there, she just lies there, I went to fish 'er out, but some people cums out of the Prospect, so I clears off. Guv she wasn't movin', God's truth. I goes to the trees hoping to frisk 'er for the papers but then you comes along. Guv I didn't do 'er in, she did it 'erself."

Rodders pressed into him again with his heel. "How did this man you were with know she would be at the post office?"

"As I ses guv this bloke knows everything, the guy also knew she would be coming 'ere. If I knew that this was going to happen, I wouldn't have come. I didn't think there would be this bother."

"Who is this guy, and where can I find him?" Rodders barked at him, increasing the pressure on his throat.

"Please guv no more please, I'm meeting him at twelve tonight, outside the gates opposite the gentleman's club in St James's Square."

Rodders eased the pressure of his foot. "I wonder who the hell this can be," he thought, "he must be a member of my club. Cloughie and I use it as our watering hole." He had to admit there were some very peculiar men in the club, but he didn't think any of them were traitors. He was about to question him further when he noticed torch lights coming toward them.

Rodney took out his pistol, and this time he would be ready for them. If they were thugs, he would shoot first and ask questions afterwards.

"Is that you Rodders?"

He recognised the voice. "Cloughie!" he called out in relief.

Since Rodders had not turned up as agreed, Cloughie had decided to search for him at the river's edge, where he knew he planned to meet a contact. They had a long-standing agreement that if either of them was attending a rendezvous with an unknown agent, each would be ready to back up the other if there was a problem.

Cloughie could see by the body on the floor and a person lying injured close by, that there was indeed such a problem.

Cloughie looked around weighing up the situation. Eager to make a move he spoke to Rodders with resolution in his voice, "Let's get this place tidied up, we cannot leave any evidence of tonight's happenings. All evidence of there being a body here needs removing along with any trace of blood from your mate over there. We'll take him with us, use him as bait, then hand him over to our gentle copper friends for questioning. They will lock him up amongst his new mates in Wormwood Scrubs, I'm sure he'll get warmly welcomed there, they love traitors."

The thug on hearing this blurted, "I'll tell you everything, please don't send me there, please not the Scrubs!"

They were finishing their task when the door of the Prospect Inn opened, and a shaft of bright light almost like a spotlight illuminated the scene.

"Shut that bloody door, don't you know there's a war on!" barked Cloughie. The door was about to close when Cloughie ran over, preventing it by jamming it with his foot. He told the proprietor he needed to use the phone urgently. Brushing the perplexed man to one side, he shouted "Where is it?" As he started to speak on the phone, Cloughie instructed the still confused man to clear off as this was none of his business. After finishing he slammed down the receiver, went outside, and helped Rodders carry Ruth's body, as with the utmost respect they placed her away from prying eyes.

Rodders removed his water-logged coat placing it gently over her. Cloughie meanwhile had unceremoniously dragged the cockney thug further down the small pier, finally placing him well away from the body. He told him he didn't want a lump of shit next to something beautiful.

They had hardly finished moving the man and GM 38's body when they heard the welcome siren of an approaching police van accompanied by another police car with two officers on board. When they saw it was Cloughie they saluted as he was well-known and respected by the authorities. He ordered them to treat the body with respect and take the deceased lady to the pathology department at St Thomas's Hospital, where there was a special unit waiting for her arrival.

As for the thug who was continually groaning in pain, he would be taken to one of the cells in their headquarters for further questioning. Rodders turned to the departing police officers and told them, in a voice loud enough for the thug to hear, that they were on a win-win situation with this cretin, he would either fully cooperate or have his bollocks mangled. The now terror-stricken man cringed in fear. As they headed toward their vehicles Rodders told the police officers that as far as they were concerned nothing had happened that night. They had stumbled on something of significant importance, so everything they had seen or heard was to be kept secret.

The van headed off to the morgue, whilst Rodders, Cloughie and the thug together with the two police officers made their way to the police car. As they settled into the car, Rodders began to shiver. The thug sat uneasily; he was also shivering.

Cloughie thought to himself that one was trembling from the cold whilst the other from fear. A wry smile lingered for a second.

Rodders caught sight of it and sharply said, "What now?"

"It's nothing," Cloughie replied as they headed back to their headquarters. The now terrified cockney told them everything they wanted to know without requiring 'persuasion.'

Eventually they arrived at the station. Rodders changed out of his wet clothes, whilst the prisoner whimpered quietly in a corner. It was approaching midnight, time to go. They drove to the rendezvous. The police car parked on the opposite side of the square to the front entrance to the Gentlemen's' Club in St James's Square. Cloughie, hid himself in the shrubbery close to the iron gate.

Meanwhile Rodders entered the club. Standing next to the antique weighing machine in the foyer, he recognised one of the late revellers as he was leaving. He stopped him as he went by and started up a conversation so as to appear normal and avoid suspicion should the traitor go by. Midnight came. There was no sight of anyone making for the exit door. Then one of the stewards, known to him, nodded as he went by. He was carrying a small member's bag, presumably to a waiting car, but apart from that the foyer remained quiet and empty. Suddenly, Rodders realised it could be him. Surely not, he thought, Hobby as he was known, was a long serving and trusted member of staff, respected and well liked. Although he would be in a good position to listen into confidential conversations between unsuspecting members, so used were they to Hobby's presence.

He followed him, keeping a careful distance. The next few seconds would be telling. Hobby was surreptitiously checking left to right, making sure he was unobserved. He slowed as he approached the gate. He suddenly stopped. He could now see his accomplice at the gate. Something wasn't right. Why was he unable to stand properly? Why was he was holding on to the railings?

He was clearly in a bad way. He panicked. Sharply turning on his heel, he spun straight into the waiting arms of one Rodney Tuxford Preston!

He smiled a greeting, but the smile disappeared as Rodney hissed, "One wrong move and I'll break your legs."

Hobby managed to tear himself away, he turned and made a run for it. He jolted to a sudden halt as Cloughie's fist drove like a steam engine piston hard into his face. Hobby and his mate collapsed to the floor almost in unison. "Great choreography!" yelled Rodders, laughing.

The waiting police car screeched around the corner, both men were handcuffed and bundled into the rear of the car. Cloughie approached, opened the rear door stared and grinned at Hobby saying, 'We've got you at last." The steward grinned back. "You can do what you like, but won't get anything from me."

Rodders approached, having heard what had been said. "Perhaps you might change your mind when things go public. Don't forget your innocent family, your wife and daughter will need protecting as a result of your treasonable activities. What you have done has resulted in the deaths of many people. One way or another we will get you to cough your guts up, sleep well!" With that the copper took out his truncheon patting it on to his hand as he said, "It's nightmares he'll be having." Everyone laughed as the car sped away. "That's another agent down." "I'm sure when they finish with him there will be more."

Chapter 16

London

They stood in the pathology lab, gazing in silence at the naked body. Agent GM-38 had now been identified as Ruth Ackerman. A German Jew who was a member of the resistance. Her skin grey, her form slender and probably the result of a meagre diet, her natural beauty was still evident. She was lost and unfortunately so was the information she had held in her mind.

Rodney looked at the papers that had been passed on to him from the War office intelligence Branch, and with a glance at Cloughie, he read out the salient points. She had been known by the Consulate members of the British embassy in Berlin prior to the war breaking out. Her partner called Max; a research chemist was working near Spandau at that time. She was of Jewish descent, having fled from Berlin to avoid persecution. Her hatred of Hitler's regime along with her knowledge of the internal organisation of the German government had promoted a keenness to join the French resistance movement. Her knowledge was a great asset to this movement which she had joined in France after escaping Germany.

During her stay in France, she had made contact with another underground operative named Joseph who worked as a general assistant in a large house owned by an entrepreneur by the name of Otto. Otto had both wealth and influence. He was an extreme admirer of Hitler's Third Reich. Joseph had befriended a young deaf-mute woman called Agata who worked as a servant close to Otto.

Otto was orchestrating a plot unknown to the authorities. He led a clandestine cohort which was planning an operation to help Germany win the war, obviously without Hitler's knowledge. There were many close to Hitler who could see that the war was turning rapidly against them, which led this small group to devise a plan that would bring Britain to its knees. The information Rodders had about their plans was short on detail, but it was clear it was potentially of great magnitude and importance. It needed to be stopped in its tracks, but unfortunately the key to that door lay hidden in the darkness of Ruth's dead brain.

They had thoroughly searched throughout her clothing but found nothing. The only items left on her body were her shoes, which were the ankle-strapped type and still firmly fixed to her feet. Cloughie unclicked the buckles carefully before removing the shoes. He examined them closely, pulling them apart to see if anything was hidden. He felt inside, examining them with a torchlight, but to no avail.

Shrugging his shoulders Rodders indicated they should leave, return to HQ and try another avenue. There was still some hope that the French underground operatives might come up with something. With respect they gently covered the body with a white sheet. Then they lifted her body onto a stretcher which fitted into a refrigeration vault. The sheet slipped revealing Ruth's feet. Cloughie was in the act of drawing the sheet over her exposed feet when he noticed something. Stuck to the ball of her left foot was a square piece of paper. He signalled them to stop, asking them to return a body to the marble table. He asked one of the medical assistants for something to peel off the paper. He hurriedly located a set of forceps.

The assistant then gestured to Cloughie, hinting to him that he would be better at removing the item, he was more expert in such matters. Frowning, Cloughie stood to the side whilst the white-coated assistant set up an angle poise lamp and, using the tweezers, he carefully unpeeled the square piece of paper before placing it onto a sheet of filter paper. After close scrutiny he told them it was a receipt for a registered mail dated on the same morning she had been pulled out of the water. Posted from St Pancras station it was addressed to W Churchill, Prime Minister, the War Office Horse

Guards Avenue, Whitehall. Wide-eyed, they stood and looked at each other. She thought of everything, she had been intent on getting a message through, one way or another.

Time was of the essence, so they grabbed their coats and headed for Whitehall. The streets were almost empty, but they would occasionally come across the odd ARP Warden who stopped and questioned them, and a quick glance at their IDs was greeted with a nod as they made their way to Horse Guards Avenue. The armed sentries at the perimeter leading to the doorway met them with greater scrutiny. Their frustration and anger at being held up from gaining access to the building was dealt with firmly and with determination, security was of the utmost importance. They eventually gained access to the building where they were ushered into the mail office. There were mountains of letters and packages being dealt with by bustling personnel. There was a plethora of young ladies sifting through the piles of correspondence, each item being entered into various record books dealing with both incoming and outgoing mail. Having persuaded those in charge of the urgency of their quest for a package addressed to the Prime Minister, a small group was designated to sift through the various boxes. There were a lot of boxes. Half an hour went by with no results, perhaps yesterday's mail had not been delivered as yet but the delivery section confirmed that all the boxes had been emptied. They looked once more, but they found nothing.

In the midst of all the commotion, a young lady came out of her office asking what the fuss was about. Cloughie told her curtly that they were looking for a missing package. It was addressed to the Prime Minister and was of vital importance. She explained that items personally addressed to senior politicians went through a separate channel. Items for Mr Churchill were dealt with in her department for security reasons. She was not at liberty to divulge if there had been such a package, let alone allow them access to it. Rodders indignantly reminded her there was a war on and pushed passed her into the office. Scanning the room quickly, his eyes fell on the package. He was about to pick it up when two armed soldiers rushed at him. He raised his arms, asking if he could take out his identification papers, and without waiting for a reply he went to remove them but as he opened his jacket the soldiers caught sight of his pistol and raised their rifles in readiness.

Speaking softly in an attempt to calm the situation, he said, "By all means remove the pistol but I do have the authority to appropriate this package. Get someone to call this number and we can resolve the situation peacefully."

After some further discussion the call was made. The clerk was told to wait by the phone, and someone would call him back. Twenty long minutes passed before the phone shrilled. The voice was unmistakable, any introduction almost unnecessary. After a brief conversation the clerk indicated that the soldiers should stand down. He had been speaking with the Prime Minister himself who had instructed him to hand over the package.

"Eureka!" exclaimed Rodders. "Now maybe we can finally unravel the information Ruth had so bravely struggled to pass on to them, sacrificing herself in the process."

Some weeks later, Rodders learned that Hobby had spilled the beans in return for the protection of his wife and daughter. They had been given a fresh identity and moved elsewhere to start a new life. Evidently, they were glad to be free of him.

As the result of the information gleaned from Hobby a network of German agents working throughout the UK were arrested. Ruth had been instrumental in bringing about their downfall. This was put on record and she was given a dignified burial attended by senior officials. She had served with courage and conviction. She was to be greatly admired and thanked for her role in helping Britain win the war.

Chapter 17

London

There was a sense of urgency and excitement as the group unwrapped the parcel. Inside was a bundle of written documents. On the initial page was a letter from Ruth which she stated that if the letter reached its destination, it was highly probable that she had been intercepted and killed. The documents inside contained a concise history of events along with vital information relating to the uncovering of terrifying plans to destroy the city of London and thus bring about an end to the war. She outlined information gleaned from Joseph's letters, and much of this had been obtained via a Polish deaf and dumb lady, Agata, who was working as a servant for "Otto".

Otto was a man of importance with contacts at the highest level. With the assistance of others, he had put together a plan designed to cause death and destruction to people in the London area. The plan would involve the launching of the V2 rocket loaded with a lethal liquid. The liquid would evaporate to produce a lethal gas. The gas could kill either by contact or inhalation. It was so powerful that it could kill in seconds by destroying the nervous system. This so-called nerve agent could wipe out thousands of Londoners almost instantly. The plan was to launch the rocket in April on Hitler's birthday.

The German supreme command was unaware of this plot. Hitler having clearly stated that the deployment of a lethal gas was prohibited at all costs, since he was fearful of a reprisal from Britain and her allies.

The parcel also contained maps, diagrams and headed note paper, all of which was accompanied by false papers. She hoped these would assist the officers in charge in their attempts to infiltrate and thwart Otto's plans. By giving as much assistance and advice as possible, she hoped to help prevent the launching of the V2 rocket with its lethal cargo.

Ruth had included the headed note paper, cunningly supplied by Agata, which bore Otto's forged signature. In the hope this would assist agents to gain access to restricted areas or organised gatherings. Since Otto was the behind-the-scenes instigator of the plot and totally in charge of the operation his signature could open doors. It appeared that the French Resistance had already made several useful contacts amongst Polish workers who were forcibly involved in the production of the rocket. They were being treated extremely badly and many died at their workplace, due to the beatings and the malnutrition they suffered.

Most of the information enclosed had been garnered by one of their own French agents. He had managed to infiltrate the factory and was employed by the Germans. His role involved the delivering of food to Jewish technicians at their workplace, according to his accounts they worked in close, cramped conditions which acerbated their already poor physical and mental state. Jewish technical workers were employed on scientific instruments and important components which were destined to eventually be assembled onto the V2 rockets.

One of these technicians collapsed due to dehydration and starvation and was dragged out of his workstation. Whilst being comforted by an undercover French agent he whispered some vital information about the significance of the guidance system. Smiling even as he died, the worker's last act was to open his clenched fist and reveal a partial diagram showing what looked like a gadget attached to a compass. He had, at least died in the knowledge that he had, in some small way, been of service to Germany's enemies.

Others were also passing on information despite the huge risks they ran.

They felt they had not much to lose, they knew if they were caught the consequences would probably be death, but that could be seen as a blessing in comparison to their terrible conditions. In a mood of defiance many had drawn the Star of David with their blood, beneath their work benches unseen by the guards.

One Jewish technician had been a professor in the development of V1 rocketry and was singled out for his knowledge. He was involved in assembling the guidance system of the rockets. Despite his seniority, he was subjected to the same abuse and maltreatment as the others. Nevertheless, he had managed to relay oral messages which agents committed to memory. The guidance system comprised something called a gimbal which could set and maintain the rocket in the right direction to strike its target; it was connected to veins which acted like fins at the rear, and also to an electrical device which controlled the veins and set the rocket's target. Without the gimbal the rocket would fly aimlessly out of control. It was one of the major parts of the rocket's technology and without it the rocket would never reach its target. Disabling the gimbal would be the best way to incapacitate the rocket.

To gain access to the gimbal it would be necessary to remove the panel situated approximately halfway down the length from the nosecone. These instruments were always the last component to be connected before ignition. In order to do this the rockets were placed horizontally on a launchpad prior to elevating it to the vertical. Just before launching an umbilical cable was plugged into the nosecone, carrying electricity which enabled the pumps to pour liquid fuel into the fuel tanks. This fuel consisted of liquid oxygen and highly flammable ethanol. On ignition, the mixture would cause a massive thrust with a loud blast, propelling the rockets upwards.

As it rose the umbilical cord was pulled out and a trap door closed behind it. The technician said that if the cable failed at this point the rocket would become quite aimless, spin and fall back to the ground. This had happened on several occasions during testing. During some tests the payloads had exploded causing death and destruction. Ruth provided further information adding:

"Although you might be aware of the date and time of the launch it has been impossible to discover the location: it will be somewhere in The Hague. Since

the British and their allies have been bombing known rocket launch sites there are now no fixed permanent locations. The German production sites for rockets are heavily camouflaged and situated deep underground. The assembled rockets are taken above ground just prior to launch. The launching takes place from very large mobile platforms which are transported at the very last minute. This makes it hugely difficult to identify where a launch will take place at any given time."

Then Ruth had added more, "Since this is a clandestine operation, you need to be aware that the rocket will not be armed with its usual explosive payload. It can be identified by a red band painted around the nose cone. This ensures that the rocket being deployed is the correct one. None of the usual launch operatives will be involved in the final launching. Otto has managed to gather a group of willing workers whose secrecy he can trust, for added security it is highly likely that these workers will not be known to one another."

Having digested the contents of the documents, everyone involved gathered round the table. It was clear that whoever had compiled the dossier had done an excellent job. It contained so much essential information on the V2, much of it unknown to the British, as well as useful guidance on how it might be incapacitated

The signature of someone called Joseph was noted amongst the documents: two senior members of the intelligence branch were present; Joseph was known to them and they determined to contact him as soon as possible. With little ceremony they told the assembly of their plan then rose to their feet and left.

Cloughie and Rodders met the next morning with other senior intelligence officials at a secret location. It was agreed that the two men would leave post-haste to try and avert the launching of the rocket. Meanwhile, another operative who was in close contact with Joseph would ask for his help in ensuring Cloughie and Rodders could reach The Hague. A coded message went out to a British agent, requesting a telegraph operator to be on duty all times for this very important operation. The vital information needed was the time and place for the launch, and without this the mission would be impossible. The technical information regarding the construction of the rocket was passed to a group of top experts in the fields of ballistics and rocketry. Rodders and Cloughie set out to meet with these scientists, travelling separately in the hope that should there be a problem at least one of them would make it through. The meeting was to be held at a secret experimental defence establishment located in Wiltshire close to the small village of Porton Down. Very little was known about V1 and V2 rockets and the scientists were excited by the challenge they were presented with. Their challenge was to come up with a way to incapacitate the rocket but in doing so it was crucial that no harm or destruction was caused to innocent Dutch civilians. One solution might be to bring the rocket down over the sea; if the missile could be plunged into deep water the toxic payload would be diluted and dispersed with minimal collateral damage.

After studying all available information, the team determined that the best way forward would be to disable the gimbal at the precise moment of launching. One of the scientists a bright young man just down from Oxford, sat with his bony elbows on the table, staring into space. One could almost see pictures forming in his mind as he mused. He had already gained a lot of respect among his colleagues for his work on developing a jet engine for fighters; but was also valued for his creative approach to problems, and his willingness to take on even the most menial tasks in contributing to projects. He was seen as a rising star in his field. Suddenly he jumped up, exclaiming excitedly, "There is a way!" Ken had the group's full attention as he began to explain: "When a rocket with this weight and power takes off, all the power of the thrust produced is needed to overcome it's inertia. This takes a few seconds during which the rocket remains vertical. Eventually the rocket rises slowly as the upward force overcomes gravity."

"Get to the point," someone heckled, but Ken just ignored this and continued.

"The vital thing here is setting the fins to ensure the gimbal remained at zero."

More muttered heckling was interrupted by Cloughie firmly telling the group he wanted to hear where this was going.

Undeterred, Ken resumed enthusiastically, "The gimbal has to remain at zero until the rocket reaches final velocity. When I was at Oxford, we were shown some film of V2 rocket launches, secretly recorded by intelligence operatives. It was possible to see that the rocket was mounted vertically and connected, as described by Joseph, to an electric cable. It was also possible to see a small door in the side – I realise now this must be the gimbal housing. The gimbal only comes into effect once the rocket had reached maximum speed which would coincide with its maximum height. We calculated what we think is a pretty accurate time of ten minutes to reach London at a speed of two thousand miles per hour. We also estimated the height reached before fuel ran out would be in the order of fifty miles: ignition to target in just a matter of minutes!"

Ken now had everyone's earnest attention. He was a tall, thin individual with keen blue eyes: the beginnings of an untidy moustache contrasting oddly with his youthful face. He had developed an unfortunate habit of grinding his teeth when excited, and those who knew him recognised that this usually coincided with inspirational ideas. His presentations were always delivered with panache, and as now revealed an in-depth knowledge of aircraft design and ballistics.

"So, the rocket runs out of fuel and gravity exerts its pull, the missile levels off and becomes horizontal. At this point, crucially, the gimbal comes into operation, setting the course to the target. In this case, London. The perfect angle as it leaves the zenith point and curves downward was forty-two degrees to the vertical: the rocket will then travel the maximum distance without thrust, in a perfect arc trajectory aimed at London. Since no fuel is needed it approaches London in complete silence. I believe we can destroy the rocket over the sea!"

One of the team jerked his head in surprise, causing in his pipe to fall onto the heap of papers; he and others scrambled to put out a shower of sparks and hot ash, but Ken continued unperturbed, totally focused on the matter in hand.

"Air pressure!" he exclaimed. "Air pressure is comparatively low at the height of fifty miles. A mercury instrument somewhat similar to a thermometer could act as a switch. The distance travelled by the mercury after the missile achieves maximum height could be calculated and used to trigger a sensitive switching device. This would activate an electric current flowing to a detonator, a small highly explosive device set close to the gimbal, causing it to fail. The vanes would then cease to function correctly, causing the rocket to spin helplessly into the sea." Ken looked toward the man still trying to extinguish the paperwork. "Rather like what happened to your pipe, Sir."

An older member of the group raised his hand, informing them that whilst his knowledge on rockets was limited, he was an expert on explosives and would immediately set to work on a device to incapacitate the gimbal. He said he could also suggest a more sophisticated and reliable method of triggering an explosion than a mercury thermometer.

Rodders stood and thanked all present for their input. Stressing that time was of the essence, he requested the two scientists to each work separately on their own design for a switching device. He would then test both and choose the most efficient. He nodded to Cloughie. There were other things needing their attention, so they collected their papers and left the room.

Ken returned to his laboratory and set to work on his mercury switch. The theory was sound, but he found difficulties in connecting the terminals and trying to compensate for temperature changes. Time was short, so he decided to cut his losses and team up with his colleague Jeff, who was working on an aneroid pressure type device. He knew they had also to tackle the issue of size – the device needed to fit into a tiny space as they had no way of knowing the dimensions of the gimbal's chamber.

A stalwart of the Ministry of Defence, Jeff was now approaching retirement: a short, rotund and genial man, his passion for good red wine had given him a rosy complexion and with his increasingly balding head he looked more and more like Mr Pickwick. Always dedicated to his work he had a genius for designing in miniature - items such as cameras much prized by field agents. He was pleased to see Ken and beckoned him over, showing him an antique silver half hunter watch. It contained a fuse movement reliant on a very fine chain in the release mechanism. The other end of the chain would be attached to a cog connected to the minute hand. Jeff and his team were attempting to create a small evacuated container that would fit inside the watch, this was proving to be very difficult.

Ken considered carefully, "If the watch could be hermetically sealed, the case itself could be adapted to change shape according to the pressure level... Maybe the glass window could be swapped for something which would also react to small changes in pressure. What do you think?"

The team agreed this sounded feasible. "Thanks Ken," Jeff said with a smile, "and if that doesn't bloody work, we'll try a bomb, a fuse and a box of matches," which lightened the mood as they got back to work.

After a night of patient toil, the task was completed and they were all delighted with the results. Not only did the device respond to pressure changes, there was now room for a small but powerful explosive. To add to the authenticity, they added a silver chain and engraved a swastika on the back of the case. Justifiably proud of their achievement, they were eager to speak to Rodders.

Chapter 18

London

Only three days to launch day. Rodders had heard from Joseph several times, but as yet they had no definite information about the launch site. He and Cloughie were on standby to be parachuted into Holland, but were still unsure of the where and when. That morning Jeff had delivered a half hunter watch; Rodders had been delighted to see him and impressed with the speed at which he had perfected the miniature explosive. He was surprised to find it was concealed inside the watch, and turning it over, found an inscription, "Capt. David Thomas," with a swastika emblazoned below.

Cloughie was curious as to the contradiction between the British name and the swastika - was this a person Jeff had known? Jeff then related the story of his father, who had been awarded a VC for heroism in saving members of his platoon under heavy enemy fire. Ducking and diving between bullets, he had made it to the enemy position and thrown in a phosphorous bomb. The poisonous fumes forced the Germans out of their trench, and they surrendered; it was not David's only courageous sortie, and he had earned huge respect from his men. Jeff explained he had added the swastika to make it look as though it had been taken from a British soldier recently, but it would please his dad that he was still having a go at the Germans somehow! At this point Cloughie arrived and was also intrigued by the inscription and the watch; he expressed concern though, "Is it safe to carry it? What if the thing detonates in our pocket?"

"Well, if you sit on it, you could end up with your testicles on the lampshade!" Jeff laughed, but added, "No, seriously, we've worked hard on several adjustments to make it safe to carry." Taking the watch, he showed them how to depress the winding button on the top, making it clear they should listen for a click before releasing it. To prime the watch, they would then depress the button a second time before placing it in the rocket. "Once the rocket reaches the correct altitude, there will be a five second time lapse before detonation; this will ensure the rocket was over the sea before igniting."

Cloughie exclaimed, "Excellent design work! Thank God you're on our side!"

Well done!" Jeff now opened his briefcase and handed them a large brown package containing instructions for the watch - how to store it, the importance of keeping it cool, and not depressing the arming button until they were ready to put it in place. "Don't be too worried - I've used an alloy of iron and nickel called Invar FeNi36, which hardly expands on heating - I used it on the small diaphragm and other sensitive parts!"

"Well, thank God for science!" Cloughie retorted.

Then Jeff shook both their hands, wished them luck as they were going to need it, and left. Cloughie immediately took the watch to the coldest spot in the house. "Let's not take any chances!" he said, and Rodders laughed.

Sitting together at the table, they now pulled out a bundle of documents from the brown envelope. Compiled by the Intelligence Corps, they included two German passports, providing them with false identities. The passports were endorsed, identifying them as scientists attached to a rocketry unit. There was a letter signed by Otto giving orders to allow them into sensitive areas to assist in the V2 rocket launch. They realised why the package was so heavy when they found two military issue pistols, loaded, a compass, binoculars and other useful items.

The final items were two small white envelopes, which they had both seen before. They contained two small capsules to attach to their molars before heading into dangerous scenarios. One hard bite would release the liquid cyanide; it was familiar territory for Rodders and Cloughie, almost reassuring to feel that if captured, they would evade torture and the possibility of giving the enemy vital information.

Chapter 19

England / Netherlands

In the confines of a small office at Manston Airport in Kent, Rodders and Cloughie sat, wondering uneasily how long the wait might be. Outside, a small light aircraft was poised to parachute them into Holland and drop them at an agreed location somewhere in the Hague. They were waiting for a Morse signal giving them details of the landing point and the launch site of the V2. Cloughie went over to his parachute, hanging ready on its peg, tapped it and whispered, "Not long now!"

The words had barely passed his lips when the speaker erupted into life; he turned and rushed toward it, but Rodders beat him to it. Adjusting his headphones, he began to scribble down the message as it came in. In the meantime, Cloughie was unfolding the map; glancing at his watch and coding grid references, he quickly pinpointed their landing zone. If all went well, signals from those on the ground would identify the landing strip. They had to be there by 12 midnight; Rodders tapped in. "Put ice in my gin and tonic."

It was now 11.15 - time to get going; he alerted the pilot and gave him the details. As they left the office with their gear, the pilot joined them. "We're all set, fuelled up, ready to go. We're in luck - it's overcast in Holland, and we'll be flying low, so that's in our favour. I know this drop off point, it's well away from habitation, and screened by trees. I will only be able to have one go at it - if we return, they'll get our location."

Both Rodders and Cloughie knew they had just one chance, but they had done this many times, and they didn't need reminding. "It's obvious from the urgency that this is something special, I wish you luck! The next you will hear from me will be at the drop off point -

no-one's mentioned picking you up, so it seems you're on your own from there!"

They both knew how hard it was going to be to make their way back by land and sea, in occupied territory... But they knew this was a vital mission, and they must succeed! There was still no information on the launch site - they desperately hoped Joseph's network was going to come through with it.

Messages had been flying between British Intelligence and the resistance movement in Holland. On arrival the men would be taken to a secret location and supplied with German uniforms and anything else needed to infiltrate the close group involved in the plot. To achieve their aim, they had to be able to get close to the rocket, they dressed for the occasion and with their forged passports and Rodder's refined, well-educated German accent, they hoped they could pull it off. Rodder's main concern was that Cloughie didn't know a word of German - he impressed upon him the importance of keeping his mouth shut at all times, and to leave the talking to him.

The plane's engine roared like an angry wasp. Flying as low as he dared over the water, the pilot passed by a pitch-dark Ramsgate. Headed away from safety and into danger. There was no turning back. The men sat in silence, deep in thought, until the pilot signalled they were approaching the drop off point, he reminded them he could not circle for fear of drawing attention. The last thing Cloughie and Rodders needed was a German reception committee. Setting his gear stick, he left the controls and moved to the exit door, telling them to prepare as he slid it open. A blast of air rushed through the plane, making it hard to breathe - they each shook the pilot's hand and grinned as they jumped, trying to keep as close together as possible.

The pilot had been right, there wasn't a single star visible, just what they needed. Suddenly a light flashed below; the pilot had landed them right on the button! They were hoping, as they dropped, that it was the partisans and not the enemy waiting for them. When they saw flashlights, they smiled at each other knowing if there had been Germans it would have been searchlights. A few months earlier, in a similar situation, there had been Germans in wait, and they had nearly been captured. They had escaped, but at the cost of some lives. They ran their tongues over their back teeth to confirm they had another way of evading capture.

The first person to reach them was Joseph, who introduced himself as they unbuckled their chutes; others appeared out of the shadows to drag the parachutes away. "We have to move quickly," whispered Joseph, "we have to get to the launch site as soon as possible!" He explained that the rocket was on the move already, accompanied by a group of around twenty personnel, most of whom were armed soldiers. "You know this operation was planned by Otto - he's a powerful man, well known to Hitler, and not a man to cross. Otto has gathered his own very loyal men, who carry out his orders impeccably; he plans things to the smallest detail, and the attack on London is no different."

Rodders and Cloughie were listening intently, getting a mental picture of Otto in case they came across him.

Joseph continued, "I have worked for Otto - sometimes as a guard, sometimes just doing odd jobs. I became friendly with a lady called Agata who worked as Otto's servant. She was deaf and dumb, and Otto considered this meant she could serve him and his officers without being a security risk. Unknown to him, she was a highly intelligent Polish woman who had studied at university and fluently understood several languages including German; she was also an excellent lip reader."

Lines of communication had been set up - Agata to Joseph. Joseph to a boy who delivered meat each day. The boy to Ruth. He knew Ruth had travelled to London to pass on all they had learnt - but she hadn't been heard of since. Rodders put his hand on Joseph's shoulder and quietly explained. Ruth had made it to London, she had got the information through, but had been intercepted and killed by a brute working for a German agent. She had been very brave, and hopefully her work would stop the plan to decimate London.

Joseph took a deep breath and shook his head. He must put Ruth to the back of his mind - there was urgent business to be done.

"The launch team consists of experts in various fields - ballistics, poisonous substances, and the technical field. They all wear the same black uniform, but with embossed insignia for their role. The three senior scientists wear white lab coats. I am sorry, we tried to get you some of those uniforms but failed."

The three men drove toward the launch site, and realised they were being followed - Joseph had considered ordering the people trailing them to be killed but had decided they might be more use to them alive, and the British agents smilingly agreed - much more use!

"The partisans will lay down their lives for the cause, and they will do all they can to protect you. But I must tell you that the prevention of the attack on London is our priority. If your mission fails, we cannot guarantee your safety I am afraid."

Rodders and Cloughie solemnly agreed, then Rodders pointed out a small track branching off the road ahead. "In here, I think!"

Joseph quickly reversed into it, and they lay in wait for the following car.

As they waited, they quickly changed into their German uniforms, sporting the insignia of rank of colonel. They discussed how to stop and capture the occupants of the car following them; even if they succeeded in this, it would be difficult to extract information in time to abort the launch - there were only two hours to go! Their uniforms might not be appropriate for the task ahead, and Cloughie's lack of German was a major problem. If caught, they would most likely be shot on sight.

They needed to keep cool and collected, and think… "And if ever there was a time for divine intervention, let it be now," they thought... "the attack on London must be prevented, if it was the last thing they ever did."

A motorbike was racing toward them, obviously in a hurry. Its headlights flashed in a sequence which Joseph returned. The rider slewed to a halt, almost hitting the car, and scrambled off the bike, blurting that a small convoy was approaching - a car with two passengers, escorted by two armed soldiers on motorbikes. As he spoke, lights appeared in the distance coming steadily toward them.

Rodders ordered the others to take cover, "Don't do anything unless I signal! If they take us down, kill the lot," he said as he dragged Cloughie into the centre of the road, laughingly assuring him he had a plan with no chance of succeeding.

He took out his pistol and held it behind his back; Cloughie did the same and muttered, "If things go pear shaped, I'll take out the ones on my right, and don't you dare miss the ones on the left,"

As the motorbikes approached, they instinctively adopted a natural pose, giving the impression of a non-urgent situation. They stood in the headlights of their car to be clearly visible, the buttons and insignia on their uniforms catching the light. The convoy was still approaching fast; for a moment they wondered if it would stop in time, but the two motor cyclists came to a stop twenty metres away. They dismounted, and slinging their automatic weapons, trained them on the agents. The riders were well schooled - they would be hard to hit in the shadows; Rodders and Cloughie were dazzled by the headlights. One of the riders shouted at them to put their hands in the air and identify themselves. Slipping their pistols into the back of their belts, the two men raised their hands in unison.

His diction perfect, Rodders stated they were under orders from the highest authority. "We are travelling to a rendezvous some miles away, on a mission of great importance; our car has broken down and we request you transport us now." One of the guards bolted a bullet into his chamber. Knowing he had the paperwork from Otto to back him up Rodders shouted, "If you do not do as we request, I will have no choice but to report you - if anything happens to me or my colleague, you will be held accountable and probably shot!" He took the papers from his breast pocket and waved them angrily,

"These are orders from high command, and this mission is of the greatest importance!"

There was an ominous silence. The guards were suspicious, but, apparently facing two high ranking officers, unsure. The stalemate was broken by one of the passengers getting out of the car. He moved cautiously to a position behind the guard on his left. He was smartly dressed in a business suit and was patently not a military man; he cleared his throat, and in a precise and confident tone, asked to hear more about their mission.

Rodders spoke: "It is of a highly sensitive nature, but I have been instructed to oversee proceedings of great importance." Holding out the papers, he began to walk toward the other man. The guards shouldered their rifles and swung them toward him. "You damn fools," bellowed Rodders, "all of you will suffer the consequences if I fail to get to the delivery on time!"

He had chosen his words carefully; if the suited man was a scientist involved in the rocket launch, by using the word "delivery" he hoped to imply he too was involved in the same exercise. It worked. The man put his hand on the guard's rifle and lowered it. He whispered he would like to talk but would do so in a position which would give the guard a clear shot if needed. He beckoned to Rodders to give him the papers, then walked into the beam of the headlights to study them. He then returned to the car and conferred with his colleague. Rodders glanced at Cloughie and winked. After what seemed an age, the other passenger came out from the car, walked quickly up to Rodders and shook his hand with gusto.

"My name is Albert - I am the principal scientist on this mission. Probably the most important day of my life! The success of this mission will bring victory for Germany, and bring Britain and her Allies to their knees!" He patted Cloughie on the back and asked him what part he was playing in the mission.

As if by telepathy, Cloughie swung and took out the guard on the left as Rodders simultaneously shot the other. The man before them fell to his knees; Cloughie trained his gun on the driver, but did not shoot. He had business with him and needed him alive.

The two English agents heard a noise and stiffened. They turned, aiming their pistols into the darkness. Joseph and his comrades appeared and came towards them.

"You cut that pretty fine," said Joseph. "We were a few seconds from shooting the guards anyway, we had our rifles pinned on them from the start."

Cloughie nodded in thanks, then turned back to the man who was now prostrate on the ground. He grabbed his collar and hauled him up. "Now I want the location of that launch site!"

The man, dressed in civilian clothes, was clearly terrified. "Please, please! I don't know! I don't know!"

Cloughie grew angry and slapped the man hard across the face.

Dropping to his knees the man implored. "Please! Have mercy - I have a family to look after... I was forced to work on this project, and it is all secret - I don't know where we were going! It is so secret, they tell us only what we need for our job - the guards were taking us there to help with the launch, but we were not in on the planning."

Rodders, hearing this, began to search the dead guards, looking for any information that might lead them to the rendezvous. Failing to find anything, he went to the car and kicked the tyres in frustration. The only people with the information they needed were dead! Then he saw the driver, still behind the wheel and shaking with fear. He wore the uniform of a Corporal. Rodders dragged him out, threw him on the ground, and placed the heel of his boot on the soldier's throat. Speaking German in a quiet and threatening tone he demanded to know where the driver was taking the car.

Croaking from the weight on his throat, the man tried to speak, but impatiently Rodders pushed harder. Clawing at Rodder's ankle to release the pressure, the corporal choked. Rodders eased off, and the driver begged for his life, "I was only told to follow the motorbikes - I didn't know anything about where we were going or why!"

Rodders was furious now, aware how much time they were losing. He pounced on the second scientist and dragged him onto the road, slammed him into the side of the car. Again, the man pleaded for mercy, and denied knowing anything about the location of the launch. Everything was hush hush - but he said, the driver had told them it wasn't far away. So, thought Rodders, smiling inwardly, the driver *did* know where they were headed. They had to get this information!

Joseph walked over and shone his torch on the scientist's face. "Yes, I have seen this one before, at Otto's house; he was at the meetings, so he must know something!" Joseph pushed Rodders aside and kicked the man hard in the groin, he screamed and rolled away. Rodders saw Joseph about to repeat the kick and stopped him. It was clear they weren't going to get the information this way.

The men were too frightened of Otto – it was not only they who would suffer but also their families. Betraying Otto was a death sentence. Rodders and Cloughie quickly conferred with Joseph; it was obvious the men did know of the launch site, but to get them to reveal it, absolute terror was required to make one crack. Cloughie signalled with his pistol for the two scientists to sit on the ground with the driver. Firing a shot above their heads he hissed, "Try anything and you'll be shot!"

Rodders told the three this was their final chance - if information was not forthcoming, there would be consequences. Then he whispered to Joseph, who grinned. The men were told they would each be interrogated separately. Joseph hauled the man he had kicked to his feet, and dragged the man away into the trees. The other two were told to sit up, listen, and watch. Rodders called out after Joseph. "If he won't talk finish him silently - use a knife, there might be military around."

Within minutes a blood curdling scream was heard, followed by desperate sobbing, an ominous gasp, then silence. Joseph returned, pausing to clean the bloodied blade of his knife in the long grass. The second civilian was next to be taken away, and again screams were heard, then moans and silence; again, Joseph wiped his blade.

"What the hell?" shouted Rodders, "you were supposed to get them to talk!"

Joseph shrugged. "There's no time to hang about - they clearly didn't know anything - I asked them both, then removed their trousers and their balls. They were in such pain that I decided to cut their throats."

"For God's sake!" uttered Rodders, "they can't have known - if they had they'd still be alive and complete." He looked calmly at the driver. "Oh dear, just this one left." Cloughie and Joseph picked up the man who was distraught and kicking, pleading and struggling.

"The wild dogs and foxes are going to have good pickings tonight," said Cloughie, laughing. "Stop, please stop," shouted the sweating Corporal. "I will take you there!"

Rodders caught hold of the driver and told him he would not be needed; they had their own driver. But he must supply them with a detailed map showing the route. Searching in the German car, Rodders found pencil and paper, then shone his torch as he laid the paper on the bonnet of the car so the driver could draw them the map. When he had finished, Rodders put his pistol to his head and pointed to Cloughie. "If there is anything wrong with this map, this man will deal with you in person - understand?"

The driver nodded nervously.

Joseph studied the map and estimated a distance of about eight miles, when a side road diverged for about a mile before presumably reaching the site. Joseph knew the area and was confident the launch site would be in a copse of mature trees. As they were about to leave Cloughie waved his knife before the driver. "This could be used to slit your throat, or set you free." He then ordered the corporal to exchange clothes with Joseph. Rodders had asked Joseph about his German, and it was apparently fluent. Dressed in uniform, Joseph could be useful in the light of Cloughie's inability to speak German, Rodders thought. Again, he reminded Cloughie, "If we are challenged, you must keep that bloody mouth shut!"

He urged Joseph to get a move on - it was probably half an hour's drive, but they didn't know what the state of the road was, or if there were any barriers set up.

As they travelled, Cloughie was keen to know how the intelligence reports had been gathered. He knew the gist of the story and congratulated Joseph on the work, praising the effectiveness and courage of those involved; without the bravery of these partisan heroes, their mission would not have been possible. He was interested to know more about Ruth and Agata's roles.

"I had only a fleeting acquaintance with Ruth," Joseph reminded him, "but she was a key figure in the operation, and without her help Agata would not have been able to escape."

Suddenly, Joseph noticed a hole in the road, and hauled on the wheel to avoid it, catching his breath. Back on track, he went on, "It was vital we got Agata away - if this operation fails, she would have fallen under immediate suspicion... she had been present at all the meetings, the only person who knew everything. Otto dismissed her as a threat because of her disabilities, you see. After leaving university, Agata had been in a car accident in which her parents were killed. She suffered serious injuries, and was left unable to hear or speak; they assumed this was due to head injuries."

"Was she German?" asked Cloughie.

"Her mother was German, but Agata was raised in Poland; her father spoke English fluently. She was very intelligent, with a real gift for languages; I was struck by her grace and character - we became close, more than friends," Joseph's voice was husky with emotion as he described their attempt to get Agata away to England, where she would be safe and useful to the intelligence services... and his voice cracked as he went on, "Ruth took her to an airstrip to meet a British plane to take them to London. The Germans had found out and ambushed us... Agata was hit in the shoulder, and fell. Ruth had no option but to jump aboard the plane and leave her to be looked after by the partisans - she had vital information for London. Weeks later I heard what followed. The partisans, with Agata, were pursued into a wood, where they had a truck concealed. She became separated but chanced upon the truck; if spotted, they would all be shot. Ignoring the pain in her shoulder, she veered away and ran down a made-up road, where she was picked up by a German searchlight. She fell in a hail of bullets. The Germans had found their quarry and killed it; they returned to quarters with their victim, and, thanks to her self sacrifice, the partisans were able to get away." Tears ran down Joseph's face and silence pervaded the car; they had reached the turning off the main road and could see the glimmer of floodlights between trees.

Cloughie turned his face to Joseph, "Now's your fucking time to get revenge!"

This was crux time; everything depended on how they were received. Would they, could they, succeed against the odds, and attach the explosive device to the gimbal.

Joseph reminded them, they were not alone - other members of his group were following, and one way or another the rocket would be prevented from reaching its target. He drove toward the armed guards with a wry smile on his lips.

Chapter 20

Netherlands

The car moved steadily onward as they neared the bright lights showing amongst the trees. Ahead of them Joseph could just make out the silhouettes of armed guards standing in a row behind powerful spotlights. The guards suddenly started running towards them with rifles at the ready and blocked their path. Joseph reminded his two passengers to put on their white lab coats, they were still in German uniforms. They had been so captivated by Joseph's story that they had failed to change their disguise. It was now too late; they were surrounded by guards who were banging on the car and ordering them out. They would just have to think on their feet.

A searchlight panned onto them bathing everything in light. Opening the window, Joseph attempted to explain their presence. The guards, in no mood for conversation, pulled open the door and dragged him out. With that, Rodders flung open his door, with a fierce glare he ordered them to stop immediately. He instructed them to release his driver, declaring they were there on important business and anyone who got in the way would answer to him and to his superiors. Seeing Rodders in his colonels uniform the perplexed men lowered their rifles and snapped to attention. Cloughie then also flung his door open, almost knocking one of the men off his feet. Now faced with two colonels, the men stood even taller.

Rodders took out the papers bearing Otto's name and speaking sharply, ordered one of the guards to deliver them to the person in charge. He ordered the others to line up at attention. Then took his lab coat out of the back of the car and calmly put it on.

Cloughie followed suit but in complete silence. Having been told that two scientists would be coming to assist with the launch everyone assumed that these were them.

Running steps could be heard coming toward them as Klaus Schmidt the officer in charge of overseeing the operation hurried towards them. He held the forged papers in his hand, on seeing two officers he saluted in the usual manner. He was somewhat puzzled to see they were senior military officers; he had been under the impression that the expected scientists were civilians. In an attempt to dispel any doubts Rodders stood to attention, clicked his heels, and loudly shouted, "Heil Hitler!"

Klaus froze momentarily but then reciprocated nervously. Not daring to question a top-ranking officer he led them into a highly illuminated open area.

There was the V2 rocket in the horizontal position. Klaus told Rodders that they had been expected much earlier but everything was on schedule for the launch.

They were now going through the final protocols prior to positioning the rocket ready for blast off. Rodders was now feeling more comfortable, his confidence in overdrive. All they had to do now was stay calm and keep up the act. There was a distinct possibility that they might, just might, get away with their plan. He asked Klaus to run through the procedures which had already been completed. After thanking him and congratulating him on a job well done Rodders announced that he would do the final check personally.

They then walked purposefully toward the rocket. A group of technicians were standing by waiting for the scientists. They had been getting anxious about the delay, and time was passing. "Let's get to it," barked Rodders, "lead me to the platform."

When they arrived more technicians were waiting, all wearing white coats except for one. His clothing was more akin to the dress of a prisoner. Although not apparently part of the scientific team he did appear to exert a lot of influence.

As Rodders climbed the steps to the platform the technicians stood to attention. "Relax," he said. "We are in this together. I am here to ensure everything goes to plan, I have faith in the team and simply needed to perform the final pre-launch check." Inwardly he thought, "This is a magnificent piece of engineering, there is nothing remotely like it in Britain. It's frightening to see how far advanced the Germans are."

Even though the tide of war was turning Rodders felt uneasy knowing that with weapons such as this, the outcome was far from certain. Drawing on the information received from the scientists at Porton Down he was able to direct the technicians to the vital component that set the rockets course, asking them to check the fin tails at its base. The man in unusual dress did so raising his thumbs to signal OK before returning to his position and standing to attention. Rodders then asked if the connection to the umbilical cord was correctly in place, once again the same man did the job giving it a nod of approval, returning to his position and standing to attention as before.

Rodders then turned and strode to the small trap door. He tapped it with his knuckles saying he wanted to check the gimbal. As expected, it was the same man who responded, he opened the door, but this time stayed put and invited Rodders to examine the gimbal. One of the other technicians spoke up, explaining that he had installed the gimbal personally and was absolutely certain it was fit for purpose.

Rodders snapped that as this was the most important part of the guidance system, he would prefer to inspect it in person. The shabbily dressed man ran to fetch a small step ladder, he quickly climbed it and unlocked the door with a key. He then stood at the foot of the ladder to assist Rodders as he climbed to the open the trap door. When he reached the top he paused, took out his watch as if to check the time and announced that everyone needed to hurry if they were going to get the rocket in the air on time.

He put his hand through the door as though he was checking the gimbal was correctly placed and jammed the watch onto the side of it. As he did so he pressed hard on the button. The second hand started moving. My God, he thought, he'd actually managed it!

He lowered himself down the ladder and was surprised to hear the oddly clothed technician whisper, "Good luck, Sir!"

Rodders did not know what to make of it but dismissed it from his mind. He was hoping against hope that the rocket would fail to reach London but there was nothing more he could do. At the bottom of the platform, he called everyone together and congratulated them on their achievements so far. Ruefully he pondered what a fantastic arsenal of weapons the Germans had amassed. Then the motors revved up as the rocket was gradually raised to its firing position. Rodders was enthralled and captivated by the sight, between this and the noise levels he was unaware of all that was happening around him. There was a hard tap on his shoulder as the engines continued to roar, he could also hear the fuel tanks beginning to fill and realised he was standing in a danger zone.

With his years of experience, he managed to present a calm appearance. He nodded his head as if in approval, took a few steps backwards then stopped and saluted the rocket. All around him were impressed by his bravery and allegiance to the German cause. They burst into spontaneous applause, acknowledging his patriotism.

Meanwhile, Klaus who had been watching things from afar, went into the field tent to dispatch a signal to a nearby substation bearing a message to Otto. This related that everything was in order, the two scientists had concluded their investigation, and all was set for launch. A message in response asked that all involved should be congratulated, especially the two scientists.

Otto had handpicked the actual scientists after meeting them at a convention for extreme reactionaries committed to Nazi ideologies. There were several such meetings promoting Germany as a powerhouse not only of Europe but of the world. It was at one of these meetings that Otto had gathered a group of likeminded individuals and the seeds of a plan using rocketry had germinated. He had also been advised of a potent liquid called sarin which was so powerful that a small amount could annihilate a city. This liquid, if placed in a sealed container could be carried in the nosecone of a rocket. When it became gaseous it would seep everywhere, obliterating everyone in its path. Otto now had all the pieces of the puzzle - the deadly chemical, the means of delivery and the scientists with the knowledge to bring the plan to fruition. He was determined the plan would work at all costs and arranged a further meeting to bring it to a successful conclusion.

Just as the Field Officer stood to view the final countdown the phone rang. It was Otto himself making enquiries about the two scientists he had chosen. Klaus told him he had been very impressed by their efficiency and patriotism but had been surprised to see they were both senior officers and not civilian as expected.

Otto was taken aback, he told Klaus angrily that the men he had appointed were not in the military, they were civilians named Hausmann and Schroeder. He commanded Klaus to find out who the hell these two men were and if they proved to be suspicious, he wanted them shot.

By now the rocket was fully fuelled, the umbilical cord leading to the nose cone had been connected to the electricity supply. It was nearing midnight; the only remaining action was to depress the ignition button. The button was on a raised platform some hundred yards away, two of the technicians led the way. Cloughie noticed that the man who had consistently persisted in helping them was trailing behind.

They were about halfway there when two guards sent by Klaus closed up on them, one called out, “Hausmann.”

Neither Rodders nor Cloughie responded.

Speaking loudly but as if in conversation he then called the name, "Schroeder."

As before, neither man responded but Cloughie realised they were the ones being so addressed, and correctly assumed that they had been rumbled and the guards had been sent to check for their identity. Swinging around, pistol at the ready just as the guards were raising their rifles.

He yelled, "Down!" and fired two shots in quick succession.

One guard fell, the second staggered but was about to return fire when Cloughie, reacting quickly, took him out. Within seconds there was a hail of bullets cracking the air around them. The men zigzagged their way toward the control platform, ordering the technicians to stay where they were. In shock the men did as ordered and stood still for a few seconds, thus acting as a shield for Rodders and Cloughie. They then threw themselves to the ground, leaving Rodders and Cloughie in the open.

They immediately recognised their precarious position however getting to the launch button was their only objective, they were prepared to risk all to reach it. Keeping a good distance between themselves they continued to swerve until they reached the base of the platform. After noting the position of the launch button on the dashboard, Cloughie shot at the overhanging lights reducing the area into darkness. Gunshots were getting closer; voices were calling for them to be killed before they could sabotage the launch.

Everyone in pursuit believed their aim was to disrupt the launch, but little did they realise that Rodders and Cloughie were desperate for the launch to take place. Some troops were almost upon the steps. Cloughie shot the first two, Rodders the third. As they neared the panel, they noticed two technicians who had previously been hidden out of sight. These men, who were not part of the military, dropped to the floor. One of them took a bullet which had been aimed at Cloughie, while the other lay terrified on the decking.

A luminous clock on the dashboard showed that thirty seconds remained before the launch button could be pressed. There was little cover as the firing continued and a second wave of guards with automatic weapons were almost upon them. Cloughie shot the leader with his last bullet but as Rodders prepared to open fire on the next the soldier suddenly collapsed in front of them. As another one also fell, they realised Joseph had taken up a position armed with an automatic rifle. Rodders dispensed with another guard using his final bullet.

Just as Joseph took up position at the base of the steps the technician crawled to the edge of the platform and fell at his feet with a heavy thud. He's not going anywhere, he thought.

Fifteen seconds remained! The firing continued as Cloughie rushed to the dashboard. To his horror he saw the ignition key was missing, pressing the button would be futile if the key had not been employed. All this for nothing!

Cloughie banged the dashboard. "We're sunk," he screeched. "The fucking ignition key is missing!" He told Joseph to make a run for it as they tried to draw the fire away from him.

The bullets continued to fly past as Cloughie took Rodders' hand, telling him their time had come. It was time to go! Both men were about to chew on their cyanide capsules when they became aware of someone crawling toward them. Rodders was about to kick out at the man but halted when he recognised him as the bizarrely dressed technician who had been helping them.

The man grinned as he continued to crawl towards the dashboard.

"It's no good," called out Cloughie. "There is no key."

In spite of this the man continued, he stood for a few seconds as he reached the dashboard, then suddenly he collapsed into Cloughie's arms.

"Poor bastard has been hit," thought Cloughie as he looked at the dying man. He then realised the man was trying to give him something. It was the missing key. He had taken it from the technician who died trying to escape from the platform. Screaming to tell Rodders he had the key, Cloughie crouched low and feeling his way in the darkness managed to fit the key into its slot.

Seven seconds to go! Holding his finger on the button he ducked as a bullet screamed by, taking off most of his ear before slamming into the framework. He felt no pain, just the warmth of the blood trickling down his neck. His mind was totally focused as he counted back from seven.

Bullets continued to rain all around. Three! Two! One! Then a nerve-racking moment before the sound of the fuel being ignited could be heard, this was followed by a deafening roar. They had done it!

Cloughie turned to Rodders in jubilation but was soon deflated as he realised his friend was pressing his hand into his shoulder in an attempt to stem the flow of blood.

As the roar of the engines grew louder and louder the whole area was lit by powerful flames. The gunfire stopped momentarily. It soon restarted but this time was not aimed at them. Joseph and his men were firing at the Germans who were running for cover.

Joseph beckoned Rodders and Cloughie, it was time to make their escape.

Cloughie helped Rodders to his feet and guided him down the steps. They could feel the ground shake beneath their feet and could not help but be impressed by the power of the rocket. It moved slowly at first but as the thrust overcame gravity its speed increased.

The rocket moved majestically into a vertical plane, growing faster and faster, sending shock waves in its wake.

Joseph hurried them away through the wooded area.

Meanwhile at the other end of the encampment Klaus called Otto, reporting the successful launch. Otto was jubilant and congratulated him.

Chapter 21

Spandau

Otto's jubilation was not to last! On the previous day he had gathered with his co- conspirators. Gathering on the eve of the Fuhrer's birthday, they had been celebrating since eight p.m. Beaming over his achievements, Otto gloated at the prospect of becoming a national hero, recorded in the annals of German history in perpetuity. He personally was about to turn the tide of this war in Germany's favour. He was conscious that there would be a backlash to the attack on London, but his guests reassured him that when Britain surrendered, he would be recognised as the hero of the hour. He smirked as they all stood to salute him reverently.

The clock hand stood only thirty minutes from midnight, and all eyes were restlessly moving to the telephone. They had been promised a call when all was in readiness to launch, and the final countdown would be transmitted to the landline in his office. Otto couldn't conceal some nervousness as he wiped perspiration from his brow. He shot up from his chair as the phone rang, listened and then punched a fist in the air, proclaiming that the rocket was now in position; he would receive a further message when firing it began. His eyes were a little glazed he rose, banged his glass on the table and cried, "Heil Hitler!" The others joined in in glee and drained their glasses again.

The phone rang again. The rocket would be launched in ten minutes. This time Otto rose to toast the good health of those present, thanking them and congratulating them on their achievement. More roars and banging on the table occurred.

With five minutes to go, there was another call; in exactly three minutes, the first sequence would begin. But a few minutes later, as midnight passed, Otto was concerned. The phone rang, and he grabbed it anxiously, although still oozing pride at this great moment... His expression changed, from joyous anticipation to rage. He crashed the telephone down. Clearly something was wrong. White faced; Otto turned to the others. Quietly he explained that the plan had failed.

"During the launch the gimbal had failed; this meant the rocket could not set a proper course for distance or height. It headed out into the North Sea where it exploded on impact with the water. The only saving grace is that it did not explode at the launch site," another of the group said sombrely

"A good job it didn't explode in the Hague - the gas would have caused immense loss of life."

Another member pointed out, "You realise, there will be an investigation. The launch was unlawful, and the gas against all Hitler's orders. He has always said he would not expose the German people to the retaliation it would engender... I fear our failure will be met with punishment.

We should consider our options – stay, or depart post-haste."

The phone rang yet again, this time, it seemed, with a hideous shrillness. Otto listened carefully to the voice at the other end of the line; it sounded exceedingly angry. "Those two officers you sent to oversee the launch probably caused it to fail!"

"What?" bellowed Otto. "I didn't send any officers, why would I involve the army?"

The voice at the other end sounded a little more composed as they said, "Well they had letters of authority on your notepaper and signed by you, to take charge of the operation."

Otto, before slamming down the phone said between clenched teeth, "I want them found and captured. But I want them alive!"

He resumed his position at the table and demanded to know if they had a traitor amongst them. If someone had tipped off the British, he wanted to know who that someone was. However, it was clear from their expressions that his collaborators were as keen as he was to succeed in the plan, and made it plain verbally. "Someone had access to this office, someone knew the details!" Suddenly his face twisted in rage as he snarled and dragged out the words, "That bloody bitch!"

Gathering his dignity, he suggested they collect together any papers, clear all trace of being at his house and go their separate ways. If blame was to be apportioned, he would take it on his own shoulders. "I will not betray you, or reveal your participation. However, an investigation will be bound to discover it. I will try to delay matters, and give you time to get away, if that is your choice. I will try to divert enquiries from you, and give you time to concoct alibis for tonight and other meetings. I wish you all well."

Each in turn embraced him as they filed out. "If only it had worked," was his final comment as he sat down alone. Slumped in his chair, he thought none of his collaborators had betrayed him; this awful situation was a result of his own mistakes. He had been blindly unaware of the cleverness of his own staff. It was only by chance, he thought, that Agata had been picked to work in the very house where the greatest scheme (as he thought) to end the war had been conceived. She had managed to uncover details of the launch programme, which she then passed on to Joseph, who was obviously a member of the Resistance. "Circumstances and ill fortune," he thought, "have dealt me a bitter blow. They have made a fool of me!"

He had compiled a detailed dossier of his plans. He had hoped one day to see it recognised as one of the finest military achievements in the history of warfare. He had not included the names of the conspirators; in case something went wrong. Now it had; he felt fear now, and wondered what would happen to him.

There wasn't long to wait; a few days had passed when two SS officers stormed into the house accompanied by four armed soldiers. Ordered to go with them, he asked why, and was answered by one of the soldiers thrusting the butt of his rifle into his stomach. The physical pain was nothing compared to the anguish and fear which flooded his mind and soul. He dragged himself to his feet, stood to attention and saluted, "Heil Hitler!" He gestured toward his jacket on a hook nearby.

"Hurry up! There are people waiting to talk to you!" snapped one of the SS officers, with a glare of contempt.

Otto walked to his coat, turned to put it on, then took a few steps away and turned to face the wall, slipping his hand to an inside pocket, feeling the cold steel of his pre-cocked revolver. Quickly transferring it to the roof of his mouth, he pulled the trigger.

Meanwhile an aircraft touched down on an air strip in the Hague. Secretively, two bankers, an important businessman and a colonel transferred to a submarine, based at Ijmuiden Port.

Its destination: Argentina.

Chapter 22

Netherlands

Except for the occasional sound of gunfire, the launch area was relatively quiet. Klaus was busy mustering his men, the site needed to be cleared of any traces which could lead to anyone associated with the launch. His first order was to assign four men to pursue the infiltrators. Klaus had a score to settle with them. In the meantime, his priority was to cover up this operation, all evidence relating to the launching of the rocket and the resulting fracas had to be eradicated.

The men worked efficiently, each man having his own role to ensure the site was cleared quickly. The rocket launch pad itself was connected to a lorry which was ready to leave. However just as they were making the final checks a message was received. The call came from an observation point on the coast directly under the path of the rocket. Otto had set up a number of such points on land and sea to track the rocket, picking up any irregularities. The first relay reported the successful passage of the rocket over its area. The second message reported a flash of light seen high in the sky on the trajectory of the rocket, the third observation post some fifty miles off shore reported hearing a loud splash ahead of them. Both lookouts had immediately communicated their findings to the command centre. They expressed concern that the rocket had failed and had come down in the sea some eighty metres from the shore.

Something clearly was amiss as there was a significant delay in the messages being picked up, probably due to the chaos surrounding the launch.

Eventually they reached Klaus who passed the communications onto Otto.

Otto's shouting and the slamming down of the phone rang in Klaus' ears as they made haste to leave the launch site.

The bullet which had torn much of Cloughie's ear had also caused some internal damage. He felt extremely dizzy, staggering as he struggled to stay upright. His sense of balance had been badly affected by the injury. Joseph took hold of him, offering support as they moved toward the cover of the nearest clump of trees.

Rodders was also having difficulties, as his wound was causing him severe pain. The three of them lurched deeper into the woods, stopping to rest as needed. They had not managed to travel far when Joseph put his finger to his lips and told them to lie down. He had heard noises which seemed like footsteps heading their way. It sounded as though there were no more than three or four pursuers but they were closing in fast. If caught they would not be able to defend themselves. They had no ammunition, plus two of their group were wounded, and they would need to rely on keeping undercover in the darkness of the night. In a whisper he told the two wounded men to stay on the ground and covered them with dried leaves. This was little more than a gesture as deep down he knew it had little chance of fooling anyone. He instructed them to listen for his signal and then count to twenty. At this time Joseph would make as much noise as possible to distract the Germans and give them a chance of escape.

The two men protested but their objections were ignored. No sooner had Joseph left when Cloughie got to his feet, wished Rodders good luck and moved off into the darkness slightly to the left of the path Joseph had taken. Rodders wasn't having any of it. If he was going down, he was going down fighting. Stealing himself against his pain he unsheathed his knife and staggered forward. If they were going to die, they would do so fighting and all together.

The three men were now moving forward, toward the enemy. One to the left, the second to the right and the third straight toward them. Their lives were now in the lap of the gods! Joseph had not got far when he saw a flickering of lights coming towards him. He saw three lights equally spaced about ten metres apart. He estimated them to be about twenty metres away. Counting in his head he had reached eight and decided to take a chance. He shifted his position to the left in the hope that the soldiers on the right flank would pass him unnoticed. They moved much faster than he expected but he just managed to lie flat on the ground so the beam from the torch narrowly missed him. Holding his breath as they passed close. His silent count had reached fifteen as he slowly and silently pursued the German officer on his right. He was concerned that the man was too far away for him to be able to rush at him and strike before being detected. Despite this he felt he had no option if he was to protect his friends.

He had now counted to eighteen and prepared to pounce. Gripping his knife, he sprung forward. At this precise moment his two companions shattered the silence with a cacophony of noise with shouts, "Charge!" and, "Kill Them!"

"You go to the right flank, you go left!"

The noise stopped the Germans in their tracks. The soldier nearest to Joseph turned and just caught the glint of his knife in the beam of his torch threw down his rifle and raised his arms in terror. He was little more than a boy and his inexperience in battle was evident.

Joseph signalled him away and he ran. The two remaining German soldiers had already fled, leaving their rifles and torches behind. Cloughie picked up a torch and began searching for Rodders, he spotted him lying face down on the ground. Together with Joseph he ran toward him, slowly turned him over and sat him upright. Blood was pouring from his right arm.

As Joseph took out his knife Rodders whispered, "You are not about to amputate, are you?"

With a smile, Joseph replied, "Maybe that's not such a bad idea, as you'd be a lot lighter to carry." He then proceeded to use his knife to cut off his rifle strap which he used as a tourniquet. When he was satisfied that the blood flow had been stemmed, they helped Rodders to his feet. Further treatment would have to wait.

They needed to get as far away as possible, but Rodders was in no fit state to walk. "We need some wheels," said Cloughie, turning to Joseph and hoping he had some ideas.

Joseph had parked the car they had used to travel to the launch site close to the entrance, concealed amongst some trees, in the hope they could use it if things went awry. If one of them could possibly get to the car, whilst the other helped Rodders to the road they might just be able to make their getaway. Rodders was in a bad way, it was clear that staying where they were was not an option if he was to survive and all of them avoid capture. It was agreed that Joseph would try to get the car as Cloughie made his way to the road, taking his partner with him. Joseph would signal, flashing the headlights as he approached, and Cloughie would respond using one of the torches kindly left behind by the Germans. Joseph grabbed one of the discarded rifles and collected a pocketful of bullets from other cartridge holders.

There was still some light coming from the launch site as it was cleared. It was however a smooth operation, quickly carried out and the lights were beginning to dim as each in turn was switched off. Finding the car would not be easy, and Joseph had a rough idea of its location and after travelling some hundred metres was relieved to see the side road leading to the site. He was delighted when turning onto this he could make out tyre tracks heading off this track. Pulling back a large branch he uncovered the car and was just about to climb in when the three young soldiers approached. He pointed his rifle at them, they froze in fear for a second time. He ordered them to lie face down with a warning that if they tried to escape, he would have no option but to shoot. He reversed the car then stopped. With his rifle aimed at them through the open door, he told them he could easily kill them but would spare their lives in exchange for enough time to get away before they raised the alarm.

"Agreed!" he shouted, and all three nodded. As he sped away, he glimpsed one of them running towards the launch site. There was little time to waste. He prayed his two mates had managed to reach the road.

Driving cautiously, he flashed his lights as he went but there was no response. After travelling some distance, he stopped. They were not to be seen, so he anxiously clambered out of the car wondering if they had lost their way, if Rodders had been too weak to make it. Looking around, he noticed a light behind him. He had to investigate despite the possibility that it might be a search party with obvious consequences should he be spotted. He turned the car around denting the rear and reducing the taillights to fragments, then sped back to where he guessed the light came from. There was no one to be seen. Opening the car door to take a closer look he was relieved to hear a voice he recognised. It was thankfully them. Despite his terrible state Rodders managed to keep his spirits high, pleased to see the car, at least he would not have to walk any further. Gently he was placed in the rear of the car, and they were soon speeding away.

They had not travelled far when Joseph saw headlights in his rear-view mirror.

The approaching vehicle was obviously travelling extremely fast whilst theirs was designed for comfort rather than speed. It was rapidly gaining on them. He pressed hard on the accelerator; it was evident that those pursuing them had to be the security guards from the rocket launch. The three escapees would be a prize catch. Otto would take great delight in having them tortured and killed for their attempts to foil his plans.

The pursuing car had closed the gap, suddenly bullets began to rain on the back of the car. Fortunately, it was armour plated, less fortunately the weight of this limited its speed. Joseph could see they were headed toward a sharp bend. He gripped the steering wheel tightly as, clenching his teeth, he took the bend at high speed. Rodders groaned in pain as the car skidded, hit the embankment, bounced off then swerved through three hundred and sixty degrees, ending in the centre of the road facing their original direction. Everything and everybody shuddered to a halt. The engine cut out and stalled. Frantically, Joseph tried to restart it, without success. After several attempts to restart it, he noticed steam pouring out from under the bonnet. The engine was not going to take them anywhere They were stuck and in big trouble!

Rodders told the other two men to make a run for it. They looked at him in surprise. He barked and reminded them he was in charge of the operation; this was not a request but a direct order. Both Cloughie and Joseph knew he was right, they sadly shook his hand. Rodders, grinning told Cloughie not to worry as the Germans would not have the pleasure of taking him alive. Cloughie tightened his grip on Rodders hand then saluted him as they left the car. No sooner had they got out of the car when Joseph dived to the floor shouting to Cloughie to get down. They were under heavy fire. They desperately needed cover!

From nowhere another set of lights could be seen heading directly toward them at speed. They were in an impossible situation. The car behind them had stopped and two soldiers from it had opened fire with automatic rifles. Joseph fired back with his pistol as they made their way to a position in front of their car which provided some cover. Joseph's fire slowed down the advancing soldiers but over their shoulder they could see multiple headlights speeding toward them. It appeared to be a convoy of vehicles; the leading truck was pointing directly at them. The driver had a decision to make, it was either the embankment or them and their car. Rodders could see what was happening and braced himself for the impact.

With its horn blasting the leading troop carrier managed to come to a screaming halt in the nick of time. So close that Cloughie and Joseph could feel the heat from the engine. The firing from the pursuing car had stopped suddenly. The gunmen threw down their rifles and scrambled aboard as the tyres spat out stones and grit. The car wheels span as it sped away into the darkness. They clearly did not want to get involved with the military

Without a moment's thought Rodders called to Cloughie to get into the back of the car and play dead. The last thing they needed was for him to be interrogated.

Soldiers with weapons jumped out of the back of the lorry whilst the following cars formed a cordon around them. With rifles pointing at them and cars around them it was clear they were trapped. Joseph helped Rodders to his feet, unsteady and in obvious pain, he posed little threat. The soldiers parted to let the officer in charge come through. He gave the order for them to lower their gun.

As he calmly approached the two men, he noticed Rodders was wearing a colonel's uniform, and he paused, saluted then continued toward them. As he did so Joseph clicked his heels together showing the proper protocol, and the young German Lieutenant nodded in response. They were in one hell of a predicament, Rodders, never averse to taking risks, decided to take advantage of the situation. The young officer had seen they had been fired at and wondered why high-ranking German officials were under fire from German soldiers. Always take the high ground, this was Rodders motto except that this time the elevation wasn't even a molehill! He introduced himself as Col. Claus Hoffman then pointing toward Cloughie named him as Col. Von Trescow, a scientist working in aeronautics. On hearing this Joseph introduced himself as a lieutenant, part of the security operation in the area.

Treading carefully the German officer explained that as this was a very sensitive area, he needed to check the identity of everyone who entered it. Joseph, standing smartly to attention, politely but drew the officer's attention to the physical state of his two colonels. They were in no fit state to answer questions, and they needed medical attention. Speaking firmly, he asked the young officer if there was a medic amongst his troops who could attend to them.

The Lieutenant was slightly taken aback but seeing high ranking officers before him realised he needed to show them some respect. He summoned one of the soldiers to fetch a medic as a matter of urgency. Joseph then helped Rodders to the front seat of the car,

Rodders quietly thanked him, winked and pretended to pass out. The medic took one look at the two injured men, told the lieutenant they were in a bad way and called for help. He instructed two soldiers to remove them from the car, placing them on makeshift beds created from greatcoats and other items of clothing.

Turning to Joseph, the Lieutenant asked what had happened and why they were being shot at by German soldiers. Joseph knew exactly what to say, with the other two not in a position to be questioned he could relate almost what had actually taken place but at the same time elevate the two injured men into heroes. He went over to Rodders who was still feigning unconsciousness, opened his tunic to remove paperwork together with his identity cards. He passed them to the lieutenant whilst explaining their present situation. The three of them had been sent on a secret mission to foil a plot instigated by a clandestine cohort led by Otto. Today was Hitler's birthday and his present would be an event which would turn the tide of the war into Germany's favour. The plan would involve deploying a V2 rocket with a course set for London. He was abruptly interrupted by the lieutenant who was eager to tell Joseph he had been dispatched from the local HQ to investigate rocket activity in the area. This was seen as suspicious since there was nothing scheduled, especially at night-time.

Joseph was more than pleased by what he was hearing, and things were working to his advantage. The lieutenant flicked through the paperwork and nodded to Joseph to carry on. Otto, he continued, had somehow managed to acquire a V2 rocket together with certain like-minded German fanatics, and the launch was now set to take place at midnight.

The lieutenant looked puzzled. "That was the time recorded but as I said there was no launch programmed for this evening. How did you come to know about it and why were we not informed?"

Joseph needed time to think. "Before we get to that there are some things you must know. If the colonels do not recover, we may never know the full story. Let me tell you what I do know, I am sure when everything is finally brought to bear officials in high command will fit the pieces together."

The lieutenant asked him to go on and thinking on his feet Joseph continued his narrative.

"As far as I know," he explained, "an agent planted in Otto's house managed to relay information to the two injured colonels."

Glancing over to where the two men were being attended to the lieutenant gestured impatiently for Joseph to continue. He was eager to learn more. The final part of the plan, expounded Joseph, was revealed at the last minute, if it was to be foiled things would have to move quickly. Fortunately, in order to infiltrate the cabal, the agent at Otto's house had managed to secure some headed paper which could be used to access the launch site. The location was unfortunately still unknown, it was only revealed after the capture of the two scientists and their driver. The two colonels had impersonated the scientists, convincing everyone on site that they had been appointed to oversee the launch. They had managed to sabotage the rocket but were unsure if they had succeeded. Their identity had been revealed by a last- minute call from Otto, revealing them as imposters. They had managed to escape but had after several encounters sustained their injuries. They had been chased to their present position and would not have got away had it not been for the lieutenant's intervention.

The lieutenant toyed with the papers for a moment before handing them back to Joseph. If all this were true, the three of them were indeed heroes and circumstances seemed to support Joseph's account. He told Joseph that a rocket had come down in the sea some distance away, but he was puzzled as to why. He was stunned when Joseph described how the rocket was loaded with a new and powerful gas capable of wiping out the whole population of London. If it had succeeded dreadful reprisals would certainly follow with Britain and her allies doing the same and worse to Berlin and other cities.

Rodders had been quietly listening in and was overjoyed to hear that they had brought the rocket down. It was now time to get away, he began to groan, hoping the lieutenant would take pity on his plight. His ploy worked and the lieutenant gave the order for him to be moved to a field hospital on the outskirts of the Hague. Joseph said he knew the hospital and would be happy to drive there himself.

The lieutenant agreed to this but insisted they be accompanied by a guard. Whilst this was not ideal, he was happy to accept the offer, hoping it would somehow provide an opportunity for them to make their escape. He was confident that their escort could be disposed of once they were far enough away.

The two injured men were made as comfortable as possible in the rear of an open-air jeep. The guard climbed up front as the lieutenant shook Joseph's hand. After saluting Joseph suggested that if they hurried, they could catch up with the launch party. It would not have travelled far since its retinue included large cumbersome vehicles which would slow progress along the narrow country roads. To everyone's relief the lieutenant agreed and their car sped away from the scene. Joseph was already working out a plan to get rid of the guard.

The lieutenant gathered his men around him, he needed to outline their next move. The men stood and listened intently; they had the utmost respect for the young officer. With a mixture of anger and passion, he told them he would hunt down the soldiers who had shot and wounded two of their own officers.

Furthermore, they were part of an organisation which could have caused disastrous consequences to their own country. He gave the order that if threatened or challenged the first response would be to open fire. The manner in which they had treated their senior officers was clear to see, the perpetrators must be made to pay for their crimes. Their first task was to clear the road; the damaged car was blocking their way.

One of the soldiers involved in moving the crashed car noticed some papers had been left behind. He gathered them up, suspecting they may be important and took them to the Lieutenant. There was no time to look at them now, he was anxious to get on with the chase so he stuffed the papers into his tunic pocket and ordered his driver to speed on.

Once satisfied that his convoy was on the way he decided to look at the bundle. It contained a roughly drawn map together with letters from Otto. "Good intelligence," he thought.

The three men had undoubtably been of great service to their country. He must make contact with them on his return. As he put the papers into the glove compartment, he noticed some handwritten notes at the bottom of one of the letters. Curious, he held it close to the light on the dashboard. It was written in English, bore Joseph's signature and addressed to someone called Rodders.

"They're bloody English!" he exclaimed. He had noted the educated German accent but had also noticed that, at times, a slight English lilt was detectable. He ordered the driver to stop, almost causing a pile up as the drivers of following vehicles slammed on their brakes. His first instinct was to turn around and give chase yet something inside told him not to do this.

Plainly, they had acted in the best interest of the country. They had almost single-handedly prevented a holocaust. Had Otto's plan worked, thousands, perhaps even millions of Londoners would now be dead or dying from some poisonous gas. The British with their allies would reciprocate, the consequence would be Armageddon.

Hitler himself had insisted that the use of any form of gas was not even to be considered. He tore up the paper, throwing it out into the darkness of the night. He turned his attention to the job in hand, the safety of one of his guards was also on his mind. He instructed his driver to drive on as fast as possible. Meanwhile the launch site had been cleared, the equipment loaded onto trucks was travelling as fast as possible away from the scene. Klaus rode in the leading car; he was keener than most to distance himself from the area so as not to get embroiled in answering awkward questions from local military. Thoughts of facing Otto were constantly churning in his brain, distracting him from concentrating on the present dilemma. He needed to getaway quickly to enable him to think clearly and assess his best options. He had seen what happened to those who let Otto down. Most had simply disappeared!

Going as fast as they dared the convoy approached the point where the two German scientists and their driver had been captured.

Joseph's men had left, fearing the worst, after waiting long over the agreed time. They had been unsure what to do with the three men in their custody. Having been instructed not to harm them they decided to tie them together and leave them by the side of the road.

The captives had been there for almost two hours when the driver of Klaus' car picked them out in his headlights. Klaus got out of the car taking two men with him, untying their bonds they took them to the truck where the men recounted their story. Klaus then realised that the two colonels he had met had been British imposters, they had convinced him with signed documents that they were acting in Germany's best interests but had in fact had their own motives for the sabotage of the launch. He was able to explain to the actual scientists that they were intent not on stopping the launch but redirecting it and bringing it down in the sea. A plan which had regrettably succeeded.

Klaus got out of the truck, ordering the driver to continue speedily on to the depot.

When the last of the vehicles disappeared into the darkness Klaus walked slowly off the road into a small clearing in nearby woodland. He knelt and ignoring an inner voice for reason, put a pistol into his mouth. He did not hear the shot that killed him!

Chapter 23

Netherlands

The car bounced along at speed, and Rodders felt every agonising bump as they drove toward town. Since leaving the convoy Joseph had been trying to work out a plan to rid them of their unwanted passenger. This would not be easy as he was young and well-built, looking as though he would pose a problem if confronted. A voice from the rear, speaking in German, interrupted his thoughts, asking if they could stop for a while and explaining that Cloughie was in a bad way. He was now totally unconscious.

His position was impeding his breathing, so he needed help urgently. Joseph looked at the guard who nodded his agreement, so he slowed the car to a halt. Keeping the engine running Joseph got out and went to the back of the car. He could see that Cloughie was bent over, making breathing difficult. He tried to lift him; however, he was too heavy. The guard could see that Rodders was in no position to help so he too got out of the car to give them a hand. As he walked around the car Rodders leant forward, screaming with pain, and slammed the front passenger door, and working precisely in tandem Joseph jumped behind the wheel, closing his door as he sped off. The guard was left standing, wondering what had just happened.

"Where to now?" asked Rodders.

Joseph replied that he was heading to a place he knew, where he had contacts in the Underground. These people could help them get the medical attention they urgently needed. It was vital that the two of them could be repatriated as soon as possible as there would be a massive operation organised to find them. If caught they would be shown no mercy.

Rodders replied that he would never allow himself to be taken alive. He and Cloughie were both blessed with a tooth fairy. Joseph drove on, musing about the strange darkness of British humour.

Bad fortune seemed never ending, a short distance ahead lights signalled that they were about to face yet another trial. This time it was in the form of a roadblock. As he slowed the car to a crawl, two flashlights shone directly into the front of car, blinding Joseph as he wound down the window. The lights then shifted to the two passengers in the rear. The patrol soldier, demanding papers, wanted to know where they were heading. Joseph impatiently replied that he was carrying two badly wounded colonels who urgently needed medical attention. They had broken away from their convoy to get them to hospital in record time. Sweeping his torch across the two wounded men was enough to convince the soldier they were indeed in a sorry state, he shouted for the barrier to be raised.

As they passed, another soldier informed Joseph that they would pass on a message to the men manning the next barrier instructing them to allow their car through without delay. Waving in acknowledgement, Joseph floored the accelerator pedal. Twenty minutes later they reached the second barrier which lifted as they approached. They passed through without being challenged and pressed on. Rodders shifting in his discomfort, wanted to know where they were heading and what plans they had for when they arrived.

Joseph reassured Rodders, telling him to take it easy. Firstly, he would be taking them to a safe house where their wounds could be treated. Many others had been successfully treated there by a local Jewish doctor who devoted himself to helping casualties in the resistance. He was a good doctor, a good man who could be trusted. Whilst they were undergoing their treatment, he would get in touch with contacts who could organise their escape. They had associates all over France, Belgium and Britain. As soon as it was safe, they would transport the pair of them to a safe destination and from there would set a programme for their passage home.

Anticipating the next question, he told Rodders that they should be there in an hour's time, subject to there being no further delays. Gently removing Cloughie's covering, Rodders could see that the bleeding seemed to have stopped but there was a huge bump where the ear should have been. Of more concern was the suspicion that part of his cranium had been broken as the bullet glanced of the side of his head. On hearing this Joseph threw caution to the winds as he raced onward.

When they arrived at the outskirts of town the car moved slowly with dimmed lights. He turned off the main road into a lane leading to a cul de sac. An imposing building which clearly needed attention, filled the whole space. It had been a clinic run by a trio of doctors. The two younger ones had been seconded to the military, only the eldest, a man in his seventies was left. He ran the practice, single-handedly working from early morning to late at night. Occasionally partisans would bring wounded activists, who he would patch up before sending them on their way. It was too perilous to keep the injured for long as German soldiers also used the facilities rather than use their own medics, especially if their injuries were received in drunken brawls or if they were in need of treatment for infections caught as result of sexual indiscretions.

Making sure that the coast was clear, Joseph moved swiftly toward the large front door. With a quick glance around he took hold of the knocker and beat a coded series of taps. He waited, allowing a few minutes to elapse before he tapped again.

He listened at the door then heard tapping from the other side. This was the signal for him to lift the knocker revealing a small hole. A beam of light shone onto to Joseph's face, and he heard the sound of several bolts being drawn before the heavy metal door slowly opened. After a short exchange, a tall man with grey hair appeared accompanied by a younger and shorter figure. Making sure there were no prying eyes, the three of them set about lifting the two wounded men out of the car. Rodders, although in severe pain, was able to walk unaided. Cloughie had to be carried on a stretcher. They rested him on a surgical bed, and he opened his eyes briefly but was unable to speak before he relapsed back into unconsciousness. Rodders was seated on an adjustable chair set beneath a powerful overhead lamp.

He grimaced, flinching as he attempted to position himself comfortably. Doctor Albert Schindler frowned at the state of his patient. His assistant passed him a pair of scissors and he cut away the jacket revealing the extent of the bullet wound. He shook his head; his patient had been hit by a dum dum bullet which flattened on impact. The entry wound was small, but the exit wound five times larger. The femur was absolutely shattered, and sadly he knew the whole arm would have to be amputated. After pumping Rodders with as much morphine as he dared, he packed the wounds with swabs to slow the bleeding as much as possible. Moving on to examine Cloughie, the doctor informed Joseph that he needed surgery urgently to prevent infection to the brain. The skull was probably fractured as the bullet deflected from the side of the head. It was critical that both men were operated on without delay as there was a strong possibility they would both die.

Albert turned to Joseph and beckoned him to come outside. The only way they could possibly survive was in a well-equipped hospital. They could not be treated there as it was too dangerous, and if found they would surely be executed. Getting them home to England was the only hope, as this would be very difficult and the doctor indicated his willingness to administer a lethal injection to save the men from dying in unbearable pain. Joseph thanked him, and said he would endeavour to make contact with members of the resistance. He felt reassured by the fact that Rodders and Cloughie were high-ranking agents, senior officials in London would go to extreme lengths to repatriate them. It was imperative that Joseph got his plans in place as swiftly as he could, so he asked if the patients could be accommodated at the clinic in the short term whilst he tracked down his contacts.

After a brief pause Albert agreed with the proviso that if Joseph did not get in touch very soon, he would have no option but to release them from their pain.

After a few quick words with Rodders about his plans he jumped into the car and was gone.

Chapter 24

Netherlands

Joseph drove through the darkness; he must reach his destination in time. It was located in an isolated area so it would be difficult to find. Unfortunately, he pondered, getting there was only the beginning as there were many other obstacles ahead. He would meet and overcome each as it presented itself. It had been some time since he last saw his contact Andre and was unsure if he was still at the same address. In this business it was often necessary to move on quickly. Even if he did manage to catch up with him it was doubtful that Andre would be able to contact agents in London who were capable of organising the complicated operation necessary to rescue his two friends. Especially since it all needed to be done in a very short space of time. Perhaps Andre could arrange shelter for them for a while but without treatment they would not survive.

If only! If only! Juggling options in his mind he pushed on, driving carefully through the villages in fear of attracting attention. All went well and he arrived at his destination without a hitch. As he approached the village, he took a turning off the road onto a track leading to a farmhouse. It was difficult to see clearly but he knew the house had a number of outbuildings. Andre lived in the furthest, close to a copse. He had chosen this position to provide cover and a quick escape from the back door. Worried about time, Joseph parked the car out of sight near the trees at the back and ran to the front of the house. He banged on the door with his fists, but there was no reply. "Damn it!" he thought, hoping to God that Andre was still there.

He continued banging for several minutes before giving up and kicking the door in anger. As he turned to leave, he was met with the barrel of a revolver in his face.

Trembling half in fright, half with hope he whispered, "Andre?", and the reply came after a short silence. "Fucking Joseph!" They embraced, each remembering the very good and the really bad situations they had faced together.

Their reliance on each other in life-threatening predicaments, the insurmountable risks they had overcome, had fused an unbreakable bond. "Pal or no pal," said Andre with a grin. "That bleeding door better not be broken!"

Hurriedly, Joseph outlined the dilemma he was in. Emphasising how important the agents were to the war effort, he described how vital it was to get them back to London. Their injuries were life threatening, and without prompt medical treatment they would not survive beyond the next twenty-four hours.

Joseph spoke passionately to Andre, "You are their last hope, I have no remotely possible way of getting two injured men back home safely." When Joseph finished speaking Andre stood and beckoned him to follow. They walked into the darkness toward a wooded area. Andre spoke quietly saying there might, just might, be an opportunity of hitching a lift on a plane.

It would be returning to England after dropping off a couple of agents. There were, however, a few issues to address. The drop off point was thirty miles from the nearest air strip suitable for a pickup. This diversion would mean they would have to use the reserve fuel, leaving little for unexpected eventualities. Andre was sure that despite this, the crew would take on the challenge. Adolph, the youngest member was, in particular, always keen for a little extra excitement. Adolph? Puzzlement was written all over Joseph's face so Andre satisfied his curiosity, telling him the young pilot had a moustache with hair deliberately brushed to one side so if the worst happened and he was captured he might be mistaken for the Fuhrer. On an earlier mission he had a near miss when one of the partisans made that very mistake and had to be prevented from shooting him.

Joseph smiled but was silently thinking that this was no time for funny quips.

They moved into the cover of the trees, stopping at a large leafless tree, its trunk devoid of bark. Andre pulled away clumps of grass from around the base, then inserting a knife prised open a small, hinged door. He took out a morse code key connected to a two-way radio transmitter. The arial was cleverly concealed running up to the topmost branch. Joseph was impressed, Andre was, by keeping the equipment away from his abode, much less likely to be caught sending or receiving messages. He sat on the ground, placing the keyboard on his lap and earphones on his head, he began signalling. In short bursts, using coded cypher, tapped away for a few moments before pausing. His call was acknowledged instantly, the network was manned twenty-four/seven. The message read:

STAND BY TWO UNITS pause IMPORTANCE CAT.5. pause INJ.CAT.5 pause IMP.

TGHT pause LOC.EO9 over. HIT OK E245HG42/37 out.

"You're dead lucky!" declared Andre. "Our pilot will be on the airstrip at six thirty am precisely."

Overjoyed, Joseph took his hand and shook it with gusto. He was eager to know where the airstrip was situated but was reminded as Andre tapped his nose that secrecy was vital. The more people who knew, the greater the chance the enemy would spoil the show.

As they made their way back Andre outlined his plan. The two men would be taken to an agreed spot at five am. They would then be transported in a German ambulance. It had been acquired some time ago and been used on many occasions to great effect. The ambulance would drop them near the airstrip where they would be met by armed members of the resistance. The pilot would make only one attempt to pick up the men. With engines still running it would take off as soon as they were safely on board. Providing all went to plan they would soon be on the way to Blighty. Once there, an ambulance would carry them to a hospital in London where doctors would be ready to start treatment immediately.

With care they got the injured men into Joseph's car, Andre, stressing the importance of keeping to the schedule, directed him to the pick-up point. Joseph was in high spirits, eager to get Rodders and Cloughie to the rendezvous on time. He had been very surprised initially when he was told that it would be the doctor in the driving seat of the ambulance, but told himself he should have known.

Albert Schindler was a cunning fox; it was surely not the first time he had undertaken such a dangerous mission.

The journey back to the doctor's house went smoothly, and so Joseph was feeling relaxed, pleased with recent events. He was, however, conscious of the threat that the clinic could be searched at any time, and the sooner they left, the better it would be for everyone. When only about a mile from his destination he came to a crossroads. A lorry carrying troops drew up just as he passed, he could see in his mirror that they were setting up a roadblock. He had missed being stopped by a hair's breadth. His heart was pounding, he had no way of explaining his presence should he be stopped and questioned. That could mean curtains for Rodders and Cloughie. He arrived at Schindler's house in a cold sweat, realizing that the only road leading to the pick-up point was now closed.

The doctor was waiting for him and the two patients, the injured men were heavily sedated and resting quietly. When Joseph told Albert about the activity at the crossroads, he responded by telling him it was time to meet Daisy.

"Who is Daisy?" asked Joseph, looking perplexed.

Making sure the injured men were comfortable, Albert led him to the rear of the building. He unlocked the door of a large garage, revealing a military ambulance. Albert clambered into the driver's seat and Joseph joined him in the passenger seat. Daisy had never let him down, Albert informed Joseph, and he only used her when there was no other possible way to help people escape. Frequent use would arouse suspicion, but this journey was imperative, the wounded agents were of significant importance to their country. He would do his utmost to get them to the rendezvous at the appointed time.

Checking his watch, Joseph pointed out that they had only just over an hour left. "We need to get going," replied Albert. "There are a few preparations to make, and we may be held up at the barrier."

He then told Joseph to jump out and lift two handles situated at the side of his seat. These released the seat from its mountings, allowing it to be removed. The sliding panel behind revealed a space filled with a variety of items. Joseph and the doctor busily unloaded these, sorting them into two piles at the rear of the ambulance. One pile consisted of planks, some with holes others with pegs, clearly designed to fit together. There were also several field stretchers and a pile of clothing both civilian and military. The second pile consisted of sacks stuffed with padding and an assortment of shoes and boots attached to stout pieces of wood.

Albert began fitting the boards together, motioning to Joseph to do the same. Joseph soon realised they were constructing long narrow boxes, the type used for burials. Two jackets were filled with stuffing and small sacks stuffed and shaped into heads. Joseph was troubled, this is all very crude, he thought, and it would not fool anybody, but he carried on following the doctor's example. The trousers were fitted with stout poles, attached to boots, everything was then fitted into the makeshift coffins. Waists were formed with military issue belts and string tied around the bottom of the trousers. Joseph was convinced they were wasting their time; a cursory glance would be enough to expose nothing but a heap of rubbish. Was he missing something? Did Albert think he could pass these contraptions off as human remains or did he have something else up his sleeve?

For an elderly man Albert moved quickly. With hardly a word spoken he briskly indicated to Joseph that he should continue to copy everything he did, making Joseph feel as a subordinate to the master in charge. They completed the task in fifteen minutes, the doctor was satisfied they were on track, unlike Joseph who was edgy and worried about the eventual outcome of all this activity. They walked back to the house, taking the two field stretchers with them.

Joseph went to help move the injured men onto the stretchers, but Albert intervened. He instructed his assistants to carefully lift the men and place them on the stretchers, securing them with belts.

Joseph watched, feeling superfluous; not a nice feeling when you are used to being in charge. Finally, he was given the task of helping carry Cloughie to the ambulance, he was not surprised to see Albert already behind the wheel. He had moved the ambulance forward to enable the placing of the stretchers in the hidden area behind the seats.

The way in which each stretcher with its occupant was put in a secure position was remarkable. This tactic had obviously been successfully used to transport injured escapees many times before. The stretcher was positioned at an angle of forty-five degrees. It was wrapped in a padded blanket which covered the patient from ankle to shoulder, preventing them from moving. There was also a helmet like fitting to immobilise the head. Cloughie was put in first since his body, apart from his head was in good condition. Rodders was then positioned at a much lower angle to prevent further damage to his shoulder. Both men had been anaesthetised with as much morphine as possible. The panel was then put back into position leaving a clearance top and bottom to allow for ventilation. As the two rough coffins were placed in the rear, Joseph realised the purpose of the holes he had noticed earlier.

These were over the spot where the boots had been arranged. Albert was in the driving seat and after one last check his assistant climbed into the passenger side. Joseph was perplexed, wondering where he was to sit but Albert waved his hand in farewell saying, "Please leave the door open I expect to be back soon. Do come and visit when the war is over."

The rain drizzled as Joseph stood watching until the taillights disappeared from sight. The men were in good hands. It would, however, be some weeks later before Joseph found out whether or not Rodders and Cloughie had made it safely home.

He had noticed a bicycle parked in the garage along with a bundle of old clothes. He was still in German uniform whilst his only papers identified him as a civilian agricultural worker, nor could he risk driving a German military car. He was now a wanted man and somehow had to get away and re-join his comrades. They would help him transfer to another partisan unit well away from this place. The ragged clothes were damp, filthy and ill-fitting but perfect for a farm labourer. The bicycle looked ancient but was well oiled and roadworthy. Feeling gratified that he had helped accomplish a successful mission to prevent a serious attack on London, Joseph jumped onto the bike and rode away through the rain.

Chapter 25

Germany

Julian Aaron Klein was returning to his home in Spandau, but had he left it too late? Most of his friends were gone, and he realized he would probably never see them again. Street by street, town by town, every city was being emptied of the Jewish communities. He could clearly see his time had come. It was in the expression on his neighbours' faces, in the paintings daubed on his front door, in broken windows and in the garbage thrown into his front garden. He would be next! He had seen this coming for some time; praying that what he had done for his family was in their best interest, hoping his daughter would forgive him. At least she was safe. With a bit of luck, when she was mature enough to fully appreciate the circumstances, she would realise he had acted in her best interests. His throat burnt and his body sagged, forcing him to sit.

Tears began to flow; he felt such pain and sorrow in his heart and in his mind. After a short time, the tears dried as an inner strength took hold. He had seen this coming. He had beaten them. The Nazis, their atrocities so great that even the good Lord would never forgive them. He rose, walking along the hallway leading to the front door, pausing by an open door he admired his precious collection. He couldn't take any of it, there was nowhere to hide his treasured possessions. The knowledge that his house would be pillaged by the enemy saddened him. He consoled himself with the hope that maybe one day his works of art, silverware, porcelain and objects d'art would eventually fall into the hands of someone who appreciated their beauty. He was tempted to take a hammer to the breakable pieces but could not do such an injustice to the artists who had lovingly created such beauty.

Some months previously, he had travelled as was his custom to meet colleagues, some of the finest diamond connoisseurs in the world. He felt privileged to be a member of their group. They had met in Amsterdam in order to discuss how best to preserve the precious stones. They were determined that their crystalline clarity and sparkling beauty would not be contaminated by the greedy, grubby hands of members of the Third Reich. The Swiss government, although inclined towards the Germans, still preserved their integrity toward individuals regardless of race or nationality.

Aaron as he preferred to be called had rested contentedly feeling his fortune was safe. He then approached the principal of St. George's School. One of the most prestigious academies in Switzerland, here he managed to secure a permanent place for his daughter Ruth. She would be a boarder there until the age of eighteen, when he hoped she would gain entrance to University. Through his contacts he also arranged to give her a new identity complete with the required documentation. It was no surprise to find that in the present situation a little financial persuasion could achieve almost anything. From now on she would be known as Ruth Mahler; a German citizen. Aaron believed Germany would win the war and she, under this identity, would be able to live her life free of fear and discrimination.

Just before Ruth's twelfth birthday Aaron took her and his wife to Switzerland, leaving them unaware that they would be there for a long time. He needed to return to Berlin for business purposes and made his farewell saying he would be able to join them at a later date.

Aaron longed for this to be true but as he said goodbye he wondered if it would be for the last time. Sadly, his fears were well founded, soon after his return the borders were closed and he along with many others was put under house arrest. He had ensured through Swiss banks that funds were readily available for his wife and daughter and Ruth flourished. It was regrettable that her father didn't see how she excelled, concentrating on languages she became fluent in German, Swiss, French and English. She moved in high society, growing into a beautiful young lady full of self-confidence. Her manners and grace made her stand out from the crowd. His wife too, had lived a life free from discrimination and fear of persecution. This had come at a price, however, she had sorely missed her husband and had to keep her Jewish faith secret, practising her devotions in solitude.

Aaron knew nothing of this, and he went sadly out of the front door of the home he had loved, locking it behind him. The tumult hit him, crowds laughed and jeered as his Jewish friends and neighbours were being forcibly removed from their homes. Onlookers pelted them with stones as they were forced into the back of an open lorry.

Young soldiers treated them brutally using truncheons and sticks with abandon. Chanting filled the air, "Jews out! Jews out!"

Eventually he was spotted by the mob who violently pulled and pushed him into the back of the lorry. He embraced his friends. He tried to console them. Quietly explaining they would probably be deported. There was no reason to be fearful. They would all come through this together. As the lorry drove off, he winced as he witnessed his front door, being battered down but was mercifully spared the sight of the looting of his precious chattels.

He and his friends were never seen again.

Chapter 26

Germany

Ruth was full of emotion as she passed her old house in Pankow Berlin. It was occupied by senior German officers after being requisitioned by the military. She didn't pause but walked stiffly by so as not to attract attention to herself. The house brought back so many happy memories; how sad it was to see the place of her upbringing reduced to a military base. She hated, really hated what Hitler and the Third Reich had done to her country, and it was clear that it wouldn't be long before Germany would be at war with the British.

Thanks to her father's endowment she had been able to fulfil his dreams, she had blossomed into an intelligent beautiful woman who excelled in languages. At the age of eighteen she had left Switzerland and returned to her own country where, with her new identity, she felt secure.

No one would realise she had been part of a Jewish family. Her mother had passed away a few months earlier and although she felt alone, she was determined to make a success of her life. She planned to fulfil her parents' hopes and aspirations, vowing not to disappoint them. She bought a comfortable house in Spandau close to the Citadel. Feeling secure and confident, she was ready to meet the challenges ahead. Looking forward to planning her future, building a career, making new friends and enjoying life free from the confines of boarding school. She had kept in contact with some school friends and wasn't surprised to hear that many of their parents held high positions in business and politics in both Germany and Switzerland.

One of her reasons behind returning to Berlin was to re-establish contact with Sophia, an old friend from her days at St. George's school. Sophia was from England, studying German and so they were each able to help the other develop fluency in their respective mother tongues. Sophia's father, Bernard, worked at the British Embassy in Berlin. Ruth was made welcome and felt at home when she visited there.

Bernard, affectionally known as Ben, also made a point of including Ruth when he visited Sophia at school. He knew her mother had been living in Switzerland and was curious about her father but never questioned Ruth about him. He was impressed by Ruth's passion for languages and her fast-developing skills in speaking several.

These attributes came to the attention of Heinrich, a German officer based in the German Embassy, who happened to be speaking to Ben one afternoon when she was present. He commented on her fluency in English and was surprised to learn she spoke French and Flemish equally well. When he asked about her occupation, she replied saying she was looking for a position. Preferably something interesting and challenging where she could use her linguistic ability, maybe teaching? He suggested the Embassy, telling her he had connections and could arrange an interview; however not to be to disheartened if she was unsuccessful as very few females were employed in such work.

Nevertheless, Ruth impressed the interview panel and was offered a position as a translator. She was given the task of translating unclassified British tapes and letters, confidential work being assigned to more senior personnel. She initially saw this as a good start but very soon the work became monotonous and the repetitive, the routine began to get her down. When she came across Heinrich one afternoon and he enquired how she was enjoying the job she told him politely but honestly that she had hoped for a more challenging role, she found the work monotonous and felt there was no opportunity to develop her skills.

Heinrich understood but encouraged her to stick with it as it was highly probable that changes would be taking place before too long. This turned out to be indeed the case when, sooner than anticipated, there was a big reshuffle throughout the building. Previously empty rooms were furnished with office equipment. Large maps of France, Poland England and the rest of Europe now covered the walls.

There was an influx of new specialist staff in all areas. Ruth was summoned to Heinrich's office to be told she was to be reassigned. Her new role would involve more weighty documents, giving her the opportunity of working with interesting and challenging material. She gladly accepted the new position, leaving the office with a broad smile. It was, sadly, a move she would come to regret.

A large part of the new work involved translating letters and other documents confiscated from the homes and businesses of Jewish and non-German residents. Most were written in coded French or English. These she was able to encrypt with little difficulty but there were also many in Yiddish. She didn't dare admit to understanding these for fear of revealing her true identity.

One afternoon, feeling sick she excused herself and rushed to the ladies' room. She just made it before vomiting, as she felt horrified by what she had just seen. She had been passed a pile of papers, which had been taken from Jewish prisoners, to translate.

Reading through the torn and ragged scripts, some written in Yiddish, she was traumatised by the descriptions of detainees being starved to the point of death, beaten and treated worse than animals. No human, she thought, could treat a fellow human in such a manner. She had disliked the German attitude to Jews, but this was sickening to the extreme. Reading between the lines, she was even more disturbed that there was a suggestion of dissidents and Jews being publicly executed. There had been a reference to someone called the head-hunter, who had a portable guillotine, going around the country and decapitating people. She tried to dismiss this, but the painful thought lingered.

Now she abhorred the leaders of the Nazi regime. The so-called cleansing of the population from anything but true Aryan blood sent shivers down her spine. Schools were "cleansed" by removing Jewish children. Towns were "cleansed" by evicting and transporting dissidents and Jews to unknown destinations. Literature, religion, beliefs and philosophies were "cleansed" by destroying, confiscating or burning books and other artifacts.

Anger burnt deep inside Ruth.

The Spandau citadel was no longer open to visitors, signs clearly warning everyone to keep out. As Ruth walked along the road, two men came out and walked over the bridge. One of them in particular caught her eye, he was a handsome young man striding confidently, and on seeing her he nodded and smiled, she couldn't help but smile back. As she walked on, he caught up with her. She felt strangely unsure of herself, a little ill at ease but with an undercurrent of excitement.

Introducing himself as Max, he explained he was a veteran of the Great War, now a chemist working in the Spandau laboratories. They fell into step, chatting with ease and getting to know each other.

They soon realised they had similar attitudes toward the Third Reich, both disquieted about the direction their country was heading in, both concerned that the forces were so strong and so well organised that there was no way to halt it.

They talked for hours trying to come up with ways to turn the tide. The conversation triggered ideas in Ruth which she did not share with Max. Could she use her access to certain information to slow down the progress?

Her thoughts turned to her friend Sophia. Could she be trusted? Would it be wiser to go directly to Ben? The burgeoning plan brought a smile to her lips.

As they said goodbye, hopeful of meeting again, her smile was broader. The chance meeting proved to be a beginning. Just like a mountain brook flowing to the sea their relationship flowed, making its way through both peaceful and hazardous stretches, until their friendship developed into a deep and passionate love.

Chapter 27

Germany

It seemed a mistake had been made. Whoever was in charge of sifting through the papers, judging their significance and passing them onto the appropriate department had clearly missed these documents. A large, sealed envelope containing a pile of papers had been sent from a member of Hitler's staff. It was addressed to a senior ambassador and when it came to Ruth's attention it had been already opened. She considered what to do, looking through the glass panel on the door, she could see everyone was busy. She could not contain herself and quickly glanced through the pages. She was dumbfounded; if what she was reading was true, the repercussions could be immense.

How would other countries react? Surely this was suicide! What on earth was Hitler up to? The headed pages in front of her were copies of communications between the German government and the Soviet Union. Hitler had earlier agreed on a nonaggression pact with Russia. The proposals contained in the secret documents described the partitioning of Poland into two zones, the North to be occupied by Germany, the South by the Soviets. In order to achieve this, the plan was a German invasion of the Northern section of Poland under the command of Fedor Von Bock, and a Russian invasion of the southern section under the command of Gerd Von Rundstedt. Scribbled annotations highlighted the fact that involving Russia in this action would pre-empt any intervention by them should Germany invade Poland alone. It was Hitler's belief that these two nations joining forces to take Poland would serve as a warning to Britain and France and discourage them from any interference.

Other notes implied that in due course, the Soviet Union, having served its purpose would be next in Germany's sights. Ruth was alarmed when she realised this was not an outline for possible future action, but a date was set. September 1st. The invasion was to begin shortly!

It was now the beginning of August and the documents indicated that plans for the invasions were gathering momentum. Absolutely stunned, she realised that such action would surely bring other countries into the war, involving the whole of Europe. Germany had already suffered defeat in a war against French and British allies and was still paying the price. Was Hitler sane? He would be leading the country into another disaster. Ruth folded the papers and placed them back into the envelope.

She slipped them under a pile of other papers on her desk; she felt overwhelmed, had no idea how to handle this information. Should she alert French or British officials to these terrifying plans? This would be an act of treason; would she be letting her own country down? Conversely should she do nothing, allowing Hitler to lead Germany into war, endangering the lives of thousands of Polish people, innocent families would be wiped out. She had to do something but what? What could she do? These thoughts were violently disrupted by Heinrich rushing through the door.

"The envelope, have you seen an envelope?" He moved toward her desk, pushing the pile of papers aside, revealing the package. Grabbing it, he looked inside and seeing the contents seemingly undisturbed he relaxed a little. Looking directly at Ruth, in order to gauge her reaction, he asked, "Did you by any chance have a look inside?"

Ruth retained her poise and replied calmly, "I am so sorry; I have been extremely busy and have not had time to deal with them. Is it important? I will start right away."

She put out her hand to take the envelope, but Heinrich pulled back and apologising for disturbing her before hurriedly leaving the room. This interchange helped Ruth decide what to do. She must alert the British authorities. She would contact Ben as a matter of urgency.

That evening she met up with Max. He could see from the expression on her face that something was troubling her. After making him promise that he would keep the information secret Ruth revealed the contents of the envelope. He was outraged. His thoughts flashed back to the time when he was in the trenches in the Great War; he remained acutely aware of the pain and suffering brought about by war and this time it would be worse. Superior firepower on the battlefield. The bombing and burning of towns and countryside, it would be like facing another hell.

Ruth began to cry and he took her gently into his arms. Through her sobs she asked what he thought they could do, adding, "We must act to stop this! Get a message to The French or British, if they know about the plan, they could perhaps stop it with a threat of retaliation."

"I doubt that would work," replied Max. "But you are right, we must do something, and anything is worth a try."

They embraced and agreed she should talk to Ben, telling him all she knew in complete secrecy. Max wiped her tears, whispering that whatever happened he would always take care of her.

Ruth smiled quietly and said, "If there is to be a war it could not come at a worse time for us. I am pregnant!"

Now Max had tears in his own eyes "Thank you!" he murmured; his voice filled with emotion. "You have just turned a very bad day into one of the happiest in my life." Their tears fell, now not in pain but in love and joy.

Later that evening, Ruth contacted Sophia and asked if she would like to get together. Sophia invited her for lunch at her home the following Sunday. After lunch, Ruth managed to get some time with Ben on his own and told him all she had learnt.

He listened carefully, thanked her for being brave enough to tell him but with a wry smile added, "It may surprise you to hear this, but we already know!"

Chapter 28

Germany

As time rolled on Ruth and Max became more and more embroiled in their relationship. Ruth had decided to stay on in her own home for convenience sake, whilst Max continued to live close to his laboratory. This had been moved out from the citadel to a secret location. He often shared his rented home with his friend and colleague Gerhardt. For the time being it suited them both. On the 22nd of September 1938, Ruth gave birth to a baby boy. She named him Aaron, after her father. As soon as she was able, she hired a nanny to care for him and returned to her work in the embassy,

Ruth's fears proved to be right. Almost exactly a year later, on the 3rd of September 1939 the whole world was turned upside down! The same day that Germany and Russia invaded Poland, France and Britain declared war on Germany. It seemed another world war was on the horizon! The usual routine matters she was used to dealing with were superseded by matters relating to the conflicts. She memorised almost every scrap of information which came her way, passing them on to Ben. She took great care in doing this, never committing anything to writing and ensuring she was not followed.

Max was very disturbed to hear what was taking place with regards to the dissidents amongst the Jewish community. His frustrations often got the better of him and he couldn't help but vent his anger when talking with his friend and colleague Gerhardt. There would come a time when he would pay for letting his passion be expressed through his tongue overriding the dangers of careless talk.

There was history of bad blood between France and Germany going back centuries. France lost the territories of Alsace and

Lorraine in the Franco - Prussian battle, meanwhile Paris was also under siege and France was forced to surrender and pay Germany the sum of five million francs. This made it possible for Germany to become the strongest country in Western Europe and the Nazis determined to use this strength to their advantage.

Little by little, the information was passing through Ruth's department and was in turn passed on to Ben, so it came as no surprise when the ill-fated day of declaration of war arrived. The British embassy received notice that the eleven a.m. deadline for the withdrawal of Germany from Poland had passed. Britain was at war. Neville Henderson gathered all his ambassadors together in the large hall and stopped the clock. He told his staff to collect their belongings, clear their desks and prepare to leave. At approximately four p.m. all the telephone lines were cut and German soldiers together with Gestapo agents arrived detaining all staff. The nearby Hotel Aldon used to accommodate staff was also raided. All but the most senior staff were then transferred under guard to the holiday resort of Bad Nauheim where they were kept under confinement, awaiting final arrangements to be made through Swiss diplomats for the exchange of German and British staff. Ruth had already been aware of the plan and knew they would be repatriated to the United Kingdom on September 7th.

Just four days away. Later that evening she went to visit Max at home. He could sense her distress at the thought of losing her best friend who was due to be sent home. He was more concerned that Germany would now be at war with both France and with Britain, but tried to reassure Ruth saying that whilst France would be soon taken by the Germans Britain was a different matter, it was part of the commonwealth and also strongly allied with America, and so her friend would be safe there. They looked at each other, fear in their eyes about what was to come.

Ruth told him she could no longer pass on any information.

He frowned, putting his finger to his lips, then putting his hands over his ears, said in a light tone of voice, "We could do with a change of scenery."

Ruth understood the hidden message and suggested they go to her home and enjoy an evening with their son Aaron.

Max's suspicions proved to be right. Gerhardt had indeed been listening and as soon as they left picked up the phone.

The phone rang for some time before it was picked up. A sharp voice at the other end snapped, "What is it? Whoever you are get on with it!" He recognised Gerhards voice, listened, then slammed the receiver down.

"The bitch is a spy!"

Gerhardt had hardly slept; he was in a sullen mood. He wrestled with his conscience. His duty to his country had to come first. Germany was on the brink of becoming an enormously powerful nation controlling Europe but part of him thought he should have spoken to Max before making the fateful call. It wasn't Max who was betraying his country but Ruth. He had developed his friendship with Ruth, but such friendships were built on trust. She no longer deserved that trust and was no longer a friend. She had betrayed her own country, the very country which had nurtured her, protected her, and cultured her. She was the traitor, not Max.

Max still was a close friend and Gerhardt made a number of calls to senior ranking officers. He tried his utmost to convince them that Max was in no way involved in treason. It was his partner Ruth who was the turncoat.

Max had not taken part in any acts of sedition, and therefore was not at fault. Gerhardt had emphasised the important contribution Max had made to scientific research. He was a brilliant scientist who had recently played a part in the discovery of a new chemical which could and would change the whole outcome of the war. His pleading to exonerate Max from any compliance in passing secret information to the enemy seemed to have worked. Col,

Schmidt had made telephone contact stating that although it seemed Max was not complicit in espionage, he must have had some suspicion of Ruth's activities as she was privy to sensitive information in her work at the German Embassy, but Max neglected to raise any concerns. He should therefore expect some form of punishment. Since it was also known that Max had expressed views which were unfavourable to Germany's policies he would be sent to a facility where he would be taught the new cultural philosophy of the third Reich.

Ruth was another matter; she would have to pay the price for passing information to the enemy. She would be given the opportunity to reveal her contacts to mitigate her offences but would be sent to a correction centre where she would be employed doing work for Germany. Her child would be raised by adoptive parents who were faithful to Nazi ideals. The Colonel assured Gerhardt that neither would be given the death penalty or indeed physically harmed in any way. These assurances made him feel more at ease with himself, at least they would not have to endure torture.

The Colonel put the phone down, then immediately dialled the number of the garrison at Spandau. He spoke to the duty officer, ordering him to meet him at the laboratories without delay along with an escort of armed soldiers. He instructed another officer to apprehend Ruth at the embassy. She was to be taken prisoner, interrogated and then shot.

Gerhardt looked at his watch. 8.30am. He felt mentally exhausted.

Max's car pulled up outside. He and Ruth had spent most of the previous day together and both felt buoyant as they said goodbye. He was pleased to see Gerhardt but thought he looked pale and tired.

When he asked if he was all right, Gerhardt forced a smile, saying he had had a busy night.

"I hope you haven't forgotten our meeting with the Colonel," said Max. "Don't forget! We'll keep to the script then I'm sure things will go down all right."

Gerhard nodded. They drove off but when they neared the laboratories Max could see that the entrance was closed.

There were soldiers everywhere.

He turned to Gerhardt who simply shrugged his shoulders, saying nothing. One of the new guards examined their papers and let them through.

Looking in his rear-view mirror, Max saw that the man was on the telephone. He began to feel uneasy.

Chapter 29

Germany

The following morning Ruth prepared to leave earlier than usual. She fondly hugged Aaron before leaving him in the care of his nanny. Max had stayed the night but left early as he had arranged to meet up with his friend and colleague Gerhardt.

Something had happened at the laboratory which needed sorting out before a planned meeting with a senior officer. Gerhardt, as senior scientist, had insisted they got their heads together to plan their presentation.

On arrival at his home Max was met by a downcast Gerhardt. He seemed sullen and unhappy. "Cheer up," cried Max as he put his hand on his friend's shoulder. "We can sort things out – we'll baffle the grumpy Colonel with science!"

Gerhardt forced a smile. As they drove away Max could see Gerhardt seemed to be in a world of his own, staring blankly through the side window.

"Don't look so glum," he urged, "he is sure to be pleased with the results. We may even be awarded a medal for our discovery!"

Gerhardt shrugged his shoulders but didn't comment.

Puzzled, Max continued driving in silence. As they approached the barrier leading to the laboratory, he noticed an unusual amount of activity. There were armed soldiers everywhere. The barrier was raised and two of the soldiers checked their IDs. Gerhardt's papers were returned but the soldier held on to Max's as he waved them through. Glancing in his rear-view mirror, Max could see the man holding his papers was on the telephone.

He felt decidedly nervous! As he brought the car to a halt, Gerhardt, having been silent for the whole journey, finally spoke, "Our friendship means a great deal to me. Early this morning I made a call. I hope in time you will understand and one day feel able to thank me." With that he opened the door and walked out.

Ben was in the middle of shaving when the phone rang. Who could that be so early? He had a great deal to do. All the senior diplomats had been given time to collect their personal belongings. Others were not so lucky; their possessions were being transferred to Switzerland. He listened, it was a short and foreboding message.

His wife Helen came toward him, looking perplexed. "What now?" she asked.

"No time to explain," came the curt reply. "Get your coat on." He interrupted her next question snapping, "Just do it!"

She rushed away. Ben dressed quickly; he ran downstairs, calling for her to hurry. Helen stumbled down, hanging on to the banister. She was still wearing her dressing gown and slippers but there was no time to change so he bustled her through the side door to the garage. There, two armed guards, one German one Swiss blocked their way.

Ben pointed to his wife as he spoke in a tone of authority, "She is diabetic and urgently needs her insulin. I have called the doctor who is ready to give her a jab."

The German soldier replied, "Jab?"

"An injection, please she needs it straight away." Ben looked at the Swiss guard. "Please, you can come with us?" Then turned to the other man saying, "We will be just a short while."

The German shook his head doubtfully, he had a limited grasp of the English language. His associate, sensing the seriousness of the situation, explained further.

Ben added, "Look! She is not even dressed; we are not planning to escape, but without the insulin she could die."

Helen had twigged. She could see that something serious was happening, and began to babble, pretending to be sick. The Swiss soldier turned to his German counterpart, reassuring him he would escort them there and back. He gestured them into the car and jumped in himself. Ben pulled away leaving a very bemused German soldier behind. He put his foot down as he needed to get there before it was too late.

Minutes later, having claimed it was the doctor's house, he was knocking on Ruth's door. It was opened by the nanny.

Frowning, Ben shouted, "Where's Ruth?"

The nanny recognised him and replied, "She has only just left for work; she cannot be far away."

"She is in danger," whispered Ben. "Get the baby ready to leave. I will try to get to her. Please be quick!"

He turned and jumped back into the car, driving along the avenue leading to the German Embassy he spotted Ruth, strolling along seemingly without a care. Not wishing to alarm her, he slowed the car then pulled up alongside, and recognising him, she smiled broadly. "Get in the car," he said quietly and calmly.

Looking in the car Ruth was alarmed to see the soldier and Helen who was lying prone, seemingly distraught, in the back seat.

"Wait!" shouted the Swiss Guard. "What is this?"

"Don't worry," replied Ben. "She is the nurse who should have treated my wife at the house."

Getting out of the car, the soldier took out his pistol.

Ben raised his arms and nodded at Ruth, saying, "Get into the car, don't worry he is Swiss. They're gentlemen, they don't shoot ladies."

"You! You!" shouted the soldier, aiming his pistol at Ben.

"Please let me explain," said Ben, speaking steadily and gesticulating with palms down. "This lady works at the British Embassy. She has a young baby, and she is married to a man - not a good man, who treats her badly. The child is not his, and to protect her we have removed her from the embassy and hope to get her back to England without him knowing." Ben stretched out his arm, pulling up his sleeves.

As he did so, the soldier's pistol clicked.

Ben paused saying, "It's OK! Look!" He revealed his watch. A white Swiss timepiece. The soldier gazed at it. "It is brand new, a Rolex tonneau shaped watch in pink gold complete with a gold strap." Looking the young soldier directly in the eye he continued, "I was presented this by William Anderson himself in return for service to the country. It could be yours. If you help this lady, get away from here and join the Embassy staff. The soldier glared as if in anger but then his expression slowly changed to one of pleasure. Nodding, he said, "I can get rid of that stupid German, leave it to me." He held out his hand for the watch. "Only when she is safely away. I give you my word!"

The soldier nodded in agreement.

They drove back to Ruth's house where she said farewell to the nanny. Handing her the keys to the house Ruth told her she could stay as long as she pleased. The nanny kissed the baby with tears in her eyes and watched as the car and its other occupants drove back to Ben's house.

As he drove, Ben clarified the situation. "This morning I had a call from someone calling you a traitor. The German authorities know you have been passing on information. Had you entered the embassy you would have been arrested."

Ruth closed her eyes, feeling helpless, what would happen to her now? "I'd better explain, nothing of significance has been given and..."

Ben interrupted her.

"Ruth! Think! They will shoot you!"

"My baby! Aaron! What will happen to him?" Her whole body shook from a mixture of fear and grief.

Ben spoke evenly in hushed tones, "There may be a way, it would be painful initially but hopefully given time matters will be resolved." Baby Aaron could become part of the repatriation group. He would easily blend in and there were several women from the embassy who could pose as his mother.

When they reached Ben's home the German guard was surprised to see them all get out of the car. The Swiss Guard explained she was their private nurse assigned by the embassy. He was going to travel with them to get the required medication and escort them to join the others facing deportation. He suggested that the German soldier re-join his unit. Ben congratulated everyone on keeping calm, however he described how they were facing an obstacle. Ruth had no papers. She was a German citizen and if discovered, her identity would be easily revealed.

At this point Ruth intervened, asking why they had gone to so much trouble on her behalf. She had played along with them, but why so much fuss? He had even given away his precious watch. Surely a gesture too far. Ben smiled. "Don't worry about that. It's a copy. Fools everyone, including his nibs the Swiss Guard." For the first time in a while, they all smiled.

"My dear." Ben regarded her with a sombre expression and a hint of tears in his eyes. "It's imperative to get you away from here to somewhere safe. Once the German regime have identified someone as a spy, they will move heaven and earth to catch them. They will have already set the wheels in motion. They will be watching the Embassy, possibly even this house but we have a small window of opportunity to evade them if we leave now. We need to act. Leave everything and go!"

They packed a few essentials into the embassy limousine. Helen sat in the rear with the baby whilst Ruth was hidden away in the spacious boot. The Swiss guard sat in the front. Hopefully his presence would act as a smokescreen.

distracting suspicious eyes. He was earning his reward simply by being there.

Fifteen minutes later they neared the rendezvous point. They planned to travel by train from Berlin to Bad Nauheim, but it would be too risky for Ruth to join them.

Before leaving, Ben had contacted a member of the secret service based in Berlin. They had become trusted partners in unearthing useful information and passing it on to British intelligence. He had hinted that Ruth may be of use to his organisation as she spoke several languages. First and foremost, however, was the task of getting Ruth to a place of safety.

Ben stopped the car on a side road and after checking there was no one around helped Ruth out. He led Ruth to a small café, leaving the others in the car. Once inside he took a sheaf of papers from his small case. He told her he sincerely hoped she would be reunited with Aaron before too long, but maybe just in case she would care to write a letter to him. He could read it when he was old enough to understand. He informed her they would do their utmost to get her back to Britain but deep-down Ruth knew they were unlikely to succeed. It was probable that she would be caught. The German hounds would now be picking up her scent. Hurriedly, she composed the letter including pieces of personal information along with some photos. Sealing it in an envelope with a heavy heart and tears running down her cheeks, she addressed it to a Jewish family who now lived in Reading, England.

She felt sick and empty. Would she see Max again? Would he miss her, or be upset when she was no longer there? What would happen to him now she was labelled as a spy? If she was in danger, so was he. She just couldn't cope with the awfulness of the situation. Her body folded as her tears flowed. The café owner rushed over in concern.

Ben calmed him by saying, "It's the war, she is frightened for her family." He understood and left them in peace.

Ruth took some deep breaths and tried to regain her composure. The tears soon dried, leaving her feeling lifeless but with an inner determination to be reunited with her son. Ben noticed the envelope, which was dotted with marks made by her tears, was addressed to Gershom and asked Ruth why it said Gershom and not Aaron.

Ruth replied with sorrow in her voice, "Gershom was the firstborn son of Moses. Aaron is my first born and will be living in a strange place. The name simply means he is living in exile in a place where he does not truly belong."

Ben was filled with emotion at Ruth's words. They held each other and the tears flowed once more.

Helen came in and touched Ben gently. It's time! As Helen and Ben left a man named Joseph came and sat beside Ruth.

Joseph ordered coffee; Ruth declined. He explained that they could not be seen leaving with British embassy officials, they would stay for a while. There are eyes everywhere just like praying mantises ready to pounce on their unsuspecting victim. After a short time, Joseph scanned the area outside the windows, satisfied they were not being watched he spoke to the proprietor, paid, then indicated to Ruth that she should stay put. He went outside, stood for a while feeling in his pockets as though something was missing then went back indoors. He took Ruth by the arm and they left together.

After walking a few paces, he led her a short distance down a narrow alleyway. They stood with Joseph in front of Ruth, shielding her from the entrance. He took out his Mauser HSc, primed it and looked over his shoulder at Ruth. "Just in case," he said with a wink and a smile. "Everything is fine." After a few moments, which seemed an age to Ruth, he peered cautiously around the corner, and once satisfied that all was clear they headed back to the café. Within minutes a car drew up and they clambered in. "Sorry about all that but we had to be sure all was well. Please keep your face away from the window, we will soon be there."

Almost a week had passed, and Ruth became very restless. There had been no news of her baby or Max. How long would she be holed up here; she needed to get away but where? Nowhere was safe anymore.

That evening Joseph returned with good news. "Your son, Aaron," he began.

"Gershom," Ruth corrected him.

"Of course, sorry. Gershom, he arrived in England on Thursday."

She jumped up and hugged him. "And Max, any news of Max?"

"He was sentenced to death but somehow managed to escape with two others. He's alive!"

Hugging him a second time she asked, "Do we know any more?"

"Only that he was found guilty of subversion but was rescued by the two men and all three seemed to have disappeared. Regretfully, I do also have some bad news."

Ruth paled.

"Your nanny was taken into custody and badly treated during questioning. Sadly, she died from her injuries. Your house has been confiscated and ransacked but whatever they were looking for, they did not find. There is a country wide search for you." Ruth was visibly shaken but Joseph hadn't finished. "The young Swiss Guard who accompanied you has been sent back to Switzerland; but not before he returned Ben's watch, which was genuine by the way. Evidently, if a soldier takes a bribe, it is tantamount to treason. In order to avoid the consequences, he was given the option of driving to the train station and returning it personally."

"That's something a little positive in all this heartache," said Ruth "But what about the German soldier?"

Joseph shook his head. "He met the usual fate for failing in his duty, he was shot."

Ruth was stiff with anger, her eyes blazed and with clenched fists she banged on the table, kicked the furniture and was just stopped in time from throwing an ornament at the window. She clawed and wrestled as Joseph held her. "The bastards! The evil, ugly Nazis. I'll kill them. I will kill every one of them."

Joseph held her at arm's length. "So, you shall," he said. "And I will help you. We are leaving Berlin tomorrow and heading for Alsace where all the action is taking place."

Chapter 30

France

As the occupation of France dragged on, the underground movement were on the defensive; the Gestapo had infiltrated their networks, resulting in many being rounded up and shot. It was now imperative that members treated everyone with suspicion, including friends and family. Ruth had a very close network which operated outside the main organisation. It included a number of people working in menial jobs for members of the Third Reich.

A new informant, called Agata, had recently been hired as a servant in the home of Otto Geiger, a senior, and loyal official in the Nazi organisation. Hired as a kitchen helper, Agata's background was interesting. She came from a distinguished Polish academic family, and at seventeen had been assessed as having a photographic memory, coupled with a high IQ. Tragically, when Agata was eighteen, the family was involved in an horrific motor accident. She lost both her parents, and she survived but her injuries had been severe. She also suffered a total loss of hearing along with her power of speech. The medics failed to find a physical cause for this and put it down to the trauma of the accident. They offered some hope that she would recover in time, but it was possible she would be deaf and dumb for life.

Now in her mid-twenties, her tall, slender figure, blonde hair and blue eyes set her apart from most Polish women. She had inherited a graceful and confident walk and demeanour from her barrister parents. She had studied at the prestigious Jagiellonian University in Krakow, where despite her injuries she had excelled in the sciences, obtaining a doctorate by the age of twenty four. As well as Polish, she spoke English, German and French, and had quickly learned to communicate with signing and lip-reading across languages. Her amazing memory unaffected by the accident, she was able to recall pages of words and pictures, almost after a glancing view. All this meant she was able to mentally store a vast amount of knowledge and communicate it to a wide range of people.

When the German army swept through Poland, she had been taken prisoner, evacuated to France and ended up as a kitchen maid in the home of Otto Geiger, a powerful financier and loyal follower of Hitler. Most Polish female prisoners were put to work in factories, or as domestic workers for the higher ranks of German officers.

Otto's house manager, looking over new arrivals for staff, had been struck by Agata's attractiveness and employed her as a dishwasher. Otto, in his visits to the kitchen, noticed her graceful demeanour and had her upgraded to serve at table. He was pleased to discover Agata was deaf and dumb as this had the added advantage of security. Many important business magnates and Nazi party members were invited to the house, carousing at Otto's table, enjoying vintage French wines and brandy confiscated from the cellars of wealthy Jewish families. The rich food and lavish hospitality frequently caused tongues to loosen. As the course of the war vacillated, and Germany appeared to be losing ground rapidly, there were often nuggets of highly sensitive information being discussed and shared. It suited Otto that the maid who waited on them could neither hear these nor pass them on.

On several occasions as she waited at the table, Otto would casually taunt and make fun of her. She played along with this, thinking to herself that they little knew what they were really dealing with. She would lean over the table, revealing her shapely bust, and even move to pick things up from the floor to show off her legs and pert backside, all the time knowing their vulgar comments made them less suspicious of her, as to them she just appeared a dumb and ignorant peasant girl.

As they drank and talked, she memorised all the information they let drop, using her lip-reading skills. As the weekly meetings went on, she gained a full insight into what they were plotting.

Chapter 31

Alsace

Otto sat at his desk, his stomach cramping with anguish, as he read through the incoming reports. The tide was turning against Germany, victory ebbing away as her enemy's gathered strength and momentum. The bombing of the US fleet at Pearl Harbour, bringing the USA into the war, with fresh troops and a war chest to renew the Allies; the catastrophic campaigns in North Africa; the lost battles against Russia; all were leading to Germany's undoing, of this he felt certain.

What would be the outcome for the German people? Defeat, surrender and humiliation, for the second time.

Otto Geiger was short in stature but lofty in power. He was now in his early forties, completely bald with bulging eyes and thin lips, which combined to give him the look of a malevolent toad when he smiled, which was rarely. The set of his head on his shoulders, with a very short neck, made his chin appear to sit on his chest, while his lightless dark brown eyes set above jutting cheeks gave him a menacing air. His personality matched his appearance - he was not a man to meddle with. His enemies were few - most of them had been disposed of along his way to power. An extremely intelligent man, he was also an opportunist, frequently pouncing before the unsuspecting victim had managed to take his measure.

He was hated and admired in equal proportion; his ruthlessness and cunning had made him the first port of call when difficult tasks needed to be completed. Those in authority relied on him to solve seemingly impossible issues, they did not look too closely at how he did it. He was fond of dogs, disliked most people and hated Jews, being proud of his own Aryan descent. Hitler was his idol, and Otto was always intent on helping the Nazi war machine to triumph; he dreamed constantly of ways to defeat the British and the Americans. His mission was to regenerate Germany, to mitigate the carnage wrought on her people, cities and industries. Germany would reignite its economic power, and the Allies would pay the price! Although Germany's defeat would leave them with a weak hand, he thought he held the trump cards, gambling on Russia being at odds with Britain and America about sharing the spoils of victory. He believed Britain would want to rebuild a broken Germany rather than see it become a foothold for the Soviets and Marxism. Berlin would be restored to its former glory, and the Russians kept at bay.

Within months, Otto Geiger's cohort had produced outline plans for the rebuilding of factories, updating of existing manufacturing plants, reconstruction of bombed areas; the industries studied included car manufacturing moving on to production of specialised machinery for essential goods. It was not possible to cover everything - they concentrated on those which would speedily renew wealth and prosperity; they were confident that even if surrender was the inevitable outcome of the war, they had the will and resolve to ensure a better future.

To achieve this, they needed to accrue a vast amount of wealth, and Otto had included two international financiers in his inner circle. As the German mark would be of little value, they needed another source, a more desirable means of exchange. Blockades by the British meant Germany was starved of raw materials and finished product - theirs would be a bankrupt country with a dejected people. But there was another way! Otto had stood before the group and explained that the financiers were part of an intricate network, their fingers fine-tuned to play a keyboard controlling every section of society.

If Germany failed, they would set up a new power hub in Argentina or South America. Vast holdings of the Jewish bankers had been confiscated, many sold and still available on the market; other assets, such as gold, jewellery and fine arts were being siphoned off in preparation for defeat. Puffing out his chest and speaking with pompous emphasis, he told them he knew of a vast honey pot!

As the weeks went by, the meetings continued, with more and more guests, but Agata noticed the format now changed, with Otto dismissing members of the conspiracy while an inner core of his group remained. It was obvious they were working on a very specific plot, and she would concentrate on finding unobtrusive tasks which brought her into the room and allowed her to lip read vital conversations. One evening, as she was pouring brandy for the guests, she was taken aback to realise this was a cabal working independently from both the military and government organisations. They were discussing means to bring the war with Britain to an end - and to do this with a devastating attack on London.

Increasingly she became extra vigilant, and careful to commit details to memory - gradually the picture emerged of a V2 rocket attack which would be launched somewhere in Amsterdam. The V2 had been developed to travel further and carry a heavier payload. The British with their aerial photography were the fly in the ointment, pinpointing where the rockets were being stored. They had also developed new shells which could pierce the armour surrounding the rocket defences. The new plan was to store the missiles on railway carriages, which could move them at short notice; importantly, Agata found out where the rockets were to be stored in Amsterdam before being moved.

Another meeting was attended by a new recruit, a high-ranking colonel whose name she had not yet discovered; he was in charge of a secret chemical factory at Falkenhagen, about seventy km from Berlin.

Whatever they were producing, it was in large quantities - a liquid with a name she could only make out as "sah-rin". Those present were claiming that if a V2 rocket were aimed at London and other cities, it would have such an impact it would end the war! An ordnance officer from the same factory, known only as RK had joined, and explained to the group that the liquid turned into a deadly nerve gas when exposed to the air; Polish workers exposed to minute quantities had died in agony at the factory. On another occasion, Otto read from a letter sent by RK referring to the workforce of Polish prisoners as "a bunch of silent walking corpses, creeping about as thin as rakes.... Or beanstalks, if that wasn't too insulting to the beans! Herr Hitler has the right idea; we must generate the perfect Aryan race... eradicating the Poles will be a good beginning!"

Agata understood, and clenched her fists. Somehow this evil man and his friends should be made to pay.

At last, the finer details began to be discussed; Otto was planning his devastating chemical attack on London for Thursday 20th April 1944 - The birthday of the Fuhrer. The rocket would be launched just after midnight - the effect of the toxic gas in darkness would enhance the panic and terror, the population of the nation's capital would be annihilated, and the British government, faced with the fact that Germany could do the same to all their cities, would be forced to surrender.

Realising this made Agata feel sick; she went about with a dark cloud over her mind for day after day. She felt utterly helpless. What could she do? How could she get this information to someone, to warn them? Her movements were monitored, and she was not allowed to leave the building. Sitting depressed and uneasy by the basement kitchen fire one cold March day, she became aware that the kitchen porter Joseph was having a conversation with the butcher's delivery man. Focusing intently on their faces, she realised Joseph, although Polish, was speaking fluent French with the man, and was detailing the movements of various personnel visiting the house. Much of it seemed trivial, but Agata realised the delivery man was paying close attention and getting as much information as possible. She realised this could be a means to get information out - it was abundantly clear to her analytical mind that this man must be involved in picking up news for the French resistance. She needed to talk to him.

Agata lay in the darkness staring at the ceiling. She couldn't sleep as there was too much at stake and time was running out. She needed a plan to get the information she had gleaned about the destruction of London out of the house and to someone who could warn Britain about the impending catastrophe. She finally decided she would take the risk and contact the butcher's delivery man in the hope he would help her. There was a problem, he could well be an informer in which case she would be signing her own death warrant.

Communication would also be a massive problem she would have to devise a way of getting the message across to him in the first instance; in order to do this, she would have to put the information into written form. Putting everything in writing would be a dangerous ploy, if the information was intercepted, she again would be in a precarious situation.

Her future at the moment held little promise, and she was prepared to take up the challenge. If she was caught sending the message the consequences were little compared to the outcome if the message did not get through. She knew the approximate time the delivery man came each morning, somehow, she would attract his attention and engineer a position to be alone with him. The chances were pretty remote, but she was determined to try. Suddenly a thought came to her, quietly she got out of bed and wrapped a blanket round her shoulders. Gently opening the door, she crept out of her bedroom. It was about three a.m. She crossed the landing and felt for the banister. She followed it along until she came to the stairs, creeping down slowly until she was at the bottom.

In the hallway there was a small pilot light, she could just make out the doorway to the games room. Quietly turning the handle, she pushed the heavy door open. As it closed behind her she was left in complete darkness. She had been in the room on several occasions serving wine to the gentleman who played at the billiard table. Stretching out to her arms she slowly shuffled toward where the table might be only to bump into a chair. She paused, totally disorientated since there shouldn't be a chair as all the furniture was usually placed against the wall, and also the chair seemed to be facing the wrong way. She cleared her head, someone must have moved the chair and not replaced it to where it should have been. Placing a hand on the arm of the chair, she moved forward with the other arm outstretched. Suddenly, on the flat seat of the chair she felt something, she smiled to herself. It was what she was looking for. Someone must have sat at the chair taking the stick of chalk they used for keeping the dartboard score with them and left it behind.

She made her way back to the door, and froze. An unmistakable faint pattern of light appeared round the door frame. Someone was opening it. With nowhere to hide, instinct made her rush to the side of the door so that when it opened, she would be hidden behind it. The door half opened, and the lights switched on. The noise of bumping into the chair must have aroused one of the night guards. She pressed herself against the wall and prayed. The door opened wider; it began to press against her. She strove to stay still and held her breath. It seemed an age, someone was holding the door open whilst scanning the billiard room. Eventually the door slowly closed, and still petrified she dared not move. She stayed there for several minutes fearing that whoever was there might still be listening. She was just about make her move when the door suddenly flew open again, she grasped in fright. A torchlight shone in her face. She fell to her knees. The shock had paralysed her.

There was a moment of silence, and she heard the door close. The light was switched on, she looked at the carpet, dreading what was about to happen. A hand took her elbow and gently raised her to her feet. Slowly she raised her head; standing in front of her now was the kitchen helper.

Luckily it was his turn to be on the night shift. Placing his finger to his lips, he turned off the light and escorted her back to her bedroom. As he led her into the room, sorrow filled him as he gazed upon her. Her whole body was shaking with fear. He sat down beside her, placing his arm around her shoulders as she cried uncontrollably. He took a hand, and as he did so he felt the chalk. He immediately realised why she had it. He had often looked at her, young and beautiful, yet trapped inside her body, behaving in a manner which exhibited no contact with the outside world. Realising the chalk would be a way of expressing herself through writing, he wondered why she hadn't used a pencil or pen. He searched into his top pocket and pulled out the pencil and offered it to her. She shook her head as she took a pencil and placed it underneath her pillow. She took the chalk and made a mark on the wooden floor, then she looked at him, wet her fingers and rubbed it off. He realised that whatever she was intending to write had to be removed instantly, and he wondered why.

She stopped crying, he looked into her eyes. Seeing they were still full of tears, he searched for his handkerchief and gently dried them. How beautiful she looked; her eyes were sad as she looked at him but for the first time, he saw her smile. He gently held her face between his hands as with both their eyes still open, he lowered his head and gently kissed her on her lips. He could feel her warm breath on his cheeks it was slowly beginning to quicken. Lowering his arms, he folded them around her and gently pulled her closer toward him.

A new kind of chemistry filled her mind and heart. Her Innocence ebbed away as he embraced her closer and closer. Her heart pounded; her thoughts were confused yet excited. He felt her warm breasts as her passion gave way to a long sigh. He turned off the lights, and they held each other in the darkness.

Chapter 32

Alsace

Within a few days, Agata and Joseph had found ways to communicate; as they worked together on the information Agata had to impart, a special fondness sprang up. Her isolation from being unable to communicate was now replaced by a feeling of purpose, but also of newfound trust and joy as she and Joseph became close. By teaching him to lip read, Agata was able to share her feelings of revulsion about the treatment of their countrymen, and anxiety about the London plan. He was horrified and resolved to do something about this. Everything he knew must be committed to memory, there must be no paper trail for Otto to find; he now realised and valued Agata's cleverness and bravery - he was in love with her and wanted to protect her from discovery.

Time was growing short, the 20th April loomed.

They now had to plan how to get time alone with Jules, the butcher's man; Joseph recognised that Jules would not be capable of memorising all the information that needed to be shared - nothing for it but to commit details to paper, but they had to seize the right moment to hand over such dangerous material. The housekeeper demanded that the butcher's boy deliver the same time every morning, and it was imperative that Joseph be in the kitchen when he called. They planned for Agata to create a diversion at the moment of handover, to distract the housekeeper and any others present. Several days passed before one cold, wet morning, the young man staggered in with a heavy basket of meat.

The housekeeper had left the room when the almighty crash of crockery smashing on the stone floor made the other maids spin round to see Agata standing amongst the debris; Joseph stepped up to Jules, pressing the note he had kept hidden into his hand, and impressing him with the vital need for secrecy. He enjoined him fiercely to get the information relayed urgently, thousands of lives depended on it. As he took the basket of meat from Jules, he patted him on the shoulder with a serious, commanding look, and almost pushed him out of the door. The housekeeper, hurrying back in to discover the nature of the commotion, noticed this unusually strict and intense manner on Joseph's part and wondered at it... But then she became distracted, scolding Agata.

A few days later, Joseph and Jules managed a few words - the message had been passed on, much to Joseph's relief. He now warned Jules, however, that he should make himself scarce before April 20th. If the plot was successfully wrecked, Otto would soon be on the warpath; there would be a witch-hunt, and it wouldn't take them long to guess how information had been leaked from the house. This meant Agata too, was at risk, he must plan for her escape; she, meanwhile, was anxiously watching the clock ticking closer and closer to Hitler's birthday.

The following evening, Joseph came to Agata in her room, and took her gently in his arms, explaining that it was time for her to go - she looked around, preparing to pack, but he put a hand on her arm and told her, "You must leave everything - someone is waiting."

Agata gazed at him, tears in her eyes; both shook with emotion as they held each other and kissed - was it for the last time? They crept through the dark kitchen and the cloud obscured garden to the tall iron gates. It was only two days now to the planned attack; they paused, and embraced again fervently, each silently wondering if they would ever meet again.

Joseph released her, whispering, "I will find you when all this is over!" and she stepped back, watching him thread his way back to the house. She felt Ruth's hand on her shoulder. Turning, she saw a warm smile, felt an understanding squeeze of her hand, and they left.

Ruth introduced herself, guiding Agata away.

Looking directly at her and illuminating her own face with the torch thus making it possible for her to lipread, Ruth comforted Agata. She said, "Don't worry, we will keep you safe, you will be in good hands, and from what I have heard of Joseph, he will move Heaven and Earth to find you. You deserve to be happy together."

Joseph and Agata had been careful to conceal their growing love for one another, so he was able to feign detachment about her escape the next day. He had been careful to remove the spare set of keys from the storeroom. Agata would have known about them, and this would explain her ability to get out of the house while he, on night duty, had been patrolling the other side. It was a large building, after all, and easy enough to avoid others in the dark. If questioned, he was ready with a story of how Agata had become increasingly unhappy, feeling claustrophobic and pleading for someone to take her out of the house; her inability to communicate had made her feel as if she was in her own personal prison. Perhaps she had runaway to kill herself.

The route Joseph had chosen for Agata led from the back gates and into a small area of woodland. Ruth and Agata had to pick their way carefully, but when they reached a clearing, Ruth stopped, and turned her torch on her face so Agata could see her. A mixture of alarm and relief flooded through Agata as Ruth explained that a light aircraft would be picking them up in about two hours' time from an airstrip; they would be taken to England, where she would be safe. There was a car nearby to take them to the airstrip.

Hurriedly, she gave Agata some papers. "These give you a new identity. If we are stopped and questioned, I will answer for you, explaining your disability - I shall tell them your deafness was caused by a bomb dropped by the filthy British swine." She smiled. "Hopefully that will get them on our side and we'll get through."

Suddenly she noticed Agata was holding some papers held together with string.

Agata offered them to Ruth, indicating they were important; with time pressing, Ruth didn't look at them but put them into her satchel.

At the end of the copse, Agata was alarmed by a figure emerging from the bushes, but looking to Ruth received a thumbs up indicating that everything was OK. They all slipped quietly into the waiting car.

Suddenly the smell of leather upholstery assailed Agata with memories of the car accident and her parents' death. Unable to explain, she lowered her head onto her knees, and prayed. The car cautiously made its way, the driver stopping before each crossroads to make sure there were no Germans present. The two hour journey felt like eternity, but eventually they arrived at an open field, and people were running around, lighting what appeared to be small torches. The strip of land ran away into the darkness, appearing to go on forever. Almost immediately, Ruth pointed up in the air to small points of light in the sky, approaching low and slow.

The aircraft landed and taxied towards them; Ruth grabbed her hand and they ran toward it as it slowed to a stop, the engine still running. The aircraft swung around and a door opened; they could see a figure inside beckoning them to hurry. This was not a place to hang around.

Suddenly the darkness was filled with light and gunfire erupted; tracer bullets were flying in all directions. German soldiers were closing in. The pilot revved the engine, with bullets ripping through the fuselage. He could see the two women running toward the plane and manoeuvred as close as he dared. Only a few yards from the plane, Agata was hit in her upper arm. Strangely, she felt no pain as her hand was torn from Ruth's grasp and she fell to the ground, the pain kicking in as she landed.

Bullets flying all around, the engine revving, and the open door just in her reach, Ruth knew she had no option but to throw herself onboard. She had vital papers that must get to London. As she was dragged aboard, she heard the resistance team open fire on the Germans, and glimpsed two figures hauling Agata away into cover.

A large hand forced her prone on the floor as bullets continued to pierce the thin fabric of the fuselage. The pilot, accelerating down the strip now found a small group of German soldiers had taken up position at the end of the runway.

All he could do was head straight toward them, turning off the headlights as he did so. Bullets glanced off the metal frame of the windscreen, deflecting them from their target, he was pleased to note. He estimated he was close to the end of the strip, hauled back on the joystick and took off into darkness. He felt a heavy thump on the wheel, one of the soldiers he hoped, but it caused the plane to waver and lose altitude, bringing it closer to the top of the trees.

"Oh God!" he shouted, as his propellor sliced branches.

Seconds later, he realised God had heard his prayer, he was clear of trees and Germans, and on his way home via the white cliffs of Dover. Feeling relaxed, he called Ruth asking her to come to the front.

As she got up one of the engines began to splutter, "Those trees, fucking trees, fucking Germans," no sooner had he cursed one engine when the other one cut out. "Get back, make yourself as safe as possible, don't worry I'll get us down safely." He held his hands firmly and pulled hard on the wheel as he tried to gain altitude, hoping the one damaged engine would enough to get them away far enough before ditching the plane. He was above the trees; he could hardly make out what lay beneath him. He knew the only clearing in the area was the one he had just landed on. Landing in the trees would be certain suicide. "Sorry love, we'll have to turn back, pray the engine get will us there, it's our only chance, hang tight."

He managed to slowly turn the plane in a wide arc, barely clear of the trees. "They won't be expecting us back, if we're captured, I'll tell them I've come back for fags."

Ruth didn't hear him, the sound of the engine and her attempts to protect herself from the crash landing were foremost in her mind. If she survived, her future was bleak, torture then execution would follow, so it was best to die on the plane. But there were the papers, and she knew she must somehow deliver them. She struggled back to the pilot, being buffeted and thrown around as the single engine, a good old merlin engine did its utmost to keep them in flight. The plane completed the circuit, the pilot was pleased to see there were still some flares alight. At least he could just make out the extent of the runway.

"Hold tight darling, I'm setting up for approach." He'd just finished, when she arrived at his side. "Get down, you stupid cow!" he said calmly in his public-school accent, which almost brought a smile to Ruth's face. Both facing imminent death and there he was unperturbed as though he was punting down the river Cam. "I need your gun." She looked around the cockpit. "In the pouch behind my seat, it's a spare one, I know you've some special stuff to deliver, don't worry we'll get it there." With that he made his final manoeuvre and headed towards the runway. "Arse up, tits down and here we go! Get down and hang on!"

With only one damaged engine, the plane rocked and seesawed as it touched down. He pulled back on the rudder and slammed on the breaks. The plane swung round almost in a full circle. Ruth bounced and rolled before coming to her feet, and she stood for a few seconds, satisfied she was still in one piece, and made for the door. The pilot was already there, he opened it and jumped out in one movement with his pistol at the ready. "Quick, he'd hardly finished the word before Ruth was at his side. "That way, head for the trees and keep going." Shots began to spray the fuselage. "Now! Go!" he yelled pushing her away from the plane. "Crawl under the plane, keep low and run, see you in Soho sometime, I'm going to be keeping them busy."

The shooting increased as she followed his instructions. The trees were close by; he'd done his best to land in the best position to give her a fighting chance. Once in the forest she ran as fast as she dared in the darkness, bumping into tree trunks and branches. She could hear the gunfire continuing, hopefully he would make an escape or be captured alive. She somehow doubted it. When the firing suddenly stopped, she knew that he'd gone.

As she continued, she was determined to get to England with the parcel, praise the pilots' braveness, and say a prayer for him in Piccadilly Circus before turning down to Soho. She could hear firing in the distance, however strangely she wasn't being pursued. Somehow, she would have to meet up with Joseph, and she had to get to London. There of course was the package to deliver, also a much more important and personal reason was her baby son Gershom. Suddenly, in all the drama and confusion she remembered, Joseph was on his way to the Netherlands. There was an underground partisan cell which would help track down Otto's conspirators. Agata, had managed to produce documentation that would give him the authority to travel distances as a personal courier to Otto. Ruth smiled as she imagined the look on Otto's face when he realised that his prized Zundapp K500 motorbike was missing.

The following morning, with Agata missing from her duties, a thorough search of the house and gardens took place. The housekeeper discovered that keys had gone missing, so Agata had let herself out during the night. The staff joined in discussions of her mood, which had changed a lot recently; she had been tense and anxious - someone suggested she had been pleading to be taken out... she had clearly decided to flee... perhaps she was unhinged.

When Otto heard about this, he was angry that the security of his house had been breached.

However, when the keys were found in the gate, he felt relieved. After all, she was only a stupid peasant mute, and would probably shortly end her days in some filthy ditch. He gave Joseph a beating and put him on permanent night watch duty. Joseph felt his wounds were nothing. He felt wonderful knowing she was now safe, but also terrible because of the anguish of continuing without her.

Meanwhile, during Ruth's escape Agata had been spotted by two partisans who raised her to her feet. They ran toward the edge of the trees, half dragging half carrying the limp Agata. Despite her wound, she made little sound except for a quiet moaning. The German soldiers were rapidly gaining on them; tempting the two partisans to leave her and make good their own escape. They lowered her to the ground.

On seeing this, Agatha, the senior resistance officer screamed out, "Don't! Don't you dare!"

The men looked toward Agatha, then took another grip on Agata. Raising her to her feet with renewed energy they pulled her into the shelter of the woods.

Agatha directed them to take her straight to the truck, saying she would distract the pursuing German soldiers. She would attempt to lead them away whilst they made their escape.

"Good Luck!" called the partisans as they headed to the track. Looking behind, Agatha saw the flashlights of the soldiers quickly closing in on her. She waved her torch toward them as she sped into the wood in the opposite direction to her comrades. Hopefully her actions would allow them enough time to get away.

Her flashlight attracted the soldier's attention. She dodged in and out of the trees as they pursued her. A hail of bullets rained all around, hitting trees, snapping branches and chipping the bark.

"Missed, You Bastards!" she muttered as she dodged and took another direction whilst continuing to flash her torch.

The gun shots were getting louder making her aware that they were closing in on her. She decided to take a risk, she had no option. Hoping her plan would work, she jammed her torch tightly into a cleft of a hanging branch. Pulling the branch slightly to make the torchlight sway, Agatha took a deep breath, looked toward the heavens then doubled back in the direction of the soldiers. After a while, she dived into the undergrowth and lay perfectly still. It was a risky tactic, but the darkness was in her favour. The soldiers would be likely to direct their lights upwards and with any luck her position would not be revealed. They were getting closer, so close she could hear the sound of their uniforms brushing against the branches. She froze, closing her eyes tightly. The running stopped.

"Where the fuck is she?"

"Over here!" came the reply.

"The light is over here." The soldiers ran on.

She waited and then rose silently and made her way back to the airstrip. When she was satisfied the coast was clear she headed down the track which led to the hidden truck.

Agata became conscious that the soft grass underfoot had changed to a hard, rough surface. Her feet hurt as she was dragged along so she struggled to stand and managed to stumble forward between her two supporters. They were relieved at not needing to support her weight any more allowing them to make better progress.

After a time, they slowed down looking around they took the risk of turning on their torches. They were relieved and pleased to find what they were hoping for. An iron gate was completely covered in bushes and other foliage, camouflaging an entrance way. Even in daylight it would be difficult to see what lay behind this seemingly dense 'hedge.' The two men listened carefully ensuring no one was around, unlocked the gated and pushed it open. One of them guided Agata through as the other closed the swinging gate behind them.

"Thank God! We've made it," said one of the men, the other replied, "Bloody ingenious, building this hideaway for vehicles so close to the airstrip." They helped Agata into the rear seat of the truck, then gesturing for her to be quiet they covered her with a soft blanket. They replaced the camouflage netting over the truck, making it almost impossible to detect in the dark. They then went and stood behind the gate listening for any activity. They did not have to wait long, soon they could pick out headlights from several trucks heading their way. The pursuing Germans! Throwing themselves to the ground they pulled their guns out at the ready. True partisans, they would do their utmost to protect their injured comrade. She had been prepared to put her life on the line.

Aware how vile Agata's fate would be, should she be captured they considered the alternative - to put her at rest if things went wrong. The noise grew as the trucks went by. The last truck in the convoy stopped outside the gate. The two men were on high alert, hoping they hadn't left anything which would identify their hideaway. Then, suddenly, all hell let loose. There was a blaze of gunfire lighting up the darkness. After a fearful few moments, it stopped. The trucks moved on but suddenly stopped a short distance away. A soldier turned a light onto a body. It was Agatha.

An almighty cheer rose from the troops. "We've got her."

"At last, we have got the bitch!" It did not take much thought for the two partisans to work out what had happened. Seeing the truck stopping at the gate Agatha must have revealed herself, possibly firing a shot to divert the soldiers' attention away from them. A senior officer shone his torch on her face. He spat on it saying, "Goodbye Agatha Merkel. You will kill no more of our men!" He then ordered the body to be thrown on the back of a truck. Her two colleagues overheard the German officer say the body would be taken to Gestapo Headquarters to be searched for any information about her person. He congratulated the men on their good work. Their task was now complete, it was time to head back to base. Later a search of Agatha's body and clothing failed to reveal anything. Her body was laid near the fountain of a local village as a warning to others.

The two partisans lay in shocked silence but the sound of groaning coming from inside the truck alerted them. Agata was in pain, and they could still save her. Agatha's sacrifice would not be in vain. Making sure all was clear, they returned to the truck. They drove away without headlights, moving slowly to reduce any noise to a minimum. Parking a short distance from the town, they kept to the shadows as they helped Agata to a safe house. They were warmly greeted and using supplies secretly provided by a local pharmacist Agata was given pain relief and her wound cleaned and bandaged.

As her pain subsided, she sat up and looked around the dimly lit room. She began to cry quietly; tears ran down her cheeks. Her silent world began to close around her. She was unable to communicate the thoughts which were haunting her. The horrors of her past, the car crash in which her parents died and she sustained injuries. Her present plight, Joseph's absence, Otto's plans, the trauma of recent events all seemed suffocating like an endless claustrophobic passageway from which there was no escape. Thankfully the morphine she had been given earlier was effective and she fell into a deep sleep.

As she slept the partisans gathered together, a group of four males and one female member, they were concerned about Agata's mental health. Her physical wounds would heal with time but her sanity was another matter. Some were surprised by her silence until her disabilities were explained and they discussed what should be done in these circumstances. Plainly Agata was in no fit state to be moved, however she was no doubt being sought by the Gestapo.

A loud banging at the back door, adjacent to an alley at the rear of the terraced houses, brought the conversation to an abrupt halt. The candles were extinguished as they rushed for their weapons. As the knocking continued one of the men cautiously approached the door whilst the rest of the group took up defensive positions. He opened the door slightly and peered out to see a young lad. The lad whispered the password, at which everyone relaxed, relieved to see it was not the Nazi soldiers they had feared.

The boy excitedly burst out, "You must all leave here at once! Soldiers led by the Gestapo are on their way. Go! Go now!"

Everyone rushed to gather their things.

"No time for that," cried the boy, "they will be here very soon."

One of the men wrapped Agata in a blanket and carried her out into the passageway. The other men followed rapidly but the lady remained. She had a job to do. Taking out a large can, she poured petrol over the room. In the meantime, the men made their way down the passageway keeping to the shadows. They headed for a narrow street leading toward the outskirts of the town where the truck was parked. They had not gone far when they heard an explosion. The soldiers had entered the passageway from the other end and were almost at the safe house. The female partisan caught a glimpse of them just as she was leaving. Rushing back inside, she grabbed another can of petrol and splashed it over the doorway. She waited. It was never known what had killed her. The hail of bullets or the blast from the exploding petrol fumes. What was known was that several soldiers had suffered horrific burns and the explosion had given Agata and her partisan escorts enough time to make their getaway.

As they escaped the town they looked back and saw smoke billowing from the direction of the safe house. They said nothing but inwardly each man said a prayer to his partisan sister. As day break approached, they split up. Agata, now able to walk, was taken by one of the men to a village a few miles away. They were heading for another hiding place; a farmhouse slightly isolated from the village itself. She was to stay there for a short time until it was safe to travel. She would then be picked up and taken to a permanent place deep in the countryside. This would be her home until the war was over. Pray to God the Germans would be defeated and they could all meet up again. She was introduced to Manfred who had inherited the farm from his father.

He had lived there alone for many years; his mother having passed away during his birth. Smiling he looked at Agata and gently shook her hand. She looked back at him taking in his worn-out clothes, battered boots, bright blue eyes and untidy hair. She judged him to be in his sixties, a tall man who walked with a limp. She later learned that this was the result of bullet wound sustained in the Great War. Despite his injury he was strong and fit, able to run the farm single handed. There was a flock of sheep on the farm which was constantly depleted by hungry villagers. Manfred tried to secure them, penning them in every night guarded by his faithful sheepdog. Hunger, however, was a strong catalyst inspiring the raiders to devise clever ways of pilfering the odd sheep. He completely understood their motives and when officials came to confiscate their share, he would claim the reduced head count was due to hungry foxes.

Having greeted Agata, Manfred invited her to the table and soon rustled up a hot drink accompanied by bread and fresh farm eggs. It was apparent that she hadn't eaten for some time. He noticed the blood soaked bandage on her arm and after she had eaten he brought in a bowl of warm water smelling of antiseptic. Smiling kindly, he removed the bandage, gently cleansed the wound then applied some diluted iodine to prevent infection before covering it with a fresh bandage. Agata grimaced in pain but bravely tried to smile in gratitude. Manfred had been told of her communication difficulties and noticing how tired she appeared beckoned her toward one of the old oak panels near the kitchen window. Drawing her attention to a curtain cord he pulled it hard. The panel spang open revealing a small space, she understood what it meant. Somewhere to hide should they have unwanted visitors.

In the living room next to the open fireplace was a large, padded armchair which could easily be converted into a bed. Again, she understood without the need for words. Manfred brought out blankets and a pillow then helped her to settle. He drew the curtains before leaving the room to let her sleep. In the kitchen he searched through the drawers for paper and pencils, leaving them on the table to provide Agata with a means of communication when she woke up.

After about a week a partisan turned up explaining there were problems but he would return as soon as he was able. Days, weeks then months went by. No one would ever come again.

The local people began to wonder about the new lady who had taken up residence on the farm. A number of folk visited the farm to buy eggs and milk and couldn't help noticing her. Manfred told them she was his niece who had come to stay with him because her family had sadly been killed in a bomb raid. Eventually some of the women noticed Agata always seemed to be wearing the same clothes so they pooled together some unwanted garments for which Agata was very grateful. She rarely left the farm for fear of being spotted by the Gestapo. She and Manfred learned to communicate through a mixture of lip reading, signing and note taking. She had accepted the fact she would never see Joseph again, indeed she didn't even know if he was still alive. Had Otto taken him prisoner? Had the Gestapo captured him? Resigned to spending the rest of her life in seclusion, she made the most of it by turning a large area of land near the house into a colourful garden. Villagers would come to enjoy the garden. Manfred built some benches and they would sit enjoying the beautiful colours and aromas whilst Agata served them cool drinks. Those villagers who could afford it would donate a few marks in return for the pleasure they drew from relaxing in the garden.

The mood of the locals began to change as the pendulum of victory swung toward Britain and her allies. One sunny Sunday afternoon, Agata was aware there was something amiss. Not one of the usual visitors had turned up. Then she understood why. German soldiers were coming toward the farm, bringing with them a group of men. A mixture of young and elderly men she recognised as local were being escorted from the village. She ran indoors, agitated and impatient as she pulled Manfred toward the window, pointing at the soldiers coming toward them. He quickly opened up the hideout gesticulating to tell her to stay there until he came for her.

As the group drew nearer, Manfred went to meet them in the hope of diverting them away from the house. The officer in charge ordered him to gather his belongings, explaining that he was empowered to conscript him into the army. They were needed to defend bridges against the advancing enemy.

His protests were answered by a blow from a soldier's rifle butt which floored him. They dragged him to his feet and pushed him toward the group of villagers. He looked at them in dismay. Some of the lads were not even in their teens. The officer took two men with him to search the house to see if there was anything worth taking such as food or weapons. Cupboards were forced open, drawers emptied onto the floor. Food and drink confiscated. The vibrations caused by furniture being thrown about alarmed Agata, who crouched in a ball, trembling in terror. Even after it all went quiet, she remained hidden, too afraid to move. Eventually she crept out, horrified by the wreckage, and wondered where Manfred could be. She quickly realised he must have been taken with the other men. She was never to see him again.

As time went by, she grew used to her life alone on the farm. Then one day as she worked in the garden a stranger arrived.

Her name was Julie-Anne.

Chapter 33

Alsace

After a restless night, Otto decided to raise some more questions about Agata. The household staff now mentioned that they thought Joseph and Agata had been getting close. They had tried to conceal it, but had more than once been seen standing close to each other, smiling as if they had a secret. At this point, they noticed Joseph was missing, and it was then revealed that no-one had seen him that morning. His room was found to be empty, and a further search revealed the keys were once again missing.

The housekeeper now remembered Joseph talking rather often with Jules, the butcher's boy, and his slightly peculiar behaviour the day the crockery was broken. Otto now realised that Agata had been picking up information, and clearly this was a system for passing it on. How she could do this when deaf and dumb puzzled him until he realised she must have been able to lip read! She would have had to write everything down, and it was then passed to Joseph to give to Jules. Doubtless, this was being leaked to the Resistance, and from them perhaps to British agents.

He called his staff together and demanded vigilance; the butcher's boy was to be apprehended on his next visit and brought to him. To Otto's growing concern, the housekeeper informed him the young man had not turned up the previous morning and as yet had not arrived. She had sent another servant to collect vegetables and the meat, and the supplier had said he hadn't seen Otto's delivery boy for several weeks. It was odd, because there wasn't another supplier in the town. Otto realised that without the boy, he would not be able to trace the suppliers - in fact whoever was supplying must be part of the resistance. Otto slammed his fist on the table...

Dammit, nothing was going right! It was vital to trace the source of the goods, and to trace Agata, Joseph and Jules. The food source was the starting point.

He pulled on his jacket and rushed out. Beginning with questioning the butcher, he was angry and baffled to find that the food supplies controlled by the military food depot had cancelled their contract. A uniformed official had stopped by to cancel the contract over a month ago. Food supply controls were stringent, Otto considered; it must be a very well organised group, and Jules was clearly not the dullard he had appeared to be. He then went to the military depot, and waited impatiently while the manager assembled his staff to enquire about any peculiarities in recent weeks. An hour later they had discovered that certain foods had been pilfered between the main food branch and the distribution centre. It appeared to be mostly the meat stocks, some of which had ended up in his house, Otto fumed. He would look into all this once his big project was over.

Returning to his house, he made some calls, starting with the main military depot. Further investigation revealed that two members of staff responsible for local food distribution had suddenly disappeared without a trace. Otto's house had been the only target of what seemed an operation to collect information to be passed on to the Resistance. The commanding officer for the distribution of food called to thank Otto for unearthing the operation. All efforts would be made to track down and apprehend those involved. He then asked Otto if there was any special reason, any sensitive information present, that might have significance to the enemy or have caused him to be targeted? Otto immediately replied, smoothly, that matters of national importance were never discussed in his house, anything at all sensitive would be dealt with in his secure business premises.

Apparently satisfied with what he had heard, the officer thanked Otto again and hung up. He wondered as he did so if Otto was up to something.

Chapter 34

Wales/Porton Down

Quiet fell over the stands and terraces, there was little time left and the game was in the balance. After a brutal and physical seventy-five minutes neither side had scored and the stalemate was making the capacity crowd uneasy, the atmosphere fraught with tension. Onlookers on both sides, started to release the tension by cheering on their team. Scarves and flags were waving, charging the moment with emotion.

An almighty cheer broke, the waving flags halted as the referee blew his whistle for a penalty against Cwmllynfell. He then glanced at his watch once more. The infringement was too far away from the crossbar to attempt a penalty kick at the posts. The Ammanford full back kicked the ball at full strength, making touch close to the opposition try line. The Ammanford supporters quietened, tense in the moment; whoever scored next would be the winners. The referee checked his watch again. The packed stands waited. The game was already in extra time which meant that a draw would force a replay.

The result of this match would decide the winners of the West Wales Rugby Championship. Both teams were from the heart of the Welsh valleys, communities only eight miles apart, where the love for rugby was fierce and passionate. Ammanford, a medium sized town on the fringes of the Black Mountains had been previous champions. Their opposition, from the small mining village of Cwmllynfell, very much the underdogs, had proved themselves to be a formidable team and a tough side to play against. The restless silence from the terraces stoked the tension in the atmosphere as the final minutes ticked by. The rivalry between town and village had been nurtured over generations; the victors would walk away warm with glee, whilst the discontentment of the losers would cast a chill over the April sunshine. Nothing like a Welsh grudge match to fuel the passions of one community confronting the other.

The resulting line out in favour of Ammanford had nearly resulted in a try, but had ended in a scrum some ten feet from the try line. Luckily for Cwmllynfell an Ammanford player had knocked the ball forward resulting in another scrum this time in favour of the defenders, right in front their own posts. This did not look good for the Cwmllynfell team who were having to defend themselves only feet from the try line. Silence fell once again in the crowd, as the players assembled for the scrum, the referee looked again at his watch and indicated that this would be the last play of the match.

With one side defending their try line in front of their posts, the other hellbent on converting the advantage to secure victory, the game was now at the critical point. The Cwmllynfell scrum-half, short but sturdy, presented the ball to the front row channel and waited for a twitch from the hooker's thumb. Signal given, he put the ball in as fast as possible, the hooker struck it with his heel causing the ball to shoot out too quickly between the legs of the back row players. The crowd gasped as one.

The scrum-half just managed to get a grip on the leather ball and dive- passed it to the flyhalf. The ball failed to reach him bouncing instead just in front of him. Another gasp! One half of the crowd groaned loudly only to be drowned by cheers from the other half. The defenders fly half was a very fit PE teacher, whose sharp reflexes and skill enabled him to snatch up the ball. Gareth, the flyhalf, nicknamed Snowy because of his fair hair, shimmied to the right and skilfully rounded his opposite number. A stunned silence overtook the Ammanford crowd as he broke through the defence. He was still dangerously close to his own try line; he needed support. The covering defence was almost upon him, fire in their eyes, determined that he would go nowhere. He heard a cry, "Now!"

Glancing to his right he saw Gershom, his winger running at pace outside him. He passed the ball; it seemed to hang in the air. The winger plucked it from the ether and sped off in full flight. The crowd erupted. Up to this point Gershom had barely had a touch of the ball, such was the ferocity of the opposing forward, and there had been limited open play. He cut inside the covering defence and then rounded his opposite wing so that nothing stood between him and the try line except for the full back. Gershom, despite his size, was an extremely fast sprinter; he held track records for his school and at district level. This was his first match against Ammanford, since he had left the area to complete his National service. They were not aware of the danger he now posed if given the space to run. He set his eye on the corner flag on the opposition try line and sprinted. The corner flag was a good distance away, but he was determined to get there. Despite his diminutive height, he was well built with a solid frame, he moved like a bullet.

The defending players were taken by surprise, realising their danger for the first time.

As Gershom ran, he could feel the uneven ground shake beneath his feet. He reached the halfway line. Still fifty yards to cover! A quick glance to his left showed the threat of the covering fallback closing on him. He realized they were on course to arrive at the same moment. He'd been here before, the smallest player on the pitch, pitted against heavier, bigger players. Their momentum had resulted in many bruises, even a broken collarbone.

But nothing would stop him now, unperturbed by their extra power he was going to get to that line at any cost. He flew toward the corner, now twenty-five yards away; the full-back was closing in fast, his angle of approach shortening the distance between him and Gershom. Seconds away from the try line, Gershom tilted his head, took a lungful of air and drove faster. In the dying yards, he decided to dive high, hoping the full-back would miss him. He threw himself into the air, arms outstretched with the ball; he felt the fullback brush under his body, as he hit the ground hard sliding over the try line. Made it! The hard baked clay surface stunned him as his head hit the ground; wavering slightly he got to his feet.

The opposing fullback had crashed himself into the advertising hoarding near the corner but signalled that he was OK. Gershom was instantly overwhelmed by a group of ecstatic Cwmllynfell players who threw him skywards, a move not calculated to ease the pains in his body, but they caught him and set him back down to earth. He became conscious of the shouts, cheers and chanting of the crowds as in unison they stamped the boards under their feet. Snowy attempted the conversion, the kick failed but it mattered little, Cwmllynfell were the new champions as the referee's whistle shrilled.

Celebrations moved from the ground into the bars and the small packed changing rooms where the beer began to flow, transforming the tensions of the game into exaltation at the result. Beer spattered the ceiling, the walls and even the chairman of the club. The chairman waited, beer dripping from his nose, to make a brief congratulatory speech. As he was about to leave after his speech, a forceful banging on the door silenced the cheers.

The players, some half-dressed, some sitting, looked bemused as a policeman entered and uttered a single sentence.

"Could I speak to a Gershom Morris?"

Chapter 35

Wales/Porton Down

The Silver Star Coach was about to leave Swansea. You could set your time by the coach's departure since it always left promptly at eight pm on Sunday evenings. The National Service squaddies provided a ready-made clientele as they travelled back through the evening to their various regiments in the South of England, the final destination being Salisbury. The bus weaved through the various towns stopping at different barracks. The halts invariably wiped the smile off the faces of the young soldiers.

They left the coach with great reluctance knowing full well that their brief idyll of freedom was now over. At the entrance to each barracks the regimental police grinned facetiously as, with heads down and with a general air of dejection, the squaddies walked toward their barrack rooms. There they would try to rest, despite feelings of being imprisoned. The thoughts of the drudgery to come the following morning would hopefully be replaced by memories of the previous hours and allow them to get some much needed sleep. However, staying positive was never easy when lying on a concrete mattress.

Gershom closed his eyes as he rested his head on the back of the seat as his own memories wandered to the past, to events that had taken place, memories of which were now causing him unrest. A great deal had happened over the last two years, and his mother Jane had died from a heart attack. This was probably brought about by overwork exacerbated by her weight and heavy smoking habit. The eldest of eleven children, she was expected to take the brunt of raising them since her own mother was frail and unwell possibly due to the stress of childbirth and poverty.

Gershom had little knowledge of how his parents had met, but was aware that at the time of his birth his mother had been living in Reading. He had seen on his birth certificate, which was not the original but a copy, that he was born in Tilehurst on 22nd September 1938. He knew his father had lived in Wales for the entirety of his life.

Somehow this made little sense to him, especially when he questioned his parents, who had glossed over it but were unable to give a satisfactory answer. His father had been a miner all his life, working in several pits in the West Wales area. His face and hands were mottled with blue scars, one of which ran from the corner of his left eye down to the middle of his cheek. He was pale through lack of sunshine, fair- haired, short in stature but with muscles of stone. He was bad tempered and uneducated, seemingly with few friends. He spent most Saturday nights drowning his miserable life with beer at the local British Legion club. Quick to quarrel, with a sharp voice, he would constantly row with Jane, who far more intelligent than he, would quietly but firmly reduce his arguments to shreds. This would only exacerbate matters, fuelling his anger. The home was not a happy one. Every payday became a battlefield, Gershom's father William, would try to forge his pay packet.

His attempt at adjusting the amount he was paid was pathetic. His lack of counterfeiting skills only superseded by his unbelievable attempts to explain the rubbings out and obvious changes to his pay slip. In stark contrast to this the manner in which Isaac tended and looked after Jane when she neared her end was a complete transformation. It was as though an epiphany had occurred, maybe due to feelings of guilt and the prospect of having to live on his own.

Whatever the reasons he stayed by her side, showing great care and diligence. After she was taken into hospital. He visited her daily despite having to travel by bus some distance from his village to Swansea. He never missed a day. Sadly, on the evening of her death, he left her side for a short while and so she died alone. The day before she died, many of her sisters and grandchildren had gathered round her in a moving family reunion. Gershom had not been able to attend as he was away on National Service. His mother was not aware of his absence but he felt he should have been there.

It wasn't surprising, he thought, that his father had never been close to him. Indeed, they hardly spoke, and in his pensive mood Gershom wondered why. His parents had hardly shown him any warmth or indeed much to each other. Endless rows and sometimes neglect had become the norm. He was often envious of his friends who had a more solid foundation of care and emotional support, making them happier and carefree. Living in a small village accentuated differences so that anomalies stood out. There were other problems in his family relationships. He had an elder brother called Dafydd, who was some nine years older than himself, who was equally distant. Dafydd too was quick-tempered, but was blessed with a warm and caring disposition.

Unfortunately, he suffered from a cognitive impairment. Gershom never knew whether his inability to reason was congenital, or the results of the consequence of mental illness.

Meningitis had swept through the village. When Gershom was four years old, he contracted the disease as a consequence of sleeping in the same bed as his brother Dafydd. Dafydd had fallen ill first and it took some time for a diagnosis to be made. He was admitted into quarantine and treated with penicillin which had not long been in use. The prolonged diagnosis may have caused some brain damage, but fortunately for Gershom he was treated much more promptly. They had shared the same intensive care ward; isolated from the rest of the hospital they could not receive visitors.

Gershom had remembered that his brother Dafydd had been discharged first. Leaving him in lonely isolation for a number of weeks. He also sadly reflected that his first cousin Margaret had died of the same disease some years later. Dafydd had few friends and a very difficult relationship with his father, their mother too seemed distant and removed from him. He was quite tall, with fair hair, but although lean he was deceptively strong. At school and around the village his peers would provoke him resulting in a build up of internal anger. His pent-up emotion often expressed itself in bouts of fighting and vandalism. It often acted as a catalyst, provoking inappropriate behaviour.

His mind turned back to the present as Gershom glanced through the window into the darkness. He saw the sign for Cardiff pass by. He recalled the many times he had watched his country playing rugby at the Cardiff Arms Park. Beating England at that hallowed ground was always met with high emotion and jubilation amongst the fans. Losing caused clouds of depression in the rest of the valley for weeks afterwards.

Rugby for them was akin to a prescriptive medication. It diverted minds away from the general depression which in those times crept into the very fabric of the villages. Every small success was a welcome tonic.

The coach rumbled on towards Newport, and then veered to the left toward the River Severn bordering Wales from England, but there was a still a long way to go he thought. With a frown he wondered why he had to report to the guard room early on this very morning.

Someone in front of the coach was being violently sick. This was not an uncommon occurrence as the young lads often met up in the Swansea pubs for a skin full, before getting on the coach with bellies full of Brains' best bitter, which as its name suggests had a profound effect on their mindsets. However, it was cheap enough on their measly pay and sufficiently palatable to satisfy their taste buds. The unfortunate lad heaved, covering himself, his seat and the unlucky passenger sitting next to him with a mixture of liquid and partially digested solids; the onlookers, delighted at the drama, laughed and jeered. The coach driver was less amused, he pulled over at the next convenient stopping point, promptly dumping him and his baggage on the pavement. Everyone cheered as they bid him farewell. Again, this was not an unfamiliar dramatic exit, Gershom was more concerned than happy as the coach moved on and abandoned the squaddie since he would not be able to arrive at his regiment in time for roll call in the morning. This would mean he would be absent without leave, resulting in punishment. The other squaddies, less concerned about his welfare, settled down for a while, then suddenly burst into song with an adaptation of 'My old man said follow the van, and don't dilly dally on the way,' but this was halted by a blast from the bus driver who threatened to throw them all out. Quietened by the threat the drunken choir settled down and peace was restored.

Having heard the unsympathetic jeering and cheering of his comrades, Gershom's mind went back to his memories. His eyes strained as he peered out into the darkness. broken only by the flickering lights of the windows of distant houses in which he reflected would be families, lonely people, young lovers starting off their lives together, some occupants happy, some unhappy all living out their separate lives. His thoughts turned to another painful and embarrassing episode which would stay with him and haunt him for the rest of his life. Why was it he thought, that whenever he looked back in time, there seemed to be few recollections of more pleasant things coming to mind. In recent years he had enjoyed being praised for his excellence on the rugby pitch. The villagers in the countryside had a passion for rugby and were more than enthusiastic in their support for their respective rugby teams. Therefore, players who excelled were singled out for praise in local shops, street corners and especially in the pubs and social clubs. Any misgivings they had once had about Gershom or his family in the past were set aside.

Gershom became a very popular character in the local area. He had been selected for national trials, and represented West Wales at schoolboy and senior levels. He was very much aware that had he not been recognised for his performance on the rugby pitch, he would definitely not have been so popular amongst his peers. The thought that rugby was possibly the only reason for his gaining esteem made him feel uneasy. His childhood had been a difficult one in many ways, certainly not the one his mother had intended for him.

These intrusions of negative thinking set his mind off in a different direction, after all he had acquired a close friendship not only with Keith, but with many other of his peers. Whilst his self-esteem was beginning to gain firmer ground, he felt uncomfortable when it came to conversing with girls of his own age. Most of his friends had developed friendships with girls from the villages whilst he lacked the confidence to approach them in conversation, and when they did include him in conversations when in groups, he became tongue-tied with nervousness. Whilst he was not an Adonis, he was satisfied that he was at least average in his appearance, however he had not been able to muster up sufficient confidence to interact with those of the opposite sex.

At the age of seventeen he was still without a close girlfriend. When in the company of his mates he couldn't help but feel left out as they talked about their conquests. Recently a local girl called Alice had sat next to him in the cinema and had put her arm around him, and after a few minutes of inactivity she had caught hold of his hand and placed it on her breast. She had yelped out loudly when he had squeezed it too tightly which had caused a ripple of laughter from those in the neighbouring seats. The combination of her anger and his blushes had caused him to make a rapid retreat just as the film was reaching its climax. He smiled to himself as he thought there had been more action on the cellulose film than on the fourth and fifth seats on the third row from the back, than in his case. Gershom contented himself by attributing this to shyness and lack of self-esteem, and resolved that the next time he would take care to treat this particular part of the lady's anatomy with more respect and tenderness, after all this soft and inviting flesh was not a rugby ball. He nearly burst out laughing to himself.

As he disentangled his mind, he recollected another more serious and painful incident which quickly dissolved any feelings of merriment. His thoughts returned back to his junior school days, to the memories of the incident which had affected him not only then but even now.

It rested with him like an ill-fated albatross around his neck serving as a permanent reminder of his position and status prior to his popularity as an all-round sportsman in the village. He recalled that during the final year of his junior school pupils had to decide whether or not to opt for the external examination which would determine which secondary school they would attend. The grammar school based some five miles away from his village boasted a high reputation for academic excellence thus opening the door to college or university. Not entering or failing the exam meant attending the secondary modern school, again a few miles distant but in the opposite direction. A case of "travel west to the grammar best" or "travel East would be least".

From the moment the young children had entered school, it had been drilled into them that education was paramount in gaining access to the professions. Higher qualifications would lead to social and economic success along with the chance of leaving the confines of the small villages for more affluent towns and cities with wider opportunities. Grammar school places were at a premium, both parents and primary schools doing their utmost to gain as many as possible.

It was now decision time, the Head Teacher gathered his papers and bustled out of his office. As he entered the classroom the entire leavers class rose to attention with a combination of respect and abject terror. The young boys and girls twitched and fidgeted with fear and tension as they stood stiff and still. He ordered everyone to sit; glaring around the class as if searching for misdemeanours, after what felt like forever, asked all those pupils who wished to be entered for the examination to raise their hands. Gershom couldn't recall how many had put up their hands, but thought it was at least half the class, including himself. Swivelling his thick neck, the Head slowly and methodically turned his head regarded each pupil with their hands raised. Pausing at each with a nod of approval, ordering them to keep their hands in the air. In his shiny dark suit, which appeared to be fighting to confine an over large frame from exploding. He revelled in his absolute power over all he surveyed. His sickly smile changed abruptly when his eyes came to rest on Gershom, giving way to an ominous scowl. Shaking his head in disapproval, he told him to put his hand down and quickly moved on to the next pupil. Gershom had been taught to obey orders, especially from the Head, so he put his hand down as he was told only to put it straight back up again. The Headmaster's eyes bulged, his leather tanned face turning red. His voice was bellowing now, the folds of fat around his stomach quivering from the guttural noise as he ordered Gershom to drop his hand.

Gershom recalled the pain and anguish he and his brother and many others before him had suffered at the hands of this bloated overpowering teacher, who it was said had only been appointed as Head when other better qualified teachers had been drafted to work in the mines or recruited for war service. Despite being untrained, unkempt and unqualified he now held a position of authority, commanding respect in the village. Gershom's thick skin was a product of years of trials; he was used to being shouted at, blamed for, threatened with the consequences of supposed bad behaviour. Years of threats and beatings from his peers and elders helped him to now stand his ground. He was certain he could pass the exam - he just needed the chance. Once more he lowered his hand then for the third time, raised it. Their form teacher, who was a gentle and lovely lady, looked on with a sorrowful expression. With white hair, blue eyes and the fairest of skin.

This boy, she thought, who had done so well in overcoming so many difficulties, was showing so much promise. He was now standing in the shadow of this unjust man, and being treated so unfairly. She admired his tenacity but worried about the consequences of his actions. All eyes in the classroom were now upon her as she rose to her feet. In comparison to the head teacher, she seemed so delicate, as if the slightest of breezes might topple her over. Everything about her appeared colourless, at her birth her parents had been told she was an albino, and she would have to be protected from sunlight for the rest of her life. Everyone in the village respected and loved her. Her short, fine hair clung to her forehead in wisps as she left her position behind the desk and moved to confront their headmaster. He was now shaking with suppressed rage, the small faces of the children looked on filled with fear and fraught with anxiety. No one had ever dared challenge him like this. His large frame swelled as he stiffened his shoulders and puffed out his chest. He turned on Gershom, roaring, his voice choked as his pharynx tightened and emerged as a childlike piping spilling a stream of abuse. No one in Gershom's family, he said, had ever succeeded in anything - his brother had been useless and so was he.

His frothing lips revealed his brown upper teeth as he spat out the words, "You are a failure and always will be. You will never pass the exam; you will be entered for the exam but without my recommendation." with that he turned, slamming the door behind him as he left.

Silence in the classroom was broken by Miss Rees, their loved and respected form teacher. She spoke gently, asking the children to take out their reading books for some quiet reading time. After a few minutes she came and sat at Gershom's side. As usual the chair next to him was vacant, as no one ever wanted to sit next to him. She had put her arm round him, pulling his head close to her. She said nothing, but held his face in her hands, smiled and nodded, with tears in her eyes. No wonder she was so loved by every child in her class.

Chapter 36

Wales/Porton Down

The coach passed over the bridge. He took a final glance at the Welsh countryside, as he left his native land behind and ventured into the old enemy's territory. Smiling to himself, he considered the present battles between the two nations, differences now settled on the playing fields of Cardiff Arms Park and Twickenham. As the game continued to enthrall spectators from the grandstands and the terraces. The difference between these encounters and ancient ones on the battlefield was that every match was celebrated by friend and foe in the neutral grounds of pubs, bars and hotels. Those recollections brought a smile to his face.

At Andover, the next stop everyone piled out again, this time in a far more sober and orderly fashion. Stretching his legs Gershom moved away from the others and their cigarette smoke; he was in no mood for idle chatter. It was now getting on for 2 a.m. and the cold air invigorated him. He moved round to the rear of the toilet area and propped his back against the wall, staring up into the sky. A cloudless, moonless night accentuated the stars; gazing at them, his mind once more turned back to his early schooldays. After the Easter break in their final term, he had felt dismay that his favourite teacher, the gentle Miss Rees was no longer there. She had been replaced by a tall male teacher.

It was clear from the moment that Mr Williams spoke, and the way that he engaged with the class, that this new teacher had something special about him. Alert and cheerful, his mannerisms and expressions kept all the young minds alert. He bounced questions quickly from one pupil to another, engaging with everyone in turn.

Gershom remembered that when it was his turn to answer a question about reading the teacher was surprised and delighted by his response; Gershom was able to talk enthusiastically about science and nature. Mr. Williams congratulated him on his topics of interest and added that these were subjects that they would be studying in the weeks to come. Later that morning in the playground, Keith, the son of a local chemist approached him and started to chat about science. It was the beginning of an enduring friendship which sustained him for many years to come. He no longer felt alone, and his spirits rose.

The day of the eleven plus arrived, questions in both Welsh and English so pupils could opt for their preferred language. Gershom chose Welsh, the language he spoke at home and in the village. He found the Maths paper easy, feeling he had answered the questions well. He enjoyed the logic questions, seeing them as puzzles to be solved. He was quietly confident that he had done enough to pass.

Miss Rees came to school the day the results were to be announced. She met with the head teacher to see them. They then both entered the room with the all-important list of names. The children stood smartly to attention as he informed them that the results were very good, and he was pleased with the pass rate. He asked the children who had not taken the exam to sit, then explained that the names of those who had passed would be read in alphabetical order. Those left standing were transfixed, hearts beating wildly. The silence in the classroom pressing on them.

Gershom grew anxious as Peter Lewis was announced as a pass. His name would be next. Dumbfounded he heard the next name... Suzanne Peters... His name had not been called. He felt lightheaded, suspecting his exam papers had not been forwarded. He wanted to vomit but held his nerve. A feeling of rage was beginning to overtake his disappointment. With tears in his eyes, he looked to his old teacher. She appeared startled and puzzled. Raising her hand, she approached the Head as he went to leave the room. He ignored her but as he reached the door, he turned his head saying dismissively that Gershom too had passed. Old and frail she might be but Miss Rees spoke with a firm yet confident voice, reminding Mr. Williams that he had failed to mention that not only had Gershom passed but his results had been outstanding. She turned to smile at Gershom, congratulating him as the Head teacher slammed the door as he left.

The months following passed pleasantly for Gershom as he cemented his friendship with Keith. He was often invited for tea and the boys enjoyed spending time in the shed at the bottom of the garden; turning matchboxes, wire, batteries and scraps of wood into electrical motors, dynamos and all sorts of gadgets. Keith, taller than Gershom, with fair hair and blue eyes was always neatly dressed, smelling clean and fresh. The loving and caring atmosphere apparent in his home struck a contrast with Gershom's experience. Life in his home was an existence devoid of enjoyment.

Stargazing now, he recalled a similar frosty evening when Keith's father had walked them to a hilltop to study the stars. The night sky seemed crammed with The Milky Way and constellations clearly visible. Brian Thomas, Keith's dad, had wandered from one constellation to another, naming them. He pointed out the Great Bear which Gershom privately thought looked more like a saucepan. Brian told them the Latin name - Ursa Major – and explained that it was the most important constellation. He showed them how to trace the two pointing stars to the Pole Star.

As the sky seemed to go round in a huge circle, the Pole Star stayed in the same position and always pointed North. For thousands of years, it has guided travellers over deserts, sailors across oceans, saved the lives of lost souls by pointing them in the right direction. He advised the boys to remember the Pole Star in their travels through life. A tall man, he knelt putting a hand on each boys' shoulder, saying, "While the Pole Star had been priceless to ancient navigators; knowledge, sound reasoning and determination should be their guiding stars on earth. They should do their utmost to follow their visions, have trust in their own abilities, setting a course for personal happiness and success." Looking at each boy in turn he impressed on them the importance of seeking sound advice, trusting their own judgement and never mixing with fools, idiots, liars, charlatans or wrongdoers. Gershom smiled to himself, thinking it was a perfect description of his Head Teacher.

The revving of the coach engine recalled Gershom back to the present. He quietly joined the rest of the squaddies clambering aboard, settling into their seats. He hoped to catch a few hours' sleep before reaching Bulford Barracks; however, the events of the last few days, the excitement of the rugby match, coupled with his reminiscences preying on his mind, kept him awake for the rest of the journey. As he tried to keep more comfortable by using his greatcoat as a pillow, he felt something hard in one of the pockets. He recalled the bulky envelope his aunt and uncle had handed to him as they said goodbye – he hadn't yet looked at it properly. His aunt had embraced him fondly and whispered that as far as she and her family were concerned, he would always hold a special place in their hearts. His uncle had joined them; the two of them had embraced him, binding all three together for a long moment.

Then releasing him his uncle slowly walked back to the house clearly upset. Gershom had glanced at the envelope; it was old and crumpled. It appeared to have passed through many hands and been opened many times. It was fastened with a scrap of tape and there was writing on the back in different coloured inks, each note annotated with signatures and dates. In his haste to catch the bus he had pushed the packet into his pocket to read later. It had slipped his mind but now was not the time to open it. He needed rest; he was apprehensive about the interview awaiting him at the guard house.

After all the stops at different regiments Gershom finally arrived at Bulford without any time to rest before reporting to the guard room.

There was barely time to shower, shave and dress in his number two uniform before reporting to the guard room dead on time. He marched in smartly, stamping his feet in front of the Duty Sergeant's desk. Speaking clearly, clipping his words precisely he informed the sergeant he was reporting as requested and awaiting orders. The sergeant looked him up and down, eagle eyes checking uniform and boots. Seemingly satisfied he opened the duty book and ordered Gershom to wait outside for a lorry which would take him to Salisbury station. The lorry would pick up others on route and take them all to Porton Down Research Establishment to take part in trials.

Gershom turned smartly about to march toward the door when the Duty Sergeant called him back. He seemed bemused, asking why the hell Gershom was involved in trials at a place like Porton Down. It had a dark reputation for research into chemical and bacterial warfare. Gershom explained; he had been approached by a Battery Sergeant with a Regimental Order paper requesting volunteers to take part in physiological trials. There were incentives – a week's extra pay and an extra weeks leave. His main reason, however, was his interest in scientific research, he hoped to study science at university after completing National Service. This would be an ideal opportunity to learn more about scientific methodologies.

With a shrug of his shoulders, he explained that they had been told it was research into the common cold; he would come to no harm.

Slapping the duty book closed, the sergeant shook his head, calling Gershom a bloody fool, saying he was clearly intelligent and should think twice about volunteering for anything which might cause him harm. This struck an uncomfortable chord.

It was the advice Keith's father had given him.

Chapter 37

Wales/Porton Down

There were only a few minutes to wait before the truck drew up with two other National Service men already on board. The main topic of conversation was the extra pay and leave they would receive. Gershom did not confide the main reason behind his volunteering. As instructed, they took the train to Salisbury, then transferred to another truck to Porton Down. High barbed wire fences formed their first view of the research centre. Armed guards manned the gates and others patrolled the perimeter. Whatever was going on there was highly secretive. They were checked and searched, but once inside were greeted by friendly service men who told them they could remove their berets and relax.

Their stay would be less regimented than life in the barracks. Thanked for attending, the three were also assured that their living conditions here would be a big improvement on those in camp!

As they were escorted to their living quarters Gershom glanced around, thinking that whilst it may be difficult for anyone to break into the encampment it would be equally difficult for anyone to break out. Once they reached their accommodation, they saw the four of them were to be together, occupying a small ward containing four single beds. The escort told them to freshen up, adding that someone would collect them to meet up with the rest of the group.

Having introduced themselves they began to chat, wondering what would happen now. They were however in a buoyant mood, thinking of the extra money they would receive along with the extra week's holiday. They thought this was going to be one hell of a jolly, and they were glad to be free of the constant orders of those senior to them. It was rumoured that food in the establishment was very good, much better than the usual codswallop they received in their respective barracks. They could now relax and treat this as a kind of holiday. The four men dived on their beds and started bouncing up and down. This was the life they thought! After their ablutions they stood together at the window watching the darkness gradually creep upon them. By the time someone had arrived to summon them, it had grown dark and the stars were bright in the sky.

Leaving the warmth of their billet they walked casually behind their leader, shivering in the chill of the night air. The Porton Down research centre was situated well away from any villages or towns, standing isolated on Salisbury Plain. Excepting the noise of their footsteps, loud in army boots, there was complete silence. The place was clearly deserted, situated far away from inquisitive eyes. Their escort stopped at a seemingly blank wall but his small torch swept over the wall, revealing a door handle. The door was easily missed, heavily constructed and tightly sealed, and it allowed no light to escape but as it opened the light flooded out, partially blinding them.

They entered what appeared to be small classroom furnished with comfortable chairs placed randomly around the room. The room itself was well lit and inviting, as everything about the place was clearly intended to put personnel at ease. They were greeted by a Sergeant dressed in military uniform apart from his beret. He introduced himself and as he did so two other sergeants entered, gesticulated toward the chairs and asked them to be seated. The two sat casually amongst them whilst the lead sergeant stood front in of them, thanked them for attending, stressing that without their help and that of those who had been before them, troops fighting to protect their country would be defenceless against unseen dangers from an enemy willing to use anything against them.

The British military took international laws extremely seriously and obeyed them to the letter. Other countries such as those they fought against had no conscience about using weapons which the Geneva Conventions had condemned. The enemies they now faced on the battlefield had developed weapons which could wipe-out whole regiments in minutes by deploying deadly gases. These horrific weapons could be delivered quickly without detection. It was absolutely necessary to find an antidote that would prevent our troops from being annihilated. He gave examples of how men in the First World War had been poisoned with chlorine and mustard gas, emphasising that the new gases now being deployed were colourless and odourless and a hundred times more lethal. It was therefore essential that chemical research was undertaken to prevent catastrophic annihilation of our troops. Without their help such research could not take place.

He turned to the film projector which showed a series of short clips depicting soldiers like themselves banded together for a common cause. One featured a terrified cat trapped at the top of the tree; it was rescued by a passing group of soldiers who returned it to its thankful owner. She was overwhelmed by their compassion and thoughtfulness and the way they worked together as a team.

Another clip focused on troops in the First World War. It showed the effects of chlorine on men who was totally defenceless as clouds of gas swept over them. The sight of soldiers coughing up thick mucus onto their tunics as they staggered with blinded eyes before finally falling and dying in agony had a profound effect on the young soldiers. The picture flashed to images of lifeless bodies strewn over the trenches. Then onto survivors walking in crocodile formation, each with his right hand placed on the shoulder of the man in front, their eyes bandaged, almost all coughing strenuously.

The room was silent, everyone stirred by the sight of so much suffering. It took little to persuade them to do what was required, they were after all soldiers, standing shoulder to shoulder with all fellow soldiers past and present.

After the presentation the group was joined by a man in civilian clothes. Gershom's interest sharpened since the newcomer could possibly be a doctor or a scientist. He was intent on finding out any kind of scientific information he could glean from this man. This was after all the main reason for his being there. The man stood behind a chair, holding on to it with clenched hands. His voice was little more than a whisper, but everyone listened intently to what he had to say. The first thing he did was to give them assurances that there would be no danger involved in the trials although some of them might experience a small amount of discomfort. Gershom, as keen as ever, raised his hand, on given the nod of approval he asked if they would be exposed to any gases and if so, what they were and how would they be administered.

The speaker paused then, without giving too much detail, explained that any substance used would be administered in minute quantities by being dripped onto a piece of cloth attached to their forearms. The skin in this area may feel cold but would not be affected in any other way. Throughout the procedure they would be in a sealed room where they would be free to entertain themselves reading, playing cards or chatting to each other. The trials would last for about half an hour, after which they would perform set tests to see how the substance in its liquid form had affected them.

Gershom followed up his earlier question, asking if they would experience any effects during or following the trial.

The scientist replied, saying, they might experience slight breathing problems and a possible tightening of the chest. He stressed there was no need to panic as after a few minutes the body would adjust to the chemical and they would recover. He also informed them that, although it was unusual, some of them may experience problems with their vision, but this too was temporary. Raising his voice, he emphasised that they would be carefully monitored throughout so there was no cause for concern.

Gershom, as inquisitive as ever, wanted to know the name of the gas and whether they would have any form of protection.

The response was dismissive. Looking at Gershom and smiling, he told him the experiment was designed to slightly incapacitate them, rather than to kill them. He added that to ensure there was no danger of anyone inhaling any excess gas as a result of evaporation they would be wearing gas masks.

Gershom hadn't finished. He wondered if they would be in a gas chamber, to which a smiling retort came from the scientist. They would be in a sealed room to prevent any leakage of the gas. Persistence was inherent in Gershom's nature and he quipped that whichever way you looked at it, that was what a gas chamber was.

Everyone laughed, releasing the tension in the room. The presenter looked at Gershom, asking if he was prepared to take an extended part in the trial by having his forearms cleansed from natural grease, prior to the liquid being dropped on.

When Gershom asked how this was different to the others, he was told that their arms would not be cleansed but that was the only difference. "Do I get extra cash for that?" quipped Gershom.

Everyone laughed. "No!" came the reply, "I can, however, arrange for an extra pudding!" The laughter grew louder.

Throughout the questions and answers Gershom noticed that the man had a strong German accent and without due thought asked what his nationality was. Surprised and somewhat taken aback he replied saying his name was Max Ackermann and that he had previously worked as a German scientist on similar projects but was now proud to be working for the British, helping other scientists in the battle against dangerous weapons. With passion in his voice, he expressed his views on the futility of war and how he was pleased to be involved in research which could save the lives of soldiers who might be exposed to chemical warfare. His address was quite moving and the room fell silent.

The four young soldiers, along with two others who had joined them for the meeting, turned their attention to the sergeant who took over the lecture. He began by again reassuring them of the safety of the trial, emphasising the fact it would only take some thirty minutes to complete. After that he explained, blood samples would be taken, and their hearing tested. They would then be transferred to the Porton Down hospital where they could rest and be well looked after. After spending a few days on the ward, they could return to their regiments where they would be discharged for a week's holiday with extra pay.

In an upbeat voice he asked for a show of hand confirming who was willing to take part in the trials for the good of their country. All hands were raised without hesitation. They were then asked to sign a document which they were told was the Official Secrets Act. Signing it prevented them from disclosing any information about the trials, and could lead to a long term of imprisonment if broken. All six men signed the document in silence.

Perhaps only Gershom now realised the magnitude of what they were taking part in; alarms bells were beginning to sound in his mind.

Now they heard that the first part of the trial would begin immediately, with drops of diluted mustard gas being introduced to a small area of skin. They filed out of the room and were directed to a clinical area, where they were instructed to roll up their sleeves, exposing the left arm. A small amount of liquid was dropped onto their forearms, allowed to dry, then dusted with Dutch powder which was rubbed over the spot.

There had been no pain, and if the rest of the trials were like this, it would be a piece of cake, thought Gershom.

After this they were allowed to leave and spend the rest of the day relaxing in preparation for further trials due to commence the next day.

Chapter 38

Wales/Porton Down

The six soldiers ambled down a hallway together, almost in silence, and were ushered into a white walled room with a glass panelled observation space sealed away from the main area. A cluster of people sat behind the glass, observing them as they came in. Gershom saw the man, Max, who he had met and chatted to the day before, now wearing a white lab coat and sitting at the centre of the group. It appeared that Max was the lead scientist, and the man in charge; perhaps he had misjudged him, he thought.

One technician lined up the volunteers, while another beckoned Gershom to one side, and after rolling up his sleeve, cleansed his forearm with what Gershom recognised as acetone.

Each soldier, wearing full battledress, was issued with a woollen hat instead of a beret. Technicians then fitted each one with a tight-fitting gas mask, and they were instructed to roll up their left sleeve. The first in the small queue went forward to sit in front of another technician, who took the left arm, placed some material on it, fixed with tape. Then a drop of clear liquid was applied from a small pipette. Another small piece of material was attached over this and again secured with tape. The young soldier was then placed at the table, facing the observation panel. He was allowed to read or play cards, but instructed to keep his treated arm extended, with the patch facing upwards.

Gershom was fourth in the line of "guinea pigs" as they jokingly referred to themselves, and like those before him, extended his left arm, which was this time closely examined. The technician confirmed that Gershom was the one whose arm had been cleansed, and applied two strips of military flannel, taping them to his arm.

Gershom asked for the name of the liquid being applied and was told simply it was a kind of nerve agent. Inquisitive as ever, Gershom asked how much was being applied. The technician cocked his head, quizzically - he wasn't used to volunteers asking so many questions - only 200mg, he said. Another layer of serge was taped over the patch, and Gershom joined the others at their table.

"All right Taff?" One of the Londoners in the group winked at Gershom, finding him a bit solemn. "This isn't half an easy job! Extra cash and a week's holiday to spend it. Cheer up mate!"

About fifteen minutes later, halfway through a game of noughts and crosses with one of his mates, Gershom complained of feeling unwell. Gazing blankly ahead he suddenly stopped speaking. His dizziness was getting worse, and as he looked about, his surroundings were becoming grey and dark, blurred and insubstantial. His head and chest felt as if they were about to burst; his breathing became difficult as his throat tightened and filled with mucus. His left arm became cold and leaden; then his arms and legs began to twitch, and he felt the warmth of urine running down his legs, felt his anus relax as he defecated. The last thing he saw before keeling over was the face of the old man in the white coat, the man called Max.

Suddenly there was panic; white coated technicians ran in to help him to his feet. For brief seconds, he seemed to recover, but then his condition pivoted into crisis. The staff rushed him through an antechamber and out to an ambulance to take him to the hospital within the complex. There, Gershom's body turned into a twisting mass of violently flailing limbs; every point of his body in spasm.

Max was trying to inject him with atropine, the known antidote to the chemical Sarin, but Gershom's violent convulsions made it difficult. Max was recalling seeing animals react in a similar way when injected with the nerve agent Tabun, which was less powerful than Sarin. None of the creatures had recovered when the reaction had been this strong. He struggled, desperate to inject the lifesaving antidote, but as he gripped Gershom's wrist he was shocked to realise there was no pulse. The technicians laid Gershom's body on the floor and attempted artificial respiration. The convulsions ceased. A senior technician, with tears in his eyes, forcibly opened Gershom's mouth to inspect his airway and found it full of vomit, slime and undigested food. In a desperate attempt to save him, more efforts were made to resuscitate, he was wrapped in blankets and hot water bottles. His legs were raised to try to restore blood to his upper body, as his face changed from grey to blue. For almost an hour and a half they battled to revive him, until reluctantly they gave up. Many were fighting tears for this healthy young volunteer as they faced the fact. They had killed him!

The autopsy revealed over a pint of blood in his abdomen, together with heavy bruising and congestion to the veins; this was caused by the furious attempts to resuscitate. His throat was full of mucus and material which would have exacerbated his other symptoms as his organs failed. Max had remained throughout the dreadful episode, horrified as well as surprised by the dramatic reaction to the small amount of Sarin administered. Previous experiments had revealed similar kinds of trauma in some volunteers, but they had all been revived after treatment with Atropine. None had exhibited the force of physical reaction which had made it impossible to inject Gershom in time.

Slowly making his way to his private room, Max wondered about the poor lad; who were his family, and how would they react to the fact, and worse, the manner, of his death? Questions would be raised, fault would be apportioned, and the very nature of their research at Porton Down would come under scrutiny. Whatever the outcome, he knew his time there would now be at an end. He tried to reassure himself that all his research had been aimed at saving life. Others he knew in the research world were hell bent on the opposite.

Back at his desk, he immediately called the admin staff to find out what they knew about the young man who had died. They were trying to contact the next of kin. His phone rang. The director of

Porton Down, in the manner of those in high office, spoke in a cold and measured tone.

"Dr Ackermann? I have been made aware of the unfortunate death of the volunteer soldier. There is a packet of papers, found among his possessions. I have sent them along to your office, and suggest you inspect them...it may have a bearing on how we move forward."

He was greeted by Julie-Anne, his secretary, looking downcast and troubled. In his office she had laid out the contents of Gershom's envelope on his desk. As he sat, he was conscious of her hand on his shoulder; it tightened and squeezed before she left him. The papers were arranged neatly before him, and he noticed a large glass of his favourite brandy, to his right. His apprehension grew, clearly something important was contained in the worn pages awaiting him.

There was an envelope, well-worn manilla, with Gershom's name on the front, but no surname. On the rear, a few dates and place names, some German and some he recognised as French. He opened a letter. His throat dried and his heart quickened; he had seen this handwriting before - he knew this writing.

"It couldn't be!" he thought, "It couldn't be!" Feverishly, he turned to a second envelope, and found photographs; images of a beautiful young woman, holding a small baby in her arms. Another photograph of her, clearly pregnant, embracing a young man as they looked at each other, warmth and affection clear in their eyes. He was looking at himself, with his betrothed, his love. It was impossible, he thought, as he gulped half the contents of his glass. Disbelieving, he turned again to the photographs, turning them over, each one confirming the reality of what he was seeing. It was her; it was him, her parents at their home, the garden, the old car, more and more evidence of the terrible truth. The baby, his baby, the bloody naked awful truth...

No! No! He had killed his own son! The letter! He had to read the letter! Maybe there was a chance, oh please God... he opened it with shaking hands; as he read he clenched his fist and banged it repeatedly onto the desk, as his eyes feverishly scanned the words...

"Gershom, my darling son,

At the time I left Germany everything in our lives was in turmoil. My friends and family had been rounded up like animals, their properties either destroyed or taken over by the authorities. The Jewish community was being singled out and persecuted by the Nazi Regime. They were blamed for being the main cause of Germany's demise during and after the Great War. Your Grandfather had been taken into captivity. I know in my heart I will never see him again. Thanks to his foresight your Grandmother is safe in Switzerland, being a neutral country, it will be free from persecution. Until recently, I was a secretary at the German Embassy in Berlin, where I came across some important documents.

The contents were so disturbing, I felt obligated to pass them on to the British Embassy. Believe me, I am not a traitor! I, like other passionate patriots, wish to bring a halt to this hateful Naziism which threatens to take over the whole of Europe. Now, I find myself in danger of being taken into custody. Even greater than any worries about my own safety is my overwhelming concern for your well-being. Since your birth you have meant the world to your father and myself and it was with great sadness that I agreed to be parted from you. My work often involves engaging with diplomats from the British and French Embassies. This places me in a precarious position. It is imperative that I evade capture. Thankfully, I have discovered that your father is alive. He managed to escape the clutches of the Gestapo who were planning to execute him.

As I write, you will have been placed in the safe care of a British Embassy diplomat, who is travelling to Britain via Switzerland. He gave his word that you will be delivered into the care of my Welsh aunt. I am heartbroken to be parted from you! I take comfort in the thought that when this terrible war is over, I will once again hold you in my arms.

Please God your father will come through this war and we can all be reunited as a family again.

In the meantime, in order to protect you we have decided to give you a new identity, bearing your new name Gershom along with your foster parents' surname. We chose Gershom for its meaning: "Not of this place." If you are reading this letter then sadly, we have not been reunited and you must have reached the age of eighteen. Information about your father and myself has been lodged in The British embassies in London and Berlin. This may help you trace us. If you find your father, please tell him I will never stop loving him and carry treasured memories of our brief time together. I am enclosing some photographs of us. One of them shows me pregnant with you. We were both overwhelmed with pride and joy. Others show family members, none of which I can name in case this letter falls into the wrong hands. The love I have for my country makes me fearful of the venomous evil of the Nazi Party. I am committed to fighting against this regime in any way I can despite any danger this will put me in.

My greatest hope is that I will hold you in my arms again but if this cannot be it will inevitably mean I have surrendered my life for my country. Don't let this cause you too much sorrow. I chose my own path but the driving force was to play a small part in making the world a better place for you and all your generation. With so much love my darling, Your adoring Mother

Max's head dropped on the scattered papers and photographs. Pain racked him as the reality sank deeper into his mind and soul. He shook and shivered as though he had plunged into icy water. His fists began to strike the table, then his face, chest, legs; anything to physically induce pain to distract from the crucifying truth that lay before him.

Over and over again came the horror. He had pledged never to use his evil creation to cause harm. Now he had broken his own taboo. He had killed his own son! And that son had never, because of him, had the chance to be known and loved as was his right, for who he really was. Guilt, remorse, anger and anguish all fighting for prominence, his feelings were tearing at Max's mind.

It was he who had assisted in the production of Tabun, the first of the nerve agents. It was he who had persuaded his true love to leave Germany. It was he who deserved to die! The brandy glass, hurled with the force of despair, shattered against the wall, and Julie-Anne ran in.

He fell into her arms, crying pitifully into her sheltering shoulder. She said nothing, just held him as his legs gave way, and they sank helplessly to the ground.

Chapter 39

Kent

The weeks passed; his ghostlike frame, the result of almost starving and neglecting himself, seemed to be dissolving into his clothing. His way of punishing himself; his spirit broken, his life in tatters, no one and nothing could console his grief. There was no hiding place for him; his tortured spirit was only relieved when mental exhaustion brought about sleep. At Salisbury station, feeling totally exiled from reality, he bought a ticket to Dover. There was no particular reason for travelling there, he was influenced by an advertising hoarding at the ticket office which promised a gateway to France and other foreign places.

Fields, towns flickered past as he gazed out of the carriage window, they meant nothing, they were just like images on a screen in a darkened cinema. Everything was changed and nothing mattered now. He was travelling in a world of no time, the whistle had blown, his game of life was over. He needed to get away from what he regarded as the murder scene, and from everyone involved in it.

The journey to London seemed to take ages; without any desire to eat, he took the train from Victoria Station to Dover Priory. Trundling toward Ashford, sleep finally overtook him again and he sank into a deep and welcome trance. He was awakened with a tap on the shoulder by the ticket inspector who, after checking the ticket still in his hand, told him he had passed through Dover and was now approaching the seaside town of Deal. Hurriedly, he picked up his baggage, stepped from the train and walked over the footbridge into the Eagle pub close by. After a few shots of whiskey, he left. The publican had recommended the Royal Hotel on the seafront as a place to stay. He made his way through the small town and found the hotel, booking in for a week.

After settling in he telephoned Julie-Anne giving her details of where he was. Promising to meet him there as soon as she was able, she advised him that he should take time out to rest and be sure to eat properly. She told him she had some important information which she would give to him when they met. Max ignored her advice, left the hotel and walked along the seafront; after turning down a side street he came across the New Inn public house which he entered in search of the anaesthetic effect of brandy. It looked Dickensian inside, furnished with blackened antique woodwork and bar; he selected a quiet corner near a small wood burning fireplace and sat down.

The rosy- faced landlady named Debbie, told him, "Sorry love, you can't sit there - one of our regulars, Ken, always sits there. There's plenty of nice snug places - did you know the New Inn is the oldest pub in Deal?" She smiled and he shrugged and moved to another chair.

The warmth, the brandy and the comforting aroma of beer coming from the wooden beer barrels gave him temporary relief from his anguish.

He turned his mind back to the time when he first arrived at Porton Down. The Secret Service and the authorities had given him clearance to assist in the specific work of scientific research involving nerve agents. On arriving there he was greeted with a mixture of dislike and suspicion, after all he was a German who was known to have been responsible in part for discovering and formulating the nerve agent Tabun, the deadly chemical which could have wiped out vast numbers of troops and civilians. However, he soon gained the respect of his new colleagues as a result of his being hard-working, meticulous and methodical in detail, whilst at the same time remaining modest in his demeanour. Whether from his military or scientific knowledge, he radiated a strong, independent and confident aura which had impressed his colleagues. It also drew the attention of his secretary Julie-Anne. She had volunteered to become his secretary, intrigued by his presence and fascinating background.

She was tall, slender with dark long hair that hung naturally at the side of her tanned face; her elegant stature drew the attention of onlookers wherever she went.

On being introduced, Max could not but help notice her features, a naturally pleasant smile which was accentuated by her wide opened dark eyes. Whilst he had admired her appearance, he dismissed it as unimportant, his thoughts were focused on scientific matters. The war weighed heavily on his mind; he had lost his would-be wife who was carrying his child. He had tried his best to find her, she seemed to have totally disappeared. There was reason to believe she had become a member of the anti-Nazi underground, and if this was the case, she would have changed her identity, many members of the underground had been captured and executed. He feared he would never see her again, wondered if she had given birth, and if so, what had happened to his child. If she had made it through the war, she would have easily found him through his friends still living in Spandau.

He coped with his loss by leaving Germany. His passion to work was now the overwhelming reason why he was there. He needed to help the British develop and understand the nature of nerve agents to counteract the possibility of other countries using it in warfare. If Britain had the agent, it would discourage others using it for fear of retaliation. His sole purpose was therefore to work, Julie-Anne was there to assist him in his research, and he only hoped that she would be efficient and totally dedicated to the important work in hand. She quickly proved to be just that, often when he worked extremely long hours she had willingly remained until late at night recording his experimental results. Their relationship was conducted in a pleasant but business-like fashion.

It wasn't until some years later, when she arrived as usual, earlier than the others, that she noticed an envelope on her desk. Inside was a birthday card from Max. In the past he had been so preoccupied by his work that he paid little attention to her personal life. He had heard in passing that today was her birthday. On the card he had skilfully drawn a bottle of champagne and glass with a single word "Lunch?"

A puzzled yet thrilling sensation touched her. Julie-Anne tapped on his door and with a cheeky grin, holding the card aloft quizzed, "One O'clock canteen?"

Max nodded with a smile, "Don't bring your notebook! Also, it is Saturday, but I am afraid you will not get overtime!"

Normally Max would work alone on the weekends, however there was a new intake of "volunteers" and he needed to ensure everything was in place for the next round of experiments with the young recruits. These experiments were sensitive, involving research on healthy exposing them to nerve agents and gas. This research which would lead to protecting soldiers in the event of a chemical attack in any future conflict.

Living alone, he had seemed detached from the others but was now revealing a more emotional side to his personality. Sitting in the New Inn by the fire, as the kindling crackled, his memory returned to that first lunch with Julie-Anne. This time when she arrived, he realised he was looking at a very attractive lady. She had changed into an elegant dress with a neckline that revealed an inviting glimpse of a softly curved breast. Her lips were moist with a red lipstick, eyes highlighted with a hint of mascara, her slender wrists decorated with simple gold bracelets. Ruby earrings which matched her lips added to her glamorous appearance.

He stood up as she walked toward him, taking her hand, he ushered her to the table, holding her chair as she sat down. He had never looked at another woman since losing his Ruth; today something was stimulating a dormant passion that he had not experienced for a long time. Stunned by her sensuality, her soft smile, the curvature of her body revealed by her dress that clung tightly, he was totally absorbed and amazed by her transformation. She would no longer be just his secretary; he felt a mixture of apprehension and excitement - where were his thoughts taking him? More importantly, was it the same for Julie-Anne?

As they dined, she played with her wine glass, rubbing her fingertips around the rim seductively, then stroking the stem in a way that left little to the imagination. During their conversation she would lean across the table, closing the distance between them, revealing her cleavage. Max could not but relish the moment. As the lunch ended, she extended her hand slightly beyond her wine glass; following her lead he gently placed his hand on hers and smiled warmly. She then placed her other hand on his, responding with her own smile. What he ate for that lunch and the moments that directly followed he could not recall. As they left the canteen, they were totally unaware of the silent eyes as others watched the drama unfold. Oblivious of others, they left hand in hand.

Instead of returning to their work place, they made their way to his quarters. At his doorway he remembered looking at her and taking her face delicately in his hands and kissing her gently on the lips. He had opened the door, guiding her inside and securing it behind him.

Max continued to stare at the open fireplace still oblivious to everything around him. Julie-Anne would hopefully be with him the next day, and he wrestled with his thoughts. His mind moved away from the present, focusing on the events of his past. In his mind's eye he saw her image wearing a warm smile. It always seemed to begin with a flicker of her eyes, then flowed over her cheeks before resting tantalisingly on her lips. Someone standing at the bar called out for service, and, disturbed by the noise, he dismissed earlier thoughts, remembering what she had said on the telephone about something important. Whatever it was, she wanted to deliver it personally. Watching the flames, changing colour from yellow to shades of blue and green. "There must have been a copper nail in the wood," he thought, "I deserve to have that nail implanted in my brain for what I have done."

He hoped Julie-Anne would be bringing good news, so he needed a break, but somehow, he suspected it might not be so.

Max finished his drink, thanked Debbie, who then had to help him as he staggered, drunkenly, to the door. He was in a stupefied state, almost unable to walk properly as he used the walls for support along the narrow paths that led from the main road. Staggering back to his hotel, his head cleared slightly as the breeze swept in icy cold from over a freezing sea. Before entering the hotel, he looked through the curtain of darkness at the coal black English Channel.

Max stood unsteadily grasping the metal bars of the railings to keep himself upright.

He could make out the lights of crossing ships heading to and from Dover. Forcing his eyes to focus, he turned his head to the direction of Dover. He was drunk. Search as hard as he could, he was unable to make out the famous White Cliffs. A solitary light caught his eye from a distant window perched on top, acting as a beacon for lost merchant travellers. He felt like a lost voyager swimming from a wreck laden with grief and destruction. Perhaps the light was indeed sending him a message, inviting him to shed his sorrows from the cliff tops. He staggered up the steps and went into the hotel. The barman was about to close, and it was clear he was far from pleased as Max ordered a double brandy and several packets of crisps. He opened a pack, soon giving up trying to unwind the blue packets that held the salt. He stuffed his mouth full of crisps, most of which landed on his clothes and the floor. He downed the brandy, while the barman seeing he had drunk more than enough, closed the bar and helped him climb the stairs.

Max dropped full face onto the bed into an unconscious state. When he finally woke up it was well into the afternoon.

He hardly recognised himself in the mirror as he shaved with trembling hands. After drinking several cups of coffee, he went to the lobby and placed a call to Porton Down. The call was returned after a short while, someone at the other end told him Julie-Anne had just left to catch the train to Deal. She would be with him later that evening.

What further news was she bringing with her, he wondered anxiously.

Chapter 40

Kent

It was 4:30 PM and already dark, Max had abstained from drinking and had forced food into himself in an attempt to reduce the effects of a raging hangover. He looked dreadful as he peered at his own reflection in the mirror. He splashed his face with cold water, hoping to restore some semblance of freshness to his appearance. Then decided to take a walk along the seashore, maybe the sea air would revitalise his depleted energy, help clear his mind and raise his downcast spirits. In the distance he could see lights from both sea and land.

Although he could not see them, the white cliffs at Kingsdown stood only about two miles away. They continued all the way to Dover. He remembered back to the time when he had first seen the cliffs, he was aboard a ferry from Calais to Dover. From the sea he had seen how the white cliffs emerged in Kingsdown then grew taller and steeper for many miles to Dover and beyond. The famous façade of the White Cliffs of Dover looking over the waters standing as a bastion to Britain's enemies, whilst at the same time their white purity reflected a welcome back to those who had left and were now returning to her shores.

On his return from his walk, he called into the Zetland Arms which stood on the pebble beach very close to the shoreline. As he entered through the doorway, he glanced back toward the cliffs, noticing there was a gate leading to a footpath which led to the top of the cliff. It looked accessible and well used. He ordered coffee and sandwiches, he was determined to remain sober and lucid, Julie-Anne had come a long way to be with him she deserved to be greeted by a sober Max. On leaving the Zetland, he walked back to the Royal hotel as darkness fell. When he arrived, the receptionist informed him there was a lady waiting for him in his room. He hurried up the stairs and on entering, hugged Julie-Anne who had been patiently waiting for him. As they embraced, she was pleased not to detect any alcohol on his breath.

After a brief conversation, Max pressed her to tell him of the news she brought for him. She led him to the edge of the bed putting her arm around his shoulder, she looked at him tenderly as tears began to run down her cheeks.

She explained that after he had left, she had made several phone calls to find out what had happened to his wife Ruth. She was finally directed to someone at MI6. After some research they discovered some interesting details about Ruth. When Max heard his wife's name mentioned, he felt a mixture of excitement and dread. Whilst he was pleased that Ruth had been traced, he could see from Julie-Anne's face that the news would not be good. Gritting his teeth and clenching his fist he waited anxiously for it to hit him. She told him that information was scant, even though some time had passed certain information was still subject to restrictions. There were still some agents working undercover in the field of operation whose safety was paramount. What was known, however, was that Ruth had become attached to the Free French Army having been transferred as an advisor from the British S.O.E. She was invaluable to them as she was fluent in German, French and English. History will one day reveal how her brave activities in espionage and subversion had led to the saving of a large number of lives. Indeed, her final valiant mission had saved thousands of civilians, even to the point where the possibility of Britain having to surrender was averted. This mission was still top secret.

Evidently the authorities were aware of Gershom's history their son, left safely with relatives in Wales. Ruth's underground activities had taken her to Alsace where she had gleaned information of great significance, a plan which could turn the tide of the war into Germany's favour. She had been summoned to travel to England and to communicate directly with a British agent based in London as a matter of great urgency. She had travelled by night on a British naval launch and landed at Dover. From there, unescorted, she transferred to an unmarked car that would take her immediately to London. On arrival she made contact with MI6 as directed and she was secreted into a safe house. Plans were made for her to meet a senior British agent at a point on the banks of the River Thames. Unknown to Ruth and the authorities, German agents were stationed at the port of Dover. They kept a constant vigil over the comings and goings of passengers, by the sheerest of chances they had seen Ruth disembark. One of the German agents who had worked in Berlin as a courier in the German Embassy recognised her immediately. She had been tailed to London, and eventually followed to the meeting point with a British agent. For some unknown reason it appears that Ruth had arrived at the rendezvous thirty minutes too early. The German agent had employed the services of a thug who were members of Mosley's henchmen to intercept her.

His orders were to follow her, and if the opportunity arose to dispose of her. He was ordered to search the body and bring back anything of significance. It appears that as he was about to tackle her, she tried to make an escape by jumping into the River Thames, sadly her attempt was thwarted and she was brutally attacked and murdered. Fearful of being seen by nearby patrons of the Prospect Inn he hastily threw the body into the River Thames, which was at low tide, then lay in waiting intending to drag her out in order to search the body when the coast was clear.

The British agent, a well trained and experienced operative had arrived at the scene before the thug could remove her from the water. He had waited for some time hoping his contact would turn up. As the tide turned, and waters began to flow, he happened to glance down and in the failing light saw the floating body. He just managed to recover the body from the water when he was set upon by the hoodlum whom he quickly dispatched.

Two other British agents turned up to see what was causing the delay, and with great dignity and respect took Ruth's body away.

One of them examined her clothing carefully, removing important information. The contents of which is still secret.

Interestingly two of the men declared that they had known her when they both worked at the British embassy in Berlin prior to war breaking out. Max was stunned by what he had just heard, he sat helplessly staring into space unable to speak.

Chapter 41

Kent

The sun had yet to rise as Max quietly gathered up his clothes and slid silently out of the room. He left a note, written the day before, which simply said:

"So sorry Julie-Anne, the evil I have created weighs heavily on my mind. This is the price that I have to pay not only for my son Gershom's life, but the dreadful certainty that many other innocent people will suffer a similar fate. I therefore have to surrender myself to God's mercy.

Forgive me, in time you will learn to forget today's nightmares as you venture deeper into the future.

God bless you, Max."

The cleaning lady greeted him, as he left the hotel saying, "Good morning sir, have a lovely day."

He barely managed a smile in response. He walked along the pebble shore; the tide was at its highest point. The soft land breeze calmed the water's surface, everything seemed so tranquil. He moved mechanically toward Kingsdown cliffs, his body totally in control now, his mind closed, devoid of thought, because soon the anguish would be over. He quickened his steps as he approached Walmer Green, the resting seagulls scattering before him.

Julie-Anne woke, felt for his body, startled when she discovered he was not there. She shot out of bed, dazed by a mixture of tiredness and the effects of the wine she had drank the night before. He had held her close as the effects of fatigue and alcohol brought on sleep. She wondered where the hell he was, then saw the note, panic gripping her as she read it. She scrambled to put her shoes on, grabbed Max's overcoat, slipped it over her night dress and ran downstairs. She almost kicked the broom from the cleaner's hands as she rushed by, asking if she had seen someone leave. The cleaner told her a man had passed some minutes earlier.

"How long ago?" she almost shrieked.

Alarmed, the cleaner replied, "About ten minutes, madam."

"There is still time," she thought.

Meanwhile Max had just passed Walmer Green, and as the darkness began to fade, he could just make out the edge of the cliff as it curved round the bay. By his reckoning it was a good mile away. He passed a group of fishermen who were busy pushing their boat along on logs soaked in black tar, as they prepared to go to sea. Max could smell the tar. For a few brief seconds it sharpened his awareness of the reality of what he was about to do. He became aware of the growing pain in his hips and legs, and his shortness of breath as he began to pant. The pain was now causing him to limp as he traversed the gravel path past the Walmer Yachting Club. There was a lot of ground to cover and the going was getting more and more difficult.

Unknown to Max, Julie-Anne was beginning to gain on him, as in her youth she had been a county champion at four hundred metres, and had broken several school records for sprinting and middle distances. The overcoat was holding her back, she tore it off and began to run faster, she knew he couldn't walk very quickly - there could still be time. Since he was heading for the cliffs, she had a good idea of what he had in mind. She had to stop him, remind him she could help, that she understood, and she loved him.

The cliffs were now fully in sight as Max passed tall Victorian houses. The fields opened up to his right allowing the breeze to increase, he welcomed its freshness. He could see Walmer Castle just ahead, nearly halfway there, and despite the pain, he pressed on. As he closed on the castle, he could just make out the cannons, the pathway now stood tall as the land to the side dropped sharply, thinking he must keep away from the edge, that he had to make it to the cliffs.

Quickening her pace, Julie-Ann began to feel the strain in her legs. "If only she had kept fitter," she thought. The fishermen Max had passed earlier, whistled as she passed them, her night dress flowing behind her. She stopped, taking a deep breath, asking them if they had seen a man go by. Seeing her distress, the urgency which caused her words to tremble they pointed, telling her that it had not been long since he had passed them. She needed to move even more quickly, but her shoes were holding her back as they threatened to slip off, so she discarded them. She felt the cold beneath her feet as she kicked them off. After a few paces, she stepped on something sharp which forced her to stop. "Damn it!" she thought, she would not make it without the discarded shoes. She hobbled back and luckily found her shoes in the growing morning light. She hurried on in pain, conscious of a warm wet liquid in her shoe. She must have cut her foot; the warm liquid was blood. There was no time to stop, she'd fix it later. She must press on at all costs. Gritting her teeth, dismissing the pain, she dashed ahead, determined to catch him.

Running down a narrow path she could make out a building ahead.

Max arrived at the Zetland Arms, pausing to get his breath back he sat for a moment on one of the wooden benches. He could just about see the whiteness of the cliffs; they could not be more than half a mile away. The sight revitalised him. He was nearing the end. He took a deep breath and stumbled on over the thick pebbles. The pathway was behind him; nothing between him and the cliffs but the shingle beach. It was heavy going, his feet dug into the heaped pebbles, slowing him down.

Each step sapped his energy and stole his breath, leaving him panting. Every muscle ached. "Not long now!" he told himself. He could see the gap between himself and the cliffs closing. He desperately needed to end things! To escape! To redeem himself!

Relief channelled through him; he was now only some two hundred yards from the base of the cliff.

Julie-Anne was half running, half hopping, leaning to one side in an attempt to alleviate the pain in her foot. It became too much, she had to stop and dropped to her knees. Removing her blood-soaked shoe, she examined her foot. A shard of flint was embedded in her sole. After removing it, the going was less painful. Increasing her pace, she passed the castle on her right but darkness still shrouded any detail. There was no sign of Max; perhaps he had turned down a side road by the pub.

However, she suspected she knew what was in his mind, he must be ahead and hopefully not far in front of her. Revived by this thought she ran on. Leaving the pathway, she started to run along the beach. It wasn't easy and she slowed but she knew the pebbles would have also hindered Max. She spotted something lying on the shingle just ahead. It was his jacket, it still felt warm. He must be just ahead! Invigorated, she pelted on.

Max had reached the gate, the path standing clear before him, the white of the chalk gleaming in the brightening sunlight. He rested for a moment; there was a steep climb ahead with no railings to grasp onto.

Part way up, all his energy sapped, he went on all fours to clamber up the path. It could not be far now to the top. He would soon be there.

Also feeling fatigued, half running, half walking, Julie-Anne closed onto the base of the cliffs. "Where the hell is he?" she muttered aloud. Fearing the worst, she reached the gate. It stood open; her heart fell as her legs gave way. She must be right; Max was intent on jumping off the cliff. "He has to be close, so close," she murmured. "I have to catch up, convince him he was not to blame. He was following instructions," She called out as loudly as she could, "Max! Max! Please stop! Talk to me.

Oh God, please stop and talk!" She ran on, still calling his name, hoping against hope she was not too late. Then she spotted his glasses on a post in front of her. Slowing down, she peered ahead and could just make out something moving. It was Max, on all fours close to the top.

Julie-Anne became hysterical screaming, pleading for him to stop. Max heard but ignored her calls.

He dragged himself along as fast as he could manage. Angry with himself for not guessing she would follow him. He drove himself on and upward, until finally he made it. He had reached the top! He paused, took a few deep breaths then lurched to the cliff edge. He could see lights in the distance. France seemed to be inviting him. He could hear Julie-Anne's pleas behind him and pangs of conscience stabbed at his soul. As he hesitated the morning clouds were clearing, revealing blue sea and sky emerging from the darkness.

In his frustration he called out, "Why?" Why for God's sake had she followed him? If she had read his note, she must understand what he must do.

Julie-Anne hauled herself toward the top of the cliff. Intent on stopping Max, she loved him with a gentle passion, more mental than physical. With a depth of love which had evolved from her admiration of his gentleness, thoughtfulness and kindness both to herself and to others. He stood out from the crowd. He must not die! She needed him too much, couldn't imagine life without him! She suddenly caught sight of him standing on the cliff edge. "No!" she screamed. She flung herself upward, grabbing at anything and everything that would help. She stumbled, slithering downwards a little way. Righting herself she managed at last to reach the top. Calling his name, she looked all around in disbelief. Max was nowhere to be seen!

Desolate, she fell to the ground, prostrate with grief, sobbing in disbelief.

Chapter 42

France

Julie-Anne returned to Paris, it appeared she had come to the end of the line, and was now quite happy to leave matters as they were. She had managed to trace Ruth and her connections, beginning with Gershom and ending with Agata. There seemed little point in carrying on, she would use up the last of her leave taking in the sights of Paris.

She sat on the edge of the bed gazing out of the window; fresh rain made the dust rise from the dirty road. The sight evoked connections in her mind - falling rain and the planned gas attack on London. RAINS, she mused, an anagram of SARIN. Her heart skipped a beat as she realised that if SARIN had replaced the rain over London, she would not be here in Paris, the whole city would have been decimated. If it had not been for the bravery of Rodders, Cloughie and others the world would now be a very different place. The authorities had made it clear that there should be a curtain of silence around the whole affair but she had decided that Andre should know the difference his bravery and that of his fellow partisans had made in obstructing the Germans. Sighing, she stood up, put on her coat and left the hotel to find him. It wasn't difficult. He spent most afternoons playing chess outside a restaurant on a boulevard close to the hotel. She was pleased to see him; Andre's smile was wide as he saw her approaching.

Sitting under a large umbrella, his tanned face, white teeth and the twinkle in his eyes accentuated his good looks. The warm summer rain continued to fall. Andre stood, gently taking hold of her hand, kissed it and led her to a seat and sat beside her, lowering his head slightly, flexing his tall frame beneath the parasol. He spoke in perfect English, meanwhile apologising to his chess partner, explaining that the lady was not fluent in French and as she would not be staying long. He wanted to bid her farewell. In hushed tones Julie-Anne began to talk about the German plot to destroy London. He put his finger to his lips in an attempt to stop her, but ignoring the gesture she continued. He tried again to silence her but she needed to communicate the value of the work he and all the other partisans had done in delaying and obstructing the enemy.

Andre glanced around and decided to let her speak. She expressed gratitude for all the sacrifices made by many brave men and women, telling him that without them it was highly probable that the outcome would have been starkly different with Germany in control of Europe. He patted her hand telling he already knew; internal intelligence had gleaned information from unnamed sources close to the operation. Many of those who had lost their lives had been honoured posthumously with medals of valour.

They rose and embraced, saying their final farewells before Julie-Anne turned and began to walk away. After a few steps she stopped, turned back, saying that in her efforts to trace partisans associated with providing vital intelligence she had visited an old farm which had been used as a safe house for agents escaping German authorities. Agata, the lady in question, had been instrumental in gathering information, and she had chosen to stay on at the farm for personal reasons. Sadly, even after all this time she was very confused and depressed; she had lost her first and only boyfriend, who had helped her manage her profound communication difficulties. Agata could neither hear nor speak but was very proficient at lip reading in several languages and communicated in sign language. Julie-Anne was able to understand her account of her involvement in bringing down the sinister plot to kill huge numbers of Londoners. She had been working close to those hatching the plot and gathered critical information which she had passed on to her boyfriend. They became separated soon after, and she had not heard from him since; she presumed he had lost his life like so many others fighting against the Third Reich.

Hearing Julie-Anne's account of her meeting with the lady, for Andre, triggered memories of Joseph, a fellow member of the French resistance. He knew Joseph had been receiving information from a lady who was a servant to Otto. This lady was also deaf and dumb and over time she and Joseph had grown very close. Joseph had told Andre that she had been shot in an act of bravery when she deflected troops away from a group of partisans. Surely this must be more than a coincidence, it was very unlikely that there would be two women with similar disabilities. Could it be that she was Joseph's lover? Could it be that she had not died but was alive and well at the farmhouse? The shooting had definitely happened, though, so how could that be reconciled with the possibility of her survival? Excited, Andre asked Julie-Anne to tell him more about the deaf and dumb lady she had met at the farm.

Julie-Anne began to describe her but Andre interrupted asking, "Her name? What is her name?"

"Agata," she replied.

Partially stunned, in a quiet voice he asked, "How does she spell her name?"

Julianne replied, "I wrote it down; it is spelt A G A T A."

"My God!" he murmured. "Is it possible? Could it be?"

"What do you mean?" countered Julie-Anne.

"Could it be a case of mistaken identity? The brave partisan who was shot went by the name of Agatha and the legend of her brave actions was passed by mouth from person to person. When the story eventually reached Joseph, he had assumed it was his Agata who had lost her life."

Julie-Anne almost jumped in excitement. "How can I find Joseph?" she blurted.

"But I know! I know where he lives!" replied Andre. He led Julie-Anne back to the table, gathered up pen and paper and began to scribble a plan of how to get there. "Take the train and then follow this sketch and you should reach him in less than an hour. The news will come as a shock, please treat him gently, he has suffered enough."

The train was just about to depart; Julie-Anne started to run, the guard spotted her and held the door open as she rushed in. She wondered how Joseph would react when he heard the news that it was possible that Agata was still alive. She was impatient for the train to reach its destination as she looked out, hardly seeing the countryside passing by. It seemed to stop at every little station and soon began to fill. Each influx of passengers brought with them a plethora of bags, packages and even dogs; there was a cacophony of sound as passengers met up with old friends. She was getting tense, she needed to see Joseph as soon as possible, hoped he would be there and not like many of her fellow passengers seemed to be, out on a shopping spree, visiting local markets. She looked at the piece of paper Andre had given her; it contained the name of the farm alongside a sketch of the route she should take to get there, complete with marker points and things to look out for. According to the map the farm did not appear to be too far from the station, but glancing out of the window she was dismayed to see the heavy rain. That's all I need. She thought, why didn't I bring a coat?

Finally, they reached her destination and she pushed her way through the throng onto the wet platform. She sheltered in the small waiting room in the hope the rain would soon subside. A porter came in, reassuring her that it should not be long before the rain eased, and Julie- Anne showed him the sketch map, asking if he knew the place. He pointed through the window and showed her the road leading to the pathway to the farm. As she looked, she realised the rain was stopping, and thanking him, hurried away. Her heart was beating rapidly as her excitement mounted. The narrow road soon petered out on to an earthy pathway. She could just make out a white farm house about a quarter of a mile away, and feeling exhilarated she lengthened her stride.

Near the farmhouse, she glimpsed a man tending a small vegetable garden. The whole area around him resembled a patchwork blanket of vibrant colours. Whoever lived there certainly had a love of flowers. As she came nearer, alerted by the sound of her footsteps, he put his trowel down and quickly straightened standing as tall as he could. He wasn't used to visitors. Who was this hurrying towards him? He had little time for strangers, small talk or any intrusions into his solitary world.

Julie-Anne introduced herself, explaining how she had bumped into his friend Andre who had told her where she could find him. She described how she was in France to trace members of the French Resistance. She was attempting to track down a very brave partisan woman by the name of Ruth who had once been close to her partner Max; he sadly was no longer alive. Her search had led her to meet some of Ruth's associates and in particular some who had worked closely with her in uncovering a secret plot targeting London.

One lady who had come to her attention was employed as the maid to an influential German called Otto. Whilst there she had served as a waitress to a clandestine group of powerful people led by him. This group was trying to orchestrate a terrible plot which could have a profound effect on the outcome of the war. Hearing this, Joseph became agitated; staring at the ground he began to chip away at the earth with the toe of his boot.

Without looking at Julie-Anne he muttered, "I know everything about that bloody Otto and his committee, the evil bastard shot himself rather than face up to the consequences of his murderous plots." He paused for a moment and then in anger, growled through twisted lips, "The woman you speak of was killed by the Nazis; she died bravely, protecting those who were trying to rescue her."

Julie-Anne looked into his eyes, softly saying, "You must be Joseph."

At this he looked at her in surprise and with a puzzled expression spoke, "I don't know how you know my name; I don't know who you are but I do know that the past is past. It is too painful to revisit so if you have a crumb of decency, you will leave me in peace. I have no wish to talk of the horrors of war. So, go! Go now!"

Undaunted, Julie-Anne stood her ground. Choosing her words carefully so as not to anger him further, she probed gently. She needed to ascertain two things in order to be certain she had got things right before she could tell him what she knew. She related how she had met up with the lady in question. Joseph stiffened, angrily declaring there had been many women employed in Otto's house and she could have met any one of them.

She replied gently saying, "Yes, but not many who are deaf and dumb. The lady I met was called Agata."

"That is just not possible," stuttered Joseph "She is dead!" He dropped to his knees, sobbing and beating the ground in frustration.

Julie-Anne knelt beside him, touching his shoulder gently and said, "No Joseph - she is alive. I can take you to her."

Lifting his head, Joseph spoke through his tears, "She was shot! She died so others could live!" Julie-Anne then disclosed what had happened. There had been a terrible mistake. "The unfortunate lady who was shot was called Agatha. Your Agata was taken away to a safe house where she remains still."

Joseph was dumbfounded, telling Julie-Anne that he needed proof. He could not believe Agata was alive until he could see her, could hold her, could feel the warmth of her body, breathe her scent. "Take me to her," he pleaded.

"That is why I came," Julie-Anne reassured him and they proceeded to make plans.

They passed the journey in silence. Joseph's eyes were constantly fixed on the passing countryside, his mind almost at breaking point. How could so much time have passed in heart ache when in fact Agata had been alive for the last fourteen years? All this sadness because of a simple misunderstanding! So many questions!

Why had instinct not told him? Why had the strength of their love, their longing for each other not reached through time and space? Why had he not searched for her? Would she still care for him? Were her thoughts still trapped in a world devoid of sound, without music and laughter? How did she cope?

At last, they were there. Joseph jumped to his feet, making his way rapidly along the corridor. In his eagerness he left his bag behind. Picking it up, Julie Anne told him to calm down. Calm down! he thought. Just not possible when his true love was so close! He longed to see her but was fearful of her reaction. What would her feelings be toward him?

They were soon on the dirt track leading to the farmhouse which stood isolated from the village. As they turned the final bend Julie-Anne drew his attention to the house on the side of the hill. On seeing this Joseph increased his pace, half walking, half running, leaving Julie-Anne lagging behind. He rushed through the gate. There she stood. He could clearly recognise her. Not knowing how to approach her, Joseph stopped and gazed, watching as she, unawares, tended a small flower patch. His throat was dry! How his heart pounded! There was a dog at her side which began yapping, jumping up at her. Alerted, Agata stood and turned. She felt uneasy, alarmed, as so few visitors came to the farm. She saw a figure standing looking at her. His tall frame, the darkness of his skin - he seemed more than familiar.

Suddenly he began to run toward her. That face, that smile, could it possibly be him? His arms were outstretched as he approached, and on an instant Agata realised it was really him, Joseph! Her disbelief and confusion fled, replaced by belief in the truth and reality of the man before her. Her soul reignited from the depths of her grief. As he came close her legs gave way and she fell into his arms. This was no dream; his physical closeness dispelled any doubts.

They held each other tight, crying and shaking, wrapped in the magic of the moment. This time there would be no parting. They separated for a second, looking closely at each other, eyes transfixed. Agata's lips trembled, she opened them and whispered softly

"Joseph." The shock of seeing him had somehow unlocked the spell of silence.

Joseph held her close, whispering reassurances that they would never part again.

Chapter 43

England/Spandau

On the flight back to the UK, Julie-Anne mulled over the events of the last few weeks. She had covered a lot of miles, and met up with some very interesting people. Her mind was agog with events and filled with an array of diverse accounts. Her mission to find out more about Max's past, had led to a fascinating history, unveiling the exploits of the partisan underground movement. The unfortunate and painful episode involving Joseph and Agata was heart-breaking, nonetheless she took great delight in being responsible for reuniting them.

Their future had dramatically changed, they would now be together once more, no longer living in the shadow of the belief that they would never see each other again. Then there were the perilous adventures of Rodders and Cloughie, who with the help of Joseph and his partisan friends, had averted a possible cataclysmic annihilation of the population of London. Was it true she thought, somehow, she couldn't get her head around the fact that such a dramatic incident had not been documented, instead it had been buried in secrecy for all these years. She suspected that the file containing the details of the intended launch of the V2 rocket on England's capital was collecting dust in some secluded vault.

She was amazed to find that Max with his friends Alex, and Fritz, had miraculously escaped from Spandau. It seemed impossible that the three of them could remain undetected even with their heads in the lion's mouth. She hadn't realised that Max had fought for Germany toward the end of the war, being captured at the end of hostilities in Tunisia.

From what she gathered he had tried to warn the British intelligence of the dangers of chemical warfare. With all this information rattling around inside her head, she felt compelled to write matters down. The loss of Max was now lying heavily on her mind, her admiration for him had grown adding to the weight that was crushing her broken heart. The point of her journey from London to Paris had been to uncover information concerning Max's past. She was leaving with some information but this gave rise to more questions each one screaming out for answers which would need further probing research. In a few days she would be back at work at Porton Down, she would make it a priority, to trace the whereabouts of the many people who had known Max. There was so much more to this man.

Julie-Anne had an insatiable appetite for finding out more.

Numerous calls, advertising, and newspaper articles unearthed a great deal of interest, the appeal for people who had known Max to come forward generated an enthusiastic response. It was now clear that it would be possible for Max's friends and acquaintances to meet together. Correspondence and communication passed between all the interested parties showing that all were keen for a reunion. This opportunity to meet up again, to share common memories would enable Julie-Anne to paint a complete picture of Max's history, helping to put her mind at rest about the way he had reacted to the tragic event of Gershom's death at Porton Down. The date was set for Saturday 21st June, which was the first anniversary of Max's disappearance. After an intensive search it was assumed his body had been swept away by the tide. If everyone turned up as promised it would be quite some gathering.

The time had come. Julie-Anne, Rodders and Cloughie travelled together, departing from Gatwick for Berlin where they stayed overnight. After breakfast the following morning they hired a car and drove towards the old farm house on the outskirts of Spandau. They came to the Citadel and stopped there for a while to appreciate the atmosphere of the place. The two rivers that bisected the area were still accessed by the ancient bridge that Max and so many of his friends had crossed over. They visited the old guard room and walked along the corridors, passing what were the laboratories used for research during the Second World War. It was exciting to feel they would soon be meeting up with many of the characters once so close to Max.

Fritz, still alive and living on the old farm, shared the place with his niece Eva and her three grown up daughters Gretel, Sophie and Helga. These four ladies helped to manage the farm which was thriving under their combined efforts. The land area had been extended and it now housed cows, pigs, goats and chickens. The cows had been carefully selected to produce the best quality milk, producing excellent cream and butter. The goat's milk was also of the highest quality as a result of their being well fed and free to roam. Not surprisingly, all the dairy products were very popular and in great demand, locally and further afield; the family enjoyed a good living as a result. Fritz was a contented man; he was surrounded by a loving family. There had only ever been one love in his life and he would always wear her ring. He had always been in the habit of keeping a diary, continuing to write about events and adventures throughout the war years and up to the present time. Often in the evenings, members of his family could be found reading his collection of writings, the tattered pages reflecting the countless times they had been browsed over. His niece and her daughters had from the very beginning decided there was only one place to host the gathering of Fritz and Max's friends. Painstakingly clearing out the old barn, furnishing it with tables and chairs from the outhouses and farm buildings. The weather forecast for that day predicted light rain with mist later on. Spit roasts of lamb and suckling pig had been set up early in the day and the aroma wafted over the fields, tantalising shoppers nearby and giving a tempting welcome to the invited guests.

They had arrived en masse, clogging up the small track. The resulting traffic jam turned into a cavalcade of horn blasting, flag waving, shouting and laughing as they lined up to park in an adjacent field, creating a carnival atmosphere. Emotions rose as they were greeted by the family, and the welcoming party began with a convivial offer of drinks; homemade wine, their own brand of beer, and an array of spirits, with soft drinks for the children. A play area had been set up, supervised by two retired teachers recruited for the task. Eva had quickly estimated that there were about forty adults in attendance accompanied by a number of children, all dressed in their best. The adults drifted into the barn, forming small groups, chatting eagerly and catching up with each other's news. A special table had been set up at the far end of the barn, reserved for three illustrious guests and placed in a prominent position so that everyone could see them and they could see one and all. They had been requested to arrive one hour later than the other guests. By this time, everyone would be in high spirits, ready to welcome the English visitors.

Eva stood up, calling everyone to attention. Her daughters had compiled a list of the various people seated in groups around the tables and after a few words of introduction Eva introduced everyone present, asking each in turn to stand and take a bow, all greeted with cheering applause. Everything was going well!

One of the daughters, waiting outside, signalled the arrival of the special guests to her mother, and at that moment Eva stood up, striking a bell to alert everyone to their arrival. Julie-Anne parked the car close to the barn, enthusiastic applause greeting the visitors as they got out. Rodders and Cloughie made their way through the gathering behind Julie-Anne, enjoying a standing ovation and shaking many eager hands on the way, feeling somewhat overwhelmed by their reception. Tears flowed freely. Rodders and Cloughie, the two old soldiers, tried hard to keep a stiff upper lip, masking their overflowing emotion. They reached their seats amid the applause and hubbub, sat quietly for a short time, then the three stood as one, nodded to the assembly and returned the welcome by two of them clapping along with everyone. Rodders joined in by enthusiastically banging the table, having only one arm.

When the room finally fell silent, Rodders and Cloughie each gave brief, heart-rending accounts of people they had met, friendships formed, and tragic losses sadly suffered by both sides. They were so pleased to see that so many of Max's friends had survived, they were greatly looking forward to reminiscing with them. The two men sat; Julie- Anne rose, she started to speak, but then froze, totally taken aback by the sincere and enthusiastic welcome she was given. The warmth of feeling coming from the assembled group overwhelmed her, tears welling in her eyes. She looked around in silence, her eyes drawn to Fritz. Physically frail as he was, his massive inner strength shone still.

He stared back at her, half smiling but with sadness in his eyes; he had been very close to Max, shared so many experiences, some happy, others very difficult; there had been joy shadowed by terror. Excitement snuffed out by pain; elation dampened by sorrow. Their bond of friendship was unequalled. Whilst overjoyed by the occasion Fritz also felt pain in his heart. Then, as he glanced around the room, someone caught his eye and his pain turned to anger. He realised there was a traitor in their midst. Fritz was transfixed; the man he was staring at shifted nervously and lowered his head. Julie-Anne could not help but notice the subtle body language passing between the two men.

As she watched the man moved uncomfortably in his seat then slowly rose to his feet and spoke.

"I knew Max very well, there was a time when we were the closest of friends. My name is Gerhardt Schrader and I am the man who betrayed him. Perhaps it would help if I started at the very beginning when Max and I were working together on a scientific project." The room fell silent and he saw confusion in everyone's eyes. Nervously, with a bowed head, he spoke almost in a whisper.

"Please let me explain. We were working on a dreadful chemical. It was so powerful that we branded it Tabun, which meant it was never, I repeat never, to be used. I am afraid I cannot tell you anymore as it is still highly classified. What we had unleashed was best kept locked away, and this was our first intention. What Max didn't know was that the laboratory was bugged, and anything we discussed was being monitored." Gerhardt's hands visibly shook but he pulled himself together. He needed to get everything off his chest; he had wrestled with his conscience long enough. Now was the time to finally face those he had hurt in the past and make amends. He continued, "Max was very unhappy about everything the Nazi regime was doing. He was passionate about his country, but loathed Hitler and his outrages." Gerhardt paused, took a deep breath, then carried on, "At that time I admired the new Nazi regime. The whole infrastructure was changing. Roads, factories and new towns were being built. There was a sense of optimism in the air, everyone made a determined effort to do the best they could for their country. Whether it meant picking up a shovel to excavate a trench or being prepared to sacrifice personal possessions for the cause, they did so willingly. Max, however, was deeply unhappy with the way everyone was being treated, especially the Jews. I was aware that he had a secret- his fiancée, named Ruth.

"His engagement to Ruth had to be kept clandestine because she was Jewish. When Ruth fell pregnant, Max told me in confidence that he was planning to get her out of the country; she had been dismissed from her job at the German Embassy in Berlin and her life was in danger. All these concerns filled Max's mind, resulting in angry anti-Nazi outbursts. When our experiments were completed the whole of the laboratory was due to be moved to another location, where more senior scientists would take over our research. It was at this point that Max's ideology would cause him to be excluded from further research; he was to be posted for training to re-join the military. He was interviewed at Spandau; I was asked to attend the meeting. Toward the end of the session, I was instructed to leave. It was sometime later that I discovered that an order had been issued for Max's execution. This sickened me!" Gerhardt paused a moment, and sipped a drink; swallowing hard, he looked out at his spellbound audience...

"I continued my work at Spandau, having moved back to the Citadel, before being transferred to the G.Faben factory at Wappertal. Here I worked with three other scientists Ambros, Ritter and Van de Linde. It was almost by accident that we stumbled across a nerve agent that was many times more powerful than Tabun. We had unleashed a real fiend, sinister and evil. We derived its name from our own names S for Schrader, A for Ambros, R for Rittr and IN from

Linde. SARIN."

Several gasps of horror and shock escaped the guests, as Gerhardt kept on, "Following this I was transferred to a new factory near Dyhernfurth which was situated forty kilometres from Warsaw in Poland. We were producing three hundred and fifty metric tons of liquid Tabun per month, intended for possible use in the war, when it was decided that Sarin would be more destructive and powerful. As a result, we were moved to a new site in Falkenhagen some hundred and twenty kilometres from Berlin, where we manufactured liquid Sarin. It was at this time I discovered that Max had somehow managed to escape from Spandau accompanied by Fritz. Whilst I was at Dyhernfurth I witnessed the horror of forced labour. Overwork, disease and malnutrition were the norm, compounded by the exposure to toxic chemicals. Hundreds of Polish workers died. As I walked through the local town, I was shocked to see so many grim-faced people with skin hanging from their bones, with barely enough energy to hold themselves upright. I passed several bodies lying ignored by the side of the road; I thought, this was not the Third Reich that I had so admired.

"During one of my trips into the town I came across a pamphlet nailed to a lamp post. It concerned a Sophie Scholl, a twenty-one-year- old student who had been guillotined on the orders of Johann Reichart. It reminded me of a distressing conversation I had shared with Max when he talked of executions by guillotine which at the time, I found difficult to believe. During my time at Falkenhagen I fully realised the extent to which Jews and Poles were being illtreated.

I will not go into too much detail but I saw men dying on their feet from starvation, severe beatings and inhumane cruelty. The final straw came when I met up with some old friends who revealed, with revulsion, how passive demonstrators, students and clerics of differing denominations were persecuted for not complying with the new "religious order" of the Third Reich. The state was claiming to be the centre of worship, a greater power than God.

"The defining moment came! I was given a number! Two thousand one hundred and twenty. This was the number of executions implemented by Johann Reichhart who had been recruited by the Nazis to dispose of dissenters. He was nicknamed "Head-hunter" and travelled with a mobile guillotine and hanging mechanism to dispose of dissenters. One of his victims was Sophie Scholl. Her final words before being decapitated were: 'Such a fine sunny day and I have to go but what does my death matter if through us thousands of people are awakened and stirred into action?'

Sophie was part of the White Rose resistance movement which was gradually taking hold throughout the country. On hearing her story, I was determined to remove myself from the research which would assist this evil, devilish regime."

Everyone in the room was stunned into silence. Heads and eyes turned in all directions before settling on the high table where the three English guests sat. Whispers began to fill the room; the atmosphere was now chilled and tense. Julie-Anne, rising to her feet again, noticed the frail, lean figure of Fritz slowly and clumsily getting up from his seat. She hastened towards him but he gestured to her to keep away, his pride resisting help from anyone. He could stand by himself! He stumbled forward, unsteady on his feet, and Julie-Anne just caught him as he slumped backwards into her arms. Anger bit as he reluctantly accepted her help, lowering him back to his seat.

"I need to talk," he exclaimed "I must say something."

She nodded. "I'll help you, but first you need to calm yourself." She smiled at him as she patted his trembling hands.

Fritz continued insistently, "I must have my say, it is important, things need settling!"

Julie-Anne picked up his glass, half full of his favourite Nierstein wine, saying, "Have a drink, then I will help you to stand and speak."

"No, you bloody well won't!" he replied with a wink and a smile. He sipped his wine saying, "If I fall, I can always blame it on this stuff!" She laughed as he slowly got to his feet, staying close as he steadied himself. He looked around the room before turning his attention toward Gerhardt. Again, the room fell silent.

"War! Filthy stinking war never determines which side is right. The cost of its outcome only reveals who is left. The sacrifice of a war is not only met by those who are dead, the living also have to bear the consequences. Everyone here has a cross to carry to Calvary! The only winners are the powerful and the rich who instigate war whilst the poor suffer death and destruction. Politicians, priests, clergy, bishops, popes justify holy wars in the name of God. When in fact they are using this as an excuse." He rocked slightly.

Julie-Anne rested her hand on his side.

Frowning, he glanced at her then continued, "I have surrendered twice, during both the Great war and the second world war, a bitter pill which is not a cure. Soldiers die, and those who live on carry many painful memories." Fritz settled his eyes once more on Gerhardt, his voice cracked with emotion as he spoke almost in a whisper. The room was so still that everyone could hear clearly as he resumed, "We live in a fractured world. All of us must try to gradually piece it together with love, hope and understanding. Hatred, sorrow, hunger, pain and destruction were all brought about by the hypnotic ideology of a powerful leader who wanted to impose his brand of Nazism on us all. If I have learnt anything from it all it is this: trying to impose Nazism on people through coercion, fear, suffering and death will never prevail. Somehow, don't ask me why, good eventually overcomes evil. Today I have heard and felt an expression of this.

"Gerhardt," he said, looking at him with eyes glistening with tears. "You have, here today, eloquently conveyed your feelings of guilt to all present. This bears testimony to all I have just said. You are living proof that good can overcome evil. On behalf of my closest friend Max, I offer forgiveness. Your actions today have further cemented a closer sense of harmony between us all." He gazed around the room and slowly sat down.

The room exploded in a mixture of applause and cheering!

Fritz looked toward Julie-Anne, who was in floods of tears.

Everything he had said brought back painful memories of the times she had spent listening to Max, hearing what he had to say when in a philosophical mood. He hated the instruments of war, especially since he himself had been instrumental in producing the most lethal and horrific nerve agent.

Fritz told her not to fret, Max would never have done anything to harm anyone, but this made her cry even more; he wondered why she was so very distressed.

Chapter 44

Spandau

The mixture of food and drink, along with the pleasant ambiance brought about by chatter and laughter chased away Gerhardt's woeful tale. Rodders and Cloughie were in high spirits, seduced by the fine fare in front of them, their mood lifted by the atmosphere. Julie-Anne suddenly stood up, recognising the couple who had just walked in and were making their way toward her. "Joseph! Agata!" she called out in excitement. They embraced. Many of the party guests having seen and heard the new arrivals were wondering who they were and the room fell silent momentarily, then whispered remarks snaked around the room.

There was an eruption of jubilant applause and cheering. It was Agata and Joseph! Even those who did not know them had heard of their exploits.

Rodders stood. The perfect gentleman as always, he extended his one arm to escort them to the table. Although they knew he had been injured, it saddened them now to see the extent of his injuries. They both wrapped their arms around him. Agata was beaming again with joy. She had heard of his and Cloughie's 'exploits and eager to express her admiration she kissed him eagerly on both cheeks. They headed toward Cloughie. He had remained seated, partly due to the results of his injuries, but more so from his intake of copious amounts of alcohol.

Chairs were brought into place, followed by wine which was quickly uncorked. They settled together excitedly around the table. Julie-Anne had been hoping so much they would come. She was as overwhelmed to see them again as they were to meet up with her once more. After a while attention was drawn to the other end of the room where Fritz, with help from Gerhardt rose to his feet.

"Everyone, please!" he called. When silence fell, he began to speak, "I've heard a great deal about Joseph but know nothing about the charming lady by his side. Can someone tell me please all you know about her?" He half stumbled; half fell back into his seat.

Julie-Anne stood and was about to begin when she noticed someone making her way toward them. "Who is this lady?" she wondered aloud. The stranger introduced herself, "My name is Sophia; I was as close a friend to Ruth as anyone could be. I have been searching for her for many years without success, and I am desperate to find her. The last time we met was here in Berlin. She was being hunted by the Gestapo. My father was working at the British Embassy and took her son, Aaron to safety, eventually reaching England. I am so sorry to interrupt but does anyone know what happened to her?"

Julie-Anne beckoned her to the table. Sophia sat, but looking around the table in the hope of hearing news of Ruth she could see from their expressions that it would not be what she hoped for.

The pit of Julie-Anne's stomach cramped with pain; her mouth dried. "Is it possible that this is Max's Ruth?" she wondered. "It has to be." She was about to speak when a hand gently touched her arm.

"Please," Cloughie whispered. "I think it best if I speak, you have been through enough already." Relieved, she sank back into her chair.

Looking directly at Sophia he began, "The lady you speak of was the most courageous person to touch my life despite the fact I never had the opportunity of speaking to her. In England she is regarded as a heroine, and had it not been for her, all of us assembled here would not be celebrating together today. We owe her so much; a damn sight more than I can say. She sacrificed everything. Her son, her fiancé Max, her freedom and tragically her life." Everyone was touched by his words and many had tears in their eyes.

Joseph took up the narrative, "We were part of an underground movement based in an area of Alsace. I endorse what has been said - but for Ruth and her resourceful bravery Britain could well have lost the war."

Sophia interrupted angrily, "I thought all along that the S.S would eventually hunt her down. When I joined your gathering today and could see she was not here I knew in my heart that it was highly unlikely that she could have survived." Breaking down, she continued through her tears. "She was the most intelligent, loyal and loving person. We were at school together and grew to be more like sisters than friends. I knew the bastard Nazis would get her in the end. I only hope she died quickly."

"She managed to elude the Nazis," Rodders began. He looked at Joseph who was about to stand up, and calmly signalled that he should stay seated. "With the assistance of Embassy staff, her baby, Aaron became Gershom, with a new identity and passport. He was eventually settled in Wales but I am sorry to say I do not know all the details."

Julie-Anne tried to intervene.

"Not now please" said Rodders. "Let's not spoil the day. There will be time enough later to fill in the details."

She smiled wryly and stayed silent.

Cloughie had so far kept quiet, unusually for him, but now he was concerned that what had been planned as a celebration was quickly turning into a very sombre occasion. He stood, looked at Julie-Anne with a wide smile, and announced loudly enough for all to hear, "Listen Everyone! Julie-Anne is about to tell how she got Joseph and Agata back together, and you are about to hear a very romantic account about these two lovebirds. Start at the beginning, Julie-Anne, as you have an amazing tale to tell."

She got to her feet launching into the remarkable story. The room was silent as everyone listened but as the story drew to a close the celebrations continued; the mood heightened by the pleasure of having heard such a romantic tale. Endless toasts followed, revelling in the reunion of Agata and Joseph. The afternoon progressed with much imbibing, laughter and singing but there came a time when the gathering came to a natural ending. A sudden chill as the wind changed toward the East brought with it a rising mist. It seemed to hang and cling as if a translucent curtain.

Clusters of old friends, joined by new friends, chattered happily as they drifted down the old track. Some were heading to their cars whilst others were making their way home on foot. A group of children seemed to almost disappear in the mist as they skipped and danced alongside their parents.

Julie-Anne stood at the window for a while gazing at the departing guests. Her eyes were drawn toward the dancing children. How happy they seemed without a care in the world. How different things might have been. How much she missed Max; life would never be the same without him.

As the last of the children disappeared from view, she was about to turn away when, from the corner of her eye, she caught a glimpse of a figure emerging from the mist. He seemed so familiar. Was it just her imagination? As he grew closer her heart began to quicken.

Surely it wasn't possible?

It couldn't be!

It couldn't possibly be!

Could it?

1938
1958
Gershom Morris
deeply mourned Son
of Max Ackermann,
5th June 1890 – 6th April 1980
Beloved Husband of
Julie-Anne Ackermann
8th Oct 1917 – 27th Nov 1995

Epilogue

It will be apparent to those who know me well that there is a lot of myself embedded in this book. Writing it has been a joy at times but also journey of catharsis.

In 1958 as a young man on National service I, like Gershom, volunteered for experimental trials at Porton Down, having been totally assured they were safe. I naively walked into what turned out to be a gas chamber and have felt the effects for the rest of my life. We were exposed to Sarin, an extremely toxic nerve agent. As a result, I have suffered from physical and mental trauma over the years, some of it quite severe. This has impacted on my quality of life, my career and other life choices. As time went by, I was persuaded to apply for a war pension and compensation. This process turned out to be harrowing. A group of veterans was formed and taking the lead I spent many hours and sleepless nights researching, compiling evidence and attending meetings. Without going into too much detail I can only say that the powers that be overturned a strong case for individual cases to be judged on their merit, instead offering a sum to be shared equally by everyone who had attended trials at Porton Down. This meant those individuals left incapacitated, some dying prematurely, were offered the same amount as others who had not been involved in the use of toxins such as Sarin, thus suffering no ill effects whatsoever. When divided between the large numbers involved the sum was minimal – almost insulting. We were also told that unless everyone accepted the offer no one would receive anything. As well as this emotional pressure I was pressured personally by those in authority to accept the deal in a full and final settlement.

Whilst the book is a fiction, much of it is based on fact and expresses how I feel about the nature of men who deliberately set about producing weapons and toxins to kill their fellow men. As well as Gershom you may in part also identify me with Max. Having gone through all that happened in my attempts to gain justice for myself and others I felt betrayed by the system. My long-suffering wife Jennifer had supported me throughout, putting up with my endless research and deliberations. She brought me much happiness as well as a few challenges.

My daughter Louise also offered much support, accompanying me to some meetings. She was reduced to tears by our failure to get justice for all.

When my wife passed away and Louise left for a new life in Australia my life fell apart. My interests in rugby, colleting memorabilia and family breaks in Spain gave way to alcohol. I, like Max was driven to go to the cliffs above Dover. Sitting on the edge I even calculated how far I would need to run before jumping in order to avoid hitting rocks which jutted out. My physics teacher would have been proud of me! Mercifully a gentle hand touched my shoulder. A quiet voice brought me back to reality. I can no longer remember the exact words but the meaning has stayed with me.

We cannot solve personal problems by imposing even greater problems on those closest to us.

She also told me she had gained solace through writing, urging me to try it. Pick up the ball and run with it instead of giving in. Her words acted like a catalyst. I determined to go on. Standing I thanked her, wished her well and with a wry smile said:

"You didn't think I was going to jump, did you?"

I am forever indebted to her and to all those who put effort into supporting my cause. Researching, writing accounts, assisting with presentations on behalf of myself and all others affected by research into toxic agents.

Also, thanks must be given for the support, patience and understanding offered by medical staff both at my local surgery and all the NHS. Over many years they have managed to patch me up, keep me going and allow me to live a rich and fulfilling life.

About the Author

Born in 1938, the son of a miner, I grew up in Wales. Money was short and life could be tough, but I thrived in the freedom of the beautiful Brecon countryside and nurtured my love of Rugby. I started my National Service at the age of eighteen and was fortunate enough to pursue the game, representing both The Royal Artillery and Kent before being posted to Salisbury.

After discharge I married, became a father of two but still managed to study, graduating in Physical Science from Exeter South Bank and later gaining my masters at The Cambridge Institute. After entering the teaching profession, I gained a lot of fulfilment from the successes of my young pupils, many of whom I am able to stay in contact with, thanks to modern technology. Rugby was not to be forgotten and I coached under nineteens for many years. This led me to becoming the chair of the London Division and the England Panel Member for this age group. Sadly, my teaching career was cut short due to ill health but I developed a strong interest in collecting antiques.

My rationale for writing a novel at my advance age was complicated. Firstly, to prove to myself I could. Having long enjoyed writing stories for my children and grandchildren I was keen to write for a more critical audience. However, the content was primarily to put some demons to bed. Some aspects of the novel are to some extent autobiographical and reflect parts of my life which have left me with feelings of frustration and bitterness.

I believe I have achieved both my aims and hope you enjoy reading this book as much as I have enjoyed writing it

BV - #0006 - 250322 - C0 - 210/148/18 - PB - 9781913839550 - Gloss Lamination